CITY MAP

CAVERNUM

OUTER WALL

FLATS

RANGE

GUARD TOWER

STABLE

PLAZA

CORE

RING

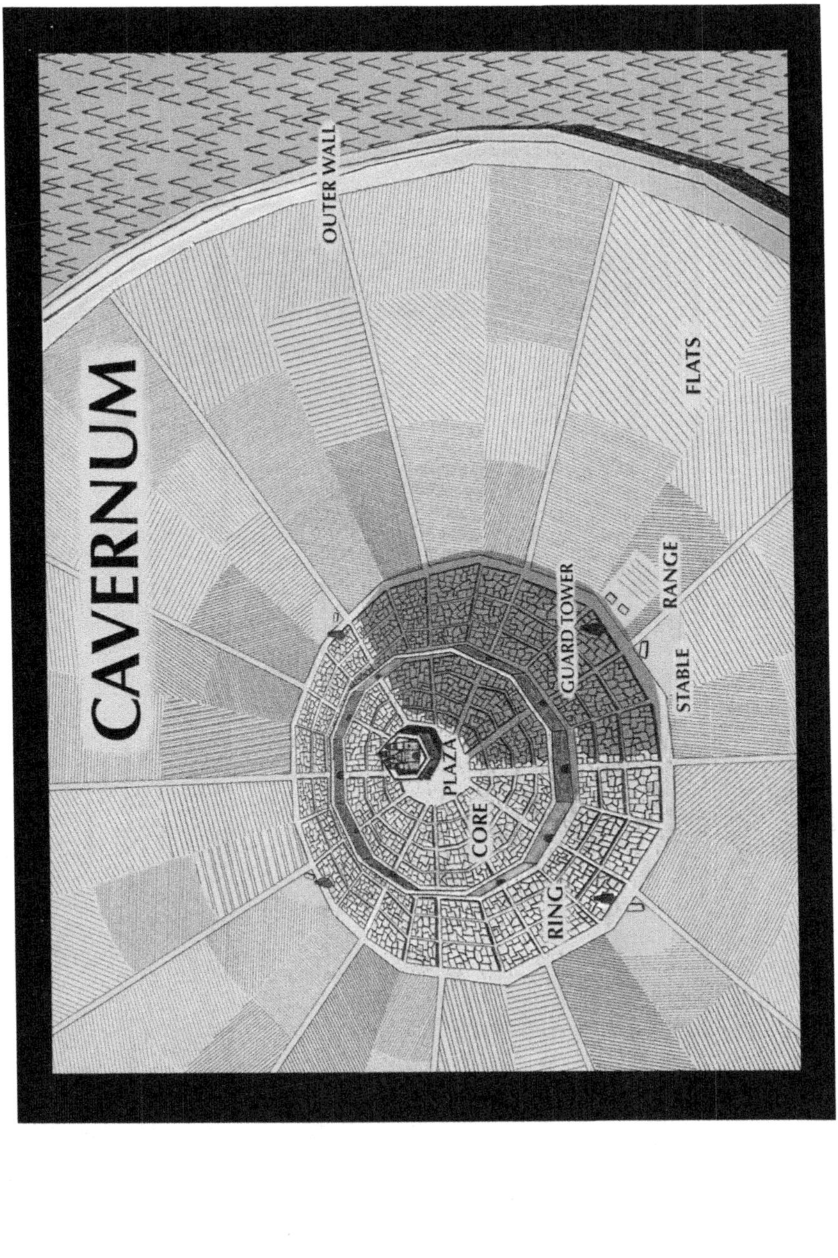

PALACE MAP

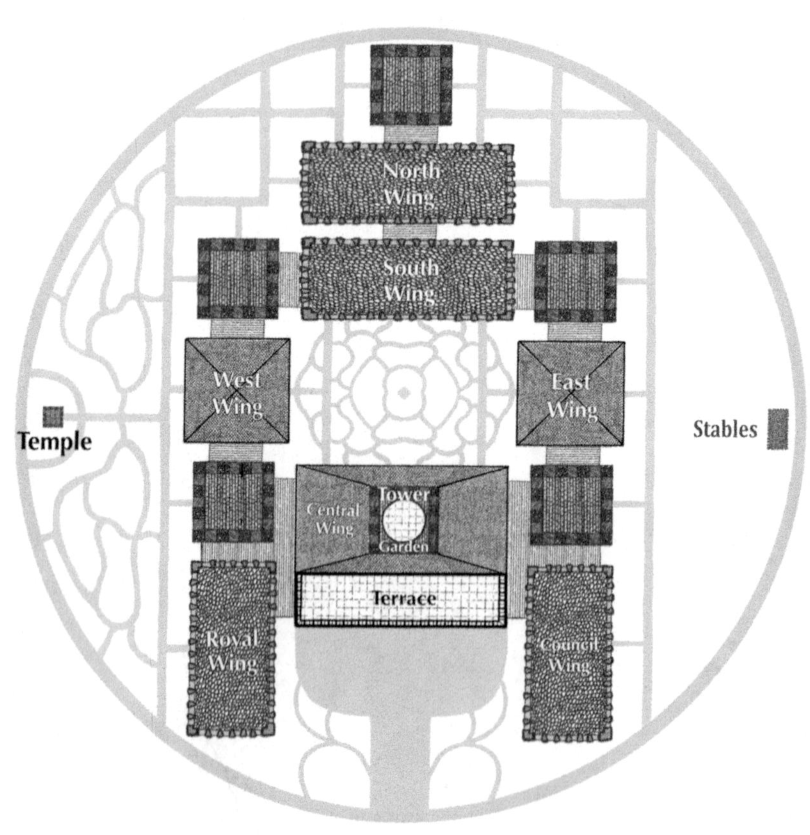
North Wing
South Wing
West Wing
East Wing
Temple
Stables
Central Wing
Tower
Garden
Terrace
Royal Wing
Council Wing

THE REVIVING

BOOK 3: PART ONE

DEVIN DOWNING

DEVIL DOWN BOOKS

CONTENTS

DEDICATION

This book is dedicated to Mel. Thanks for helping me navigate this new way of seeing the world.

THE REVIVING: PART ONE
First edition. Nov 18, 2023

Cover design by Ricardo Montaño Castro

ACKNOWLEDGMENTS

I'd like to acknowledge you patient, equanimous readers out there. Thank you for staying interested even after I delayed this book for several small eternities. Medical school was nearly the death of my writing career, and I never would've found the motivation to keep writing without you guys cheering me on.

PREVIOUSLY

Previously in The Dividing:

- Prologue reveals that, 18 years ago, Jenevrah fled from Hogrum with her baby boy named Ezra (who is Matt).
- Fast forward 18 years, Matt is exploring the "power plant" (the ruins of Hogrum) when he is attacked by a feeder (nicknamed Hood). He is subsequently saved by Zane.
- Meanwhile in Cavernum, Rose gives a speech for Remembrance Day. She is attacked by a mob, and is rescued by her boyfriend, Commander Antai Elsborne, who also happens to be King Dralton's apprentice.
- Dralton reveals several letters from Rose's father, Zezric. Zezric sent the letters from Hogrum, where he was living with his pregnant wife. He was sent there by King Dralton to infiltrate a demon cult. According to the letters, Rose's mother (Violet) died during childbirth. Shortly after, Hogrum was invaded by feeders. Zane (who was a guardian in Hogrum) managed to escape with Rose and Antai. His family, however, didn't survive.

- Upon arriving in Cavernum, Matt was brought to the healing loft where he was healed by Kendra. That night, he met Lynn (the princess's alias).
- Matt, Diego, and Lynn try out for the guard and are accepted. They begin training with Proticus (Tick for short).
- While training in the Trench, Vyle and his goons attack Matt and Diego, but Rose intervenes.
- Zane tutors Matt, helping him learn dominion. He also confirms that Matt is a Demon (someone with a specific Adamic tattoo, allowing them dominion over human-beings).
- Another sanctuary, Lycon, sends out a distress call. By the time reinforcements arrive, Lycon has been ravaged by feeders.
- Vyle assaults Rose, searching for her hidden amulet. To protect herself, she reveals that she is the princess.
- For the Final Assessment, the recruits compete in the dueling pit (a giant cavern located beneath the Royal Plaza). Matt defeats Vyle. Vyle then forfeits rather than fight Rose. Lastly, Rose defeats Matt, earning herself the prized position of Royal Guardsman.
- That night, the recruits celebrate in the Beyond. Feeders ambush the party, killing dozens. Tick (the head trainer) is killed by a demon, and his corpse is possessed. Velma is killed as well. In order to save Rose, Matt possesses a demon, but quickly loses control. An unknown man (later revealed as Matt's biological father) kills the demon before fleeing into the forest.
- At the graduation ceremony, Diego recognizes the man who killed his mother. He and Matt follow the man into the Palace, unearthing an attempt to raid the Palace Vault. Matt confronts and fights a demon named Iris (later revealed to be his sister). He shoots at the fleeing Equalists, hitting one (who is later revealed as Diego's father).

- Meanwhile, Rose's true identity is announced. An assassin (Jack) shoots her, but she is saved by her Adamic armor. A massacre begins in the plaza, and Antai (who is actually Jack disguised by a shape-shifting relic called the Morphmask) leads her through the tunnels.
- Rose is forced to open the Inheritance Box and discovers the spoken spell "Faza Le Bakanzah."
- Antai (the real Antai) confronts Jack. Jack possesses Rose and forces her to shoot Antai (first in the chest and then in the head).
- Great-grandpa Titan uses a spoken spell to resurrect Antai. Antai's heart begins beating, but he does not wake up.
- Diego's father is hanged. Diego gets himself expelled from the guard for trying to save his father.
- King Dralton uses an amulet with the demon spell to interrogate Jack. Infiltrating Jack's memories, he sees that the Holy One is underground. (The king assumes that the Holy One is under Cavernum, but it is later revealed that King Dralton is mistaken. The Holy One is actually under Hogrum.)

Previously in The Surviving:

- Prologue reveals that, 18 years ago, Rose's father (Zezric) had a terrible nightmare. When he awoke from the dream, he discovered that he had accidentally stabbed his wife in his sleep. As she lost consciousness, he promised her that he wouldn't let her die.
- Back in the present, Matt and Rose are beginning their careers as full-fledged guardsmen.
- Matt discovers he is a mystic (someone with the rare gift of soul-travel—to untether their soul and move strictly as spirit). Matt uses this gift to visit Rose in her dreams.
- Meanwhile, Iris is punishing the 'wicked' in the name of the Holy One. She (being Matt's sister) is a mystic as well,

entering dreams and judging people for their sins. If guilty, she marks their doors with blood; then, she slaughters them in their sleep.

- Several survivors from Lycon (the sanctuary that was destroyed in book 1) arrive in Cavernum. One of them (Gideon) brings the soul-anchor of a fallen Guardian.
- The High Council decides to bestow that soul-anchor on a current Guardian's apprentice, thus creating a new Guardian. Quill (Vyle's older brother) is selected.
- To fill the newly-available apprenticeship, The Surviving is organized. Matt, Rose, Diego, Vyle, and Crasilda are among those chosen as champions.
- For the first challenge, each champion must defend the laborers during the Lumber Haul. Feeders attack, and Rose speaks the "Burn" spell (Havaknah Ra), accidentally killing both feeders and laborers alike.
- Quill's door is painted with blood, marking him for death.
- Kendra begins training Matt to heal. Things quickly become romantic.
- For the second challenge, the champions must defend various citizens that have been marked for death. Matt is assigned to defend Quill. Iris attacks, but is subdued by Quill. Before Quill can kill her, Matt stabs him in the head. Iris escapes.
- Matt meets Great-grandpa Titan. When he sees Matt, he freaks out, somehow calling Matt by name before Matt was even introduced. Reading his mind, Matt discovers that Titan doesn't have regular dementia; he purposefully erased his own memories.
- At Judy's request, Matt attends the Fall Ball with Rose. That night (Hallow's Eve), he helps to retrieve Antai from the Veil (the barrier between the physical and spiritual realms). Antai finally wakes up.

- That same night, Jack escapes from the Pit with the help of Commander Noyen. Noyen is captured and sentenced to death for his crimes.
- Jack (also a mystic like Matt, and thus able to possess people using soul-travel) possesses Octavian (a royal guardsman) and uses his body to kill Great-grandpa Titan.
- From various clues, Dralton suspects that the Holy One is hiding beneath the ruins of Hogrum.
- For the third challenge, the recruits are sent to Hogrum to spy on the Holy One. Vyle tries to prevent Rose from going to the Palace. He reveals that he knows there will be an ambush because his father is in cahoots with the Holy One. When Rose threatens to tell the High Council, Vyle attacks Rose, freezing her beneath the canal surface.
- Matt visits Kentville to say goodbye to Judy before she passes. Then, he hurries to Hogrum, arriving moments after Rose is frozen. He subdues Vyle and rescues Rose from the water, using the Breath of Life (a healing kiss used to transfer some of the soul) to revive her.
- As Rose recovers, Matt ventures into the Palace where he is captured by the Holy One. He awakens in Hogrum's underground prison (analogous to the Pit) alongside Nevela, Diego's mom, and several strangers. Hood (the same feeder that bit Matt in book 1) appears, claiming to know Matt's father. He betrays the Holy One to help them escape.
- They return to Cavernum. Unbeknownst to Matt, the other escapees are possessed, marked with tattoo spells that can destroy the sanctuary walls.
- They arrive in time for Rose's coronation ceremony. Before King Dralton can crown Rose, Diego (possessed by a demon) shoots Dralton with an Adamic bullet. In the end, Dralton dies, and Matt is framed for the assassination.
- Matt is exposed as a demon and sent to the Pit, but Rose sets him free and gives him the Morphmask to help him escape.

- After seeking Iris's aid, Matt manages to perform an exorcism on Diego. Matt, Diego, Rose, and Antai split up and pursue the other possessed escapees. They manage to stop some of the bombers (namely Crasilda and Diego's mother) but two others get away. They activate the spells, destroying the inner and outer walls.
- Rose meets up with Zane in the Flats. General Kaynes (openly serving the Holy One) confronts them both. He uses light dominion to create illusions, eventually catching Zane by surprise and stabbing him through the chest. Before Kaynes can capture Rose, Mystery Man (Matt's dad) decapitates him.
- Rose gathers the survivors and leads them safely to the Palace. Matt does the same with Kendra's family, but feeders intercept them in the Royal Plaza.
- Vyle arrives and stabs Matt in the stomach. Before Vyle can deliver the finishing blow, Rose shoots him in the neck with an arrow. Matt takes the opportunity to feed on Vyle, using the dominion to keep Kendra alive.
- Kendra arrives safely in the palace, but Matt (being a feeder) can't enter. He chooses instead to go with his father (who is also a feeder) and Iris.
- Hours after the battle, Rose stands on the Palace Wall, looking out at the plaza. She sees the Holy One, recognizing him as her father from his portrait.

PROLOGUE

18 years earlier...

Jenevrah stumbled down the mountain, dodging rocks and roots in the darkness. Her muscles ached and burned, but she barely took notice.

The forest was unchanging. Each mile seemed like the last—an endless array of shadowy branches and lopsided soil. Her throat was raw, and her arms burned from the weight of her infant. She just needed to make it to Kentville, and Ezra would escape.

Go to Kentville. Zane will be waiting for you.

That's what Kildron had told her, but with every step, she began to doubt the plan.

I should be there by now.

She was about to lose hope when street lights pierced through the leaves. She dashed out of the trees and onto the asphalt, sprinting across the highway towards Center Street. The tiny town had only a few roads, and in a single glance, Jenevra took it all in. Some curious eyes peered out from between closed curtains, but no one ventured outside. The streets were bare.

As she studied the town, her heart sank. The gas station was on the corner, but Zane was nowhere to be seen.

I'm too late. They left me.

Jenevra clenched her fists. Only the baby in her arms kept her from lashing out in frustration. She stumbled to a standstill, suddenly exhausted. Ezra had given up crying, and Jenevra felt like giving up too.

She thought of her husband, fighting for his life against the feeders. She thought of her children and their future. If Zezric won, they would be in jeopardy.

Finally, she looked down at Ezra. "Looks like you're staying here," she whispered.

She spun in a circle scanning the city. The closest house was just a hundred yards away. The lights were on. Most importantly, a large wooden M was hanging on the front door. Jenevra let out a sigh of relief.

That's the one.

She crept to the door and held her face next to Ezra's. She stared into his brilliant blue eyes. She would be back for him. She would help her husband and return for her baby before dawn.

Jenevrah sighed. She wanted to believe it, but deep down, she knew it was a lie.

This is goodbye.

As quietly as she could, Jenevrah lowered her baby onto the doormat. Then, she unbuckled her sheathe, setting the Adamic blade on the porch a safe distance from Ezra.

Finally, Jenevrah stood, her jaw clenching as the tears saturated her eyes. Seeing him lying on the floor made her heart squeeze. The sooner Ezra was inside and warm, the better.

She pounded the door with her fist.

"I love you, Ezra. I'll always love you." She took a step to run, but paused, looking back one last time.

"Goodbye, Matt."

1

MATT

Pain radiates from my side, permeating down the length of each limb. It's as though my nerves are in hyperdrive. Every point of contact is constant anguish. My body weight feels like a hydraulic press, flattening my bones against the stone floor. I have a blanket, but it does little to cushion the grit beneath my skin—a hundred pins stabbing into my spine.

Worst of all is the itching, like a colony of ants tunneling through my insides, traveling over my intestines like a highway. I know it means the worst.

My wound is infected.

It's been three days since Vyle stabbed me… three days since I fed on his soul. I've tried to heal myself, but Kendra never taught me how to battle bacteria—not on this scale, anyway. I've done everything I can to amplify my immune system, but my soul is wrung dry like a kitchen rag. The energy I felt from feeding was spent days ago. Now, I don't know what else to do.

Even breathing has become an uphill battle. My heart patters in my chest, rapid and desperate. With every inhalation, the pain only intensifies, and I still can't get enough air. I'm slowly drowning, lungs filling up with my own internal fluids.

I'm dying.

The only thing keeping me alive is the soul anchor clasped between my clammy fingers. Iris lent it to me at Kildron's command, no doubt saving my life in the process. Normally, a soul-anchor can't be borrowed thanks to its unique bonding spell, but our tattoos happen to be identical—given by our mother.

I groan as another wave of nausea crashes over me, my agony echoing off the cave walls. The only other noise is the trickling of a small cave stream.

"Hey, Matt, you okay?" Iris asks. "You want any water?" The soft glow of light dominion emanates from her hand. The yellowish light illuminates my surroundings, showing nothing but jagged igneous rock.

"I'm fine," I wheeze, only to wince a moment later. The effort of expelling air from my lungs sends a cascade of agony pulsating through my diaphragm.

Iris frowns, disturbed by my current state. She knows the feeling first-hand. She was stabbed a few weeks ago.

It's almost poetic. Two siblings, stabbed by two siblings—Quill and Vyle Kaynes. Not to mention, Zane was stabbed as well. General Kaynes drove a blade through his chest. Unlike us, Zane didn't survive.

General Kaynes.

The thought sends memories rattling through my skull—unfamiliar, invasive memories. General Kaynes singing me happy birthday. General Kaynes slapping me in the face, his palm flat and firm. In those memories, I don't call him General Kaynes; I call him dad.

They're Vyle's memories—pieces of his soul I've consumed. His thoughts—his insecurities and fears— swim in my consciousness, constantly reminding me of the taste of his blood.

I murdered him.

"Matt? You okay?"

"Hmmm?" I open my eyes to find Iris still watching me, the gentle yellow light illuminating her blonde bangs.

"You were breathing fast," she explains. "You alright?"

"Yeah, I'm fine." I squeeze my eyes shut, wishing I could just cease to exist. Part of me wants to sleep, but another part fears that my nightmares will be as painful as reality.

"Where's Kildron?" I finally choke.

"He went to go… feed," Iris admits. She dangles her necklace—a small crystal hourglass—in front of her face and gives it a flick, watching it swing back and forth.

I stay silent. It wasn't the answer I was hoping for.

"He should be back soon," Iris guesses, giving the hourglass another flick. "Hopefully, he'll bring more food. You should get some sleep in the meantime."

It won't make any difference, I think to myself. *I'm dead either way.*

Regardless, I close my eyes. I reach deep into my mind until I find the sensory center of the thalamus—a trick Kendra once taught me. With a single command, I turn off the outside world.

Sleep!

In an instant, my connection to the world vanishes. The rocky floor dissolves below me. The trickle of a distant stream falls silent. Most importantly, my pain evaporates.

Still, discomfort creeps across my skin, but it's far less intense—from a fire hose to a water fountain.

I'm floating in an endless void, yet I'm lucid. I can hear my thoughts, and I use them to form the space around me.

Home!

Light erupts in the void of my mind, forming cream-colored wallpaper and a thick brown carpet with oak baseboards. I step onto the kitchen tile and take a seat at the dinner table. A ham sandwich is waiting for me, cut in triangles and perched on a paper towel. Beside it is a tall glass of Judy's fresh-squeezed limeade.

I pick up a sandwich and take a bite before the lunch meat grows warm. Though it's a year since she's made me one, my subconscious remembers the flavor.

"I'll be in soon." Judy's voice carries through the screen door. "Just planting some petunias."

I can see her from the dinner table, stooped over a planter box in the back of the yard. The sight is calming, even knowing it's a fabrication.

"So that's your adoptive mom?" a voice speaks from behind me.

I whip around, knocking over the glass of limeade in the process, sending the juice waterfalling off the edge of the table.

Kildron only laughs. He stands in the corner of the kitchen, looking curiously around the house. "Nice place you got here. Very… modest."

"What the heck. What are you doing in my head?"

Kildron ignores the question. Instead, he motions through the screen door at Judy. "That's your adoptive mom, right? She seems like a nice lady. Maybe I'll have to introduce myself."

"What, no!"

"Hello, there!" Kildron slides open the screen door and waltzes into the garden. "The name's Kildron Kaimor, pleased to meet—."

Disappear.

In the blink of an eye, Judy flashes out of existence. Kildron blinks, frowns, and turns back to me. "Bummer. Maybe I can meet the pops instead?"

"What's wrong with you?" I demand. "You can't just barge inside my head."

"It was risky." Kildron laughs as he struts across the kitchen and into the family room. He lifts a picture frame from the fireplace mantle. "I was a little worried you'd be dreaming of that girl of yours. Talk about awkward."

Disappear.

The picture—a photo from 8th grade graduation—vanishes, leaving him scowling at his palm.

"Seriously, get out!" I demand. "My dreams are private."

Kildron looks at me, and grins. "Oh c'mon. Don't act like you've never crashed a dream without permission."

I have, of course, which only infuriates me more.

He holds my gaze and grins wider. "See, no need to be so judgy. Now, take a seat. We have some catching up to do." He spins the dining chair so that it's facing backwards and sits straddling the back-rest—exactly how Zane used to.

"What makes you think I want to talk?"

His smile droops, and he genuinely seems disappointed.

"C'mon. I changed your diapers, kid. I mean, aren't you a little curious where I've been? What I've been doing? How I survived all these years?"

"You've been feeding." I say it with more disdain than I intended. "What else is there to know?" I refuse to look him in the eye, instead watching a hummingbird in the garden.

"Not just feeding," Kildron insists. "Saving lives. Bringing down the Order. Hunting them one by one. They call me the Archangel for a reason, Ezra. I've never hurt a single Adamic." He emphatically holds a finger in the air. "Not one Adamic hair was harmed. Not one!"

"Congrats," I mutter.

"Alright." Kildron stands and wanders over to the fridge. "I see you're not interested in me at the moment. That's fair. Let's talk about you." Kildron opens the door and grabs a gallon of milk, taking a swig straight from the carton. "What about that girl we saved? The blonde?"

Kendra.

The thought of her leaves me feeling empty. Helpless. I managed to save her, but I lost her in the process. Now, as a feeder, the very power of Adamic separates us.

I shrug. "What about her?"

Kildron is still looking through the fridge. Manipulating my dream, he forms a spoon in his hand and scoops a bite of Judy's potato casserole. "You tell me," he says between chews. "Last I saw you, you were picking flowers for the princess. I suppose you had a change of heart, not that I can blame you. The blonde is quite a catch. Besides, healers really know their way around the bod—"

"Shut up! Please! Can you just stop?"

Kildron closes the fridge and licks the spoon clean. "Look, I get it. You have a lot to process. That's why I'm here. I've been through this before. I know what it's like."

With every word, I feel my pulse rising. "What? Because I'm a feeder, you think you know what I'm going through?" I feel so much rage inside me, I don't know what to do with it. Maybe it's the fact that I'm dying. Or maybe it's Vyle's anger, growing inside me like a parasite.

"Not just that," Kildron says. "All of it. I know what it's like to be a demon. I know what it's like to be separated from the girl I love. I know what it's like to watch a city crumble. To lose everything you hold d—"

"I'm nothing like you," I hiss, desperately wanting to believe it.

Kildron falls silent. I can feel his emotions radiating toward me. Confusion. Frustration. Indignation. Disappointment.

Finally, he sighs. "I'm trying to save Cavernum, just like you. I'm protecting people, just like you. Tell me how we're different."

"You choose to feed. You do it everyday. I only did it because I had to."

Kildron laughs. "You think I feed because I want to? God, you're naive. My feeding saved your life. It saved your girl too. You should be thanking me."

"I'm a feeder," I stammer. "I may as well be dead."

Kildron's hand shoots forward, grabbing me by the throat. He doesn't squeeze, but the pressure is enough to scare me. I can feel my pulse thumping against his thumb. I try to pull my arm away, but he only tightens his grip. "Don't ever say that..." Kildron seethes, his eyes filled with a burst of madness. "Not in front of me." He releases my neck with a shove. "Nothing is worse than being dead," he hisses. "Your mother is dead, and you're not. You don't get to compare the two."

"Doesn't feel that way," I spit back at him, massaging my airway. "Pretty soon we'll all be dead. For all we know, the Holy One already has the Library."

"He's still looking," Kildron states. "I confirmed it from a feeder today. We can still stop him."

"You're lying to yourself," I insist. "He has an army. He speaks Adamic. The second he sees us, we're dead."

"He only speaks one phrase," Kildron argues. "Maybe two. Neither spell can kill us, as far as I know."

"Wonderful. Problem solved," I mock. "Can you please leave me alone now?"

"Why? So you can soul-walk your way to the palace? I know that's what you're planning; It won't work, Ezra."

"You don't know that."

"Oh, yes I do! Trust me; I've tried a million times to soul-travel through the walls. It's impossible. From the very first time you feed, your soul is marked. The sanctuary spells can sense it. Even soul-walking, you can't pass through."

It doesn't matter what Kildron says. I can be at the palace wall in a matter of minutes. I have to at least try.

I urge my soul out of my body.

"Stop!" Kildron grabs my wrist, and I feel his soul—a metaphysical force—anchoring me to my body. I try to pull away, but he doesn't budge. Even in my own dream, he's stronger than me.

"Let me go," I try to twist out of his grasp, but his nails dig into my wrist.

"You'll die," Kildron hisses. "If you leave your body when you're this weak, you won't make it back. If you really love the girl, you won't risk your life for something so stupid."

I pull again, and he finally lets go.

"Don't be foolish, Ezra. You have to think of the bigger picture."

"What bigger picture?" I throw my hands in the air. "I'm dying, and you know it. I could be dead by tomorrow."

I expect to see a flicker of sadness, perhaps some regret. Instead, Kildron smiles. His lips part, showing a full view of his pearly whites. "Oh, give me some credit. You really think I'd let you die?"

"As if you have a choice," I sneer.

"I do… I do have a choice, Ezra. I choose to feed."

I turn, locking eyes with Kildron. "What does that have to do with anything?"

"Wake up, and I'll show you." He smiles, a mixture of pride and mischief. "It's time I taught you the Laying on of Hands."

"The what?"

"You heard me. C'mon." With that, he turns and walks toward the wall. He passes through the wallpaper like a cartoon ghost, his consciousness slowly fading from my presence.

With no other option, I close my eyes. It takes all of my focus.

Awake!

The moment my eyes open, consciousness is excruciating. As my senses reboot, the pain takes hold of my focus. It radiates from my wound, causing my bones to ache. With every breath, a knife digs deeper into my side. I breathe as shallow as possible, but that only makes my head hurt worse.

"Iris, can you give us some light?" Kildron calls in the darkness. "I want you to see this."

Immediately, our little cavern illuminates with pale-yellow light.

Iris steps closer. "What's going on?"

"I'm giving Ezra the Laying on of Hands."

"The what?" Iris asks, and I'm grateful I don't have to utter the words myself.

"Really? Zane never… okay. Allow me to explain. It's a method to transfer one's soul, almost like the breath of life. Historically, prophets used it to heal the sick."

He kneels down in the dirt next to my bedroll. "A healer can only transfer a fraction of their soul. The benefits are modest at best. As a feeder, however, I'll be transferring many souls. It should be enough to stabilize Ezra."

I think of the prison below Hogrum. There, the Holy One was feeding on his prisoners, passing the power to his followers. *This must be how he did it.*

"Will it feel like feeding?" I wheeze. "Will I see their memories?"

Kildron shrugs. "Good question. You'll have to let us know. You ready?"

I nod.

"Get comfortable. This may take a bit." Kildron places both hands palm-down on my forehead. He lets the entire weight of his arms press into my skin, driving the back of my skull into my makeshift pillow.

Then, I feel the energy. The dominion flows into me like a babbling brook. The moment I get a taste, I'm filled with an unbearable thirst. As the energy flows in, my soul reaches out, lapping desperately at every drop of energy. I catch glimpses—a feeder holding down his victim by their hair, a feeder chasing a boy down an alley—but there's no rage or insatiable hunger. It's like I'm watching a movie rather than living it.

Still, I can't help but lap at the trickle of souls. After a minute, I notice that the pain has subsided, suppressed and compressed back into my stab wound. My muscles feel rejuvenated, and my head is clear.

When Kildron finally lifts his hands, my heart sinks. I still thirst.

I need more.

"Wait!" I beg. "Just a little more."

Iris gives me a strange look, and Kildron shakes his head. His face is extra pale in Iris's light.

"Sorry," Kildron gasps. "That's all I have. It'll have to do for now. You should sleep. Keep resting."

I sit up, amazed by the absence of my pain. Once again, my body is a tool, not a prison. The dominion buzzes within me, promising to obey my every command.

I focus my soul around my wound, commanding my immune system.

Amplify.

A subtle itch intensifies, but the pain is suppressed, carrying with it the promise of improvement.

"I actually feel pretty good," I insist. "Thanks." I carefully roll onto my hands and knees, climbing to my feet. A wave of dizziness washes over me, but it quickly passes.

"Ezra, don't be stupid," Kildron begs. "You need to rest."

"I will rest; there's just something I have to do first." I stagger away from my bed, making my way toward the labyrinth of lava tubes. "Iris, can you show me the way out of here?" I ask.

"Kildron's right," Iris says. "Kendra can wait. It's not worth the risk."

"This isn't about Kendra," I say. "It's about Zane. He deserves to be buried."

Kildron snorts somewhere behind me. "We don't bury the dead; we burn them."

"All the more reason you should come. The flames might attract feeders. We'll be safer as a group."

"C'mon, Ezra. This is idiotic," Kildron breathes.

Before I can stop it, my anger begins to flare. "Don't you care that his body is just laying out there? After all he's done for us, doesn't he deserve better?" I take a few deep breaths, hunching over as the pain reawakens in my gut. This time, I lower my voice. "Don't you want to say goodbye?"

Kildron clenches his jaw, finally nodding. "Fine. But not now. It's midnight. We'll leave at dawn."

2

ROSE

I stand on the wall, overlooking the Royal Plaza. I've been here for nearly two days, wondering if my father will return, yet praying he doesn't.

He's the Holy One, Rose. Your own father did this.

Every time I think of him, my throat gets tight. My father killed Grandpa. He captured Nevela, and sent a demon to take her place as my maid. He sent feeders to my graduation party, killing Tick… killing Velma. He manipulated Iris, turning her into an executioner to punish the 'wicked.' He unleashed feeders on the sanctuary, massacring thousands.

All the deaths… all the suffering… it's all his fault.

Why, Dad? How could you do this?

Now, I see why Grandpa didn't tell me. Despite everything, I want to find my father. I want to understand. *He isn't a monster. He can't be!*

I pull my cloak closer. The sun has risen, but I can hardly feel its warmth. Frost still coats the outside of my clothes.

"Rose," Antai calls out to me as he climbs the steps to the wall. "I brought you breakfast." He holds out a large bowl of soup, if I can even call it that. It's 90% broth with some corn and turnips floating on the surface. I take it, relishing the warmth of the ceramic.

Antai smiles, removing a cloth from his pocket. He unfolds it, revealing a partially smashed slice of cornbread. “They only had a few of these, but I managed to snag you one. It’s still warm.”

“You should have given it to one of the children.” I mutter.

His smile droops. “You don’t want it?”

“It’s fine,” I say, not wanting to hurt his feelings. “I’ll eat it. You can set it down on the ledge.”

Antai places it gingerly on the stone parapet as I take a few sips of the soup. I know they’re rationing, but this hardly seems adequate. Morale is low enough as it is.

Antai rests his elbows on the stone and leans over the parapet, scanning the horizon. Over his guard uniform, he’s wearing a light gray cloak—the color of ash—not for the cold, but for the funeral. Everyone wears gray to pay their respects. It’s tradition.

“You’re still not coming?” Antai asks.

“We’ve talked about this, Antai. He’ll see the smoke. He’ll know what we’re doing. It would be the perfect time to strike.”

“I know. I just… It's your Grandpa's funeral, Rose. I guess I figured you’d change your mind.”

I squeeze my eyes shut, hoping it’ll prevent the tears from spilling out. “Sometimes, sacrifices have to be made.”

“And sometimes they don’t,” Antai says. “We need you on the throne, Rose. The High Council is making decisions without you.”

“So fill me in,” I say.

“Fine,” Antai groans. “The food count is final. Most of the harvest is in the outer granaries. We only have two months if we ration. We’re allotting extra calories for the guardsmen to avoid fatigue on watch.” He looks away, almost ashamed. “Also, to conserve resources, we’ve decided to execute all prisoners of the Pit.”

My stomach sinks. A few weeks ago, I would’ve been appalled at the notion. But now… I can see the logic.

“Is that all?” I ask.

“We’ve tripled the wall patrol. They’ve been instructed to shoot on sight. And we’ve sent four messenger hawks to the communication bunker. Two returned with the message unopened. The other two are still unaccounted for. Without the bunker, we have no way to contact the other sanctuaries. That's about it."

"Sounds like it's going fine without me," I mutter.

"It's not," Antai gripes. "I have to fight them on every little thing. I need you with me." He sighs, meeting my gaze. "Answer me this... what makes you so sure he'll return?"

"I just... I have a feeling, alright? I need to be here when he arrives. I can reason with him, Antai. I know I can."

Antai flares his nostrils. "And what if you can't?"

I don't say anything. I don't have an answer.

"Okay," Antai huffs. "That's fine. I just think this is a waste of time. That's all. If your father wants to talk, he'll find a way. He obliterated the sanctuary for heaven's sake. I'm sure he can manage a simple letter. You don't need to stand here day and night. Not while so many people need you, myself included."

"Maybe," I breathe, "but I can't risk it."

Antai grimaces, trying hard not to express his frustration. He shoves his hands in his waistband, his thumbs drumming on the leather. "I get that, Rose. I do. But... I think you're overestimating yourself."

I scrunch my nose, letting him see my disapproval.

"Your..." He lowers his voice. "Your father knew you were here, and still, he tried to bomb the palace. If we hadn't got to Nevela in time, he would have succeeded. The man killed Dralton—his own father. He slaughtered thousands of innocent people. How do you plan to reason with someone like that?"

"I... I have to try." I insist, trying to conceal my own doubt.

Antai presses his palms to his temples. "Look, Rose. You know I worry about you, and I'm trying not to let that dictate my actions. You're the queen. You can take care of yourself. But I will say this. It's your grandfather's funeral, for God's sake. What will the people think when you don't show up? You're supposed to give the closing remarks." His head ever so slightly shakes back and forth. "Tell me you'll at least think about it."

The truth is, I think about it constantly. I won't admit it, but I'm at my breaking point. My back aches, my feet throb, and my elbows are bruised from leaning on the stone. More than anything, I'm exhausted from my own anxiety—constantly entertaining new scenarios in my mind, three days of hypothetical conversations with my father. *I can't take it anymore.*

I stare out over the plaza, unsure of how to respond. "I'll think about it," I promise.

Antai sighs. "It starts in an hour. You still have time to change your—"

"I said I'd think about it," I snap.

Antai bows his head before drumming his thumb on his holster. "Okay, well, I hope to see you there." He begins backing away. "If you need anything before then, send a messenger. I love you."

I watch him go, unable to say it back. I do love him, or at least I used to. Since his coma, we've hardly had time to speak, much less rekindle our relationship.

Don't get me wrong. I would happily spend the day with Antai, living out my girlish fantasies of sleigh rides through the snow and cuddling in front of the fire with of cup of hot caramel, but not today… not anytime soon.

Love can wait.

I stare out at the plaza, wrestling with my fears. Except for the dead, the plaza is abandoned. The feeders are out of sight, hibernating in their stolen dens, most likely gorging on this year's harvest. Meanwhile, the bodies begin to rot. The smell is subtle, but I know it'll get worse.

I breathe into the base of my gloves, attempting to warm my frozen fingers. The sun is setting, and the temperature is beginning to plummet. For the third day in a row, my presence on the wall has been fruitless.

Don't give up, Rose. He'll return eventually.

I want to attend the funeral—more than anything—but my worries won't let me leave. I have this terrible dread that he'll charge the moment I step off the wall.

Where are you, Father?

Twang.

The sound of a bowstring splits the silence, originating from somewhere behind me. Turning my back to the plaza, I peer over the edge of the wall.

Twang.

Gideon pulls back his bowstring and releases another arrow into a hay bale. He flashes a smile when he sees me watching. "Don't mind me, My Queen. I am but keeping the muscles warm," he sings in a thick French accent.

For the first time today, I feel a smile pulling on my lips. Over the last month, Gideon has proven himself a trusted friend. Not only did he train me in archery, but he offered wisdom when I needed it most.

I hesitate before climbing down the steps of the palace wall. If Zezric comes, I'll be a short dash from the wall. Unlike the funeral, the risk is minimal.

As I reach the grassy landing, I meet the obsidian eyes of Gideon. He pulls back the string and releases another arrow.

"Decided to join me for some shooting, have you?"

"Not quite," I say as I approach. "Do you have a moment to talk?"

Gideon smiles, slinging the bow over his shoulder. "For you, I have many moments. I must admit, I've been missing you at our daily practice. It is not as fulfilling to train alone."

"I'm sorry, Gideon. I've been… busy."

"Of course, My Queen. No apologies needed."

"Can you be honest with me, Gideon?"

"Always, My Queen."

"Does everyone think I'm going crazy?"

"Hmmm." As he thinks, Gideon strums his bowstring like a harp. "Perhaps some, Your Majesty. To be frank, many suspect you are depressed. Or rather, they suspect that you've given up. Most of the survivors have lost hope, and they are looking to validate their own despair. I believe they find that validation in you."

His words sting, but I expected as much.

"Does it look like I've given up to you?"

Gideon furrows his brow and looks me over, studying my

demeanor. "Sometimes, Your Majesty, we must give up to survive. When the Holy One invaded Lycon, I fought to save my people. I fought with all my heart. However, at a certain point, I gave up. I stopped fighting, and started running instead. If I hadn't given up, I would've died with my brethren. Sometimes, in order to survive, we must give up on one goal and adopt another."

He looks up at the palace, climbing the spires with his eyes. "It seems to me, Your Majesty, that you've given up on being queen. You've abandoned your duties for something else that takes precedent. I have no qualms with that."

Antai was right.

"And what if I don't want to give up on being queen?" I ask.

"You still have the throne, don't you?" Gideon chuckles. "All you have to do is take your place. Otherwise, I imagine they will choose a leader in your absence."

I think for a moment. Grandpa knew who the Holy One was. He knew it was his own son, and yet he never managed to make contact, at least not that I know of. Perhaps, I'm not any different... Perhaps, I'm wasting my time after all.

Why is Antai always right?

"Thank you, Gideon. Thank you for being blunt with me. I'm afraid I have to cut our conversation short. It's time I resumed my duties."

Gideon smiles. "Very well. In that case, shall I expect you for archery tomorrow?"

I'm about to decline when several memories come to mind. The arrow that pierced Vyle's neck, saving Matt in the process. The arrow that dropped a feeder before it could kill Diego's family.

"We'll see," I say.

I take one last look at the wall, and swallow my rising apprehension.

If you want me, father, you'll have to come find me.

I watch as the flames consume Grandpa's body. The King of Cavernum is finally being cremated.

The entire palace is gathered outside the temple where a funeral pyre has been erected. It holds less than a dozen bodies, including Grandpa's, but they represent the whole of Cavernum—thousands and thousands of deceased.

A large crowd is gathered around the pyre. They're one part elite and two parts commoner. Not many laborers made it to safety, save those Equalists who were armed with amulets.

Now, they watch the fire with the same hopelessness I feel. They know their loved ones are scattered throughout the sanctuary, slowly rotting. They need hope; they need it desperately.

The priest has already given his speech, and a remnant of the orchestra is playing a dismal melody. As the flames grow smaller, the last violin vibrato falls silent.

Antai gives my hand a quick squeeze before letting go. It's his way of saying 'it's time.'

I position myself between the temple and the pyre, facing the crowd. *This is it, Rose. Just be honest with them.* I take a deep breath, and let dominion amplify my voice.

"To be honest, I haven't given this speech much thought. I want to say the right thing—something to ease your pain and give you hope. It's what I'm sure you're all expecting from a queen. If my grandpa were here, it's what I would expect of him."

I take a deep breath, hearing the crackle of the embers as I collect myself. "You want answers and promises, and the truth is, I don't have them. I'm no different than you. I don't have any hope to share with you. I don't know what's going to happen. For whatever reason, the Holy One—" *My father...* "—has decided to spare the palace." *For now.* "The future is... uncertain. At this point, I can't make you any promises."

I look over at Antai who purses his lips. I can tell he isn't a fan of my speech.

"I'm not trying to be bleak," I insist. "I'm trying to be transparent. We have much to overcome if we're going to survive, and I can't promise perfect solutions. I can only promise one thing: that you're not alone. Whatever you are feeling—your suffering, your pain—someone else is feeling the same… I'm feeling the same. We are in this together."

I look back at Antai who gives an encouraging nod. His expression is more optimistic now.

"I can't speak for all of you, so I will speak for myself. I feel lucky to be alive—and I want to feel grateful—but at the same time, I feel guilty. I feel guilty for celebrating life when so many didn't make it. I feel angry. I want to fight back; I want to kill them for what they did, but I'm afraid I'm not strong enough. Most of all, I want to have hope, but I'm afraid I'm only lying to myself."

The crowd listens with solemn faces. If they disagree with my words, they don't voice it.

"And while my words carry no promise of the future, I'll make you a promise of the present. I will do everything in my power to protect you. I will give my life if necessary." I look down at the smoking pyre —at my grandfather's ashes. "My grandfather had a saying, a personal mantra, if you will. He used to say, 'A servant is subject to his master, but a king is subject to all." He lived his live according to those words, and he died in your service. In the wake of his death, I've inherited his throne… so from this moment forward, I will live as he lived. From this day forward, I will be your servant."

I step away from the fire, resuming my place in the audience.

Antai wraps his arm around me, bathing me in his body heat. "You did well."

"Thanks," I whisper as I nuzzle into his shoulder.

We stand in silence, listening as the orchestra plays one last song. I lean my head on Antai's shoulder and nuzzle into his neck. Meanwhile, my mind wanders beyond the wall.

Part of me wonders if my father can hear the music. He would probably recognize it as a dirge. Is he listening now, from somewhere in the Core? Does he regret killing his own father?

DING!

The bell tower rings out, disrupting the musicians. Some lower their instruments while others attempt to keep playing. Within seconds, the song falls into disarray, and the music falls silent.

I hold my breath, waiting for another toll, fearing the worst. Three tolls means imminent danger. Perhaps the Holy One has decided to kill us after all. Another Adamic bomb could blow at any moment.

Silence.

One toll: friendly arrival.

"Matt." I whisper his name loud enough for Antai to hear.

His eyes widen. "You think?"

I don't bother responding. I turn and run for the palace gate. Using dominion, I amplify my muscles, reaching speeds unattainable for the average human.

I'm almost there when several soldiers remove the iron crossbeam. A moment later, the gate swings slowly inward, parting in the middle. The doors create a small opening—no more than a foot or two—when a body slips inside.

That's not possible.

General Kaynes brushes the snow from his iconic silver cloak. He stands tall and grins, reveling in the commotion his presence provokes.

My mouth falls open as I stare.

There's no way!

I saw General Kaynes get decapitated. Matt's father cut his head clean off. I watched it happen.

General Kaynes turns, and his eyes find me. He ignores the other soldiers, approaching me with a swoosh of his cloak. "Hello, My Queen."

I'm frozen in place as he bows at my feet. Then, he takes my hand and kisses my knuckles. My heart races, and my hand quivers. My gut tells me I'm in danger, but I don't know what to do.

Finally, General Kaynes lifts his head. He stands and leans in, whispering in my ear. "Your father sends his regards."

3

MATT

I squint down the tunnel, partially blinded by light. Leaning against the wall and caked in cave dust, a wooden ladder ascends to the surface world.

Kildron stops, dimming his light dominion slightly. “Alright, Ezra, before we go up, I want to make one thing clear. You can’t show an ounce of weakness. You can’t limp. You can’t give them any reason to target us, do you hear me?”

“Sure,” I mumble. I touch my hand to my face, or rather, to the morph mask I’m wearing. Rose gave it to me to help me escape from the pit, and I’ve had it ever since.

I command the mask, imagining the features of the feeder who first bit me.

Hood!

Immediately, an earthquake erupts across my body, the mask at the epicenter. My nerves tremble and my clothes transform into a black, tattered cloak. Most convincing are the tattoos. Adamic armor covers my skin from head to toe. I know it won't actually protect me, but it sure looks convincing.

Kildron studies me. The corner of Kildron’s lips turn down, and I see the recognition in his eyes.

"You knew him, right?" I ask.

Kildron sighs. "Yeah. I've known Mutalah since we were little. Before Zane even. He was my only friend in the Order."

"The Order?"

"The Order of the Firstborn. It's a church. More of a cult, really. It's fairly popular among feeders. Only devout followers can receive the Mark of the Beast."

"You were a believer?"

Kildron shrugs. "My parents certainly were. It wasn't the best childhood, but Mutalah made it manageable." He motions at my appearance. "How'd you know him, anyhow?"

"I wouldn't really say I knew him," I explain. "When I first discovered Hogrum, he was there. He tried to feed on me, but Zane showed up and saved me. Then the council sent us back to Hogrum—that was a few weeks ago. The Holy One captured us, but—" I've already forgotten his name. "—your friend set us free. Looking back, I assumed it was a trap—you know, so that we'd bring the Adamic Bombs to Cavernum—but now I don't know what to think."

"There are no secrets with the Holy One," Kildron says. "He knew Mutalah. He knew he'd try to set you free. He probably planned it from the beginning." Kildron sighs. "Anyway, you should change disguises. Mutalah is too recognizable."

"I don't know any other feeders," I say.

"Here." Kildron reaches over and touches his hand to my morph mask. A second later, the familiar wave of pins and needles washes over me.

Iris cringes.

"I'm hideous, aren't I?" My voice comes out in a garbled croak. My tongue slips into the gaps where my teeth should be. "I feel like my skin is falling off."

"It is," Kildron laughs. "Some feeders live so long, their bodies begin to rot. The power of feeding sustains them as their skin decays."

Iris points at my cheek. "Is that… a maggot?"

I raise my hand to my face and feel something small squirm beneath my finger. My nausea returns.

"They're not real," Kildron says. "It's just an illusion."

"They feel real," I complain. "I can feel them wiggling."

"You can remove them if you want." Kildron says.

"How?"

"The mask can only imitate real people, but the accessories are changeable. Clothes, jewelry, even weapons. It would be a pretty useless relic if you could only imitate a single outfit."

"Weapons?" I ask.

"Here. Give me that." Kildron reaches out and grabs my chin, slipping his fingers under the morph mask. At first it resists, firmly suctioned to my face. Then, the mask lifts away and peels from my skin.

Once free from my face, the fleshy color drains from the mask, returning to its natural silver hue. Now, it's a simple metal oval with slits for the eyes and mouth.

Kildron presses the mask to his face, instantly transforming. His curly hair recedes, shortening in length, but remaining the same color. His frown lines disappear, and I find myself looking at my own reflection. He's wearing an identical blood-stained guard uniform.

"You're me," I gasp.

"Observe," Kildron speaks in my voice. Suddenly, his clothes transform into a black tux. Then, they gradually morph into tattered blue jeans and a t-shirt. "See, I control the outfit."A moment later, his clothes transform into fireman gear, complete with a helmet and respirator. Lastly, his outfit morphs back into my blood-stained guard uniform.

Kildron grins proudly, showing my teeth. "What do you want to see first? Knives? A sword maybe?"

Starting in his palm, a silver blade materializes, extending into the air from a simple metal hilt. The steel glistens in the Adamic light.

"Does it cut?" I wonder.

Kildron swings the sword at the wooden ladder. It slices an inch into the wooden beam, breaking off a few splinters.

"The spell is a powerful one." He swings again, chopping into the wood once more. "Everything you create exerts a force. Your clothes feel genuine, your weight actually changes, and yes, a knife will cut. But there's a catch…"

Kildron lets go of the hilt, and immediately the blade vanishes, dissolving like dust in the wind.

"Once an accessory leaves your hand, the spell loses effect. Sadly, that means projectiles don't work. You can form a gun." He raises his arms, bolstering a massive shotgun. "But it won't fire bullets." He looks at me and grins. "Oh, I forgot. You can even fake injuries." Suddenly, the skin peels open the side of his neck, forming a perfect feeder bite, and the blood begins to gush.

"Go ahead," Kildron coaxes. "Touch it."

I reach out and poke the stream of blood with my index finger. Exactly as expected, it's warm and wet. However, when I lift my finger, it comes away clean. There isn't the faintest trace of blood.

With that, Kildron peels off the mask and hands it back to me. "I think that about covers it."

Iris eyes Kildron suspiciously. "How do you know all this?"

"It's a royal heirloom. The mask once belonged to the King of Hogrum; he was my uncle-in-law. Jenevrah showed it to me when we were dating. We… uhhh…" He smiles mischievously. "Well, I won't go into details."

"Gross," Iris says, looking away.

Once I put the mask back on, Kildron touches his hand to my forehead and the familiar chills spread over my body, returning me to the form of an ancient feeder, this time without the maggots. A moment later, I'm wearing a long black cloak—the same type of cloak Hood once wore.

"Why the cloak?" I ask.

"It's customary for members of the Order. Everyone ready?"

"Don't you want an amulet?" Iris asks. She holds up her spare amplifier, composed of two simple symbols.

Between the three of us, we have three amulets. Iris has two, her soul-anchor and an amplifier. I have the other—the amplifier Kendra gave me as I kissed her goodbye.

"Nah," Kildron says. "I'm a feeder. It wouldn't do me much good."

I blink. "Why not?"

"You're serious?" Kildron says. "Zane never explained this?"

I shake my head.

Kildron points at the amplifier in Iris's hand. "You ever wonder why feeders don't use amulets? Hypothetically, they could amplify the souls of a dozen victims, becoming unstoppable, right?"

Unsure, I take a guess. "Y—"

"Wrong!" Kildron interjects. "Amulets are smarter than that, or Adamic is, I suppose. They can differentiate between souls. Amplifiers only amplify the soul of the user, not the foreign souls they consumed. Most feeders never even strain their original soul, making an amplifier useless. Same goes for soul-anchors. I can use one, but it won't do me any good until I'm down to my bare soul. Make sense?"

"Yeah," I say.

Iris nods.

"Good. Let's get going."

Kildron holds the ladder as Iris ascends, illuminating the tunnel with dominion. The wooden rungs creak with each step, but it easily holds her weight. She reaches up with her hands to twist a wooden latch above her head. Then, she places her palms flat on the tunnel ceiling and shoves.

A trapdoor swings upward as the dust rains down. The opening unveils nothing but more darkness. Without a word, Iris disappears through the opening she created. After a second, her voice hisses in the silence.

"Clear."

"Now you, Ezra," Kildron directs.

My side hurts, but I don't voice it. This was my idea after all.

I take hold of the ladder and grit my teeth. As I lift my foot to the first rung, I can feel my side splitting open. More than the pain is the fear—fear that I'm undoing days' worth of healing. Or worse, fear that I haven't improved at all. Fear that I'm doomed to a slow, agonizing death.

"You good?" Kildron asks.

"Mmhhmm." I grunt, biting through another step. Then another. I'm about to take a third when Iris peers down from the top of the ladder.

"Screw this," she mumbles. The air ripples below me, lifting me gently towards the surface. As I pass through the hatch, Iris takes my hands and pulls me to my feet.

"Thanks."

I can feel my pulse in my forehead, and have to swallow the vomit rising in my esophagus, but I'm still on my feet. That alone is a victory.

Iris eyes me up and down. "You okay? You don't look too good."

"Yeah, I'm fine," I lie, directing my focus to our new surroundings. I'm in a small storage closet. There's a broom and some rags in a bucket. On the floor next to the hatch is a crumpled rug, just big enough to conceal the opening.

Kildron emerges from the hatch, closing it behind him before sliding the rug over the top.

Iris pushes open the closet door, and we emerge in the saloon of Bob's Brew. Immediately, I'm hit with the stench of human excrement. It's coming from the bodies. One is draped over the bar, blood staining the wood next to its neck. Another could pass as a pile of laundry, crumpled in the corner.

I reach to cover my nose, but Kildron shakes his head. "Don't. You can't act appalled. This is an average day for a feeder. We're lucky it's cold, or the stench would be worse."

I nod. As we move toward the exit, I take note of the damage. Several barrels lie on their sides, the contents either consumed or tipped out. The streetside windows are broken, and the piano—the one Rose played for us—has a human-sized crater in the top.

We don't speak as we move through the doorway and into the street. It's quiet, much quieter than I thought it would be. The feeders have finished their rampage. Most likely, they're relaxing after such a feast, sleeping in their victims' bed, eating their food, trying on their clothes…

We walk in silence, the snow crunching beneath our feet. Up ahead, a feeder staggers across the street. I straighten my back and lift my chin, but my efforts aren't necessary. The feeder doesn't even give us a glance.

From Bob's Brew, we weave through the alleys until we intersect with Eastern Avenue—a direct path to the flats. We follow it downhill, pretending not to notice when feeders wander close.

We trudge through the snow, easily a foot or two thick. It fills my shoes, wetting my socks and seeping between my toes. In the distance, the Flats wrap around the sanctuary—an endless field of white.

That's when I spot them: a pair of feeders moving toward us—a man and a woman. They walk in the middle of the road, holding hands. Suddenly, the woman looks up and meets my gaze. The man does the same a moment later.

I look away and instantly regret it. From the corner of my eye, I see they're no longer holding hands.

Show no weakness.

I try to ignore them, focusing on my gait. Despite the pain, I manage a smooth stride. Kildron and Iris continue walking as well, pretending to ignore the feeders.

The couple is only a stone's throw away, whispering to one another. The male feeder closes his eyes, continuing to mouth something I can't quite hear. I use some of the dominion Kildron gave me to amplify my hearing. Their words become audible.

"The girl isn't one of us. And the boy is a feedling. Perhaps we didn't miss the fun after all."

"But there are three of them," the girl hisses.

"The boy is weak. We can take them. Follow my lead."

I glance at Kildron, unsure if he heard them, but he gives no indication. He paces toward the feeders, undeterred.

My heart pounds with each step. "Kild—"

Shhhh! I know. His thoughts echo in my head, and his confidence floods my mind.

In stride, Kildron steps around me, putting himself closest to the feeders. Then, he continues walking as if taking a Sunday stroll.

The feeders are close now. 20 feet away. 10 feet.

They pass by Kildron, only a few feet of clearance between their shoulders. As soon as the feeders are behind us, the male feeder turns, pointing a hand at Kildron.

TZZZZZ!

A brilliant beam of light flashes, moving too fast to track. It happens so fast, my eyes can barely make sense of it. Blue tendrils of electricity crackle in the air around us, deflecting in an arc around Kildron, yet leaving him untouched.

Suddenly, the lightning disappears as the air ripples, and the cloaked feeder is thrown back. He collides with a stone wall with enough force to crack both brick and bone. For a split second, he hangs in the air before flopping into the snow.

I look back at the woman feeder just in time to see her raise an arm. Then, she stops. She stands completely motionless, fingers aimed at Kildron.

I blink, but nothing changes. The woman hasn't moved a muscle.

That's when I see it. The changes are subtle. Her eyes are glossy. Tiny ice crystals cling to the corners of her open mouth.

"What did you do to her?" Iris asks.

Kildron motions at the statuesque woman. "What does it look like? I froze her."

"You froze… her blood?" I ask. I've never seen anything like it. I've seen people encased in ice, but this is different. From the outside, she looks completely untouched. The freezing was done from within.

"Not just her blood," Kildron corrects. "All the water in her body. Blood, pee, spit, you name it."

"I didn't know you could do that," I breathe.

"Seriously?" Kidron narrows his eyes at me. "Dominion over mankind? Ring any bells? There's no way Zane never mentioned it."

"I'm not stupid," I insist. "I know we have dominion over people. I just… I figured that meant possession. I didn't know we could do…" I motion at the feeder. "That!"

"Of course we can. It's one of our great advantages as demons," Kildron says proudly. "We can command their flesh as we do the elements. We can boil their blood, melt their bones, even turn them to stone. You ever heard of Medussah?" He turns and continues his trek toward the flats.

I limp after him. "You mean…?"

Kildron grins. "A powerful demon, killed by the prophet Perseus. After feeding, she turned her victims to stone." He shakes his head. "I can't believe Zane never taught you this."

I glance at Iris. "Did you know this?"

She shrugs. "I had a hunch."

As we reach the flats, the snow grows deeper. It isn't packed from the foot-traffic of feeders. I retrace my steps, trying to remember where Zane fell. He was defending Rose. They were on the road when General Kaynes stabbed him in the back. Somewhere around…

"There," I say, pointing.

The body is 30 yards away. I approach Zane slowly. The snow is piled on his back like a turtle shell. The wind has cleared some of the snow on his neck, but his flesh has a sickly blue hue. The rest of his features are face down in the snow.

Delicately, I brush the snow from his back. *Why, Zane? Why did it have to be you?*

"Wait here," Kildron instructs. I watch as he hurries over to a nearby barn. He returns a minute later with a rudimentary wheelbarrow.

Kildron parks the wheelbarrow beside Zane. Then, he bends down and tugs on Zane's arm. "Oof, he's heavier than I remember. Give me a hand, Iris." Kildron motions to Zane's feet.

With a grunt, and a little dominion, they manage to heave Zane into the wheelbarrow. His arms are frozen in an extended position, and his feet hang off the end of the barrow. Nothing about it is reverent. Nothing is how I hoped it would be.

"This way." Kildron wheels Zane over to the barn, leaving the wheelbarrow outside the front door. Then, he starts stripping planks from the structure and tossing them in a pile. Iris joins in, and soon they've assembled a massive stack of kindling.

When he's satisfied, Kildron grabs hold of the wheelbarrow and tips Zane into the center of the stack. He outstretches his hand, and a stream of flames engulfs the entire pile. It instantly ignites the wood, burying Zane's body in a continuous torrent of flames.

As the wood begins to char, Kildron grabs a few more planks, piling them up against Zane's torso. Satisfied, he dusts his hands off on his cloak. "Would anyone like to say a few words?"

Iris steps forward. She bows her head in silence before whispering, "You… you were good to me. Thank you for finding me a family. I hope you're reunited with yours now."

It's short, and sweet. With a slight bow of her head, Iris steps away from the bonfire.

I'm about to step forward, but Kildron beats me to it. He steps up to the wheelbarrow and looks out over the Flats. "There weren't many people like Zane. He was on another level. When he said he had your back, he had it, no matter what. I wish we could've had more time." He looks down, finding Zane's frozen face. "I'm going to miss you, Z." He laughs to himself. "You look good with a beard by the way. I'm sorry I couldn't be there for you. I hope you're with Zoey now. I hope Laya and Amanti didn't grow up too much without you. I hope… I hope you're happy, wherever you're at. And thanks for watching my kids while I was gone. It means more than you know. I couldn't have asked for a better friend."

I let out a snort. It's unintentional, but I can't help but roll my eyes.

"What?" Kildron asks.

"Nothing," I say, looking away.

"No, really. Tell me. If you have something to say, just say it."

"Nothing."

It's subtle, but I feel his presence as he slithers into my head. It's as though he left the door to my head wide open, and a small draft is blowing through my brain.

"Demons! Get out of my head!"

"No, I want you to say it," Kildron insists. "I can feel your resentment, Ezra. I know you have something to say. So spit it out. Let's put this behind us."

"Fine. You want to know what's bothering me? You say he was your best friend, but you didn't even recognize him. You were making jokes as he bled out. Hell, you recognized his sword before you recognized him. Some friend you must have been."

Kildron glares back at me, his face cold and unreadable. "I hadn't seen him in 18 years… he'd changed."

"And that's another thing," I retort. "You abandoned him for two decades. This whole time, he thought you were dead. You could've at least sent a letter."

"That's what you're mad about? That I didn't play pen-pals with my childhood buddy?" Kildron laughs. "I see you have your mothers theatrics."

"What is that supposed to mean?" I ask

"You're pissed because you think I wasn't a good friend? Cmon, Ezra, this doesn't even involve you."

"My name's not Ezra!" I snap. "God! You don't get it. You're not just a bad friend, you're a terrible father. You abandoned us too. For 18 years, Iris thought you were dead. You knew she was in Cavernum, and you never once reached out."

"It's not that simple, Ezra."

"Really?" I seethe. "It seems pretty simple to me. Zane worked in the convoy. He was constantly in the Beyond. You could've paid him a visit just one time. Told him you weren't dead. He could've arranged a meeting. How hard is that?"

"I had my reasons," he mutters, face taut, jaw strained.

"Did you?" I challenge, "Or did you stop caring? Did you get so caught up with your feeding that you forgot Zane even existed? You forgot about your own children?"

"SHUT UP!" Kildron shouts, raising his hand as if he's about to strike me. In my weakened state, I can't help but flinch.

When he sees me cower, his eyes soften, but the rage remains. "Just shut up!" Kildron repeats, slowly lowering his hand. "You don't know anything. You want to know why I never visited Zane? Because of her." He points at Iris, who stands with an unreadable expression. "She'd learn I was alive, and then what? She'd want to visit me in the Beyond, where the feeders roam. Once may not be a big deal, but she'd want to see me again, and again, each time putting her life in danger. There were only two options. Let her believe I died, or put her life at risk. Do you think it was an easy choice? Do you?"

I say nothing.

"It was torture. So yes, I tried to forget at times. I tried to forget I had failed everyone I love, that my daughter was being raised by strangers. That my baby boy had been killed and my wife was likely tortured to death. I tried to forget, but I couldn't, no matter how many times I fed—no matter how many memories I stuffed my head with—I couldn't forget. So stop acting like you would've done better. I did the best I could!"

I bite my tongue, but I can't stop the words from forming. "I did do better," I hiss, little more than a whisper. "I tried to find you. Everyone told me my parents didn't want me. They told me not to look for you, but I didn't listen. I spent years looking. YEARS! Don't you get it? I posted ads on the internet. I googled every symbol imaginable, trying to figure out what my tattoos meant. I emailed linguists and egyptologists. One year, I called every tattoo parlor in Colorado, asking if they'd ever tattooed a baby. Do you know how many tattoo parlors are in Colorado? Hundreds! I was going to call Nevada's next, but Judy took my phone away. So don't tell me I couldn't have done better. I *did* do better. I never stopped looking!"

Kildron grits his teeth, staring at Zane's bonfire. The wood shifts, and Zane's body drops a few inches, sending embers into the sky.

"You're right," Kildron finally sighs. "I'm not the father you deserve. Is that what you want to hear? That I'm a shitty dad? I'll admit it. I'm the worst. But reality is, I'm not here to parent you. That ship has sailed. And I certainly don't care if you're mad at me. Rage is good. It'll keep you vigilant. Hell, I don't even care if you like me. All I care about is keeping you alive."

Like you did for Zane?

Kildron stiffens, his presence retracting from my mind before I ever noticed it was there.

He steps closer, his eyes are wide and wild. "You want to put the blame on me? That's fine. Put it on me! Everything is my fault! I let him die. Does that make you feel better? Good! Blame old Pops so you don't have to blame yourself."

But it doesn't make me feel better. Nothing does. Deep down, I know why I'm so angry: *I wish Zane lived instead of you.*

Kildron nods his head, once again eavesdropping on my inner thoughts. "So that's what this is about?"

I have a chance to refute it, but I don't bother.

Kildron bites his lip, his nostrils flaring. "You know, Matt, we have that in common. Zane was always better at this. He'd know what to do. He wouldn't have failed you like I did. Maybe if he was here, you wouldn't be a feeder." He stares at the flames, his voice trailing off. "I'd trade places with him if I could, but I don't get that luxury. We're not gods. We can't decide who lives and who dies."

Finally, he pulls his eyes off the fire, shaking his head as if waking from a dream. He spins in a circle, surveying the horizon. "We've already been here too long. If you have something to say, say it quick." With that, he wanders away from the pyre.

Iris looks awkwardly over at me. "I… I'll give you some privacy." She follows Kildron through the snow.

Alone, I approach his burning body. Fortunately, the flames obscure his bubbling flesh.

"Hey, Zane. It's me, Matt. I… I'm sorry for everything." I want to cry. I want to feel something, but all I feel is emptiness—emptiness and rage.

"For what it's worth, I tried to find you," I tell Zane's body. "I went to the veil last night. You weren't there. I guess that means you moved on. That's good. You deserve to be happy."

The right words don't come, so I just stand there, watching his body burn. It all feels so inadequate. No urn for the ashes. No eulogy or music. Just my stupid, worthless apology and a little fire for his frozen corpse.

I feel my anger rising once more. *Why? Why did it have to end like this?*

"You'd probably hate to hear me say this, but I wish I could speak Adamic. If I could, I'd bring you back, because I need you, Zane. I don't know if we can do this without you… Well, I guess this is it. If you see Judy, tell her hi for me. Goodbye, Zane."

I look out over the flats, trying not to stare as his skin boils and hisses. That's when I see it: a tiny drop of gold amid the endless snow. An object is buried—a tiny golden sprout piercing the icy soil. I bend my knees, trying not to crease my torso, and tug on the gold. It's heavier than I expected. The snow falls away, revealing a hefty gold crown—the king's crown. On the inner surface, I see an engraving.

Unfortunately, a large dent intersects the Adamic symbols, disrupting the spell.

I look up to see Kildron walking over.

"What'd you find?" he wonders.

"The royal crown, but it's scratched."

"Toss it," Kildron suggests. "The thing is useless without its spell."

"Shouldn't we return it?"

"Do whatever you want. Wear it for all I care," he says. "Just make sure no one sees it."

Not wanting to abandon it, I place the crown over my head, the weight of the crown disappearing as the morph mask strips it from view.

Suddenly, Kildron grabs my arm. "We need to move." His eyes are trained on the outskirts of the city. Cloaked in dark robes, three figures walk along the road, seemingly headed our direction.

"Stay behind me," Kildron commands. "We have company."

We move in a triangle formation—Kildron in front and Iris at my side. Kildron leads us briskly back toward the Ring, traveling directly toward the cloaked trio.

One feeder walks slightly in front of the others. He holds a metal spear in his right hand, plunging the dull end into the snow with each step like a walking stick. It's subtle, but I can make out a row of Adamic symbols on the spearhead.

When we're a dozen yards away, the feeders stop, spreading out in the road to block our path.

"I've been waiting a long time for this, Archangel," the spear-wielding feeder exclaims with a grin. He's young, maybe my age, but the lower half of his face is covered in thick, ropy scars. The fibrous tissue doesn't stretch, making his smile more of a grimace. Even more distinct are the black symbols tattooed across his forehead: the Mark of the Beast.

"Nice ink," Kildron mocks. "Very… bold. Personally, I prefer the ol' tramp stamp; it's a tad more discreet."

The demon puffs out his chest. "I am not ashamed of my birthright. I will not hide Satan's glory from the world."

"A zealot. How refreshing." Kildron takes a step closer. He holds his hand flat above his brow like a visor and squints into the morning sun. "Do I know you from something?"

"My name is Insidivon Wraik. My father was Clawkin Wraik, High

Priest of the Firstborn," the demon announces proudly. "You slaughtered him in the temple of our Lord." He points to the scars on his face. "You spared me. That was your mistake. Now, you must suffer Satan's opposition."

"Yeah, yeah. Let's get this over with," Kildron says nonchalantly. He lifts his right hand and places it over his heart. "Before these witnesses, I invoke the Firstborn's Judgment." Without waiting for a response, Kildron removes his cloak, tossing it on the ground beside him. He reaches down and unsheathes Zane's short sword.

Insidivon smiles. "As Cain struck down Abel, let the righteous prevail." He spins his spear, stabbing it point first into the snow. "May Lucifer's light shine on the victor." He lets his cloak fall from his shoulders. The feeder isn't wearing a shirt. Instead, his torso and arms are covered in the familiar tattoos of Adamic armor. They begin at his throat and end at his wrists like a geometric turtleneck.

Kildron quickly turns his head to address us. "He agreed to a duel. Don't intervene."

With that, he gives the gladius a few warm up swings. "Come on, Ugly. Your father won't avenge himself."

The demon snatches his spear from the snow and gives it a wide swing through the air. As the spear arcs, it drags the snow behind it, sending a six foot wave of ice careening toward Kildron.

Kildron extends his sword and, with the help of dominion, parts the wave down the middle. At the last second, he twists sideways, allowing the two separate snow mounds to rush past on either side.

With his sword still extended, Kildron smiles. Blue tendrils of electricity leap from the tip of Kildron's sword, surging at the young demon.

Insidivon plants the tip of his spear into the snow a moment before the electricity collides with the steel. It crackles through the spear and dissipates into the ground.

Kildron is already in motion, rushing forward and slashing at Insidivon's torso, but the demon deflects the blow with the shaft of his spear. They're a blur as they strike at each other, their movements connected in a deadly dance. Kildron swings and Insidivon ducks. Insidivon stabs and Kildron blocks.

The steel rings out, setting the tempo of the dance. Cling! Ting! Cling! Ting!

Insidivon makes the first mistake. He thrusts at Kildron's chest, but Kildron is prepared. He deflects the speartip with the side of his gladius, and before Insidivon can retract the spear, Kildron grabs the shaft with his free hand and pulls. As Insidivon stumbles forward, Kildron kicks him in the knee. It buckles with a pop.

Insidivon falls to one knee, and Kildron swings his gladius in a powerful overhand stroke.

Ting!

At the last moment, Insidivon manages to raise his spear, catching the gladius on the spear shaft midway between his two hands.

Then… nothing. Neither man moves. I see the muscles bulging in Kildron's neck—his biceps bulging—but his sword remains motionless against the spear shaft as his muscles quake. It looks as though he's fighting his own body.

Possession.

Insidivon is possessing Kildron. It's the only plausible explanation. As demons, they're both on equal ground. The strongest soul will succeed.

For several seconds, they remain in place, like an equally-matched arm wrestle. Then, ever so slowly, a smile twitches on Kildron's lips. The gladius tilts to the side, its razor sharp edge sliding across the surface of the spear shaft. It strikes Insidivon's fingers, slicing easily through all four digits. Then, before Insidivon can recover, the blade sweeps through his neck, decapitating the boy in a single swing.

As his head hits the ground, the two remaining feeders scramble to action. They take two steps toward Kildron before going rigid, arms quivering at their sides.

"Cut them down," Kildron chokes through clenched teeth. "I can't… hold… them both." His eyes are closed, and his arms convulse in a rhythmic motion. Whatever he's doing, he's losing control.

I extend my soul, reaching toward Insidivon's spear.

Thrust.

The spear tip lurches, driving itself deep into the feeder's chest. Iris offs the other with an icicle through the eye socket.

Kildron sucks in a gasp as the feeders fall to the floor. He reaches momentarily for his face, as if his own eye was skewered. Panting, he spends the next few seconds with his hands on his knees.

Iris watches Kildron, a mixture of fear and amazement in her eyes. "Did you… possess them both?"

Kildron nods. "Feeders aren't what they used to be, let me tell you. We killed most of the big leaguers in Hogrum. Compared to them, these guys are more like nibblers."

He bends down and retrieves the Adamic spear, tossing it to Iris. "Carry this, will you?" Finally, he sheathes his gladius and turns his attention to the Ring. "Come. We should get back to the tunnels."

"Uuuughh," the feeder with the icicle groans. Lying on his side, he rolls into a ball like a startled pill bug. His good eye flutters open.

Iris doesn't hesitate. She raises the spear, aiming for his throat.

"Wait!" Kildron lifts his hand, causing the air to ripple around the feeder, pinning him to the ground. "Free dominion," he mutters.

The feeder struggles helplessly, causing the air to reverberate. He may as well be a fly, cocooned in spider silk and ready for eating.

I turn away as Kildron descends on him, grabbing him by the head and biting his neck. I hear a nauseating slurp as Kildron devours his soul. The feeder, still half conscious, groans helplessly beneath his jaws.

In search of a distraction, my eyes find the young demon, Insidivon. His head is lying in the road, glossy eyes looking in my direction. He was my age—probably younger—and Kildron cut him down without mercy, decapitating him the same way he did General Kaynes.

General Kaynes! How could I forget?

I turn around, racing back toward the Outer Wall.

"Matt," Iris calls, showing a hint of concern. "What are you doing?"

I stop beside the road, a few feet from where I originally found Zane's body. Squinting, I study the snow. There's a barren patch of dirt, completely devoid of ice, as if something had been there, but was moved. It's about the size of a body.

"He's gone," I gasp.

"Who?" Kildron asks, reluctantly trotting over.

"General Kaynes. The guy you decapitated."

"The bastard who killed Zane," Iris clarifies, scanning the snow around us.

"He should be right here, right?" I point at the bare patch of dirt.

"Hmmm..." Kildron says, scanning the snow around us.

"Did someone move him?" I wonder. "Why would they move him? To feed?"

Kildron shakes his head. "You can't feed on the dead. Feeders have no use for a body."

"That's not true," Iris says. "I've heard stories about—"

"We don't have time for this!" Kildron barks, beginning his march back toward the cave. "We shouldn't be out here. Besides... Necromancy is a lost art."

"You're sure?" Iris asks.

Kildron spins to face us, seemingly holding his breath. "It wouldn't matter either way. The city is full of the dead. If they want bodies, there's nothing we can do to stop them."

4

ROSE

"What did he say?" Antai asks.

"He said, 'Your father sends his regards.'"

Antai frowns, walking by my side. "That's it? No explanation?"

"That's it. Then, he started talking with the guards."

We turn a corner, and Antai waves to the guardsmen as we enter the Royal Wing. The hallway is oddly busy now that the spare rooms have been filled with refugees from the Core.

Antai leans in, whispering into my hair. "And you're sure he was dead?"

"Of course, I'm sure. I saw him, Antai. His head was cut clean off. It was sitting there in the snow. I saw it."

"You think he resurrected him… like Titan did to me? Maybe he already has the Book of Life?"

I bite my cheek. "I suppose it is possible, but I doubt it."

"Yeah, you're probably right." Antai says with a low voice. "If he found the Library, he'd have no reason to send Kaynes. He'd come himself."

"I've thought about it," I add, "and there's no way he'd resurrect Kaynes before bringing back my mother."

Antai nods his head. “Okay, let’s assume Kaynes isn’t resurrected. Why send him at all? To kidnap you? To spy on us?”

“That’s what I’m going to find out.”

I stop in front of my quarters and remove the Adamic key from where it dangles around my neck.

Before he died, Grandpa enchanted my room with powerful symbols. They are carved into the center of the oak door.

Only two keys open it—one in my possession and the other with Antai.

I hold the door open for Antai, then step inside, using my Adamic key to lock the door from the inside.

Without wasting a moment, I reach for the relic on my nightstand—a silver band with two misty orbs set on either side of a nosepiece.

Antai furrows his brow. “What’s that?”

“A relic. Grandpa called them Seerglasses. It lets you spy on a person in real time.” I hold it up so he can see the symbols.

Antai lets out a nervous laugh. “You’re telling me you can see anyone you want, right now?”

“Almost anyone. You have to know them personally. I tried it on my father, but it didn’t work.”

Antai grins as he watches me fit the seerglasses over my head. “That’s amazing. Does Kaynes know about these?”

“He shouldn’t, unless my father somehow told him. I only found out about them recently.”

"And what, you plan to spy on him all day?" He muses, a glimmer of a smile on his lips. "Who knows what you'll see."

I roll my eyes. "As long as it takes to learn what he's up to."

I lower the relic until the misty white glass obscures my view. I hear Antai step closer.

"How do you use it?"

"You have to describe them to the relic," I say, "both body and soul. The glasses do the rest."

I imagine General Kaynes. In my mind's eye, I picture his slicked gray hair and narrow face. His pointed nose and arrogant eyes. I think of his pompous nature—his sophisticated intelligence and his obsession with reputation. I think of how he never left his quarters without his cloak ironed. I think of the way he treated Vyle—as if his own son was insufficient, unworthy of the family name.

To my dismay, nothing happens.

I think of his charisma and charm, the way he could talk circles around the other diplomats. The way he outsmarted Zane, conjuring a mirage of himself. He was clever, capable, and selfish.

For a moment, the seerglasses stir, filling with a collage of colors, but a clear image never forms.

"Hmmm, that's weird. It should be working. I feel like I know him pretty well."

"I can try, if you want," Antai says.

"One sec."

As a test, I imagine Kendra, her long blonde hair always curled in neat symmetry. I think of her green eyes and her desire to help everyone she can.

Immediately, the glasses fill with color, swirling and rearranging into a face. I watch as Kendra, wherever she is, offers a sympathetic smile. Then, she closes her eyes, outstretching her hands as she heals someone. I can't see the other person, but a part of their foot is visible, resting in Kendra's palm. The underside of their toes are bloodied and stripped of all skin.

"I can see Kendra, but it won't show me General Kaynes," I say.

"You want me to try?" Antai offers again.

"Hold on."

This time, I picture Matt, with his wavy blonde hair. I think of that night when he entered my dreams—the night he shared his soul with me. I think of the firestorm of emotions that swept me up and singed my heart. I picture our kiss, brief yet tantalizing.

Then, I see him in the glass.

Impossible.

When I checked on him last night, he was unconscious, clinging to what little life he had left. Now, he's walking in the snow, somewhat briskly I might add. There's a slight lean to his posture, favoring his left side, but he looks well. He looks really, really well.

"Rose?"

Flustered, I toss the relic to Antai. "Fine. You try."

Antai puts on the glasses and falls silent. I wait in silence as he attempts to summon an image of General Kaynes. After a minute, he removes the glasses. "Yeah, that's weird. I got it to work on General Katu, but not Kaynes."

"Maybe we don't know him like we thought we did," I theorize. "Proticus once told me he tortures feeders. Maybe there's more we don't know."

Antai shrugs. "Maybe." He drums his fingers in his holster. "Whatever it is, we'll figure it out. One thing at a time, okay?"

"I guess."

He looks at me until I meet his gaze. His eyes, like a rich cup of cocoa, soothe my nerves. He opens his arms and wraps me in a warm bear hug. "Come here." His muscles compress the anxiety swelling within my skull, equalizing the mental pressure.

"Better?" He asks.

"Mmhhmm. Thanks."

Still holding me tight, he waddles us over to the desk. "Here, sit down. Just for a minute."

I plop onto my desk chair, and Antai steps behind me. Next thing I know, his thumbs are pressing into my shoulders, working out the knots.

"Mmmm, that feels nice." The longer he works, the more guilty I feel.

"Hey, Antai?"

"Yeah?"

"I'm sorry I haven't been the most pleasant lately."

He hesitates, perhaps wondering if he should disagree. "You have a lot on your mind," he finally says.

"Still, I want to—"

"Shhhh," he tips my head back until it's nearly upside down and silences my apology with a kiss. My soul sighs, and I let my lips sink into his mouth, sweet surprise culminating in tactile delight.

Tap. Tap. Tap.

Nevela's timid knock echoes from the maid's door.

Antai's face hovers above mine. "Do you need to get that?"

"Ugh," I groan. "I probably should."

Antai lets go of my face and takes a step back.

"Come in, Nevela" I call.

The door jostles softly, but doesn't open.

"Sorry, one moment." I forgot about the lock. Ever since I began keeping relics in my room, I began locking the maid's door as well.

Removing my Adamic key, I unlock the door, and pull it open.

Wendy enters first, carrying a tray of diluted pork stew and a small serving of crab apple salad.

Nevela follows close behind with a heaping bundle of linens. She hesitates when she sees Antai. "Oh, are we interrupting?"

"Not at all," Antai says. He looks over at me. "In fact, I'll go talk to Octavian. He knows which guards are still loyal to the crown. Maybe we can get some eyes on… our person of interest."

"That's a good idea. Thank you, Antai."

"Anytime... I mean it," he winks as he unlocks the front door and slips into the hallway. A moment later, I hear it lock from the outside.

"Sorry, Rose," Nevela winces. "Normally, I'd do this while you're away, but with the doors locked…"

"No problem. Pretend I'm not even here," I insist.

Once Wendy sets down the tray, she joins in as well, stripping the sheets and remaking the bed.

"And how has your day been, Your Majesty?" Nevela hums as she tucks the sheet under the base of the mattress.

"You don't need to do that, Nevela. Surely, there's more important tasks."

Nevela fluffs the pillows. "The head housekeeper insists we keep up the old routine. She says it'll give a sense of normalcy."

"Seriously, don't worry about it, Nevela. I insist."

"Oh, okay." Nevela finishes plumping one last pillow before stepping away from the bed. "You never answered my question. How was your day so far?"

"Unexpected," I sigh. "But it could be worse. Listen, I want to apologize to both of you. I know I've been distant the last few days. I want you to know I'm here if you need anything, or if you want to talk."

"Oh, don't you worry about us," Nevela says. "You just focus on your duties."

"Well, I'm sorry regardless." I set the seerglasses on my desk. "What about you both? How has your day been?"

"The funeral was beautiful," Nevela gushes. "I loved what you said. So stoic. The commoners have been talking about it. They're worried of course, but they're so resilient. You should see what they're doing. The sewers guild is stripping the drapes to make blankets for the refugees. The theater curtain alone made over 100 blankets. Thick ones too. And did you see the line outside the Glass Temple yesterday? Brother Stonlak is holding free marriage ceremonies for the unwed. It's really quite beautiful."

The truth is, I hadn't seen the line. I'd been so focused on my father that I'd missed everything within the walls. "That's thoughtful of him," I say. "What else has been going on?"

Wendy doesn't look quite so enthusiastic. She looks down at her belly, which seems even bigger than I remember. "We've been busy the last few days. They expect us to serve the entire palace."

"I heard the palace population has tripled," Nevela interjects.

"Meals are a nightmare. The chefs claim we have food to last till spring, but the kitchen staff says otherwise. They estimate a month or two, which explains the rations."

For a moment, I think she's finished. Then, her eyes widen. "Oh, I almost forgot. Look at this." Nevela lifts the gray maid's dress, exposing her bare stomach. To my surprise, her skin is exactly that: bare. There isn't a single tattoo on her flesh, not even an ink stain. Not even a scar.

"Diego removed them with dominion. The whole thing was Wendy's idea."

"Diego thought of it first," Wendy deflects. "He's already done the same for his mom. He was happy to help."

"How nice of him," I agree.

"He's so serious; he almost reminds me of Zane," Nevela rambles. "He didn't say much, but the Equalists love him. I heard them talking by the stables yesterday. They treat him like a hero, which is odd considering he's a guardsman."

Of course they idolize him. They think he killed the king.

I've learned more in five minutes with Nevela than I have from one of Antai's updates. Simply put, the girl has a knack for gossip.

I can't help but smile. "How do you do it, Nevela? How do you stay so positive, after everything?" *After being held captive. After being possessed and sent on a suicide mission.*

She pauses, taking a moment to think it through. "I don't know. More than anything, I feel lucky. What's the saying, 'you don't know what you have until it's gone?'"

"The healer really helped a lot," Wendy adds.

I raise an eyebrow. "Healer?"

"Her name was Kendra," Nevela remembers. "She said she could heal the mind—that the brain is an organ, and can be injured like any other. I don't know what she did, but I've been feeling much better. It's strange. So many terrible things happened, but… they almost feel insignificant, like a dream I can barely remember. She really has a gift, Rose. Perhaps you should give her a visit?"

I smile. "Perhaps I will."

Suddenly, a key clicks within my door. Antai bursts in a moment later. He doesn't look happy. "Kaynes just called an emergency meeting."

"Right now?"

"Right now," Antai repeats. He glances at my maids before looking back at me. "He says he has news about the Holy One."

The throne is cold and uncomfortable. The polished stone saps all heat from the back of my thighs. I tug my dress lower, trying to get fabric between the stone and my skin.

Surprisingly, I was among the first to arrive. The other diplomats wander in gradually. Most give me dirty looks as they pass the throne. General Katu seems relieved to see me, and Gwenevere gives me a smile that almost appears genuine.

General Kaynes arrives last, his robes swishing as he waltzes into the room.

"I'll be damned," Chancellor Bolo laughs. "It's a dead man walking."

Kaynes rolls his eyes. "Yes, yes, I'm well aware of what's been said about me, by the Queen's own mouth, no less. I shall do my best to address it shortly."

He chooses the seat directly to my left and sits down. His eyes skip around the table. "That's everyone, correct? Shall we begin, Your Majesty?"

I look to Antai, who merely shrugs. With no other options, I oblige.

"Welcome, everyone. Thank you for attending so promptly. As I'm sure you are all aware, due to the passing of General Zane, we are now a body of eight. As such, five will be our new majority. In the case of a tie, my vote will take precedence."

I face General Kaynes and take a deep breath. "You called this meeting, General Kaynes, and will have ample time to address your concerns, however, I have a few questions first. As the council has heard me testify, I witnessed your death, which makes me very uneasy seeing you now."

"What are we to think?" Chancellor Quine asks. "The queen has lied to us? Clearly, he lives. We can all attest to that."

"I know how this looks," I interject. "But I don't rescind my testimony. I can only think of one explanation... his corpse is possessed."

"Possessed?" Gwenevere frowns, clearly unconvinced.

General Kaynes merely laughs.

"I've seen it," I insist. "When feeders attacked the guard graduation party, there was a demon. He killed Proticus Tyre, and then possessed his remains."

"Bahh! This is madness," Bolo bellows. "Does that look like a corpse to you?"

"I'll admit, it doesn't," I acknowledge, "but you may not be familiar with self-dominion. It involves manipulating your own body with dominion. Hypothetically, a demon could use self-dominion to add color to the skin. Add warmth. They could make a corpse seem alive."

"I thought he was decapitated," Chancellor Quine says. "Living or corpse, General Kaynes does not appear headless to me."

"A head can be reattached with dominion," I reason. "It's possible."

"Possible does not equate to probable," General Kaynes asserts. Smiling, he protrudes his chin and tugs his collar downward. "Look at my neck. There's not even a scar, Your Majesty. You expect them to believe my head was... reattached?"

General Katu runs one hand along his throat. "I'm sorry, Your Majesty, but I do not know any healers who can reattach a head. Limbs, perhaps, but not a head. This theory seems... unlikely."

General Kaynes sighs, standing up. "Allow me to put this conspiracy theory to rest. Come here, Your Majesty. Feel my pulse. Listen to my heart. Let me prove to you I am alive."

He extends his arm, and I hesitantly lean forward. I press my index finger to his wrist.

Bum. Bum. Bum.

A steady pulse drums against my finger. At the very least, his heart is beating.

Impossible.

I'm speechless for a moment before I find the words. "This doesn't prove anything. Self-dominion could be used to make the heart beat."

"Your Majesty," General Kaynes raises his voice. "Listen to yourself. What you are suggesting is mad. You claim I am manipulating a dead corpse. I am controlling every muscle fiber, every reflex. I am making the heart beat and the blood flow, and I am doing all this simultaneously while maintaining a conversation. I suppose you believe I am manipulating digestion as well? Do I need to eat a meal in your presence? Do you need to study my feces to be convinced? Surely, Your Majesty, you hear the lunacy?"

I do. I hear it. What I am suggesting is impossible. But that only leaves one other option.

The Holy One resurrected General Kaynes!

The blood drains from my face. I can't find any words.

"Rose?" Antai watches me with narrowed eyes—nervous eyes. His glance has a clear message: *say something!*

"Very well." I clear my throat and take another deep breath. "Thank you, General Kaynes. You have addressed my concerns."

Don't show weakness, Rose. You must act the part.

"So, the queen fabricated her story?" Chancellor Bolo concludes, his double chin wobbling like a turkey. "That's all there is to it. Are we all in agreement on that?"

I bite my tongue, trying desperately to contain my rage. At this point, anything I say will only act against me.

"It's true, the queen did lie," General Kaynes explains. "But not in the way you think. I believe it's time you heard what really happened the day of the invasion."

General Kaynes pushes back his chair, rising to his feet. He paces in front of the city map as he speaks. "As I'm sure you all remember, Matthew MacArther was imprisoned the day of the invasion. He was a demon. He served the Holy One."

Several heads nod in agreement. Others, like General Katu, frown.

Kaynes continues. "At some point that day, our queen snuck into the Pit and released this demon. Not only that, she accompanied him into the Ring. By this time, I had realized the demon had escaped, so I pursued them. I caught up to them in the Flats when I heard the first explosion. As the feeders ransacked the sanctuary, she stood by her demon lover. The feeders ran past them both as if they were an ally."

"What?" I gasp. "That's absurd!"

"Shhh!" General Kaynes holds a finger to his lips. Somehow, he's perfectly calm. "That's when Zane returned. He saw the carnage and confronted the queen. At that moment, they turned on him. Soon, another demon arrived—Matthew MacArther's father. Together, the three of them overwhelmed Zane, cutting him down without mercy. Then, they turned on me."

All I can do is bite my tongue and shake my head. Antai is equally distraught. I can hear the drumming of his fingers from below the table.

General Kaynes feigns embarrassment, the corners of his eyes turning down. "I tried to fight them, but they were too strong. So instead, I created an illusion with dominion. The queen didn't lie when she said I was decapitated. She saw it happen. She saw the demon—MacArther's father—cut off my head… but it was only an illusion. I even condensed the air to provide some resistance to the blade. The demon, in his foolishness, believed I had fallen. I managed to sneak away as they continued their killing spree."

It was an illusion!

My jaw drops open.

Kaynes wasn't resurrected, because he was never dead at all. It was an apparition the entire time. It's the only thing that makes sense. The more I think about it, the more the color drains from my face.

"These accusations are bold," General Katu says with a sadness in his voice. "Do you have a rebuttal, Your Majesty?"

"I've already given my testimony," I choke. "It's possible we were tricked. Perhaps it was an illusion as General Kaynes says, but everything else was true. I swear it. He came after me in the name of the Holy One. He admitted it himself."

"Our current predicament," General Kaynes says, "is very simple. We both claim the other is serving the Holy One. Only one of us can be telling the truth."

Gwenevere furrows her brow. She studies me with her beady eyes and bird-beak nose. "Why would the queen condemn her own kingdom?"

General Kaynes' lips part in a toothy grin. "I thought you'd never ask. As you all know, I've been without the palace for nearly four days. I've been spying on the Holy One, and I've discovered something unbelievable. I saw the man the feeders bow to, and to my surprise, I recognized him. You all know his name…"

The breath catches in my throat. My entire body goes rigid.

Kaynes looks slowly over the Council, letting the suspense build. His eyes stop on me. "The Holy One is Zezric Malik, the queen's own father."

I hear a collective gasp. All eyes are on me, waiting for me to dispute, but I can't form the words. It's the truth, after all.

General Kaynes smiles tauntingly. "Go ahead, Rose, tell them I'm lying. Or have you known for some time now?"

"It's not what it sounds like!" I cry. "I saw him on the night of the invasion. I've never spoken a word to him. That's why I was waiting on the wall. I thought if he saw me, he wouldn't attack. I thought I could change his mind. I don't serve him, I swear it upon the Creator."

"I've heard enough!" Bolo bellows. "This is treason of the worst kind."

"Silence!" Antai stands, his voice booming through the room. "What is happening here? You've heard two sides of a story. Both appear plausible. And now you're jumping to condemn your queen? On what evidence?" He glances at the oak doors and lowers his voice. "Yes, Rose believes she saw her father, but that isn't evidence of treason? Not one person—apart from General Kaynes—saw her serving him in any capacity. It is his word against hers. So how can you speak of punishment?"

"She has motive," Bolo argues.

"Motive isn't proof." Antai growls, fury in his eyes. "I have motive to knock you on your ass, but that doesn't mean I'll do it."

Bolo's opens his mouth only to close it again.

"She lied to the council," Chancellor Quine says. "How can we ignore that?"

Antai shakes his head. "She didn't tell a single lie. She simply withheld information, and for good reason. Imagine if the public found out. Zezric, their beloved prince, is the man who massacred their families. That would cause chaos. The people would turn on their queen, exactly as you have. So please. Let's think rationally for once. I beg of you." With that, Antai takes his seat once more.

For several seconds, no one speaks. Gwenevere stares at the table, chewing her lip. Katu rubs his temples. The other diplomats look angry.

"I've heard enough." Bolo slams his fist on the table. "She conspired with a demon and aided his escape. How can she sit on that throne?"

"We could impeach," Quine says.

General Kaynes shakes his head. "Impeaching the queen will cause chaos and confusion. We can't lose the people's trust."

Quine looks disappointed. "What would you suggest?"

General Kaynes smiles. "Something more… subtle. I propose a conflict of interest. We are at war with the Holy One, who happens to be the queen's own father. Surely that qualifies. Until the conflict of interest is resolved, I vote to suspend the queen's participation on all council matters, to take effect immediately."

"What? You can't do that!" I cry. "You don't understand!"

"All in favor?" General Kaynes asks.

General Kaynes raises his hand first, immediately followed by Chancellor Bolo and Chancellor Quine. Chancellor Turnag, who hasn't said a single word, raises his hand high.

That's four.

I look at Gwenevere, who is still staring at the table. Her lips are sealed tight, compressing themselves into thin lines. Her jaw is taut with indecision. Eventually, hesitantly, she raises her hand.

"It's final!" General Kaynes gleefully declares. "Until the conflict of interest is resolved, the queen will be suspended from all council matters. We are now a council of seven, with a majority of four."

"But—" Antai starts.

General Kaynes silences him with a glare. "I appreciate your loyalty, General Elsborne, but the matter is settled." Kaynes looks over the council once more. "While I have you all here, I want to make one last suggestion. Since the betrayal of our former-commander Noyan, we've been without a Palace Commander. Commanders Hunt and Zurg both passed in the invasion. We need more leadership."

"And who would you propose?" Gwenevere asks.

"Crasilda Lumb comes to mind." Kaynes shrugs, as if it only just occurred to him. "She was Bolo's champion, if I recall correctly. A fiery girl. We could use that kind of passion."

"I concur," Bolo barks.

"All in favor?" Kaynes says.

Hands raise around the table. Only Antai and General Katu oppose.

"Wonderful. This has been a fruitful meeting. If there is nothing else…"

There's so much I want to say, but I know it's futile. Somehow, Kaynes has stripped me of my power in a single meeting. And he did it all without a spell or amulet.

"Meeting adjourned," Kaynes says, standing briskly and striding out of the room. The other chancellors follow suit.

Antai leans over, whispering in my ear. "I'm going to consult with the lawyer guild. There has to be something we can do. I'll meet you in your room later tonight."

"Okay," I breathe. "See you then."

I can't muster the energy to leave, so I sit on the throne with my head bowed. One by one, the diplomats shuffle past me and out of the room.

To my surprise, General Katu lingers in his seat. He gives me a curious glance as Chancellor Bolo hobbles out of the room, making us the only remaining diplomats.

"Captain Guzon," General Katu calls to the guard outside the door. "Can you give us some privacy for a moment?"

The guard steps through the doorway. His eyes linger on us as he tugs the massive doors shut one at a time, sealing us alone inside.

I study Katu. He's a small man, with thin limbs and a vivacious smile. Unlike the other guardians, he carries a certain humility.

"I was hoping to have a brief word, Your Majesty. I was grieved to see the council treat you with such disrespect. I—"

"How can I help you, General Katu?" I say it coldly, with little patience. I'm not in the mood for sympathy.

"Quite the opposite. I think I can be of service to you." He reaches into his robes and removes a single piece of parchment. It's folded in half and sealed with a wax stamp. "Your grandfather gave me this the morning of your coronation. He instructed me to deliver it to you on the day of his funeral, and not a moment sooner." He places the parchment on the table. "I looked for you after the ceremony, but you'd already left." Bowing his head, he begins to back away. "I'll leave you to it."

I snatch up the letter, starting in disbelief at my grandfather's royal seal—God's hand reaching down through a cloud.

"Katu… thank you." I call after him as he retreats from the room. "This means more than you know."

"My pleasure, Your Majesty." He closes the council room doors with a soft thud, leaving me in solitude.

I don't wait a moment. With a soft tug, the paper peels from the wax, falling open. Grandpa's eloquent handwriting blankets the page.

My dearest Rose,

It pains me to write this letter. I don't want to imagine a future where I'm not there to support you, yet I know it is coming. By the time you read this letter, it will already have come to pass.

Do not misunderstand my words. I will resist my fate, but some battles are doomed from the start. That is why I must write this letter.

There is so much I've not told you. I've lied, Rose, I've lied more than I wanted to, but I always had your best interest in mind.

If I haven't told you already, it's time you know. The Holy One is your father, Zezric. I've tried to stop him. I've even tried to kill him, but I've failed. Now, I'm afraid that task falls to you. He mustn't find the Book of Life. You must stop him at all costs.

I haven't prepared you as well as I should have. There's still so much I need to teach you. So much I want to tell you, but the circumstances prevent me.

I'm sorry, Rose. I wish I could've told you these things in person, but I fear I would've revealed more than was prudent. Even now, I imagine you are wondering why I can't be plain with you. I'm afraid that, too, must remain a mystery. There are still some things you must not know.

As for the Lost Library, I don't know where to find it. But there is one way I can help you. A poem—or rather, a riddle—has been passed down the royal line for generations. My father recited it to me when I was your age. It is the same clue I gave to Zezric. I pray you will have more luck deciphering it than I did.

Deep beneath your feet is the power you seek
It takes a word to open, but you cannot speak
It is an ark of salvation when the future is bleak
But beware, once opened, destruction will leak

I love you, Rose. I know you will do amazing things as Queen.

Until we meet again,
Grandpa

Ps. Memorize the clue, then burn this letter.

I sit on his throne, rereading the letter over and over, This page is his final farewell—his dying words.

Goodbye, Grandpa.

I lift the letter into the air and let it fall.

Burn!

The letter ignites all at once, burning up in a quick flash of smoke. Once it's gone, I continue reciting the poem in my head.

It's not much, as far as clues go, but it's a start. I recite the first line in my head.

Deep beneath your feet is the power you seek.

That much is clear. The Lost Library is underground. At this very moment, my father is out there searching for it.

I simply have to find it first.

5

MATT

Kildron lifts his hands from my head, and the steady trickle of power immediately runs dry. "How do you feel?" he asks.

"Better." I take a deep breath in, letting my abdomen expand. Miraculously, I feel no pain. "Much better. I actually feel good."

"It better be better," Kildron scoffs. "That was the entirety of our friend we met on the road, plus two more from yesterday."

"I thought feeding on feeders was like eating crumbs?"

"It is," Kildron says. "But the feeders are so full of power right now, it's like a feast of crumbs. And, in my benevolence, I'm giving that dominion to you, so be grateful."

"Thanks… I guess." I lift my shirt, studying my stomach. The outside of my wound has closed, but the skin is still puffy and irritated. I know the bacteria rages beneath my skin, but I can barely feel it. My muscles buzz with the power of dominion.

Iris is sitting in the corner, illuminating the cave with her soul-anchor. She's pretending not to care, but I know she's listening to every word. She leans back and removes her hourglass from where it was hidden in her shirt. She gives it a flick and watches it swing back and forth like the pendulum of a grandfather clock.

I stand, and for the first time in days, I don't feel the urge to vomit.

My appetite is slowly returning. "I feel good," I say, twisting slowly from side to side. "I might be able to fight."

"Not a chance," Kildron says. "The power will sustain you, but you can't risk dominion. If you go burning through souls, you'll be back where you started."

Kildron turns, and his eyes bulge. "Wha-where did you get that?"

Iris furrows her brow and lifts the hourglass higher. "This? I've always had it. I thought it came from you and mom."

Kildron blinks. "It was Jenevrah's. I thought it was lost forever."

Kildron reaches for the hourglass, but Iris pulls it back. "It's mine. She left it with me."

Kildron's jaw falls open. "But…I—" he blinks and looks down, collecting his thoughts. "I made it myself," he says softly. "It was a gift for our engagement—a symbol of our time together. We had this saying, 'eternity isn't enough time.'"

Iris purses her lips. Finally, she holds out the hourglass. "Fine. Take it. I don't even care." She shakes it impatiently.

Kildron snatches it up, grasping it in his fist as if it were the last token to heaven. "Thank you," he breathes.

Iris stands, still clearly upset. "What now? I'm going crazy down here. Shouldn't we be doing something? Looking for the Book of Life? Anything?"

Kildron pockets the hourglass. "Are we ready for this discussion?" he asks, looking over at me.

I nod.

"Alright." Kildron straightens. "I think we all know the plan. To stop the Holy One, we have to find the Book of Life. And to find the Book of Life, the royal family is the key. Anciently, they were tasked with defending the Language. The king's father, Titan… he should know where it is."

"He's dead," I say matter-of-factly.

"What? You're sure?"

"I'm sure," I growl. "I watched him die."

Kildron nods. "What about King Dralton? Does he—"

"Dead!" I say. "They're both dead."

Kildron frowns, his forehead folding along the creases. "Someone has to know. What about the princess?"

I shake my head. "She doesn't know."

Kildron squints. "You're sure we can trust her?" His voice is coated with suspicion. "She hasn't sided with the Holy One?"

His tone makes me uncomfortable. "What kind of question is that?"

Kildron stifles a laugh. "You don't know, do you? Satan's Glory, you really don't know?"

"Know what?"

"Who the Holy One is."

My eyes widen. "You know who he is?"

Kildron sneers. "Obviously. I fought him, numbnuts. His name is Zezric Malik."

Malik! It takes a second for the name to register.

"No!... You're serious?"

Kildron nods.

"But… how… why would he…?"

"It's a long story…" Kildron sighs.

Iris looks around the cave. "We have time."

He waves his hand. "It was so long ago, I barely remember the details."

When he sees me raise my brow, he sighs. "You know what? Fine. Here's the gist of it."

Kildron repositions on his bedroll and runs his fingers through his hair. "It all started with a feeder named Asmodeus. I'm telling you, this guy was ancient—maybe the oldest man on Earth. I'm talking thousands of years old. Anyways, Asmodeus started a church in Hogrum—called it the Order of the Firstborn. To reward loyalty, his disciples were given the Mark of the Beast."

"The demon tattoo?" I clarify.

"That's right."

"Hold on," Iris interjects. "You said Asmodeus was a feeder? How did he get into Hogrum?"

Kildron's eyes light up. "That's right. I almost forgot; he had this relic called the Shackles of Redemption—said he found them hidden in the ocean. Somehow, the relic let him pass through the wall. Anyway, at some point over the years, Asmodeus converted our ancestors, and the Kaimors have been demons ever since."

"He chose them because they were mystics?" I wonder.

"Maybe," Kildron shrugs. "Or because they believed the doctrine. Who really knows."

Iris rolls her eyes. "What does this have to do with the Holy One?"

"I'm getting there," Kidlron insists. "This is where I come in. I was raised a demon, but I didn't believe their teachings. As a teen, I wanted to forsake the Order, but dissenting was too dangerous. Instead of deserting, Zane convinced me to be his spy. So, over the next few years, I worked my way into Asmodeus's inner circle. Big surprise, he was after The Book of Life. He thought it was hidden in Hogrum, and he was willing to destroy the place to get it."

"And the Holy One?" Iris nags.

Kildron smiles. "Now, we get to the Holy One. I was actually spying for Zane when I first met him."

"He was part of the Order?" I ask.

"The opposite, actually. Zezric was sent from Cavernum as a spy. He was trying to infiltrate the Order, just like me. He was supposed to be an ally, but he turned on us. Somewhere along the way, he decided he wanted the power for himself. He destroyed the sanctuary and unleashed the feeders, all in the search of a library that was never there." Kildron sighs. "I tried to kill him that night, but he escaped in the chaos. As for your mother... That night was the last time I saw her."

"Let me make sure I have this straight," I say. "Zezric was a good guy, helping you fight Asmodeous—a bad guy. Then, he turned evil and destroyed Hogrum, but the Book of Life was never there?"

"Bingo," Kildron says.

"Okay, so how do we find it?" Iris asks.

Kildron frowns. "You don't."

Once again, my anger begins to rise. "But you just said—"

"It's locked," Kildron says. "It won't matter if we find it. Only the royal family can open it."

"So? We can still look," I insist. "What if we find it? We can tell Rose. Maybe she has a key. We can use the language against him."

"It won't matter," Kildron sighs. "Zezric has hundreds of eyes on the palace, inside and out. The second Rose leaves, they'll follow. We'd lead them right to it."

"She has an invisibility relic," I argue. "She could—"

"Matt!" Kildron shouts. "It. Won't. Work. It won't! Whatever relic she has, the Holy One will know about it. He'll be one step ahead; he always is. As long as he can read your mind, there's no point in searching. You'll only be aiding his cause. Any knowledge you acquire becomes his knowledge."

"Why don't we just kill him?" Iris asks. "Get close with the morph mask and catch him by surprise. Wouldn't that be easier than finding some library?"

Kildron shakes his head. "It won't work. He'll see it coming."

'How?" Iris demands. "You act like he's omniscient."

Kildron rubs his eyes, emptying his lungs in a long sigh. "He might as well be. He knows things before they happen. It's like he has eyes in the back of his head."

I frown. "But he doesn't... right?"

Kildron sighs. "What he has is better. It's some kind of power—one I don't completely understand. The King of Hogrum called it Foresight."

"Foresight?" I furrow my brow. "Like, he can see the future?"

"I'm not quite sure," Kildron admits. "Whatever the gift is, he can predict any attack. I tried to kill him once, but he was always a step ahead. It was like fighting a ghost. Even without the Book of Life, his power is Godly."

"How did he get Foresight?" I wonder.

"Supposedly, it's inherited, passed down through Cavernic Royalty. His father, Dralton, had it too."

I frown, suddenly confused. "King Dralton had Foresight?"

"Yep," Kildron confirms. "He was the only man that Zezric ever feared, and now he's dead."

Iris perks up. "This gift runs in the family line, right?" She turns to me. "What about the princess?"

"I'm not sure," I say. "I don't think Rose has it. Or if she does, she doesn't know it yet."

Kildron inhales through his teeth. "In that case, he's untouchable. Facing him is a suicide mission."

"This is stupid," I complain. "We can't kill him, and we can't find the library. We might as well surrender now."

Kildron furrows his brow. "I never said we can't find the library,"

"Yes, you did," I insist.

"You weren't listening," Kildron stands, brushing the bottom of his jeans. "There was a condition. I said there's no point in searching so long as he can read your mind."

"Same difference,"

"It's not the same. Shield your mind, and the search can commence."

"What are we supposed to do?" I demand. "Find me a soul-anchor just lying around?"

Kildron shakes his head. "Soul-anchors can be removed. I have something else in mind. There's a technique to shield your thoughts. It can be quite effective, but it takes some practice."

"Okay. So teach us," I insist.

"I was planning to." A sliver of a smile creeps onto Kildron's face. "What do you say, Iris?"

Iris shrugs, "Sure. I'm listening."

"The technique is called Durebrum," he explains. "For the sake of simplicity, think of the soul as air, filling the space inside you. When a demon possesses you, the two souls overlap, filling the same space. This allows the demon to access the mind, memories and all."

"How insightful," Iris grumbles sarcastically.

I expect Kildron to snap back, but he only grins. "To protect the mind, you must condense it—compacting the soul until it becomes solid… impenetrable. Two gasses can share the same space, but a solid will always disperse the air around it."

"That sounds easy enough," I say. "We just condense our soul?"

"Simple in theory, but tricky in practice." Kildron looks back and forth between us. "Now, who's ready to give it a try?"

When Iris says nothing, I shrug. "I will, I guess."

"Great. For starters, get comfortable." Kildron motions at my bedroll. "Lay down. Eliminate all distractions. Then, just draw your soul inward. Pack your mind in a tight little ball."

I lie down on my bedroll and close my eyes. "What are you gonna do?"

"Same thing the Holy One would: scour your mind in search of secrets."

"I'm not sure I have any secrets," I admit.

"If you do, I'll find them," Kildon says confidently. "Now, go ahead and give it a try. I'll give you a headstart."

I do as Kildron directed, trying to compact my soul. Instead of reaching out, as I would to use dominion, I reach inward. Like inhaling a big breath, I suck my soul deeper, drawing it into my abdomen. My soul resists, like elastic. The more I pull it in, the more it rebounds against me. The discomfort is strange—beyond physical. My consciousness—my very psyche—is being crushed. My soul wants to expand… needs to expand.

Knock Knock! Can I come in?

Before I know what's happening, Kildron is in my head, driving his consciousness through my thoughts like a battering ram. Memories begin to surface as he picks his way through my mind.

Suddenly, I'm at the movies with my 8th grade crush. I leave my hand palm up on the armrest, hoping she might take it. Unfortunately, her hands stay tucked under her thighs as if they're cold.

A second later, I'm in the Urgent Care, getting stitches on the side of my finger.

Kildron flips through my mind as if it were a magazine, glancing briefly at each memory before turning the page.

No!

I take my soul and draw it closer, wrapping my mind around my memories like an armful of laundry fresh out of the dryer. The more memories I grab, the harder it is to hold them all.

I feel Kildron's consciousness ramming into me. With every jostle, another sock of a memory falls free from my grasp.

As they fall, Kildron snatches each one, giving it a quick gander. *Let's see…*

Before I can stop him, Kildron dives into the memory, taking me with him.

I find myself standing on a grassy field at Lincoln Elementary. My classmates huddle around me, each one accompanied by a grown man —their fathers.

What do we have here? Kildron's words echo in my head. Like me, he's a helpless observer, sharing the view from my eyes.

My 5th grade teacher, Mrs. Noonan, stands in front of the crowd, holding a bucket of supplies in her hand. "Before we begin, I just want to thank all the dads for coming out today." She looks over the crowd, briefly making eye contact with each one of the men. "And I know we have a few grandfathers and brothers as well. Thank you. It means the world to these kids. I promise, it'll be a day they never forget."

Mrs. Noonan offers one last gracious smile before clapping her hands together. "Alright, class, who's ready for the Dad Olympics to begin?"

"Me! Me!" my classmates cheer, jumping up and down around me. A few fathers echo their excitement, but I say nothing, choosing instead to look at the grass.

Mrs. Noonan tips over the bucket and dumps a pile of rope onto the grass. It's not one big strand, but dozens of individual 4-foot segments.

"Okay everyone, pair up with your dads. We're going to start with a three-legged race. Take one of the ropes and tie one leg together. When you're ready, line up in front of the soccer goal."

I don't know what to do, so I just stand there, looking down at my feet.

Mrs. Noonan notices, putting a hand on my shoulder. "Hey, Matt. We can be a team if you'd like. I don't know if we'll win, but I'm pretty fast. What do you say?"

"No thanks," I sigh.

"Are you sure? It'll be fun."

"I'm okay," I say softly.

Mrs. Noonan studies me a moment longer. "What if I make you the referee? Does that sound fun?"

I shrug my shoulders.

"Great. Why don't you walk down to the other soccer goal. That will be the finish line. When we're ready, you can say go."

Slowly, I make my way across the field, dragging my feet in the grass. By the time I arrive at the finish line, everyone is lined up and ready.

"Okay, Matt," Mrs. Noonan shouts. "Tell us when to go."

"On your marks…" I mumble

"Louder, Matt," Mrs. Noonan shouts. "Everyone needs to hear you."

I take a deep, shaky breath. It's not a shout, but I manage something audible this time. "On your marks… Get set… Go!"

Several dads erupt forward, nearly dragging their children with them. The rest follow close behind, laughing and cheering as they stumble forward in an uncoordinated hobble.

I bite my cheek as they run toward me. Every dad is smiling, coaxing their child with patience and love. Every child is laughing.

Everyone but me.

In the middle of the pack, a girl suddenly trips and falls flat on her stomach, stopping her father in his tracks. The rest of the duos run past them.

"Hurry, Ashley!" Her dad picks her up and sets her back on her feet. "They're getting away," he laughs.

Together, they take two steps before she trips again, almost pulling him down with her.

Meanwhile, the first daddy-duo makes it past the finish line, followed closely by another.

Once again, Ashley's dad picks her up and sets her on her feet. "New plan," he announces. "Step on my shoes." With their legs still bound, he spins her so she's facing his stomach and lets her step onto his shoes. "Hold on tight."

Ashley hugs her dad's waist as he runs, jostling her up and down with every step. They're a decent way behind the other kids, but they're catching up quickly. As they approach the finish line, they overtake the second to last duo by a foot or less.

"Yes!" Ashley squeals as she jumps up and down. "We beat Cameron!"

"Cameron got last," another kid teases.

Cameron's face turns red. "I did not! Ashley cheated!"

"Hey, now," Cameron's dad says, putting a hand on Cameron's shoulder. "It's okay to lose, buddy. They beat us fair and square."

"But…" Cameron huffs. "We didn't lose!" He looks around until his eyes lock onto me. "Matt did! His dad didn't even come."

"Cameron!" his dad scolds. He crouches down to whisper in his ear, but I can still make out what he's saying. "We shouldn't say things like that, buddy. You might make him feel bad."

"But it's true," Cameron whines.

"It doesn't matter," his dad says. "Some dads can't take time off work. He probably wishes his dad could be here, and you might make him feel worse."

It's too late. The tears start to stream down my cheek, and my chin quivers as I try to compose myself.

"Look," One of my classmates whispers to another. "He's crying."

Everyone is staring at me now, children and parents alike. None of the fathers say anything. After all, they aren't my dad. It's not their place to console me.

"My mom says he doesn't have a dad," Michael whispers to another classmate.

"Why not? Did he die?"

Michael shrugs, holding his palms to the sky with bent elbows. "How am I supposed to know?"

Mrs. Noonan scrambles to action, stepping in front of me to shield me from their gaze. "Alright, everyone. Up next is kickball, dads versus kids. Why don't you all wait at the dugout, and I'll be right over."

Once the crowd has moved away, Mrs. Noonan turns to face me. "Are you alright, Matt? I know this must be a tough day for you."

I sniffle, unable to form words.

"I think you might feel better once the kickball game starts. All the kids are together on one team. You won't be alone this time."

"I wanna go home," I choke.

"Are you sure?" She frowns. "But we have such a fun day planned."

"I want my mom," I sniffle. "I wanna go home!"

Mrs. Noonan nods. "Of course, Matt. Let's go call your mom."

Suddenly the memory ends as Kildron retreats from my mind. My eyes snap open, but tears blur my vision. I quickly blink them away.

"That…" Kildron clears his throat uncomfortably. "That was a good start, but it needs work."

Iris is already lying on her bedroll. She narrows her eyes as I wipe the moisture from my cheek. "What… what happened in there?"

"He failed," Kildorn says quickly, wanting to change the subject. "It's your turn now."

Iris tucks her hands behind her head and closes her eyes, as if lounging by the pool. "Go ahead."

Kildron stands over her, staring right at her face. Suddenly, his eyes glaze over, and his mouth goes slack.

Silence.

As the seconds tick by, Kildron's breathing becomes deeper, almost ragged. A minute goes by. Then another.

Just as I start to grow bored, Iris begins to twitch. Finally, her eyes snap open and she bolts upright, arms spreading wide like a startled panda. Immediately, she composes herself, rolling onto her stomach and climbing to her feet.

Kildron purses his lips. He almost looks concerned but hides it with a compliment. "That… that was good. I'm impressed."

Iris sits up, a proud smirk on her face. "Admit it, you almost gave up."

"Don't get too cocky," Kildron warns. "The Holy One is a different story. If I can pierce your defenses, he'll blow right through them."

My eyes open slowly, appreciating the simplicity of my bedroom. The ceiling fan spins overhead, filling the room with a soothing hum. An animated poster of Spider-Man watches me from the wall by the window. It was a birthday present when I was twelve. After all these years, I never took it down.

I kick off my covers and roll out of bed. "Mom?"

No one answers.

I shiver as I pass under the ceiling fan. I'm only wearing basketball shorts—my preferred form of pajamas. I grab a t-shirt from its place on the ground and pull it over my head.

"Mom?"

I wander into the kitchen and peer through the sliding glass door. That's weird. She's not cooking breakfast and she's not in the garden.

Something nags me from the back of my mind. Something about Judy that I just can't recall.

CHK-CHKKK!

Behind me, someone racks a pump-action shotgun.

I spin around, coming face to face with Judy. She aims the shotgun at my chest. "Mom! There you are. What—"

"You have two seconds to get out of here before I fill your lungs with lead."

"What? Mom, it's me. Are you okay? Put the gun down."

Her finger tightens on the trigger. "One…"

"Mom!" Panic pierces my heart, sending it into overdrive. "Please, stop. It's me, Matt… your son."

Judy looks me up and down, narrowing her eyes in the process. "You're no son of mine. You're one of those… things. You're a monster."

"What?"

"I know what you did to that boy. You're not my Matthew. You're a monster."

"Mom—"

"Get out!" She screams, jabbing the barrel at me like a spear. "GET OUT, YOU MONSTER!"

In the blink of an eye, everything crispens. My mental fog dissipates.

Finally, I remember what's been nagging me. My jaw falls open.

"But… you're dead."

Judy pulls the trigger!

Freeze!

It's not my command, but Kildron's. I can sense his consciousness as he halts the diverging buckshot, freezing a dozen pellets in front of my face. Judy is frozen as well, her hatred preserved in a teeth-exposing grimace.

Kildron materializes at my side, eyeing Judy's frozen figure. "So, this is what you think about feeders, huh?"

"It's just a dream," I insist as relief floods through me. *She didn't hate me. It's just a dream.*

"Sometimes, our dreams reflect our feelings." Kildron scoffs. "You fed in self-defense, you know. It doesn't make you a monster."

I can tell he's trying to console me, but the way he says it only feels condescending.

"I didn't ask your opinion," I bark. "Why are you even here? I thought we agreed my dreams are private."

Kildron frowns, annoyed with my own frustration. "I could hear you gasping and holding your breath. I figured you were having a nightmare."

"That doesn't mean you can barge into my head."

"I know," Kildron says. "But it's more than that. We really need to talk. I figured we'd do it here, let you rest while we're at it." Kildron closes his eyes, and suddenly the world spins. The colors around me stretch in long brushstrokes before condensing back into a clear image.

I'm standing in a luxury hotel room, or maybe it's an apartment suite. A massive row of windows display a panoramic view of the city night. Skyscrapers tower over the distant roads, their windows a checkerboard of yellow and black. From this height, the distant cars hardly seem to be moving. The rest of the apartment is decorated with generic, fancy decor—abstract paintings and thin-legged end tables.

"Where are we? New York?"

"Seattle," Kildron says. "This is where I lived the last few years."

"This was your house?" When I imagined Kildron as a feeder, I imagined a bum, wandering through the streets. I didn't imagine a penthouse suite.

Kildron nods, strolling over to a stainless steel fridge. "Sure beats the cave, am I right?" He pulls open the fridge door and grabs a beer. "Want a drink?"

"I'm fine," I say.

"Suit yourself." Kildron flops onto a black leather couch and kicks his feet up on a glass coffee table. Using his teeth, he pries off the beer cap and gives the bottle a swig. "Not gonna lie, I love this apartment. Though I don't care much for Seattle. Too crowded… and too much rain."

"Why live here then?"

"It's the closest city to Cavernum. You'd be surprised how many feeders flock here to feed."

"And you feed on them?"

Kildron shrugs. "The bad ones, yeah. Someone has to." He kicks off his shoes, sighing with satisfaction. "Satan's glory, it feels good to relax. Come sit, Matt."

Even in the dream world, a fraction of my fatigue persists, and my bones ache. Begrudgingly, I take a seat on the opposite end of the couch.

He eyes his beer, but he doesn't take a sip. "Hey, Matt. About what you said yesterday…"

I stiffen.

"I've been thinking, and I think you're right. I should've tried harder to find you. I'm sorry."

"Is that all?" I ask.

Kildron frowns. "I said I'm sorry. I… I'm taking responsibility. What more do you want me to say?"

I shrug.

He rubs his temples. "God, this is harder than I thought it would be. Look. I just want us to have a fresh start, okay? A clean slate for everyone. I'll forget what you said yesterday if you forget all the things I said."

I watch him, trying to decide if this is all an act. After a second, I lean back into the sofa cushion. "What things?"

A smile slowly grows on Kildron's face. "Alright then." He lifts his bottle as if in a toast. "To fresh starts." He takes a sip.

"So," I say, looking around. "What else did you have in mind?"

"I thought we could talk, just the two of us. I have some questions for you, and if you're anything like your mother, I'm sure you have some too."

I resist the urge to decline. *Clean slate*, I remind myself.

"Sure," I say. "What do you want to know?"

"Everything. How'd you end up with that old lady, Junie? How'd you find Cavernum? Tell me everything."

"First of all, her name's Judy. She found me on her doorstep the night Hogrum was destroyed. She raised me ever since."

"She seems nice," Kildron notes. "I'll have to thank her sometime."

"She's dead," I remind him.

"That's right, I… sorry. That must've been hard for you."

I know he's trying to sympathize, but it feels forced. "I don't want to talk about it."

Kildron almost looks relieved. "Alright… so, how'd you find Cavernum?"

I give him a quick summary. When I finish, he asks about The Dividing next, my capture and escape in Hogrum, all the way up to the invasion. I tell him everything.

He gives his beer a little swirl. "That's quite the little anecdote you've got."

"Yup."

Kildron narrows his eyes, setting his beer on the table. "I uhhh, I wanted to ask something else… about Jenevrah," He says it reluctantly, a hint of disappointment in his voice. "I saw a memory when you were attempting Durebrum… something the Holy One said. It was only a glimpse. I thought maybe you could elaborate… please."

"Sure," I take a second, thinking back to my discussion with the Holy One. "I don't know much. Only what the Holy One told me. And I'm not even sure he was telling the truth."

Resting his elbows on his knees, Kildron leans forward. "Go on."

I clench my teeth, refusing to look at Kildron. "The Holy One said he killed her. He wanted something she had, but she erased her memories. In the end, he thought she was too dangerous to be left alive."

Kildron's head droops, like a wilting flower. I can see the pain in his countenance, but it's subtle, tempered by decades of mourning. His chest swells as he takes a deep breath. "That's it? I was hoping for a little more."

"That's it." I say.

Kildron picks back up his beer, taking a sip. "Did he say what he was after?"

"No."

"Hmmm," Kildron stares into the darkness, lost in thought. "Interesting… Have you mentioned this to Iris?" Kildron asks.

"Yeah, I told her."

"How did she react?"

I shrug. "I don't know. Intrigued, I guess."

"Hmmm," Kildron hums. "She didn't mention a relic or anything like that?"

"Why would she mention a relic?"

"No reason." Kildron purses his lips. "Can you do me a favor, Matt? Don't mention this conversation to Iris. I want to keep this between us."

"How come?"

Kildron bites his lips, choosing his words carefully. "Iris was a servant of the Holy One. At some point, she believed in his cause. I worry that her loyalties are still… questionable."

I frown. "After all she did, you don't trust her?"

"It's not personal. I don't trust you either… not until you learn to shield your mind. This knowledge is dangerous, Matt. Your mother erased her memories for a reason."

"Fine." I look at Kildron. "What was mom like? I asked Zane once, but..."

"What was she like?" he echoes. He closes his eyes and his lip twitches into a smile. "Why don't I just show you?"

In the blink of an eye, a figure appears at Kildron's side. She's tall for a woman, with long brown hair. She resembles Iris in some ways, but her nose is more petite, and she lacks Iris's muscle. Oddly enough, she's only a few years older than myself. Then I remember: Kildron hasn't seen her in 18 years.

"Hi, Mom," I mutter softly. "It's me, Matt. You probably know me as Ezra."

The woman smiles at me shyly, stops smiling, then smiles again. Her shoulders slowly sway from side to side, playing in a continuous loop like some kind of video game character.

"What's wrong with her?"

Kildron looks away. "I'm not sure I remember enough. I don't even remember the sound of her voice. It's been too long."

"Oh... okay." Still, I watch her, absorbing every detail. Her scarlet lips and scattered freckles.

When Kildron sees my disappointment, he sighs. "She was perfect, your mother. I never deserved her, and everyone knew it. She was clever, and kind, a little timid, but she could win over anyone with a single conversation." Kildron smiles to himself. "She was an angel, but she wasn't a pushover. She'd speak her mind if she had to."

I smile. I'd love a story, but I can't bring myself to ask. *Why get attached when she's already gone?*

Slowly, the image of my mother fades like fog in the rising sun.

"Anything else you want to know?" Kildron seems more relaxed now, content to be conversing with his son.

"Yeah. I've actually been thinking about something lately. When I was in Hogrum, the Holy One said something weird. He said... that I would serve him someday. We would fight side by side. Is it possible he could know that? You know... with Foresight and all?"

"Hmmm," Kildron scratches his chin. "As far as I know, Foresight only works in the short-term, whatever it is. And time-dominion is impossible without a relic. Believe me, I've tried. But… maybe…" His voice trails off as he stares into the air above my head.

"Maybe what?"

His lips pinch into a thin line. "Nothing. It's probably nothing."

"No, what? I want to know."

"I just… maybe he didn't see the future, but the past."

"What do you mean?"

Kildron shakes his head. "Forget it. I shouldn't have said anything."

"What? Just tell me," I beg.

"I can't. I really shouldn't have said anything. I'll tell you when you master Durebrum."

"But—"

"That's final," Kildron asserts, not an ounce of doubt in his tone.

Annoyed, I look out the window, watching the cars pile up at a stoplight.

Kildron repositions in his seat. "So… tell the truth. Did you try to visit the healer girl?"

I look away, bothered by how predictable I've become. "You were right. I couldn't get through the wall."

Kildron smiles. "You're persistent, even when the odds are against you. That's good." He looks at me, waiting for me to meet his gaze. "Tell me about the girl. You two serious?"

"I guess."

"How long have you known her?" Kildron says, before taking a sip of his beer.

I'm almost embarrassed to say it. "Four months."

Kildron sits up, choking on his beer. "What!" He laughs. "You had me risking my life for a summer fling?"

"She's not a summer fling," I insist, but my voice lacks assurance. I thought the same thing about Rose, and I was wrong.

"Have you two…?" he raises an eyebrow at me.

"What, no!"

Kildron raises his hands, leaning back in his chair. "Hey, I don't judge. I'm just trying to get a sense of things." He scratches his chin for a minute. "Have you guys merged?"

"Merged?"

"I don't know what the kids call it these days. Mind-splitting. Body-sharing. Rubbing-souls. If you know, you know."

"You mean, like… possession?"

"No, no, no. We're talking about two different ends of a spectrum. Possession is on one end—violent and invasive. Merging is gentler. You bring your soul to the edge of their consciousness. You both can decide how much you want to expose. You can simply share a dream, like we are." Kildron motions to the room around us. "We call this dream-hopping. Or you can… merge deeper—exposing your inner thoughts and feelings."

My mind wanders to Kendra. The euphoric feeling as our souls intertwined. As the memories surface, I can't keep the blood from rushing to my face.

Kildron's jaw falls open. "Really? You merged… before you even…" he shakes his head. "Wow. No wonder she loves you."

"It's not a big deal," I say.

Kildron shrugs. "If you say so. How many times did you do it?"

"I don't know."

"Yeah, you do. One time? Three times?"

"Most nights."

"Most nights! Satan's Glory. No wonder you're obsessed with her."

"I don't get it. What's the big deal?"

"You're letting your souls converge. You're opening up your mind. Your desires. Your intentions. There's no secrets after that. Building trust in a relationship can take ages, but merging goes beyond trust. It grants a perfect knowledge of your inner thoughts."

"Alright. I get it."

"I'm just saying, four months is fast. Not to shame you or anything. You could be merging with multiple girls for all I care."

My face gets warmer.

Kildron's jaw drops open. "No… you didn't… With who…the

princess?" He beams a proud smile. "You filthy little animal," he laughs. "No wonder you were picking her flowers."

Something about his reaction puts me at ease. I feel a smile tugging on my lips.

"It just kinda happened," I admit. "I didn't even know what merging was."

Kildron raises his palms. "Like I said, I'm not here to judge. Who you merge with is your business." He stands from the sofa and stretches, arching his back with his arms above his head. "Let me ask you this. The healer girl, do you love her?"

"Yeah, I do."

"And what about the princess?"

I open my mouth, but I don't quite have an answer. "I thought I did. Now, I don't know how I feel."

Kildron nods his head, satisfied. "I'll tell you what. Next time I go out to feed, I'll find a pen and paper. You can write a letter to this girl, and we'll deliver it together. Sound good?"

"Yeah."

He frowns as another thought enters his mind. "And write the princess too. If we want to stop the Holy One, I have a feeling we'll need her help."

6

ROSE

From my perch on the wall, I watch the Equalists gather south of the stable. It's a large stretch of relatively bare earth, perfect for practicing dominion.

Bob—the owner of Bob's Brew—leads them in a series of drills. First, they all form fireballs in unison. Then, I see the subtle rippling of energy shields. Throughout it all, Bob wobbles through their midst, giving smiles and words of encouragement.

Watching their progress is more entertaining than I anticipated. I can almost forget that the council is meeting without me. I can almost forget how they banished me from the throne.

Ka-Crack!

I flinch as a bolt of lightning erupts from Bob's fingertips and branches into the air. He demonstrates again, pointing a flattened hand at the clouds.

Ka-Crack!

I must admit, the feat is impressive. Many guardsmen fail to summon lightning in their lifetime. For a bartender to do so is unheard of.

The sound of heavy footsteps approaches, stopping directly behind me.

"Hey, Rose," Diego stammers. "I'm on wall duty. I thought I'd see how you're doing."

I turn, looking over my shoulder at Diego. He's in a white Royal Guard uniform, the chain of an amplifier disappearing underneath his collar. He stands a few feet away with his hands in his pockets, as if afraid to approach. Everything about him has an air of unease.

"Hi, Diego. Did Antai put you up to this?"

"No." Diego shakes his head vigorously, then falls still. "Actually, it was Wendy… and Nevela. They wanted me to check on you."

Of course they did. Even after all they went through, they still manage to look out for me.

"You're welcome to join me," I offer. "I'm just watching them train."

Diego steps up to the parapet beside me, resting his elbows on the stone. "Not bad, right?"

"Growing up, I thought only the best of the best could exercise dominion. Apparently, I was wrong."

"Most of them never had the chance. Bob calls them his untapped potential." Diego shifts his weight from one foot to the other. "Some people are talking. They think the council wants to take away our amulets. Is it true?"

I sigh. "To be honest, Diego, I'm not sure. I'm suspended from the council... but if it makes you feel better, Antai won't let that happen. We need as many soldiers as we can get."

"Cool." Diego nods his head up and down, his shoulder relaxing. After a second, he turns around and stares out at the Core. "Do you think he's okay out there?"

I know who he's referring to.

Matt.

"I think so," I state. "I'm convinced he'll pull through."

"I sure hope so," Diego breathes.

"How's your family doing?" I ask, unsure what else to say.

"Good, I guess... They're alive. That's better than most. Mary is doing good. I have nothing to complain about." He says it all with a solemn expression.

"And yet it feels hopeless," I say.

Diego nods, his lips pressed thin. "Sometimes I wonder if dying to the feeders would have been better. Matt once told me it felt like falling asleep. At least it would have been quick. Now, they'll slowly starve. It'll take weeks…"

I don't argue with him. For all I know, he's right. In our attempt to save the sanctuary, we may have simply prolonged their suffering.

I decide to change the subject.

"Nevela told me what you did for her, removing the spell and all. Thank you."

"No problem," Diego says. "You should know. I removed mine, too, and my mom's. I know we disabled the spells, but I thought we should remove the symbols, just in case. Crasilda is the only one left. "

I find myself nodding. "That's good. Thank you for doing that."

"No problem." He rubs his palms together, glancing nervously around us. "Hey, Rose?"

"Yeah?"

"I've been meaning to tell you this, but I haven't really had the chance. I'm sorry for what happened to your Grandpa. I—"

"You don't have to apologize," I interject. "I know what it's like." I swallow loudly. "When the palace was raided a few months back, I was possessed by a demon. He made me point a gun at Antai and forced me to pull the trigger. I tried everything to stop myself, but I couldn't. I know you're not the one responsible. So please, don't apologize, Diego. There was nothing you could've done."

To my surprise, Diego shakes his head. "I'm not so sure about that."

I raise an eyebrow, my breath catching in my chest. "What do you mean?"

Diego looks away, suddenly ashamed. "I'm not so sure our experience was the same, that's all."

Matt's sister—Iris was her name—she called Diego's possession something special. Permanent possession… true possession. Perhaps there was more to it.

"What was it like?" I ask, "if you don't mind sharing."

Diego looks around, making sure we're alone. "It wasn't like you said, like he was controlling my body. It was different than that. It was like…" He looks around again, increasingly paranoid.

"It was like our minds got mixed together," Diego breathes, disgust in his voice. "It didn't feel like we were fighting for the same body. It felt like we joined souls. We became one… you know?"

"Huh," I mutter. "That's… interesting."

"This will sound crazy," Diego admits, "but once he got inside me, it was like we thought the same. I don't know how to explain it. We weren't me, and we weren't him; we were something in the middle: a new person. A mixture. When it happened, I wanted to shoot the king. I wanted him to die." He shakes his head. "I know it wasn't me, but at the same time, it felt like me. I couldn't tell the difference."

"I'm sorry, Diego. I can't imagine what that must've been like. Still, I don't blame you. It wasn't your fault."

"It doesn't feel that way." Diego says, staring out toward the Ring. "When Matt read my mind, I called out for help. It was as if, in that second, my emotions took control. I wanted to save my family more than he wanted to serve the Holy One. I stopped him from using the spell, but I couldn't stop him from pulling the trigger. Together, we wanted the king to die more than we wanted him to live. So, yes, I want to apologize, Rose. I'm sorry. I'm sorry I didn't fight harder."

"It's okay," is all I can mutter. My eyes are already clouding with tears. I don't know what to make of what I'm hearing, but I know I shouldn't speak, or I'll say something I'll regret.

"I just… I thought you should know," he says, defeated.

"Thank you, Diego." I manage to keep my voice composed, looking away and wiping a tear on my shoulder. "I appreciate the information. If you'll excuse me, I should—."

"Wait, there's one more thing," he says quickly. "I know the demon's gone, but sometimes it feels like he's still inside me, you know? Like his thoughts became a part of me. I talked to my mom about it. She feels the same. We can fight it, don't get me wrong, but sometimes it's… confusing. My point is, I worry about Crasilda. She always wanted power. And now…" he lets his voice trail off.

"You think she might be dangerous?"

Diego nods. "I think she might be on his side."

I sigh, tucking my hair behind my ears. "Well, as of yesterday, she's commander of the Royal Guard. Commander Kaynes is a traitor as well, and he practically controls the council. He may as well be king at this point."

Diego looks over at me, his nose wrinkling. He opens his mouth and closes it again. "Can I give you some advice, Rose… as a friend?"

The question makes me nervous. "Okay."

He looks up at me, a cold intensity in his eyes. "The Holy One doesn't play by the rules. That's why he's winning. As long as you do as you're told, he'll have the advantage."

"What are you suggesting?" I frown. "I assassinate General Kaynes?"

"Not exactly," Diego says. "You said that General Kaynes controls the council, right? So what? The council isn't your only source of power."

"I'm not sure I'm following you." I say.

Diego sighs. "My point is, don't be afraid to break the rules. The council makes the laws, but they don't control the people. Take matters into your own hands."

"You think I should… what? Plan a coup?"

"Maybe. It's definitely an option. My point is, you can't wait for the council to come to their senses. By then, it might be too late." He falls silent as another guard marches past us. "Okay, I should probably get back on patrol."

"Thank you, Diego. I appreciate your honesty."

"Of course. I'll see you later, I guess. If you need anything, let me know."

"I will." With that, Diego turns and marches away.

I think of Grandpa. He made a demon-amulet, knowing that the council would condemn it. He kept them in the dark, knowing they'd disapprove of his actions. He did what he thought was best, no matter the consequences.

It's time I do the same.

It's noon, but the storm clouds shield the sun, giving my room a somber, dusky atmosphere. Snowflakes salt my window, sticking together in clumps. To make up for the insufficient sunlight, several candles are lit around my quarters.

"Who are we missing?" Antai asks, scanning the room. "Octavian?"

Wendy and Nevela sit in the reading nook by the window. Diego stands next to them, arms folded. Gideon sits in my desk chair, and Antai paces in the middle of the room.

"He's keeping watch on General Kaynes," I say. "We're only missing Kendra. I'll give her another minute, and then we can begin."

Antai continues to pace, checking his watch constantly. Eventually, he holds up his wrist so that his watch is visible. "It's been two."

I stand from the foot of my bed, looking around at my makeshift council of trustees. It's smaller than I would've liked, but it's all I've got.

"Welcome, everyone. Thank you all for coming. As you may have guessed, this meeting is somewhat of a secret. In light of recent events, I no longer trust the High Council. I'm certain that General Kaynes is a traitor. He's loyal to the Holy One." *To my father.*

I should tell them. I should explain everything, but I don't have the energy to explain myself—to defend my allegiance on account of a father I never knew.

Next time.

I collect my thoughts. "The truth is, I no longer hold any power as queen, so I've gathered you here to discuss our options moving forward."

Antai stops pacing, he stands in front of my bed, facing the group. "The way I see it, our options can be divided into three broad categories: take the offensive, flee the sanctuary, or do nothing and hope for the best. Fighting and fleeing will lead to casualties—

possibly even massacre—and staying here means almost certain starvation. Sorry to be so blunt, but that's the current predicament. Right now it's a matter of minimizing the consequences. Any suggestions?"

For a minute, the room is depressingly silent. Gideon is the first to speak.

"Not a suggestion, I'm afraid. Merely a question about this new Guardian, Crasilda. It's my understanding that Kaynes was the one who first recommended her. Do we believe she serves the Holy One as well?"

"He was," Antai says, "so I wouldn't be surprised."

"I don't know…" I speculate. "The Holy One killed her father. I can't see her letting that go."

"Not to mention the whole Adamic bomb thing," Diego adds.

That's right. I nearly forgot. Crasilda was among those my father tattooed with a sanctuary-destroying spell. One of his demons possessed her, forcing her to use her body as a bomb. She's only alive because Matt intervened.

"Diego's right," I agree. "She has every reason to hate the Holy One."

"She's not a guardian; she's a lapdog," Antai says. "I don't think there's much to it. Kaynes is using her as an extra vote. The other diplomats are no different. He has them all convinced that he's saving the sanctuary from the rogue queen."

Gideon nods at Antai. "Thank you. That answers my question."

Antai looks around the room, his finger tapping on his holster. "So, saving the sanctuary… any ideas?"

The room is silent.

When no one speaks, Gideon clears his throat. "Your Majesty, could you elaborate regarding our resources. I am under the impression that the amulet vault remains partially unused."

I nod. "Lieutenant Octavian dispersed most of the amplifiers during the invasion. They remain in the possession of the Equalists. We also distributed the Adamic blades. Diego, Matt, and Octavian each have one. There might be one or two left in the vault. And then there are the soul-anchors. They would be invaluable, but I don't know the bonding spell. Without being bonded, they're worthless."

Gideon massages the bridge of his nose. "Have we considered making more Adamic blades? If we could arm every soldier, that alone could give us a fighting chance."

Diego suddenly sits forward. "What about an Adamic bullet? That's how the king was killed. You could make one too, like the Holy One did. Or several. If someone could get close enough, maybe it could do the job."

Antai brightens at the thought of it. "That's... a really good idea. Use his own invention against him. What do you think, Rose?"

I bite my lip. "The arrowheads I've made are much bigger than a bullet. I'm not sure if I can make a spell that small... but I'll try. I can start on it tonight."

"Hmmm," Gideon hums. "Any other weapons at our disposal? Relics, perhaps?"

I hesitate, looking down at my thumb. I'm wearing a silver ring composed of two bands, one overlaying the other. Each band is engraved with two Adamic symbols. At the moment, the outer band is positioned so that the symbols don't align.

You trust them, Rose. That's why they're here.

I reach down to my thumb and twist the outer layer of my ring, aligning the symbols.

Nevela gasps as I disappear.

"We have an invisibility ring," I say, my voice the only indication of my presence. "It's proven useful, but there's only one."

I twist the ring again, materializing in the same place. I don't mention the seerglasses. They don't feel relevant.

Wendy stands, scrunching her nose as she thinks. "Can it work on multiple people?"

"Yes, but you have to be touching my skin." I reach out my hand, and she takes it. Then, I twist the ring.

Nevela gasps again, clapping her hands together softly. "It works!"

I twist the ring again, misaligning the symbols.

"We could ferry people out," Wendy says, "In groups of five or six. It would take a while, but it would save lives."

I frown, not wanting to crush her hope. "We'd leave footprints in the snow. And the feeders might sense our presence with Adamic. We'd never make it."

"What if we used the tunnels?" Antai wonders. "One of the passageways connects to the Pit. It collapsed, but I bet we could dig it out."

Gideon looks intrigued. "I was under the impression that the tunnels were unnavigable."

"The Equalists mapped out some of them," Diego offers. "Bob said they used to smuggle weapons into the sanctuary. Maybe he knows a way out."

"Can you talk to him tomorrow?" I ask Diego. "Find out what he knows, and report back."

"No problem," Diego says.

"Any other ideas?" I ask.

When no one speaks, Gideon raises an eyebrow. "We've yet to hear your input, My Queen. Surely, you haven't gathered us here without some sort of scheme."

"I only have one idea," I admit, "but it's sort of a long shot. The Holy One is looking for the Lost Library, which supposedly contains the entire Adamic Language. If we find it first, we can use it against him. With the Library, we can't lose."

"Are we sure it even exists?" Wendy wonders.

I bite my tongue, looking at Antai. He nods.

"I wasn't certain if I should share this," I say, "but I trust you all. Before he died, my grandpa left me a letter. He told me about a riddle. Supposedly, it reveals the Library's location. He never solved it, but maybe we'll have more luck."

"What do you mean by riddle?" Diego asks. "Like a riddle, riddle? Like for kids?"

"I suppose so." I walk over to my desk and pick up a thin slate chalkboard. I begin writing as I recite the poem.

Deep beneath your feet is the power you seek.
It takes a word to open, but you cannot speak.
It is an ark of salvation when the future is bleak.
But beware, once opened, destruction will leak.

"That's it?" Diego asks, blinking in disappointment.

"That's it," I say solemnly. "Some of it is fairly straightforward. The Library is underground, that much is obvious. The only thing beneath our feet is the lava tubes. And a word opens it—presumably an Adamic word—but you cannot speak. That would only leave a written word, right? So, a written spell opens the library. The rest of the riddle seems…

"Useless," Diego mutters, squinting at the chalkboard.

"I was going to say cryptic, but yes, unhelpful at the very least."

Gideon tilts his head to the side. "'An ark of salvation' is an allusion to Noah's ark, I believe. When there is no hope for survival, Adamic will save us, just as the ark saved Noah from the flood. However, the last line is contradictory. 'Once opened, destruction will leak.'"

"Destruction will leak?" Antai shakes his head, his finger tapping on his holster. "They really wanted that rhyme, didn't they?"

"Sounds like a booby trap to me," Diego says.

Wendy nods. "Yeah, it kinda does. Maybe we shouldn't find it. There could be a curse for whoever opens it— a punishment for their greed."

"It's possible…" I agree, "but we can't be sure. The warning might be philosophical. Adamic can save us, if used correctly, but it can be used for evil as well. Power to both save and destroy."

"The riddle is meant for the royal family, right?" Diego says excitedly. "They live in the palace. Beneath the palace is the Pit!"

"I searched it this morning," Antai says. "There's no sign of the Library."

"This is impossible," Diego groans. "If it's not in the Pit, it must be in the tunnels, right. Well, the Equalists have been down there for years. They haven't found anything."

Gideon frowns. "How do you know what the entrance would look like? If Adamic is the key, there is no need for a keyhole. No need for a doorknob, or even a door for that matter. The entrance could be anything… anywhere. I worry this isn't the best use of our time."

Antai drums his fingers on his holster. "In your opinion, what would be a better use of our time?"

Gideon clears his throat. "This has been a necessary tangent, but I worry we are ignoring the inevitable outcome of invasion. As we stand, we won't survive another attack. We need to increase our odds… prepare our soldiers."

"They're trained and armed," Antai argues. "What more can we do?"

"They are armed; this is true," Gideon holds up a finger. "But not all weapons are created equal."

I know what he's implying. "You want me to make them Adamic weapons?"

"You don't have to make them yourself, My Queen." Gideon says. "Your time is too valuable, and to be frank, your fingers are slow. You should delegate. Perhaps find someone better suited for the craft."

I consider this a moment before nodding my head. Suddenly, it hits me. "Klinton's dad is the palace painter, Mr. Enemary. And his son is his apprentice. I bet we could trust them. I could teach them the armor piercing spell…" I frown. "But we don't have a forge in the palace. Where are we going to get the weapons?"

"I can take care of that," Diego offers. "I've been practicing my metal dominion. I think I could shape a simple sword."

"Arrowheads too," Gideon adds. "And I will start crafting bows. Imagine what a wall full of archers could achieve. With your permission, General Elsborne, I'd like to begin mandatory archery training."

"I'll see what I can do."

"Alright," I beam. "I think that covers it. Diego makes the weapons. The painters make the spells. And Gideon will cover archery training."

"Ahem," Nevela grins ear to ear. "Aren't you forgetting something?"

"Uhhhh." I don't have the slightest clue.

"I'm a seamstress," Nevela hints with a smile. "Teach me the armor spell, and I can sew Adamic armor."

"That… is a really good idea. Alright then. And Nevela with the armor." Slowly, I erase the chalkboard. "If no one has any other ideas, I supp—"

Thud. Thud. Thud.

"It's me, Kendra," a voice calls from the other side of the door.

Antai unlocks the door, and Kendra shuffles in. Her face is flushed. "Sorry, I'm late," she pants, looking around the room. "General Kaynes requested a private healing session. It took longer than I anticipated."

"Why did he need healing?" I ask, my voice more eager than I intended.

Kendra hesitates a moment, then relents. "Cervical radiculopathy… nerve pain in the neck," she explains.

I stiffen at the news, and Antai briefly meets my gaze. He's thinking the same thing I am.

It can't be a coincidence.

"We were just discussing our options," Gideon informs her.

Antai nods. "So far, we've considered assassinating the Holy One with an Adamic bullet and searching for the Lost Library ourselves. Got any other ideas?"

To my surprise, Kendra nods emphatically. She looks at me, her cerulean eyes eager and glistening. "Actually, I do." She opens her notebook and begins flipping through the pages. "Has anyone heard of the Blood-eye Plague of 1971?"

"I have," I say. "It was an epidemic in the Ring, right? Estimates put the death toll over 2,000. They sealed off the palace for nearly six months to help curb the spread."

"That's right," Kendra says excitedly. "The plague was highly infectious. Symptoms were mild to begin with—cough, nausea, diarrhea, fatigue—but grew more severe. By the second week, it caused hemorrhagic fever and mucosal bleeding." Kendra takes several pages from her notebook and spreads them out on the desk. Every sketch is virtually the same: a bedridden man or woman crying tears of blood.

Nevela cringes, covering her mouth with both hands.

Kendra points to one of the sketches. "The final symptom is bloody discharge from the eyes, hence the name. From there, 90% of patients recover completely. However, 5% will die, and 5% are left permanently blind."

"Did you draw these?" Wendy asks.

"Madame Xantone did," Kendra explains. "She was a new recruit when the plague hit. This is what she remembers from the outbreak."

Antai scowls. "I'm not sure I understand. What does this have to do with us?"

"Everything," Kendra gushes. "After the plague ended, Lady Xantone specialized in virology. She treats the High Council for every flu and common cold, but she can do more than cure a virus. She can recreate one. I've been talking with her, and she believes she could reproduce the Blood-eye Plague. She even claims she can alter it… make it more lethal."

"You want to start a plague," Antai breathes. "Infect the feeders with it. That's brilliant!"

Kendra beams. "If we can just infect a few feeders, the plague will spread. In a few weeks, with any luck, we can reduce their numbers and leave them crippled. At the very least, it'll weaken them."

"How do we infect them without infecting the palace?" I ask. "Something tells me Madame Xantone won't step anywhere near a feeder."

Kendra shifts her weight, her eyes turning downward. "Unfortunately, we'll need a sacrifice. We can infect someone here in the palace before sending them outside the wall. The feeders won't be able to resist. They'll feed and contract the virus. From there, the plague will spread. The incubation period is only a few days."

“So what, we find a volunteer?” Antai asks.

Suddenly, an idea pops into my head. “Kendra, if I can get you a volunteer, how soon until Lady Xantone can infect them?”

“Whenever. We could do it as soon as tonight. Why? Do you have someone in mind?”

“I think I might.” Before I can elaborate, there’s a knock on the door.

“Kaynes is in his chambers,” Octavian whispers through the door. “You’re safe to exit anytime.”

“Got it,” I call, just loud enough for Octavian to hear me. “This was a good start,” I announce, looking around the room. “A very good start. Thanks everyone. Any last ideas before we split up?”

Gideon clears his throat. “There’s one last option that we haven’t explored: requesting aid. Perhaps another sanctuary could offer reinforcements.”

“Which one?” Antai doubts. “Beskum is struggling as it is, And Domalamora only has two guardians. They don’t stand a chance against the Holy One. If we ask for help, we’ll be condemning them.”

“So?” Wendy interjects. “If the Holy One wins, they’re doomed either way.”

“I had something else in mind,” Gideon admits. “I’m sure you’ve all heard of Atlantia—the Sunken Sanctuary of the Sea. From what I’ve read, the Prophet Posedonah became its first king. He was a powerful Adalit. If they preserved his knowledge, who knows the power Atlantia may hold. It may be the only force to rival the Holy One.”

“If it still exists,” Antai says. “No one’s been to Atlantia in a few hundred years. We don’t even know where it is.”

“Antai is right,” I say. “The last person to visit Atlantia was my 5th great-grandfather, King Vorkumic. Dralton always wanted to go, but Vorkumic never recorded its location.”

Diego blinks, shaking his head in disbelief. “Hold on. Back up. Are… are you guys talking about Atlantis?”

“Atlantia?” I repeat.

“Atlantis,” Diego emphasizes. “In the Beyond, we have legends of a lost city, Atlantis, sunken in the ocean. Everyone's heard of it. They've made movies about it and everything."

"Do they know where it is?" Wendy asks.

"No way. I mean, they have theories and all, but no one's found it. Everyone thinks it's made up."

"What are the theories?" I wonder.

Diego shrugs. "The guesses are all over the place. Some think it was frozen under Antarctica. Some think it was swallowed by the Bermuda Triangle. Others think it's a sunken island in the Mediterranean. Stuff like that."

"I didn't understand a thing you just said," Wendy laughs.

"It's geography in the Beyond," I explain. "Antarctica is a frozen continent near the bottom of the planet, and the Mediterranean is a sea. I've never heard of…" I glance at Diego. "the Bertuma Triangle?"

"The Bermuda Triangle. It's kinda hard to explain," Diego says. "It's an area in the Atlantic Ocean, right off the coast of Florida where a ton of ships and airplanes have disappeared. They just vanish, and no one knows why."

"Why do they think Atlantia is there?" Antai questions.

"It's just stupid theories. Some people think that Atlantis had futuristic technology allowing people to live underwater. One theory is that their technology got so advanced that they created a portal to another world. Supposedly, Atlantis got sucked through the portal and disappeared. They think the Bermuda Triangle is a side effect of the portal. It swallows airplanes and boats, dragging them into another dimension, just like it did to Atlantis. Crazy, right?…"

His eyes glaze over and his jaw falls open. For a moment, he stares into empty space. "Holy Freak! They were right?" Diego starts pacing back and forth in front of my window, staring at his shoes. He mumbles quietly to himself. "It's the spell. They fly right over it."

"Diego?" I ask. "What are you talking about?"

"It all makes sense," Diego gasps, suddenly snapping to attention. He looks around the room. "There are stories of pilots who fly through the Bermuda Triangle. They all tell the same story. Their compasses stop working, and their equipment malfunctions."

"Meaning?" Antai asks.

"Meaning, it's the walls!" He waves his arms as he speaks. "Renshu told us that the walls create a magnetic field, right? It ruins technology. That's why the communication bunker is so far from the wall. That's gotta be it. Atlantis has a magnetic field that interferes with airplanes. That's why the pilots get lost." Suddenly, his eyes light up. "Maybe it's not underwater. Maybe it's on the surface! If Atlantis has a spell like Cavernum, you won't be able to see it from the outside, right? Boats would hit the wall without seeing it. It would sink the ship. That would explain so much!"

Gideon scratches his chin. "This is promising. Do you think it can be located?"

Diego frowns. "Maybe… but it wouldn't be easy. The Bermuda Triangle is huge. I don't even know how big. I'd have to Google it. Finding the sanctuary could take forever, assuming I'm even right."

"Let me get this straight," Antai sighs. "You think you might know where it is, in theory, but you don't think you could actually find it."

Diego shrugs. "Maybe I could find it. Maybe not. You'd never know for sure until you looked."

"It would take too long," I state. "Traveling in the Beyond, finding a boat, searching the ocean. This could take months. The Holy One will be Adalingual by then. Not to mention the impossibility of escaping the walls."

"What if Matt went?" Kendra proposes. "I could use the invisibility ring and find him. I'll tell him about Diego's idea, and we could look for it. He's trapped outside the wall, anyways. We might as well try. If Atlantia is what they say it is, it might be our only hope."

"I don't know, Rose," Antai warns. "The invisibility relic is powerful. Do we want to waste it on such a gamble? It might be our best chance at an assassination."

Everyone looks at me.

I grasp the ring and pull, slowly slipping it over the knuckle. "My grandfather couldn't defeat the Holy One," I remind myself. "He was the most powerful man I know. If he couldn't do it, I don't think I can either. Assassination sounds as unlikely as Atlantia, maybe more so. If you want my opinion, yes, I think we should try it."

I hold out the ring and drop it into her hand. "How soon are you prepared to leave?"

Kendra smiles. "I'll pack my things."

7

MATT

I clutch the letters tightly, one in each hand. They're nothing fancy, a single sheet of parchment folded into fourths. "Deliver to Kendra Eck" and "Deliver to Queen Roselyn Malik" are written in bold print.

We're almost to the palace now. I follow Kildron, a few paces behind. Iris trails us both, guarding the rear.

With each swing of my arms, my hands come into view. My fingers are long, with bulbous, walnut-sized knuckles. My skin is ulcerous and peeling, but Kildron insists the disguise is necessary.

We shuffle through a small alley stepping over the bodies. The corpses are a common sight, half covered in snow. I'm almost used to them now.

"This is close enough," Kildron whispers, "Any closer, and they'll see us."

Beyond the alley, the palace wall towers over the surrounding structures. We're only a short dash from its base. From this angle, I can only see the heads of the guardsmen as they patrol the wall. They bob up and down with every step, moving counterclockwise around the palace. Every now and then, they lean over the wall, peering down at the road below.

"The letters?" Kildron holds out his hand.

"I can do it," I offer.

Kildron shakes his head. "You need to save your energy. What if they spot you and start firing? What if they have Adamic arrows?"

"Fine." I hand over the letters.

"And the morph-mask?"

I reach to my chin, peeling off the mask. My skin quivers as my body returns to its normal form.

Kildron presses it over his face, but the mask doesn't morph. It remains a silvery sheet.

"You pick the disguise," Kildron instructs. "Make me someone they won't shoot… just in case."

Reaching out, I rest my fingers on the mask. I already know who he should impersonate. Someone the guardsmen trust. Someone they wouldn't question. Someone who commonly writes to the princess.

Antai Elsborne.

Kildron's pale flesh is instantly replaced with olive skin. His spine compresses, and his muscles expand. Finally, his black robe retracts, morphing into a guard uniform complete with the double red lapels of a guardian.

"How do I look?" Kildron asks.

"Like a douche," Iris says.

"Good." Kildron walks to the edge of the alley. There's a 50 foot stretch of bare cobblestone between the alley and the base of the wall. He'll be completely exposed the entire way.

Kildron closes his eyes, and the air around him begins to grow misty. A cloud of white fog builds around him, condensing like the dew on a cold glass. The fog grows thicker and thicker until it perfectly matches the snow around us. Even from a few feet away, I can barely see Kildron at its center.

"Here goes nothing," Antai's voice whispers from within the foggy cloud.

Moving at a walking pace, the cloud slowly drifts out of the alley and into the open. I expect him to rush the wall, but Kildron creeps instead. The cloud drifts at a snail's pace, indiscernible from above.

Suddenly, a head bobs into view on the wall walk. The guardsman leans over the edge, peering directly at Kildron's cloud. He sniffles, clears his throat, then spits off the wall. After sniffling once more, the soldier continues his patrol.

I watch as the cloud reaches the base of the wall. Immediately, the mist dissolves, revealing Antai's body pressed up against the stone . He peers up the face of the wall, and immediately begins to levitate.

I don't see the air ripple. I don't see any tugging on his clothes. It's as if gravity is turned off completely. He drifts upward as if riding an invisible elevator.

As he approaches the top of the wall, Antai's body slows to a stop. He hugs the wall as another guard shuffles past. Then, he levitates a few inches higher, peeking over the top of the parapet. Finally, like a frisbee, he tosses the two letters over the stone railing and onto the wall walk. Without waiting for a response, he drops like a stone.

Right before hitting the ground, Kildron rapidly slows, landing in a crouch. Still wearing Antai's body, he bolts across the clearing and slides into the shadow of the alleyway a moment before a guard peers over the wall. The guardsman frowns, noticing the footprints, and scans the city once more. When he doesn't spot anyone, the guard steps away from the ledge and moves out of sight.

"Do you think he saw the letters?"

"He saw them," Kildron says. "There's no way he missed them. They'll get delivered. C'mon."

We move briskly, retreating through the Core. As always, Kildron takes the lead. He's abandoned Antai's uniform, replacing it with a tattered black cloak. From behind, I can't see what face he's chosen to impersonate.

We turn onto Benediction Boulevard, slowing as we pass a gathering of feeders. They're assembled outside a slaughterhouse called Pixie's Porkchops, drinking apple whiskey straight from the bottle. In the middle of the road, an open fire roars. A full-grown pig roasts over the top of it.

The feeders hardly bat an eye as we shuffle by on the far side of the road. They're too engrossed in the conversation.

"You should've seen the girl I found," a feeder smirks. "One of them pampered-types. Her hair was like silk. Oiled skin and everything. I kept her for a few days until I got bored of her. Looking back, I should've kept her longer. I didn't realize how much I'd miss her."

I can't see his face, but Kildron clenches his fists. Our pace slows.

"I could never keep pets," another feeder casually comments. "Once they start whining, I have to put them down. The noise drives me nuts."

"It's not so bad," a third feeder says. "If you train them well, they won't make a peep. You just have to be consistent."

We turn the corner and Kildron stops. He's wearing his own body, and I see murder in his eyes.

"Iris, get Matt back to the cave. I'll meet up with you soon."

"You're going to feed?" she wonders.

"Not on that. I don't want that filth inside me. I have something else in mind. Just get to the cave. I'll be back soon."

Without another word, he turns and walks back toward the gathering.

"C'mon," Iris says, hurrying down the road. "Whatever he's about to do will attract attention. I don't want to be here when it does."

"What if he needs our help?"

"He won't," Iris says coldly. "You saw him possess two feeders at once. He'll be fine."

As we walk, I listen for the crack of lighting, or some indication of a battle. I hear nothing but the howling of the wind. The sound is eerie, whistling between the buildings like demented whispers.

We move in silence, sticking to the smaller alleys. I have no idea where we're going, but Iris leads confidently, hardly pausing at the intersections.

"What was it like growing up in Cavernum?" I finally ask.

"Fine."

"Just fine?"

"It was fine," Iris barks. "What more do you want me to say?"

"Sorry, geez. It was just a question."

We continue in silence. Every few minutes, I can see Iris glance at me from the corner of my eye.

Finally, she sighs. "Cavernum sucked, okay."

"How come?" I press.

Iris rolls her eyes. "Seriously?"

"What? I'm just curious."

"Fine…" Iris stares down at the snow as she walks. "I guess I never really felt like I belonged. Bob saw through this city's bullshit, and he taught me to do the same. He raised me as an Equalist from the day I could walk. Even as a kid, I attended the meetings, helped pass messages, find new recruits, everything. Dad kept me out of the action, but I did whatever I could. Still, it was lonely. I was the only kid."

"That sucks. How come?"

"The Equalists have a rule," Iris explains. "No one is allowed to join until after they're divided. Too many people change loyalties once they get a taste of wealth."

"But Bob let you join?" I point out.

Iris shrugs. "I think deep down, he knew his days were numbered. He wants me to lead the Equalists eventually, so he figured I better get an early start. He had this saying, 'the best habits are made in infancy.'"

"Sounds rough," I say.

"It was." She looks up at an intersection, turns left, then continues to stare at the snow. "I only had one friend growing up. She was my first crush. We did everything together, and yet, she couldn't know about the Equalists. As I got older, I used to dream about telling her everything. About the Equalists. About my tattoos. Our plans for Cavernum. Eventually, I did… She didn't take it well."

Iris sighs. "We never talked after that. She just ignored me, as if we never knew each other. The next few months, I worried that she'd turn us in. I laid in bed at night, waiting for the guard to bust in and steal my dad away. I thought they would torture him and hang him, all because I couldn't keep my mouth shut. I pushed everyone away after that. It was easier to be alone than to lie."

"Then what happened?"

"Then, I met Jazon. He showed up in the tunnels one day, wandering blindly through the labyrinth." She doesn't smile, but I can hear a change in her voice. “He heard that the Equalists were down there, so he went searching in the tunnels, knowing he’d get lost. By the time we found him, he had been down there for two days. Of course, he begged to join, but he was only seventeen at the time. Bob turned him away, but he kept coming back. When he finally turned 18, he didn’t show up to The Dividing. He accepted a spot in the fields to make sure he could join us. My dad said he was stupid, but I know he loved him for it. The rest was history. I finally had someone I could trust. Someone who understood me. He’s the best man I’ve ever met… and he’s gone.”

She looks over at me. “Let me ask you something, Matt. Do you think he deserves to come back?”

There's no good answer. “I… I think lots of people deserve to come back. But that doesn’t mean they should.”

“Why not?” Iris demands. “Because it’s wrong? It’s unnatural?”

“Well… sort of,” I breathe. “What do you want me to say?”

“I want you to actually think about it. Why is the Holy One wrong? God did the same exact thing. He flooded the Earth for the greater good. How is this any different?”

“I don’t know.”

“Isn’t that a problem?” Iris asks. “If you don’t know, then why are you fighting against him?”

I think hard. “Maybe God isn’t perfect. Maybe he made a mistake with the flood. It seems like he regretted it. He only did it once, after all. Demons came back, and he hasn’t flooded the world again, right? Maybe God stopped interfering because he knows it’s wrong. An omnipotent God shouldn’t toy with our lives.”

Iris rolls her eyes. “How can you say he shouldn’t interfere with life? He created us. Do you think that was a mistake as well?”

Once again, I have to think. “Creation is different from control. Our parents created us, but that doesn’t give them the right to control us… or kill us for that matter. I don’t even get what you’re arguing, Iris. You think he was justified in doing this?” I motion in a circle around me.

Iris looks away. “I wanted to stop it, but we failed. The damage is already done, Matt. The price is paid. They're all dead. The Holy One has already won. Now, he has the chance to rebuild. With Adamic, he can undo everything. Bring back life. Undo pain. Why not let him? He can bring back Zane… Judy."

"They wouldn't want that," I say. Judy said so herself, and Zane was no different.

"It's not just them, Matt. This is about everyone."

"What about those girls?" I ask. "You heard what the feeders did. The Holy One let that happen. He destroyed the walls and let them loose. How can you defend him after all that?"

Iris clenches her jaw. "I… I can't change the past, okay. I can only improve the future. He's going to find the Library, Matt. He can make a world without murderers and rapists. He can fix this… and I'm going to help him."

"What are you saying?"

Iris stops. "I'm sorry, Matt."

I look around. I'd been so engrossed in the argument, I hadn't realized how far we'd walked. We're somewhere in the Ring, but I don't recognize the neighborhood. As I spin around, I see feeders watching from the rooftops. There are eyes in the alleys as well. They were waiting for us… expecting us.

She led me here on purpose!

Now, I understand. The cold shoulder. The quiet indifference. Iris never wanted to be friends. It's easier to betray a stranger.

I'm about to run, when a door opens. A man stands in the doorway wearing a simple black vest beneath a gray suit. His beard is short and perfectly trimmed. His dark eyes see right through me, and his smile is oddly comforting—as if I'm an old friend who happens to be in town.

"Come on in, Matt." The Holy One steps to the side and gestures at the open door. "We have some catching up to do."

8

ROSE

I stand in front of the cell, my face centered between the bars. It's difficult, but I try not to pity the man I see before me.

Commander Noyen stands in the middle of his cage, his tawny mustache now surrounded by caramel scruff. Once, he was a boisterous man with a hearty laugh. Now, his eyes sag and his head droops.

Most concerning is his skin. It has a sickly yellow hue, no doubt from his failing kidneys. Without his daily healing session, Noyen is quickly succumbing to disease.

"I have a proposal for you," I say. "It's not much, but I think you'll find it better than the alternative."

"Alright," Noyen groans. "I'm listening."

"First, let me be clear about your current predicament. You have been found guilty of treason. You have been sentenced to death by hanging. The gallows are unavailable, so that method has been altered to a firing squad. This will take place tomorrow. Your wife and two sons will be there. Before you die, they will announce you as a traitor. That's the last thing your sons will ever think of you."

Noyen sits there, mouth agape, hollow eyes envisioning his fate. "And your proposal?"

"If you agree to my terms, Antai Elsborne will return within the hour. He will set you free, and escort you to the healing loft. There, you will receive one last healing session from Madame Xantone. Afterward, Antai will escort you to the palace wall. You will be given the chance to flee into the Beyond."

"Feeder or firing squad? That's my proposal? I think I'll take the firing squad, thank you very much."

"I didn't finish," I say. "If you accept, your boys won't have to watch you die. Instead, they will be told that you were sent on a special mission—a mission that could save us from the feeders. They will always believe you to be a hero."

"Which is a lie," Noyen grumbles, genuinely confused.

I want to tell him the truth, but I can't risk it. If a demon reads his mind, our plan will be spoiled. He can never know his contribution.

"It will be real to them," I reason. "Isn't that enough?"

Noyen flares his nostril and sighs his contempt. "I'll do it..." he finally croaks, "on one condition. I want to say goodbye to my family."

"Alright, but ten minutes is all you get, and it has to be before the healing."

"Fine. You have a deal," Noyen agrees.

"Perfect. Antai will be here soon enough. I hope you make it," I lie.

I turn and march through the darkness of the Pit, climbing the slick stone steps to the ground floor. I'm almost to my chambers when I stop. There's a guard standing in front of my door, staring straight at me. He looks nervous, holding a folded piece of parchment.

"Your Majesty. A moment, please."

I step closer, preparing myself for bad news. "Yes?"

"I have a message for you, Your Majesty. I found it on the wall walk. It just appeared out of nowhere."

I snatch the paper, looking at the title "Deliver to Queen Roselyn Malik."

Matt!

I recognize the handwriting from his previous letter—when he asked me to the Hallow's Eve Ball.

"Have you read it?" I demand.

"O-of course not, Your Majesty. I would never!"

"And you haven't shown this to anyone?"

"No one, Your Majesty."

"How long ago did you find it?" I wonder. *Maybe he's still near the wall.*

"About two hours ago, Your Majesty. I've been waiting for you here ever since."

"Thank you, lieutenant. You're dismissed."

I wait until he leaves before unlocking the door. Then, I dash inside and lock it behind me. Unfolding the paper, I take a seat on the edge of my bed.

Dear Rose,

I'm assuming this letter might get passed around before it reaches you, so I'm going to be careful about what I say. First of all, I'm alive and well. You don't need to worry about me.

More importantly, my father knows the Holy One's identity. I'll try to be vague, in case this letter is intercepted. He says the Holy One is someone who used to pick Marigolds. Do you know anything about that? I imagine this must be hard to believe, but my father seems confident.

Second, my father knows quite a bit about the Holy One. He says he has a special ability that makes him difficult to kill. He called it foresight. Have you heard of this before? He thinks you might have the gift as well. Apparently, it runs in your family. For our sake, I hope you do.

Lastly, do you have a plan? I want to help somehow, but I'm not sure what we can do from out here. Let me know if you have any ideas.

I hope you're doing well.

To respond, drop your letter from the westernmost point of the wall, directly adjacent to the glass temple. From this point on, I'll write my responses and be holding them at sunset. You should be able to read them with the seerglasses, right?

I hear the door jostle as Antai unlocks it from the outside. It creaks as it swings open.

"I got a letter from Matt." I say, never taking my eyes off the page. "I'll explain in a second."

I should warn you, my father suspects that there are spies in the palace. Be careful. If he's right about the Holy One, he'll be watching you closely.

I miss you. Thanks again for breaking me out of prison.

Sincerely,
Matt

Suddenly, a shiver runs down my spine. Antai hasn't said a word.

A silky, pompous voice speaks from behind me. "Tell me, how's our friend Matthew doing?"

I leap from my chair, turning to face General Kaynes. He's seated on the edge of my bed, one leg crossed over the other. In his hand he holds an Adamic key.

Fir—

I'm about to set my bed ablaze when I see it. He's holding his soul-anchor in the air, pinching the chain between two fingers. With a dramatic flare, he opens his fingers and drops the amulet onto my bedspread. "Let's not do anything rash, princess. I'm not here to hurt you. I'm merely the messenger."

Pull.

His amulet whisks through the air and into my open hand. Still, he could have a hidden amulet. I don't take any chances.

Shield.

The air ripples between us.

Kill him, Rose. I think to myself. *This is your chance. Claim it was self-defense.*

"How did you get in here?" I demand. "Where'd you get that key? Where's Antai?"

"Oh, you think this is Antai's key? Don't worry. Antai is perfectly fine. No, the Holy One made this for me." He points at the symbols on the door. "Correct me if I'm wrong, but Dralton copied these spells from the amulet vault—a spell the Holy One knows quite well. He's a very capable Adalit, more skilled than Dralton, some would say."

Suddenly, it makes sense. The vault robbers had a key. This whole time, I worried Grandpa was involved, when my father was the one at fault.

"What do you want?" I demand.

"Like I said, I'm merely the messenger," Kaynes says nonchalantly, tapping his foot in the air.

I narrow my eyes. "What's the message?"

"The Holy One would like to formally invite you to breakfast tomorrow. Antai is invited as well, of course. You'll be his guests of honor, under his protection."

"How stupid do you think I am?"

"The Holy One suspected you would need further… motivation. You should know, he has dear, sweet, Matthew in his possession. If you comply, Matt will immediately be set free. On the contrary, if you decide not to join him tomorrow, he will remove Matthew's hands. The next day, it will be his tongue, then his eyes. On the fourth day, Matt will lose his life."

"You're lying," I say confidently. "He sent me a letter not two hours ago."

Kaynes smiles, motioning to the seerglasses on my desk. "Are you sure about that? Go ahead. Take a look."

I hesitate. Putting on the seerglasses would obscure my vision, leaving me vulnerable. My gut tells me I shouldn't risk it.

"Oh, don't be like that, Rosey. When have I ever hurt you?"

My stomach sinks into my gut. General Kaynes would never call me Rosey. Not in a million years.

Realization races through me. The neck pain. The reason I couldn't see General Kaynes with the seer glasses. It wasn't because I didn't know him well enough. It was because his soul and body were mismatched.

I take a step back. "Jack?"

"Atta girl," His voice still sounds like General Kaynes, but the intonation suddenly changes. Now, he speaks with an Australian accent. "I thought I'd have to spell it out for ya, but you figured it out all on your own."

I take another step back. "But… how are you breathing? The illusion was a lie, wasn't it? Kaynes really was decapitated."

"Necromancy," Jack beams. "A rare form of possession. Quite poetic actually. You know what they say, an eye for an eye, a tooth for a tooth… a life for a life."

"But… how?"

"Sorry, mate. I'm afraid that's a trade secret. If you really want to know, you'll have to ask your ol' man at breakfast tomorrow. He did the procedure himself."

Procedure?

The maid door jiggles. Nevela's voice calls through the oak. "Rose? Are you okay in there?"

At the sound of her voice, Jack lights up. "Nevela," he whispers. "What a sweet girl. I saw her in the hallway today, happy as can be. Isn't she just a godsend?"

"Rose?" Nevela calls again, her voice increasingly panicked. The door jiggles again, this time faster.

I step up to the maid door. "I'm fine," I shout into the wood. "Just wait in your room. I'll explain everything later."

"You're sure?" she squeaks.

"Yes, I'm sure. Just give me a minute. Everything will be fine."

"Bless her heart," Jack says, placing a hand over his breastbone. "I miss impersonating her innocence. Honest, I do. Those were good times, back when we were buddies, you and I. Simpler times."

"You're sick."

"So you've told me." Jack uncrosses his legs, standing abruptly. "Whelp, that's the message. Oh, I almost forgot. The Holy One wants his relics back. The seerglasses and the Ring of Soronan. That's part of the deal."

"I don't have the ring anymore. I gave it away."

Jack frowns. "Hmmm, what a shame. I'm sure your father will understand. He can be rather merciful when he wants to be."

Jack hops up from the edge of the bed, his Australian accent vanishing. "Now, if you'll return my amulet, I'll be on my merry way." He holds out his hand.

"You're never getting this back," I seethe. "I should kill you right now."

Jack grins, showing General Kaynes' perfect teeth. "You certainly could, but I'm sure you'd regret it. If I'm not present tomorrow, Matt will suffer for it. If you don't return my amulet, Matt will suffer for it. Rebel in any way, and Matt will suffer for it. If you care for his life, which I know you do, you won't test the Holy One. It will only bring you suffering. That much, I can promise you." He lifts his hand, opening his fingers wider. "My amulet, please."

I heave the soul-anchor at him, which bounces off his shoulder and lands on the floor. "There! Now get out!"

Jack slowly stoops over and scoops his amulet off the floorboards. "I really have missed you, Rose. I'm glad we got to spend more time together. I'll see you tomorrow." He gives me one last smile as he closes the door behind him. I hear a click as he locks it from the outside.

As soon as he's gone, I scramble for the seer glasses, fitting them over my head.

Matt!

His image forms. Wherever he's at, it's dark—nearly as dark as the cave. I can barely see his outline. He's lying on his back with his arms and legs spread eagle. His eyes are shut, and he appears to be sleeping. He looks fine to me—unhurt.

Then, I notice it. His arms are hyperextended, and his hands are hidden from view, sunk beneath the surface of the stone floor, completely enclosed in the limestone. His knees are slightly bent, and his shoes are submerged in the floor, anchoring him to the ground.

Jack was right. Matt is a prisoner to the Holy One.

I no longer have a choice. If I want Matt to live, I must face my father.

9

MATT

I follow the Holy One up the staircase. His gray slacks swish with each step, and his dress shoes clack loudly on the stone.

We're in an old apartment building, typical for the Ring. The stairs are warped, and the limestone walls appear to be shedding their skin, small piles of sediment accumulating in the corners.

My mind races with possibilities. I could run. I could blow a hole in the wall and see how far I make it. Or maybe, I could surprise him with combustion dominion—take off his head with a sudden explosion. Who cares if I die with him? The trade would be worth it.

It won't work, The Holy One whispers in my mind. *You'd only hurt yourself.*

Already, he's lurking in my thoughts, testing my intentions. He's like a shadow, undetectable in my darkest memories. I look, but I can't find him. Or maybe he's gone?

I'm still here. He laughs, chuckling out loud as we climb the final flight of stairs.

For a second, I consider using Durebrum, but as soon as I think of it, I've given myself away.

Durebrum? Don't flatter yourself. You know nothing of any use to me.

The Holy One stops at the top of the stairs and opens a door on the left. He steps into a two-room home. The entire place is ransacked. Pottery pieces blanket the floor, big chunks collecting along the walls. In the corner, a straw mattress has been gutted, its contents spilling out like entrails. Fortunately, I don't see any blood in the room. The occupants must have escaped before they were slaughtered.

In contrast to the chaos, a small, circular table is erected in the middle of the room, glazed in a reflective lacquer. A decorative centerpiece sits in the middle—a woven twine mat with a single candle on top.

The Holy One takes a seat at the table and sips from his glass. A spherical ball of ice floats in the center of a yellow-liquid. Beside his glass is an unlabeled bottle of liquor.

"Cavernic Bourbon," the Holy One says. "I found some in the 3rd district. Empowered as I am, the alcohol has little effect, but you can't put a price on nostalgia. It was my father's favorite."

"What do you want from me?"

The Holy One smiles, staring out the window. "You are a means of motivation, Matthew." His voice is deep and syrupy, like someone you'd hear in a cologne commercial. "So long as Rose obeys, I'm not going to kill you."

"So, what—I'm a hostage?"

"Indeed you are. My daughter cares for you a great deal. She'll do just about anything to keep you safe. If all goes well, you'll be released tomorrow morning." He swirls his glass, watching the ice ball spin like a tiny planet on its axis. "Though I must confess, that's not all I want from you. Before I set you free, I want to offer you a fresh perspective. Give you a chance to reconsider my offer."

I'll never join you.

"Never? That's hardly an open-minded approach, is it, Matthew? No matter. The truth is self-evident to those who can reason. Do you mind if I share an observation with you?"

I say nothing.

"It's really an interesting pattern I've observed. My father, Dralton, married a refugee. My wife, Violet, was a refugee as well. And now my daughter, Rose, has developed strong feelings for you, another refugee. What do you think, Matt? Is it a coincidence? Or is there something about refugees that draws our attention? Hmmm?"

"I don't know," I say.

"I have a theory," he says, dragging his finger along the rim of his glass. "I think it's an ideology they develop in the Beyond—a conviction of human rights that attracts us. In Cavernum, there are no rights. Rights are a result of power. The king has rights. The Elite have rights —the right to do as they please. Everyone else is subject to the power of their oppressors. Refugees, at least in the beginning, don't believe this way. They are taught that rights are god-given. Humans are simply born with them. The right to privacy. The right to freedom… the right to religion, self defense, a fair trial, I could go on and on."

Zezric looks out the window, staring into the distance. "Refugees believe they are entitled to a happy life, simply for being born. It's refreshing, this view. Idealistic. A tad naive, perhaps, yet tantalizingly quixotic. I, myself, was drawn to it. I still am, Matthew. You see, I believe I can create this world. A world where every person is protected. Every soul is happy. Where humanity has rights that can't be violated. Where the powerful can't take advantage of the weak. Where the innocent need not suffer. Tell me, Matt, don't you like the sound of that?"

"I…" *I do.*

"I know you do," the Holy One says, "but you have apprehensions. Why?"

"No one should have that much power," I assert. "There's a saying in the Beyond. 'Power corrupts, and absolute power corrupts absolutely.'"

The Holy One nods his head. "Sir John Dalberg-Acton. Brilliant man. The Adamic have a similar saying, 'Make man a God, he'll become the devil as well.'"

"You think they're wrong?" I ask.

"On the contrary. I think they're wise beyond measure. You see, Matt, humans are self-serving by nature. In a world of finite resources, the powerful will always exploit the weak. Take the Elite, for example.

They have the power to distribute resources, yet they hoard them. They feast while the laborers starve. But if you're trying to compare earthly power with heavenly power, the analogy is incompatible. Corruption doesn't apply to godhood. With Adamic, there's no limit to resources. Infinite power. Infinite control. There will be such abundance that everyone's needs can be met. Do you understand, Matt? I will be able to give at no expense to myself. When resources become infinite, corruption becomes… impractical."

"And what about the suffering you've already caused?"

The Holy One grins, taking another sip of his bourbon. "I think you know the answer to that."

I don't do anything that can't be undone. That's what he told me when I was captive in Hogrum.

The Holy One nods. "Exactly, Matthew. All of the damage will be repaired. All the suffering will be rewarded 100 fold. Not only can I bring back Zane, I can bring back his daughters and his wife. I can make sure they never fall ill. They never get robbed or raped or beaten. I can give them a pain-free life—an eternity of happiness. In comparison, their current suffering is a drop in the ocean."

"How can you guarantee they'll never get hurt?" I demand. "You can't control how people act."

"With Adamic, I can do anything, Matt. There is no limit."

"How? You're going to remove certain choices?"

Zezric nods. "And the world will be better for it. Rapists will be subdued. Killers will be restrained. You see, much of humanity's suffering is self-inflicted. Humans hurt each other, and therefore they must be kept in check. By limiting sin, we can eliminate suffering."

"You're wrong," I say. "You can't eliminate suffering. What if someone gets heartbroken?" Scenarios swim through my head. "What if their partner doesn't love them back? What if someone insults them? Offends them? What if they get bullied, or left out? I get that you want to stop killers and rapists, but where do you draw the line? Controlling language? Controlling relationships? Controlling how people treat each other? These are the things that make us human. You can't take that away."

The Holy One sets down his glass. "An excellent question, Matt, one we should discuss together. That's why we need a council. That's why I need you. Together, we can draw that line."

"No, we can't!" I feel my frustration rising, only my fear keeping it in check. "No one can draw that line. We're talking about restricting freewill. The morality, the ethics of it… it's all philosophical."

The Holy One smiles. "Now, you're getting it, Matthew. Philosophy is what separates man from beast. Like animals, we eat, we sleep, we reproduce. Not even our love is unique. A deer loves her fawn. A dog loves her pups. Love isn't what makes us superior. It's our philosophy. Our speculation and imagination. We are creators. We wish to control… perfect… transcend. We were meant to rule from the very beginning. We are gods, Matt. Surely, you feel it deep within you."

"I don't… I'm sorry. I don't believe it."

The Holy One sighs. "I know, Matt… but you will someday. Think about it. Truly think about it. Every time someone you love suffers, think about what could be. Think about the world you can create at my side. Think about the lines you would draw. The safeguards. Begin building your world, and see if you don't like what you discover."

The Holy One tosses back his glass and downs the rest of its contents. "Thank you, Matt, for a stimulating discussion. I can't tell you what a bore these feeders have become."

"What will you do with me now?"

"First, I must mitigate the risk of housing you here. Don't resist," the Holy One warns. "You'll only make it worse." As he speaks, my amulet slithers across my chest, slowly lifting over my head.

I raise my arm to grab it, but his soul fills my limbs, taking control. My muscles flex, but my arm doesn't move.

"Shhhhh," the Holy One whispers. "Don't resist."

His soul retracts as my amplifier floats through the air, landing on the table.

Satisfied, the Holy One stands. "Kildron has empowered you with his feeding. I'll need to drain your dominion. Not your original soul, of course, simply the excess. This should only hurt a little."

I stumble back until my shoulder blades crash into the stone wall.

Combus—

The Holy One is already in motion. He touches his palm to my forehead, pushing my skull against the stone wall. Then, I feel it. It's like a crevice has opened up inside me—a drain at the very bottom of my being. Immediately, my energy flows, pouring out of the drain and into the Holy One. My insides become hollow, and my soul grows hungrier. Starving. My pain reawakens. My body aches.

I try to resist. I pull on the energy, trying to draw it back, but it's no use. His gravity is stronger, drawing away my energy like a black hole.

Then, it's over.

With his hand still pressed to my head, the Holy One speaks a single command.

"Sleep."

Instantly, the world goes black.

10

ROSE

Feeders peer at us from rooftops and through broken windows. They watch, amused, as Jack parades us through the Ring.

Antai walks at my side, positioned between Jack and I. His hand rests on his holster at all times. To my surprise, he doesn't scan his surroundings. He stares straight ahead, taking long strides. We may be at the Holy One's mercy, but Antai doesn't play the part of a prisoner.

His composure is comforting. His hand is steady, and his face, unreadable. When I take his hand, he finally looks over at me, offering a hesitant smile.

To my surprise, Antai didn't resist this meeting. I merely had to agree to three rules. One, we don't remove our amulets under any circumstances. Two, no matter who Zezric threatens to harm, we don't comply. If necessary, I should let Antai die before I do my father's bidding. And lastly, as soon as the opportunity presents itself, we kill my father, no questions asked.

Jack stops outside of an apartment building. He motions at the door, his silver robe swishing. "The Holy One is waiting on the third floor, first door on your left."

Everything is going to be alright, Rose. We're just going to talk, nothing more.

I climb the steps, my head throbbing. My throat constricts, and I taste stomach acid.

Antai puts a hand on the small of my back, his gentle touch steadying my emotions.

I stop on the third floor, taking a deep breath before pushing through the door.

"Hello, Rose."

My father sits at the table, watching me with distractingly dark eyes. His smile is wide and charismatic, nothing like his portrait. He's immaculately groomed, sporting a fitted vest and dress shirt, sleeves rolled to his elbows. A suit coat hangs neatly on the back of his chair. As I study him, his eyes dance across my features.

"You have your mother's eyes," he happily reports. "You're exactly as I imagined you'd be."

As I look at his grin, my fear evaporates, burned away by a boiling rage. He should be racked with guilt for what he's done. He should be ashamed to stand before his daughter. Instead, he's grinning like a child on Hallow's Eve.

Zezric watches me with amusement, no doubt trying to read my emotions. His elbows rest on the table, hands clasped above a porcelain plate. Around us, the table is fully prepped with sausage, eggs, and buttercakes.

"Please, take a seat." He gestures at two empty chairs opposite him. "We have so much to discuss. You can leave the seer glasses on the table."

I do as he directs, setting the relic beside a pitcher of orange juice. Then, I sit, never taking my eyes off my father.

"Wonderful," he sings. "I can't tell you how excited I am to have you both here. I've been waiting for this for quite some time. It's all I've been able to think about the last few weeks."

He's so lively… so animated. It's not what I expected. I imagined him cold and heartless—calculating and corrupt, not cordial. Somehow, his civility is more off-putting than the alternative.

He clasps his hands over his plate. "Let me preface our discussion with a bit of a disclaimer. I'm not here to hurt anyone. I know you perceive me as threatening, so I'd like to mitigate any intimidation you may feel. I've decided not to confiscate your weapons. So long as you wear your soul-anchors, your thoughts will remain private. In fact, I quite look forward to the ambiguity. Reading minds can become quite dull after a while."

Zezric leans forward, his eyes boring through my pupils. "I've so much to tell you, Rose. I don't even know where to begin." He picks up a wine glass, moves it towards his mouth, but sets it back down without a sip. "And I'm sure you have stories of your own. I want to hear everything."

He massacred your people, Rose, don't forget what he's done.

"I'm not saying another word until you let Matt go," I hiss through gritted teeth.

The Holy One grins wider. "I'd expect nothing less. Very well... Jack!" he shouts.

The front door creaks open, and Jack steps inside. "Yes, my Lord?"

"Release Matthew. He's free to leave the premises. Make sure the feeders know he's under my protection."

"Yes, my Lord."

I wait as Jack scurries into the nearby bedroom. I hear a slapping noise, followed by a groan.

"Wakey wakey," Jack coos. "Time to go home."

My father takes a sip from his wine glass. "When I found Matt, he had quite the infection: clostridium difficile. His bloodstream was swimming in it. It took some effort, but I managed to heal him." He looks up from his wine glass, finding my eyes. "I wanted to heal him, Rose. I did it for you. I want you to know that."

Matt suddenly stumbles out of the bedroom, groggy eyes snapping open. "What..." He spins in a circle to survey the room. Finally, his eyes settle on me.

"Matt!" I try to say more, but the words don't come out.

"Rose?" He takes a step forward.

"Get out of here, MacArthur," Antai commands. "Get somewhere safe and stay there. That's an order."

Matt hesitates, looking in my direction.

"Listen to him, Matt," I mutter. "You need to go! We'll be fine, but you need to get far away."

For a second he simply stares, eyebrows contorted and mouth agape. Then, he fumbles to the door, pausing in the threshold. He pats his chest as if looking for an amulet. "But…"

"Go!" I insist.

Just when I think he'll do something stupid, his jaw snaps shut and his eyes narrow. Without another word, he pushes through the front door and stumbles down the stairwell.

"There you go," Zezric sighs. "Free as a bird. Now, we can enjoy my little feast. I've made sure to include some variety. It's a classic breakfast in the Beyond." He reaches down and plucks a sausage off his plate, taking a bite. "I cooked everything myself. We have whole-grain pancakes. Maple sausage. Bacon and eggs. Hash—"

"I'm not eating," I hiss.

"Oh, please, you think it's poisoned?" Zezric frowns.

"Could be," I say.

"Let me reiterate: I don't want to kill you, Rose. I don't want you to suffer, nor do I want you to fear. Am I understood? You are alive, because I want you to live. Your friends are alive because I want them to live. I'm not the villain you think I am—some monster who delights in death and bloodshed. If that were the case, I would've burned the palace to the ground."

"Could've fooled me."

His shoulders stiffen. "Yes, I've been forced to do atrocious things—things that will forever haunt me. I'm the first to admit that. But you must believe me, Rose. I've only ever done harm to secure the Book of Life. So please, don't act as if I'm here to harass you. I find that offensive."

"Offensive? Offensive!" I seethe, standing from my chair. Antai takes my wrist, but it does nothing to restrain my rage. "You slaughtered children… babies! You don't get to talk about offensive!"

The Holy One takes another bite of sausage and nonchalantly dabs his lips with a napkin. "You're shouting, Rose."

"Fuck you," I spit. I've never said those words before, but here, facing him, it sums my emotions perfectly.

Zezric sighs. "I know you must think I'm abominable. You think I'm the most horrid man alive. That's precisely why I planned this meal. I want to explain things in person. You deserve that much."

I shake my head. "There's no explaining what you've done. You can't justify it. You killed them! You killed them all! How can you expect me to pretend nothing ever happened?"

"I don't expect you to pretend, I expect you to understand," Zezric says, raising his voice. He quickly takes a sip of wine to compose himself. "Everything I do, I do to make the world better. Every life I take, I will restore. Is that too hard to comprehend? It's not just for the greater good, it's for the *utmost* good. It's for a world without suffering."

I groan, rubbing my temples. "You can't honestly believe that. You're delusional!"

Zezric sits forward, opening his mouth then closing it. After a moment, he slowly shifts his weight back onto his seat. "How about this… give me one good reason I shouldn't find The Book of Life. One reason, and I'll abandon the cause. But you have to really convince me. My argument is simple. All the pain I've caused will be remedied with Adamic. And I won't stop there. Millions of hungry children need my help. Millions of sick and afflicted. The suffering in the world is so much bigger than Cavernum, Rose. Tell me why I shouldn't help them?"

I glance at Antai, who says nothing. His hand is still resting on the holster. Finally, I look back at Zezric.

"Go on," Zezric urges. "I'm listening."

I take a few moments, collecting my thoughts.

What would Grandpa say?

I sit in silence, forming my argument. "Okay… okay." I speak slowly, trying my best to emulate Grandpa's wisdom. "You talk of a perfect world, one without suffering, but what would that mean for humanity? Everything bad that's ever happened to me has made me who I am. With every trial I overcome, I become stronger. As painful as it is, suffering helps us grow. You can't get rid of it. It's a necessary part of life."

The Holy One raises his eyebrows, nodding his head. "An interesting argument: every mistake we make is a learning opportunity. If you take away suffering, our progression stops. Does that sum it up?"

I swallow. "That's right. Losing Velma was excruciating, but her death taught me so much. I wouldn't be who I am today without her sacrifice. I wish she were here, but I wouldn't change the past, even if I could. Suffering can result in good. You know it's true."

Zezric takes another sip of his drink, a subtle grin tugging on his lips. "I'll admit, it is a compelling argument, but flawed, nonetheless. Allow me to refute it with a simple question: if I were to kill Antai this very moment, would you become stronger? Hmmm? And more importantly, would your growth outweigh the cost of his life?" Zezric raises an eyebrow at me, flashing a dangerous smirk. "Should I kill him, Rose? Should I end his life this very second?"

"No," I breathe, fearing his threat is more than rhetorical. "That's not what I'm saying."

"Are you sure?" Zezreic raises an eyebrow. "If your argument stands, killing Antai will make you a better person. Why should I not kill him and bless you with further growth? Hmmm?" Zezric looks at his wine glass, giving the contents a gentle swirl. "I'll go one further. Why should we not use suffering as a means of instruction? Torturing a child would make them stronger, correct? It would teach them discipline… endurance… mental stamina? Surely, the benefits of their growth outweigh their suffering? Would you not agree?"

"That's not what I meant."

"Of course it is," Zezric laughs. "You said you were stronger for losing Velma. You said you prefer her dead. Her death helped you grow more than her life would have."

"That's not what I said! I said I wouldn't change the past!"

"Yes, a past where she died," Zezric reiterates. "You're implying that personal growth is more valuable than a loved one's life. If that's true, I'll kill Antai this instant. I'll abandon my search for the Book of Life and let death abound in the world."

"You're twisting my words!"

"I'm emphasizing the flaws, Rose." He swirls his drink some more, causing bubbles to simmer on the surface. "Perhaps my point is best conveyed in a story. Do you know where we are… specifically, I mean?"

We're in a laborers home, that much is certain. Beyond that, I'm unsure.

Zezric sets down his wine glass and gestures around the room. "Your mother lived in this very home, back before we met. You see, she was—"

"A refugee. I know."

"I imagine you would," Zezric says. "She moved here when she was only—"

"14 years old," I interject.

Zezric leans back and interlaces his fingers behind his head. "Why don't you tell me about Violet, if you know so much about her?"

"Fine," I say, thinking back to grandpa's stories. "Violet moved here with her parents when she was 14. The only thing she brought with her was her violin. She played constantly, only stopping to go to class."

Zezric watches me, his face eerily pleasant. He nods along with each detail.

"When she turned 18," I continue, "Mom competed for a spot in the Royal Orchestra. The conductor was blown away. They gave her a soloist position. In fact, Grandpa said you attended her first concert solo—The Dawn of Creation. That's where you both met. Grandpa said her performance was flawless. After the concert, you found her backstage and asked her on a date. You were married two years later. Three years after that, I was born."

The Holy One nods. "You're not technically wrong, but you're missing some important details. You see, Violet would've told a vastly different story."

He rests his elbows on the table, his eyes narrowing. "Her parents were good people, Linda and Michael. Together, they ran a coffee shop in Oregon. When his cousin was killed by a feeder, Michael decided the risk was too great. He abandoned his coffee shop and moved his family to Cavernum.

"When they arrived, Michael was immediately sent to the fields. At first, he was okay with it—a small sacrifice for Violet's safety—but over time, he grew bitter. He began drinking to cope with his disappointing life. Then, he drank more. Some nights, he'd get angry… break stuff. Eventually, he became violent.

"He never touched Violet, thank God, but her mother, Linda, wasn't so lucky. When he was upset, Michael would hit her, right in front of Violet.

"As you can imagine, this weighed heavily on Violet. To distract herself from it all, she had a special way of coping." Zezric points down at his feet. "She'd stand right here, in this exact spot, and play her violin, staring out this very window."

I follow Zezric's gaze. Across the street is a massive building with four marble pillars and massive double-doors. The building looks newly renovated, complete with new shutters and a fresh coat of paint. I recognize it as a courthouse.

Zezric points out the window. "As she played the violin, Violet would watch the judges arrive every morning, pulling up in private carriages, wearing spotless purple robes."

Zezric turns away from the window, as if too disgusted to watch any longer. "In that courthouse, Violet saw an opportunity. While her father was slaving away in the Flats, she went before the judges and gave her testimony. She explained how her father was hitting her mother. She poured her heart out, yet the judges didn't care. 'A man has dominion over his wife,' they told her. They denied her pleas without any investigation."

He sighs, bowing his head. "Well, you can guess what happened next. Michael found out that Violet testified against him. Before long, he was drunk, and this time, he didn't hold back. He beat Violet's mom with a wine bottle. Violet hid in the bedroom, but she knew what was happening. She could hear her mother's cries, begging for her life. He didn't stop until the bottle finally broke."

I cringe at the thought of it. This is my grandmother he's talking about. *My grandmother being beaten by my grandfather!* I scrunch my nose in disgust.

Zezric watches me with tender eyes. "Yes, Rose, it's horrifying. I'm sorry if this disturbs you, but I refuse to censor her history." He takes a deep breath. "When it was over, Violet found Linda on the floor. She was missing teeth. Her eyes were swollen shut, and her entire rib cage was purple. They didn't have money for a healer, so they kept her in the kitchen by the fire, feeding her mashed potatoes and broth. Miraculously, she survived the attack, but she developed pneumonia shortly after—a complication of the fractured ribs. Winter came, and her health deteriorated."

Zezric grows quiet, picking up his wineglass and downing the contents. "Linda passed away in the spring," he solemnly reports. "Michael took his life a few weeks later… not that he deserves any sympathy."

I tuck my hands between my thighs to stop them from shaking. Antai says nothing, simply watching my reaction.

Zezric pours another glass of wine. "Her parents were gone, and Violet was left behind to pick up the pieces. She kept practicing the violin, not out of passion, but out of desperation. She worked harder than she ever had in her life. She persevered, and yes, she was accepted into the orchestra. She learned she could do impossible things. Some might even say she was stronger because of it." Zezric looks at me, an intensity in his eyes. "That was your argument, wasn't it? Violet's suffering made her stronger."

Reluctantly, I nod my head.

"And what of her father?" Zezric asks.

I hesitate. "What do you mean?"

Zezric shrugs. "He suffered too, didn't he? His life was ripped out from under him. He abandoned his successful business only to be sent to the Flats, working from dusk till dawn, getting whipped and treated like scum. He sacrificed everything for his daughter—a daughter who he rarely saw. He suffered quite a bit. Did it make him stronger, Rose?"

I say nothing.

"No," Zezric looks down at his glass. "It made him bitter and abusive. His suffering made him a monster."

I bite my cheek, desperately looking for a rebuttal.

"You see, Rose," Zezric continues. "Some, like my father, might look at Violet and see a success story. Some would argue it made her tougher, stronger even. I would have to disagree. Her past was a wound—one that never fully healed." He speaks slower now, his eyes half closed. "It wasn't her poise that caught my attention that very first concert, nor was it her talent; it was her melancholy. She was the only musician that looked miserable."

Zezric meets my gaze, his ink-drop eyes glistening with grief. "She was so beautiful, Rose, even miserable. I wanted to see what she'd look like with a smile. I wanted to protect her from whatever tragedy she had endured." He sighs, taking a sip from his wine glass. "My point is, your mother was still hurting. A part of her had been killed by her father. She lost a certain lightheartedness.... joviality. True, she became desensitized to life's pain, but she also became numb to some of life's beauty. Do you think that's a beneficial trade? Do you truly think trauma is a blessing?"

"No." My response is barely a whisper, but it's the truth. I was wrong. Suffering isn't anything to be desired.

Zezric nods silently, satisfied with my response. "Very well. Can you give me any other reason I should abandon this course?"

I try to conjure up another rebuttal. I know he's wrong—I feel it deep inside me—but I can't concentrate. My grandmother's story fills my mind, cluttering my thoughts and scattering any reason.

"Excellent," Zezric says, placing a pancake on his plate. "Perhaps we've found some common ground, after all."

"You're insane."

Zezric glares daggers at me, his jaw quivering. "Do you know how many times I've heard that? I'm insane. I'm deranged. I'm delusional. Let me tell you what's insane, Rose. Every time Michael got drunk, Violet prayed. She begged God, asking him to intervene. And then, when it happened a week later, she prayed again. Every time he picked up a bottle, she prayed, and God didn't answer. Not once. That's what I call delusional."

I frown. "You think Mom was delusional?"

Zezric suddenly stands, pacing back and forth. "Not Violet, humanity! Do you know how many people pray to God and get no response? Their loved ones die. Their children suffer. Their lives fall to pieces, and God stays silent. A God who has infinite love and infinite power—a God who knows everything and can do anything—he lets his children suffer. And you know what, Rose? We worship him for it. *That* is insanity! *That* makes no sense! And here I am, trying to be a better god—a god who helps, a god who won't abandon those in need—and you label me the villian. Do you see the irony in that? Tell me you can see it! Tell me!"

He slams his fist into the table, knocking over his wine glass. The noise snaps him from his outrage. He takes a deep breath, letting his shoulders sag. "I apologize."

With a wave of his hand, the spilt wine floats into the air and back into his glass. Suddenly, Zezric looks over at Antai. "And what do you think of all this, Commander? You've been awfully quiet."

Antai grits his teeth. "I'm not sure yet."

"Typical." Zezric slumps back into his chair. He picks up a strip of bacon with his fingers and takes a bite.

I take advantage of the silence. "How long until you find the Book of Life?" I ask.

Zezric holds up one finger as he chews. Finally, he forces a swallow. "Dralton shared the poem with you, I imagine."

I nod.

"Deep beneath your feet is the power you seek; It's quite explicit. We're scouring the tunnels, mapping as we go. I suspect we'll find it within the month. Then, the real work begins."

The real work? "What do you mean?" I ask.

"Finding the library is simple," Zezric claims. "Learning Adamic will be considerably more challenging. The original manuscripts are in Hebrew. In the last decade, I've grown proficient, but it won't be a walk in the park. From Hebrew, I must memorize another language in its entirety. Godhood doesn't come in the blink of an eye, Rose. It comes gradually, one word at a time."

"How long will it take?"

"Currently, I only know 5 spells—eight or nine distinct Adamic words. Records estimate 15,000 words in the Adamic language. I think I can grasp the basics in a few weeks, but fluency will take years."

He suddenly sits up, staring at me with his endless, charcoal eyes. "In the meantime, I want to establish some ground rules." He finishes the bacon strip in two quick bites. "Jack will remain in the palace, inhabiting General Kaynes. He will keep an eye on you. Each night, he will report to me. If he feels you threaten my plan in any way, I will destroy the palace. I will kill everyone; do you hear me? On the contrary, so long as you don't interfere with my efforts, no one will get hurt. Is that understood?"

"Yes," I breathe.

"Good." Zezric picks up another strip of bacon. "You really aren't going to eat? I heard you were rationing in the palace."

I clench my fists, ignoring his taunts. "How'd you bring back his body without Adamic?" I demand. "General Kaynes was decapitated? It doesn't make sense."

"Ahhh, yes. Necromancy… an interesting art—one the Order has hidden for centuries. It's not about raising the dead; only Adamic can perform a true resurrection. No, necromancy is different. It involves transferring a life force from the living to the deceased. A life for a life."

"Jack called it a procedure."

Zezric smiles. "I suppose it is. You really want to know?"

"Yes."

He leans forward. "First, you find a viable corpse. If the body is damaged, it must be repaired. In the case of General Kaynes, his head had to be… well… capitated. His spinal cord, trachea, esophagus, muscles, arteries, everything needed reconnecting."

"Where'd you find the healers?" I wonder.

"You mean healer," Zezric corrects, holding out his arms in an act of self-display. "You're looking at him."

"That's impossible."

Zezric smirks. "You don't have the slightest inkling of what's possible. I'm empowered by thousands of feedings, more than any feeder you'll ever meet. I can do things you wouldn't dream of."

"But… healing isn't about power, it's about knowledge."

"You're exactly right," Zezric beams. "I taught myself in the Beyond. Matthew may have told you what happened. My body was destroyed in Hogrum, damaged far beyond repair. So, I inhabited another body… permanently. I decided I would reshape it with self-dominion, but it proved to be a difficult feat. The human body is miraculously complex. So, I began studying in the Beyond. Their knowledge of medicine has far surpassed our own. I learned to do more than heal. I found ways to manipulate the human body, design it to my liking. After what I accomplished, decapitation was hardly a challenge."

I'm stunned. If Zezric is telling the truth, he's far more powerful than I ever imagined.

We don't stand a chance!

Zezric finishes his glass of wine and immediately pours a third. "I'm a little disappointed. You never asked about my spells. Aren't you curious?"

Antai narrows his eyes.

Zezric flashes a harmless smile. "I know what you're thinking. Adamic is power. Why would I give up such an advantage? Well, consider it a display of good faith." He meets my gaze. "You may oppose me now, but if you join my council someday, we should be equals, should we not? I trust you'll do good with the power I bestow."

Suddenly, he stabs a pancake with his fork and holds it in the air. He whispers just loud enough for me to make out the words.

"Havaknah Ra."

Burn.

I clench my eyes shut, expecting to be incinerated. Instead, I only hear Zezric's laughter. When I open my eyes, I see a blackened pancake on his fork. Thin strings of smoke trail off the sizzling embers.

"But… how?" I gasp. The last time I used that spell, I cremated an entire forest, feeders and laborers alike.

"Adamic requires specificity," Zezric explains. "With this spell, I am commanding the elements to burn, yet I lack the vocabulary to specify *what* should burn. Thus, every element within earshot will obey me. To prevent total destruction, I must specifically command otherwise."

"And how do you do that?" I ask.

"Well, I can't speak Adamic, so I must communicate with my soul. You see, Rose, it's merely a matter of combining non-verbal dominion with the spoken language."

Havaknah Ra. I repeat the words in my head. I could speak them right now and ignite my father. If Zezric is telling the truth, I could exclude Antai and myself from the carnage. All I have to do is specifically command that we not be burned.

It's too risky!

Titan failed to kill Jack with the spell. Odds are, Zezric would survive too. Or worse, Antai might not.

"And the other spells?" I ask.

"During my time in Hogrum, I learned a particularly interesting spell," Zezric says. "Allow me to demonstrate."

He stands from his chair and closes his eyes. "Inumkuh Lene Maratagah."

Immediately, my soul understands. *Be still and Unmoving.*

The words seem to fill the air around me, constricting my movements. They press upon my chest and squeeze my head from all sides. My jaw is locked in place, my fingers immobilized. I can move my eyes, but my eyelids are stuck wide open.

Across the table, Zezric watches with fascination. "A strange spell indeed. The prophet Malazotah used it to calm the tempests, but it does much more. It inhibits all movement, completely entrapping those within the sound of my voice."

I try to speak, but my tongue is frozen in place. All I can manage is a garbled grunt.

"Claustrophobic, I know. The first time I used the spell, I forgot to exclude myself. Fortunately, it wears off after a minute or so." He reaches down and picks up a butter knife from beside his plate. "I imagine you must feel completely defenseless, but it isn't as it seems. The borders of the spell are gradual."

He pulls back his arm and throws the knife at my face. The second it leaves his hand, it begins to slow. The knife only travels 3 feet before it creeps to a stop, suspended motionless in the air. Next, he grabs his wine glass and sloshes the wine at Antai. The globs of liquid disperse in the air, slowing gradually to a standstill. They hover, perfectly suspended, a few feet from Antai's nose.

"I may have you trapped," Zezric says, "but I can't harm you—not while the spell is in effect. In a way, you're safer than I am. By exempting myself from the spell, I also leave myself vulnerable to attack. Go ahead, try it… try to kill me."

For some reason, I waver. He invites violence so casually, it almost feels like a trap.

Antai must not hesitate, because a pillar of fire engulfs Zezric in a sudden whoosh. It lasts only a second. As quickly as the flames appear, they flash out of existence, like the quick pinch of a candle wick.

Zezric stands in the same spot, completely unharmed. Smiling, he pats a few smoking embers on the corner of his suit coat. "A valiant attempt, Commander. Anyway, I believe I've made my point. The spell should be wearing off any moment now."

As soon as he says it, I notice the knife begin to slowly drift toward the floor. The water droplets sink as well, like weightless soap bubbles. They descend in a straight line, until they land softly on the floor, collecting into a small puddle of wine. It takes some extra effort, but I manage to turn my head. Then, I blink. Finally, the spell gives way, and I suck in a deep breath, my rib cage moving freely.

Zezric studies us. "It's terrifying, isn't it? The power in a single phrase. A single word." He turns and faces out the window, looking once more at the courthouse. "Imagine the good we can do when we're fluent. 15,000 words of absolute power. A perfect world is just around the corner."

Before I know what's happening, I see a blur of movement to my right. Antai has silently risen from his chair, drawing his pistol and aiming it at the back of Zezric's head.

He only hesitates for a moment before squeezing the trigger.

11

MATT

Jack follows me as I stumble down the staircase. Using my shoulder as a battering ram, I burst through the exit and onto the street, squinting in the brilliant sunlight.

Feeders loiter on the sidewalk, smiling in my direction with their pointed teeth and bloodless lips.

Jack stops in the doorway behind me. "The Holy One extends his mercy to this man. He is not to be harmed." With that, he slams the door shut.

"Come here, boy," a zombie-looking feeder calls out to me. "The Holy One has spared you. Let us give thanks to our Lord of Opposition."

I take a step back, scanning my surroundings for a feederless escape route.

"Awww, he's scared." A bald woman says softly, a devious grin spreading from ear to ear. "Come to mommy, boy. I'll take care of you."

I find my exit and make a run for it, stumbling into an empty alley. My knees are stiff from being imprisoned in the stone, but it doesn't matter. The feeders don't follow.

Then, it dawns on me.

My side!

Even as I sprint, I can't feel any pain. It feels as though I've been healed entirely.

I run for several blocks, taking turns as sporadically and randomly as possible. Finally, I turn into an alley and tuck my body into the doorway of an apartment. I try to slow my breathing, listening for any footsteps. I hear the crunching of snow somewhere nearby, but no feeders round the corner. Finally, when I'm sure I haven't been followed, I lift my shirt and inspect the wound.

Impossible.

My skin is flawless. Not even a scar remains. I push on my side, digging my fingers into the underlying gut, but I feel nothing.

He healed me!

I sit there another minute, trying to make sense of my situation. Iris betrayed me; there's no denying that. But why? Did he brainwash her? Did he get inside her head? And then there's Rose, trading her freedom for my own.

BANG!

A gunshot pierces the silence, echoing from the direction I just fled. It wasn't loud for a gunshot, nothing larger than a pistol by the sound of it.

BANG! BANG! BANG!

I step out of my hiding spot. Looking back up the slope of the sanctuary.

Rose!

Intuition tells me she fired the shots, but even if she miraculously killed her father, she'll have to face his army of vengeant feeders.

She needs me! I take a step in the direction of the gunshots.

Out of nowhere, a hand takes hold of my wrist. A feminine voice whispers from behind me. "Oh, no you don't,"

Panicked, I swing my arm, smacking something solid and eliciting a whimper. The hand releases my wrist. However, as I frantically look around me, I don't see a soul in sight. That is, until I notice the footprints in the snow.

Kendra materializes beside me, her blonde hair falling flat around her shoulders. Her fingers grasp a small silver ring on her thumb. The other hand gently dabs her upper lip which is bleeding and already a bit puffy.

"Kendra? But… how—"

She throws her arms around my neck, letting all of her weight hang on my shoulders. In this moment, I forget everything else. I lift her feet off the ground, breathing in the scent of her hair, relishing the contour of her body.

After a few seconds, I lower Kendra back to the ground. She's not looking at me, but scanning our surroundings.

She takes a step towards the Flats. "C'mon, we need to move fast."

"I left Rose with the Holy One. We need to go help her."

Kendra winces. "We can't. We need to keep moving."

"But..."

"We can't help her, Matt! No one can. We don't stand a chance."

"You want to leave them?"

"That's exactly what I want. Rose has a mission for us. There's no time to explain!"

She twists the ring, immediately disappearing. Then, she takes my hand. I can still see myself, yet I can feel the spell buzzing around me, warping the light around my skin so that it never reflects off my body.

Next thing I know, she's pulling me toward the flats, guiding me with the tug of her invisible hand.

"Where's your dad?" she eventually asks.

"I'm not sure. Last I saw him—"

We exit the alley and stop dead in our tracks. A landscape of crimson jolts my senses. Blood stains the snow before us, turning the entire expanse of the roadway red. It looks as though a cement truck poured blood through the street. Then, I see the bodies, six or seven of them lying amid the stained snow.

"Oh, God!" Kendra's voice calls out from the air beside me.

The bodies are mutilated in a way I've never seen before. They're shrunk, almost dehydrated. Their eyes are sucked deep into the sockets, and their lips are shriveled like raisins—pale and bloodless. Every inch of exposed skin is wrinkled and pruned, like fingers after a long bath.

Then, I spot movement on the side of the road. A single feeder sits on the porch of Pixie's Porkchops, directly beside the roast pig. In his hands, he holds a massive pork chop, stooping over to take bites with his mouth.

I let go of Kendra's hand, materializing in the blood-soaked snow. "Kildron?"

The feeder's head snaps up. "Matt?" Immediately, his body transforms, growing a full head of blonde locks. When he sees the look on my face, he comes bounding off the porch. His eyes widen as Kendra materializes next to me.

"What happened? What's she doing here?" He asks, frantically scanning the street. "Where's Iris?"

"She…" I don't know how to break the news.

"She betrayed us." Kendra says matter-of-factly. "There's no time to explain. We need to get to the Communication Bunker."

Kildron doesn't react except for the slight flare of his nostrils. "We lost her sooner than I thought," he says coldly. "What happened?"

"Didn't you hear me?" Kendra exclaims. "There's no time for this. We need to get to the Communication Bunker. Please! I'll explain everything on the way."

"Fine. Bunker it is," Kildron says, beginning a steady march toward the Flats.

I don't budge. "And what about Iris?" I demand.

"What about her?" Kildron spits, his voice laced with disgust. "If all goes well, we'll never see her again."

"How can you say that?" I demand. "She's your daughter."

Kildron stops in his tracks, shoulders shaking beneath his cloak. "Not anymore," he hisses. "She's no daughter of mine."

12

ROSE

Zezric is already in motion as the gun goes off. Without turning around, he whips his head to the side, tucking his ear to his shoulder.

BANG!

The bullet—our only Adamic bullet—shatters the window, passing through the space where Zezric's head had just been. It was our only hope, and it missed.

Antai pulls the trigger three more times.

BANG! BANG! BANG!

This time, the air ripples a few inches from Zezric's skull. The remaining bullets—regular, everyday bullets—deflect to either side of his head, passing through the empty window frame and ricocheting off of the courthouse across the road.

To my surprise, Zezric hardly reacts. He continues to stare out the window.

"An Adamic bullet…." Zezric calmly muses, still leaving his back exposed. "I can't say I blame you."

Suddenly, Zezric tenses. It's as though he can somehow sense the impending danger. "I wouldn't do that if I were you."

In the blink of an eye, Antai drops his pistol and draws an Adamic blade. He swings for Zezric's neck.

Shlink!

Before the blade makes contact, the air ripples, slicing effortlessly through Antai's forearm. The Adamic dagger, still clutched firmly in Antai's severed hand, flops to the floor.

"Agghhh!" Antai lets out a guttural cry, looking down at his amputated hand. Then, with his left hand, he reaches into his waistband and draws a second Adamic blade.

Once again, he lunges, this time stabbing at Zezric's back.

Shlink!

The air ripples again, cutting clean through Antai's wrist. The dagger clanks as it strikes the stone floor, followed by the thump of Antai's hand.

Crying out, Antai cowers back, knocking into the table and sending dishes crashing to the floor. Blood pours from each arm, trickling onto the seat of his chair.

"I warned you," Zezric sighs, slowly turning to face us. "Now look what you made me do."

Antai grits his teeth. His eyes flicker downward at the Adamic blade on the floor. The blade twitches before launching into the air. It travels in a perfectly straight trajectory, aiming for Zezric's nose.

Zezric is already in motion. He sidebends to the left, barely moving out of the dagger's path. The blade passes an inch from his ear before embedding itself in the stone wall.

With his body still contorted, Zezric smiles.

Shlink!

A ripple of force cuts through Antai's knees. His legs buckle, and he immediately topples onto his side, holding out two arm stumps to slow his fall.

I gasp, my hands shaking at the sight of his amputated legs. *This can't be happening!*

Before he can scream, Antai's body lurches into the air, his back slamming into the stone ceiling. The air ripples around him, pinning what's left of his arms and legs to the ceiling. The stone immediately begins to mold, like fresh dough, around his severed limbs.

Do something, Rose!

I backpedal into the wall. I want to defend Antai, but I'm frozen with fear. *He's too strong!*

"Ahhhhh!" Antai lets out a bloodcurdling scream as he struggles against the force dominion. Ripples cascade over his torso as Zezric presses him into the ceiling.

Antai's breathing grows shallow as his lungs compress. His face turns red, despite the blood loss.

Finally, I find the courage.

Fire!

A few sparks ignite on the top of my fingers, but before the flames can form, Zezric is there. His consciousness commands the very same molecules, suppressing the flames and chilling the air around me. The weight of his command hangs on the atoms. They recognize his authority, choosing to obey him over me.

Impossible!

Ignoring me, Zezric reaches up, slipping his fingers under the chain of Antai's amulet. With a quick yank, he tears it free and tosses it onto the table.

"You're lucky my daughter loves you, or you'd already be dead." Zezric stands directly below Antai's face, staring up at him. With the low ceiling, their noses are only inches apart.

Zezric reaches up again, placing his palm flat on Antai's forehead. "Sleep."

At the command, Antai's eyes flutter, snap open, and finally droop closed. His head slowly goes limp, dangling from his suspended body.

Zezric grins, resuming his seat. "Now, for the bleeding." Flowing like a liquid, the stone ceiling recedes, exposing the severed tip of each limb. Immediately, the bloodied stumps begin to boil. Then, after a second, they burn, releasing a thin stream of smoke into the air.

I look away as the sound of sizzling bacon fills the room. The smell is putrid, irritating my eyes and itching the back of my throat.

"That should do it," Zezric says. Slowly, the stone retracts. Rather than letting him plummet, Zezric slowly lowers Antai's body to the ground with dominion, depositing him next to the table. "He'll still need healing when you get back to Cavernum, but he won't bleed out."

This can't be happening!

I fall to my knees beside Antai, unable to look away from his shortened limbs. Both arms are nearby. I can see his severed legs out of the corner of my eye. "You can reattach them!" I blurt. "You have the power. Please! I'm begging you!"

Zezric shrugs. "You said it yourself, Rose. Our suffering makes us stronger. This was a blessing for Antai. Right?"

"No!" I choke. "I was wrong! Please, just heal him! Please, Dad! Please! I'm begging you!"

Zezric looks down at Antai, his face pained yet resolute. "This will be a good reminder for you, Rose. Everytime you see him struggle, everytime you see him suffer, you'll remember why I'm doing this. You'll remember that a perfect world—a perfect Antai—is just around the corner."

"Please!" I gasp. "Please!" The tears blind me as I sob. "Please don't do this, Dad! Pleeeeeaase… please." My voice gives out as the sobs take over.

Zezric picks up his wine glass. "Come. Let us finish our discussion. Antai needs his rest."

"No! I won't do anything—" my throat constricts, causing me to cough through my sobs. "—until you heal him. I'm not leav—"

"ROSE!" Zezric screams, sending a jolt of fear through my body. "It is done!"

He sighs, composing himself once more. "Stand up and come sit. Stop acting like a child. I know it looks gruesome, but he won't die. I give you my word."

"He needs a healer," I whimper. " Please. It can't wait. Let me take him to the palace. I can't lose him."

"Demons, child, he won't die. Have some faith."

"You don't know that," I cry.

Zezric rolls his eyes. "Fine." He directs his gaze at Antai and closes his eyes.

After a second, Antai's limbs begin to quiver. Independent bands of muscle, like thick red slugs, bulge from his wounds and ooze over the severed stump. The muscular slugs crawl over exposed bone before knitting themselves together. Finally, his skin begins to stretch as if pulled by a string. It slowly wraps itself over the glistening muscle, coming together at the apex of each stump. By the time it's all done, each of Antai's limbs are completely encased within a flawless layer of skin.

Zezric picks up the wine bottle, filling his glass to the brim. "There. Now come sit."

I can't take my eyes off him. Antai's body is lying on the floor. His face is pale, but he appears to be sleeping soundly. I can see his chest rising and falling. Up and down. Up and down.

He's alive, but his limbs! The sight feels wrong. He's incomplete. How will he walk? How will he live?

What has he done to you, Antai?

"Rose?" Zezric warns. "I won't ask again." He motions at my seat. "I know this hurts you, but it will be alright. I don't do anything that can't be undone."

I push off the floor, rising shakily to my feet. My head swims as I stumble to the table, falling into my chair.

Be strong, Rose, I tell myself. *Just talk to him. See what you can learn. Do it for Antai.*

I take a deep breath and wipe the tears out of my eyes. "Tell me… tell me about Foresight."

"What has Dralton taught you?" Zezric asks.

"N-nothing," I admit, fighting to slow my breathing. "I've only heard rumors… People think you can see the future. They say it's a gift, and that it runs in the royal family."

Zezric smiles. "Not a gift, Rose, a technique. No one is born with foresight. It must be learned. The prophet Izekiah taught our ancestors when we were entrusted with the Book of Life. We've passed down the knowledge ever since."

Keep asking questions, Rose. Don't think about Antai.

"H-how does it work?" I manage.

"I can reach a few moments into the future," Zezric says nonchalantly. "I knew Antai was going to shoot before he even drew his weapon."

I take a deep breath, calming my diaphragm. "Can you teach me?"

Zezric laughs. "I certainly can, but I choose not to. Foresight is the ultimate advantage. In some ways, it is more powerful than Adamic. If you can foresee a spell, you can counter it. Go ahead, try a spell on me."

It's not that I don't want him dead. I want it now more than ever. Still, I hesitate. Antai's body is on the floor. One mistake, and he'll burn.

"Hava—"

The air thickens in my mouth, making me gag. I heave forward, trying to spit whatever object appeared inside my throat, but there's nothing there. The force dominion has already dissolved.

"See," Zezric says calmly. "A spell is useless if you can't pronounce it. So long as I have foresight, a spell will never be uttered in my presence."

"Ha—" As soon as I try to speak, the force reappears, choking me once more.

"Don't waste your breath," Zezric laughs. After a second, the force in my throat disappears.

I cough, clearing my irritated esophagus. "What about the other spells?" I ask. "You said you knew five."

"Indeed. The last three spells are the most important. Tell me, Rose. What do you know of the Lost Libraries?

"Libraries?" I wrinkle my nose. "As in plural?"

"Of course. Why do you think we have a sister sanctuary? There were always two. The prophets wanted to preserve Adamic, but they wanted to restrict it as well, so they added safeguards—two that I can thing of.

He smiles to himself, swirling his drink, "The first is really quite clever. They separated the Adamic language into two categories—

words that act and words that are acted upon. Words that act were preserved in one library, and words that are acted upon were preserved in another."

"Nouns and verbs," I whisper.

"Precisely. The verbs were hidden in Hogrum. The nouns in Cavernum. Each offers power, but you need both to achieve godhood."

He pours his fourth glass of wine and gives it a swirl. "Once complete, the libraries were sealed, only to be opened or closed with Adamic. Each royal family was charged with their protection. It's really quite clever how they designed it. The Cavernic king—your many-great grandfather—was entrusted with two phrases. One was a generic spell. It could seal either sanctuary, should they ever be opened. The second spell was sanctuary-specific. It could only open the library in Hogrum—a library he didn't have access to. Likewise, the king of Hogrum was given the sealing spell, yet he could only open the library in Cavernum. Checks and balances, as they say in the Beyond."

"You only had the phrase to open Hogrum?" I realize. "That's why you attacked Hogrum first."

"Correct, but it didn't matter. When I got to Hogrum's Library, it was empty. The contents had already been relocated—-presumably to Cavernum. Now, the entire manuscript is contained in a single location. For the last 18 years, I had a problem; I didn't know the spell to open it… but Titan did. He was the one who put it there."

Zezric looks at me, smiling gleefully. "Before erasing his own memories, Titan hid the spell in the Inheritance Box, which posed a real issue. As you know, my body is no longer my own." He extends his arms, looking from one to the other. "Despite my reconstruction, no royal blood flows in these veins; so, I needed a pawn. I couldn't fool Dralton. He's too clever for that. That's why I needed you, Rose. Only you could open the Inheritance Box."

My mind swims, drowning in the information. "You mean…"

"You were smart to burn the paper, but then you attempted the spell on Jack. Of course, you mispronounced it—the tonicity can be tricky—

but I managed to work it out from what he described." He smiles victoriously. "Faza Le Bakanzah."

Immediately, my soul understands.

Unseal Bakanzah.

"Turns out," Zezric explains, "Bakanzah is a proper noun—an Adamic name for the library here in Cavernum. Now, all I have to do is find it. And when I do, the world will be made right... Antai will be made whole... your mother will be revived."

Suddenly, an idea comes to mind. "Mom is in heaven—a perfect paradise. What if she doesn't want to come back?"

To my surprise, Zezric raises a finger excitedly. "Ahhh, yes. A fair argument indeed. I'm glad you brought it up. You see, I was taught that heaven is the highest form of happiness." He takes a slow sip from his glass. "Frankly, that is a lie."

"Excuse me?"

Zezric nods. "Heaven exists, yes, but it's no paradise. It's a prison."

"How can you say that?"

"With confidence, Rose. Heaven is a prison. Think about it. Once a year, on the night of Hallow's Eve, the veil is lifted, correct? One night a year, the spirits of the dead are free to roam. The Adamic recognize this. They refuse to sleep, fearing that they'll be haunted in their dreams by the damned. Don't you think it's strange, Rose, that we aren't visited by our loved ones? The damned come to haunt us, and yet our loved ones don't visit from their heavenly homes? There's only one logical explanation: they're trapped."

"They're not trapped; they're happy," I insist. "They don't want to leave."

"That's what Dralton taught me as well. If you ask any Adamic, they'd say the same thing. They accept this measly excuse without a second thought. They attribute more truth to tradition than they do to reason." Zezric shakes his head. "But with a little logic, it all falls apart. Think about it, Rose. If you died today, would you want to visit anyone on Hallow's Eve? I certainly would. No infinitesimal joy or heavenly bliss could stop me from coming back." He looks up, his thoughts wandering heavenward. "No, not in a million years. If the roles were reversed—if I was dead, and Violet was here on Earth—I would endure endless suffering to spend a night with her. I would abandon unfathomable bliss to hear her voice. I would do anything, Rose, and I know she would do the same for me. I know it! That only leaves one remaining possibility: she's a prisoner. Your mother is held captive, and I'm the only one who can set her free."

I look down at Antai's body, tears threatening my vision once more. "I can't do this anymore. Can I take him home now?" I beg.

Zezric holds up a finger. "Almost. You never asked about the second safeguard."

"What's the second safeguard?" I croak.

"I'm glad you asked," he says sarcastically. "Every time the Libraries are sealed, they are inactivated for one solar revolution. For an entire year, not even the proper spell will open them. A tad simplistic if you ask me, but I suppose it has its place."

He looks me over, frowning. "I apologize. I've tormented you enough for one morning." He turns toward the door. "Jack!"

The front door immediately opens, and a swoosh of silver robes step into the room. "Yes, my lord?"

"Can you send in Iris? We're just about finished."

"Of course, my lord," Jack bows before closing the door. I hear his footsteps retreating down the stairwell.

Zezric directs his attention to Antai. "While I was healing dear Mr. Elsborne, I happened across a particular memory. If I'm not mistaken, you entrusted a certain healer with the Ring of Soronan. She was given instructions to find Atlantia, was she not?"

I say nothing.

"As you can imagine, that threatens my plans. I can't let your search party run amuck in the Beyond."

The sound of creaking footsteps grows louder from the stairwell. A moment later, Iris opens the door. "You summoned me, my lord?"

"I did," Zezric says. "I have a task for you—an opportunity to display your reclaimed loyalty. Your brother and Kendra are headed for Atlantia. I want you to find them. Take as many feeders as you need."

He reaches across the table and picks up the seerglasses, tossing the relic to Iris. "And take this. Use it to track their movement."

"What should I do when I catch them?" Iris asks.

"Bring your brother to me; I want him alive. The healer too. But not Kildron. Go ahead and kill him for me. When you bring me his head, you can join me as an equal."

13

MATT

I rap my knuckles on the top of the bunker hatch in a musical rhythm—the classic one from spy movies.

Tink….tink….. tink tink… tink……... tink.. tink.

Silence. I knock again.

Tink. Tink. Tink.

"Helloooo," I call. "Klinton? You in there? It's me, Matt!" I tug on the latch, but it doesn't budge.

Kildron kicks the bunker hatch with his boot. "I'll give them ten seconds."

"Klinton!" I knock again. "It's Matt! Open up!"

"Eight… nine… ten," Kildron counts. He steps forward, slapping both hands flat on the hatch door. He closes his eyes, investigating the inner workings with dominion. After a moment, he rotates his hand to the right as if turning a key. I hear the clank of metal as the lock slides out of place. Finally, Kildron yanks the lid upward, and the hatch swings open.

"Klinton?" I lean over the hole, peering into the darkness. "You down there?"

"Matt? Is that you?" I hear a flurry of footsteps as Klinton sprints to the base of the ladder. He squints up at us through thick-framed glasses and a rat's nest of curly brown hair. "Matt? You made it!" He turns his head. "Ron! Wake up! Matt is here. He's alive! You gotta get up!"

"We're coming down," I call, feeding my legs into the mouth of the hatch and scurrying down the ladder. The second my shoes hit the floor, Klinton has his arms around me.

"I thought you guys were dead," he says as he squeezes my ribs. "We were freaking out down here. We thought we were the only ones left."

Ron stumbles out of the bedroom, still pulling a pair of sweats over his boxers. The moment he sees me, he starts laughing like a madman.

"No way! You did it, you little bastard! Thank God! We're saved!" He nearly tackles Klinton and I, pulling us both into a three-way hug.

"I told you!" Klinton laughs. "I never doubted. Not once."

They release me as Kendra hops off the ladder, diving at her like two untrained puppies.

"Kendra!" Klinton cries.

"Hi," she laughs back. "I'm glad you're both okay."

Ron shakes his head, blinking in disbelief. "How… we saw the wall go down. How are you still alive?"

Kendra winces, the corner of her eyes drooping. "The feeders are still out there, but the Palace Wall is intact. Some survivors are safe there… for now at least."

Clunk!

The hatch door echoes as Kildron slams it shut. He descends only halfway down the ladder. Then, he jumps, shaking the floor on impact. Standing tall, he stares blankly at Ron and Klinton.

Ron raises an eyebrow. "He with you guys?"

"This is my dad, Kildron," I say. "Kildron, meet Klinton and Ron."

"Hi," my dad mutters.

"Nice to meet you, sir," Klinton says, giving a little wave.

"Kildron and Klinton," Ron grins. "Say that five times fast."

Klinton leans to the side. He looks past my dad and squints at the sealed hatch. "What about my brother? Did Kowen—"

"He's safe," Kendra interjects. "I saw him in the palace. He's doing well. The rest of your siblings too."

Klinton breathes a sigh of relief. "Good. That's good."

"Is it just you two?" I ask, peering down the hallway.

"Captain Renshu was here, but took off in the helicopter."

Kendra looks appalled. "He left you here?"

"He offered to take us," Klinton clarifies, "but I wouldn't leave without Kowen, and Ron wouldn't leave without me."

"So, what now?" Ron asks. "You're here to take us back, I'm guessing?"

Kendra looks at me, and I look at the floor. "Actually, I can't go back. I'm, uhhh… I'm a feeder now."

Ron's jaw swings open. "Damn! You're serious? You mean you… Holy shit."

I shrug. "Yeah, well, it is what it is."

"To be honest, we need some computer help," Kendra says, coming to my aid. "We're searching for Atlantia."

Klinton frowns. "Atlantia, as in the Sunken Sanctuary?"

Kendra nods. "We need backup. With their help, we might be able to stop the Holy One. Diego thinks it might be in the Bermuda Triangle."

"If we can find where the ships go missing, we can find the sanctuary," I add. "At least… that's the theory."

"I'm sorry, but you've lost me," Ron admits.

I point down the hallway. "Just get me on Google. We'll take care of the rest."

"Can do," Klinton says, leading us to the computer room. "Just give me one second." He grabs the mouse and clicks to exit out of a movie. In seconds, he has a Google search bar on the screen.

"It's all yours," he says motioning to the chair.

"I can help too," Ron says, sitting down at another computer. "What are we searching for?"

"We're looking for anything strange in the Bermuda Triangle," Kendra explains. "Missing planes, shipwrecks, anything like that. Specifically, we want coordinates—somewhere to start looking."

"You're going to look for it? Like, in person?" Klinton doubts.

"That's the plan," Kendra sighs.

I start with a simple search, 'List of missing ships in Bermuda Triangle.' I sift through the results, clicking on a Wikipedia article.

As I scan, I'm mostly disappointed. Most of the missing ships have unremarkable stories—their disappearance attributed to stormy seas or inexperienced captains. They don't point to an unseen sanctuary like I anticipated. I search for missing aircraft next and get similar results.

For the next hour, we sift through the internet's infinite information, jumping from page to page. Klinton reads over my shoulder, pointing at the links he thinks I should click next.

"Ummm, guys," Ron looks up from his monitor. "I think I found something."

"What is it?" I ask, leaning over.

He reads aloud. "'On December 5th, 1945, a group of five US bombers left Fort Lauderdale for a short naval exercise. However, mid-flight, they sent out a distress call.'" He looks up. "Listen to this. The pilot is recorded saying, 'Both my compasses are down. We can't find West. Everything is wrong.'"

"You might just be onto something," I stand to get a better look at his screen. "Both his compasses broke?" I echo.

Ron nods. "That's not all. There were four other bombers with him. They should've taken over navigation, but they didn't. It sounds as though all of them had malfunctions. With two compasses each, the odds of that happening are basically zero."

I nod in agreement. "It has to be the magnetic field. What else could it be?"

"Tell me you have coordinates?" Kendra begs.

"Right here. This is a map of their flight path." Ron clicks to enlarge the map. "They were traveling east along latitude 26 degrees north. And this is where they made the first distress call." He points to a red star on the map. "Search in that area and you might just find something."

I turn to my dad, "What do you think? Worth the gamble?"

He shrugs. "It won't be easy. First, we need a way to get to Seattle.

Then, we'd need to fly to Florida. From there, we'll need a big enough boat… not to mention we'll have to navigate the open ocean with no naval training. And even if we do all that, odds are we'll sail right past it and never even know it."

"Captain Renshu left his truck," Klinton interjects hesitantly. "His keys are in the kitchen. I think it still has gas."

"See! We already have a plan," Kendra says excitedly. "The sooner we get going, the better."

"But… we just started researching," I voice. "What if there's a better lead? We could be looking in the wrong spot."

"We'll keep searching online," Klinton offers. "If we find a better clue, we'll call you." He opens a drawer and fishes through an assortment of cell phones. "Here, take this." He selects an iPhone with a matching charger and hands them to me. "That way we can keep in touch. Our number is in the Contacts under 'H.Q.'"

"You don't want to come with us?" I ask.

Klinton slowly shakes his head. "I can't leave without Kowen. Besides, we'll just slow you down anyway." He looks down at my bloodied uniform and frowns. "Is that all you have to wear?"

"For now, yeah."

"You can borrow some of my clothes."

Kildron's footsteps clank behind me. He clears his throat. "I've got the keys." He gives them a shake, eliciting a faint jingle. "Grab those clothes quick, then we should hit the road. Kendra's right; we've got a lot of ground to cover. If we hurry, we can make it to Seattle by nightfall. I have something there I want to show you."

"Like what?"

He smiles. "When was the last time you went to church?"

14

ROSE

Antai stirs, and for a moment, I think he might wake up. It's been hours since the incident, and he still hasn't opened his eyes.

Just looking at him makes my heart twist in knots, wringing itself of blood and making me feel faint. I resist the urge to look away.

Each hand is amputated mid-forearm. His legs are symmetrically severed as well. They end a few inches above what should be his knees.

Madame Xantone rests her hands on the stump on Antai's thighs and closes her eyes. After a few seconds, her jaw drops open. "This job is remarkable. If I didn't know better, I'd think his injury was a decade old." Her eyes remain shut as she slides her hand over the amputation. "There's sufficient soft tissue to cushion a prosthesis, and the femur bone is already prepped for weight-bearing. I'm not sure there's anything to improve upon. For all intents and purposes, he's healed."

"You're sure?"

"I wouldn't say so if I wasn't," Madame Xantone insists.

"Well, thank you regardless. Your opinion puts me a little more at ease."

"Anytime." Madame Xantone bows. "I'll be in the healing loft should any concerns arise." She struts across the room and opens the door. "Oh, hello, Lieutenant."

Octavian is outside my door. His mouth is set in a tight line and the bottom of his eyelids are tense. He looks straight past Madame Xantone and finds my eyes. "My Queen, would you accompany me to the High Council Wing? There is a matter you should attend to immediately."

"I'm sorry, Octavian, but I need to be with Antai. Can you settle the matter yourself?"

The bottom of his lip turns downwards. "I'm sorry, Your Majesty, but this is *urgent*." He stresses the last word in a way that makes my stomach sink.

I nod. "Madame Xantone, can you keep Antai company for a moment?"

"I suppose I have some time. How long will you—"

"Not long." I'm already out the door. Octavian, with a long stride and swinging arms, leads me down the hall. He isn't running, but I need to jog just to keep up.

"What's going on?" I demand.

"General Katu is dead," he says.

I stop in my tracks, dread paralyzing me. "But…"

"Come, Your Majesty," he takes my hand and guides me down the hall."

"How?" I choke.

"He passed in the night. His wife found him deceased when she woke this morning. She doesn't know what happened, and we don't yet have a cause of death. For what it's worth, I was watching General Kaynes last night. He never left his room."

Several guardsmen are gathered outside Katu's chambers. There are a few healers as well. They try to console Katu's wife, handing her a handkerchief to wipe her tears.

I walk right past them and into the room.

Katu's corpse hasn't been moved. He's on his back in the bed, eyes closed. The covers are pulled away, exposing his bare legs and torso.

A single healer sits at the edge of his bed, one hand resting on his breastbone, eyes closed. She's in her thirties with coiling black hair and prominent cheekbones. Her hoop earrings are heavy enough to create a concerning stretch in her earlobes.

I watch in silence. After a minute, she opens her eyes.

"Oh!" she gasps and retracts her hand in fright. "Forgive me, Your Majesty. I didn't hear you come in."

"Sorry. I didn't want to interrupt. Are you in charge of the autopsy?" I ask.

"I am." The healer straightens her shoulders. "I'm Jephora, palace pathologist."

"Well, Jephora, What can you tell me?"

"For starters, his blood gasses are all over the place. He's hypoxic and hypercapnic."

"I'm sorry. I'm not a healer," I say.

"Of course. My apologies, Your Majesty." She blushes. "His blood has low levels of oxygen and excessive carbon dioxide. I also noted some fluid in his lungs—nothing alarming, but more than I would've expected. Also, if you look closely, you can see petechiae in his conjunctiva."

When she sees me squint, she blushes again. "Allow me to explain." She reaches up to Katu's face and pulls down on his lower eyelid, "See these little red spots. They're tiny broken blood vessels. Petechiae, we call it."

"Okay. So what does it mean?" I ask.

Jephora sits up, "Interestingly enough, everything points to asphyxiation."

"You think he was murdered?"

Her eyes double in size. "Oh, heavens no. There are no signs of a struggle. No bruising or laryngeal damage. My first suspicion would be drug use. Certain compounds can cause respiratory failure, but I didn't find any opioids in his system, so it's currently unconfirmed."

"What about dominion?" I wonder. "You can suffocate someone with dominion. Suck the air from their lungs. They wouldn't have bruises."

I shiver at the memory.

Jephora ponders this for a moment. "Hmmm. Even dominion would leave signs," she finally concludes. "A vacuum in the lungs would damage the alveolar tissue. I just don't see any indication in my autopsy."

"And there's no other explanation?"

"There is one explanation… According to his chart, he had sleep apnea. Asphyxiation is a rare complication, but it's certainly possible. Essentially, you choke on your own tongue as you sleep."

"Mystery solved!" General Kaynes calls from the doorway, waltzing through the door with a swoosh of his robe. "Personally, I can't think of a better way to go, passing painlessly in my satin sheets."

He strides audaciously across the room, stopping at the foot of the bed. "It's a shame God had to call him home so young. He was such a good man, always loyal to the crown."

I bite my tongue and lower my voice. "If you had something to do with this…?"

General Kaynes exaggerates a look of surprise. "Me? How could you imply such a travesty? I was in my chambers all night as I'm sure you've been informed." He leans in closer, whispering softly in my ear. "I'm telling the truth, Rosey. I had nothing to do with this. Well… almost nothing. Surely, you believe me?"

I've heard enough. I push past General Kaynes and stumble into the hallway. I spin in a circle, looking for Octavian, but he's already gone.

"Everything alright, miss?"

"Huh?" I turn, spotting the source of the voice. Bob stands beside a framed tapestry. His beer belly is barely contained in a wool coat, and his sandy beard is braided in two separate strands.

"You okay?" he croaks. "You don't look so good."

Everyone is watching me, including Katu's wife and the plethora of guardsmen. "I'm sorry, I need to get back to my room," I stammer as I take off down the hallway.

"Wait up, m'lady!" Bob hobbles to catch up with me, swinging his weight with each step. "I'll accompany you… if you don't mind, of course."

"Actually, I think I prefer—"

"Wonderful!" Bob bellows, before I can finish the sentence. He increases his stride to match my own. He doesn't huff or struggle as I expected. In fact, he's quite nimble, turning his hefty body to dodge a patrolling guard who failed to move out of the way.

We walk in silence until we turn the corner. Bob twists to get a look behind us. "Coast is clear. Kaynes didn't follow."

His voice is different than I remember. When I first met him—back at Bob's Brew—he had a drunken slur and a brazen lack of awareness. Now, his words are crisp and direct, perhaps sobered by the direness of our situation.

"You know," he whispers. "I've been meaning to speak with you, m'lady. Our mutual friend, Diego… well… he told me about that plan of yours. I think I can be of service."

"You mean, in the tunnels?"

"That's right. It'll take me a couple of days, but I'm pretty sure I can find a way out. I'll bring a few men with me to excavate the collapse. With our amulets, we should have it cleared in a few hours. Once we verify an exit path, I'll return to the Pit, and we can start the evacuation."

"That's… That's wonderful! Is there anything you need from me?"

"Now that you mention it..." He falls silent as we approach a group of commoners. He waits until they pass. "You need to make sure the Pit is guarded by men you trust. I don't want them raising any alarms. We'll begin excavating in two days. That should give you time to make any changes you need."

"I can do that," I say, "Consider it done."

As Antai's door comes into view, Bob slows to a stop. "I was sorry to hear about what happened to Antai. If you ever need a break from it all, you can come find me. I have a lemon-ginger beer with your name on it."

He remembered. It was the beer I requested my first time in Bob's Brew.

"Thanks, Bob. I might just have to take you up on that."

Bob stops. "There's one last thing. I tried to talk to you earlier. I came by your chambers."

"I was with Antai," I explain.

Bob waves his hand dismissively. "I know that now, of course. The point is, when I came by your room, I saw a girl sneaking out. Bwuah! What's her name? One of the Champions from The Surviving. Skinny little thing. Red hair."

"Crasilda?"

Bob snaps his fingers. "That's it!"

"She was in my room? You're sure?"

"Sure as the day is long."

"Thanks, Bob. I appreciate this."

"Anytime." He thumps me on the shoulder. "Welp, keep hang'n in there." With that, he tramps away.

I grab Antai's door and push it open.

Antai is sitting up in bed, a pillow propped behind his head. "Hey, Rose." He fakes a smile, glancing down at his body. "Guess things didn't go as planned."

"Antai! Thank God, you're awake." I look around the room. "Where's Madame Xantone."

"I sent her away."

"What? Why?"

"Why not?" He shrugs. "It's not like I need a babysitter."

"Oh… I guess not." I change the subject. "How… uh… how are you feeling?"

He bows his head, scanning his injuries. "It doesn't hurt." After a second, he grimaces and looks away. I think he's going to say more, but he stops himself, shrugging instead. "I'm fine. I'm alive, aren't I?"

I nod. "What do you remember?"

"More than I'd like to." He looks up, searching the archives of his mind. "I remember trying to shoot him. Then, he dis-armed me." Antai cracks a smile. "Next thing I knew, I was de-feated." He raises an eyebrow.

I can't bring myself to laugh. "I don't really want to joke about this, Antai."

He furrows his brow. "Not that funny, huh?" He looks down. "I guess without my arms, I can't make a very good punchline." He cracks a smile.

"Can we be serious for a minute?" I beg. "I'm worried about you, Antai."

His smile wilts, quickly transforming into a scowl. "What? You don't like my jokes?"

"I just… it's too soon for me. Nothing about this is funny."

His scowl darkens into a glare. "Well, maybe I need a little laughter. Maybe I need something funny right now. Did you maybe consider that?"

"I'm sorry. I just—"

He raises his arm stumps in the air. "What else am I supposed to do, if I can't make a joke? It's not like I can do anything else!"

"I'm sorry," My voice comes out as a whisper. "It just… It hurts me to—"

"Oh, so now we're talking about you again? Forgive me," he sneers. "I forgot your feelings take precedence. Clearly, you're the one in need of coddling. Your boyfriend got turned into a talking torso. Poor little princess has the inconvenience of replacing him. Let's all pity her, shall we?"

"Antai!" I gasp.

"Of course, it didn't take you long last time," he adds. "What was it, a month to find a replacement? Less?"

I'm speechless. I've never heard Antai talk this way. The words refuse to register.

Antai exhales through his nose. "Even as a feeder, he probably looks like the better option about now." He leans his head back on the pillow, staring up at the ceiling. "Maybe that was your plan all along. Let your father cut me down so you could run back to MacArthur. Right? I mean, you didn't even help me. You just watched."

"STOP IT!" Something in me snaps. "Just stop!" The tears openly stream down my face, but they're accompanied with a sense of indignation—betrayal even. "None of that is true, and you know it. I choose you, Antai. Even now. I…" I take a deep breath, my jaw quivering. "I don't care if things are different. You're my best friend. I want you. I…"

"You still can't even say it," he sneers.

"Say what?"

Antai says nothing, refusing to look me in the eye.

"Say what? 'I love you?'"

He says nothing.

"You don't think I love you?" I demand.

He shrugs, his lips tense—ready to retaliate. Finally, he meets my gaze. "Do you?"

"Of course I do!"

"Then why don't you say it?"

"I…" I'm not sure I have an answer.

He rolls his eyes. "That's what I thought." He turns his head, looking out the window. "Your dad should've finished me off—save us both the time."

I open my mouth to respond, but stop myself. *He's hurting, Rose. Stop bickering and be there for him.*

I take a deep breath. "Listen. I know it seems bad now, but we'll get through this. It'll get better, we just have to give it some time."

His eyes harden again, mad that his despair is being debated. "Look at me, Rose! I can't walk. I can't fight. I can't even hold your hand. I can't do anything. I'm not a person anymore. I'm just… meat."

"You have dominion," I remind him. "You'll adapt. Madame Xantone says she can fit you with prosthetics. You'll be back on your feet in no time."

He looks down at the foot of the bed, eyeing the space where his feet should be. "Doubt it."

"Hey!" I say, waiting until he looks at me. "You're still you. You're still Antai. I know it seems bad right now, but we're gonna get through this. I promise."

He says nothing, letting his eyes wander back to the window.

Tap. Tap.

A teenage servant pushes the door open with his hip. He's carrying a bowl in each hand—mashed potatoes and a vegetable soup.

"Hi, General Elsborne," the servant strides confidently into the room. "I'm here to assist with dinner."

I stand, allowing the boy to take my place at the bedside. After setting the bowls on the nightstand, he spoons a bite of mashed potatoes and holds it in front of Antai's mouth.

Antai frowns, looking at me rather than the spoon. "Maybe you should come back tomorrow, Rose."

"You want me to leave?" I can't keep the sting from my voice.

Confused, the servant lowers the spoon.

"It's just…" Antai looks away. "It feels weird with you watching."

"Antai, there's nothing to be ashamed of. You—"

"Please," he says. "Just leave."

I exhale my frustration. "Okay… And when should I come back? Tonight?"

"I don't know."

"Tomorrow?" I ask.

"I… I just need some time," he solemnly replies. "I'll let you know when I'm ready."

With every second, I'm beginning to second guess myself. I'm hiding in Crasilda's wardrobe, sandwiched between a ball gown and a fur coat. The air reeks of sage perfume, and the temperature is unbearable. My body heat, combined with the moisture from my breath, has turned the oversized cupboard into a sauna. Every few minutes, I have to use dominion just to cool off.

Chill!

Goosebumps erupt on my arms as the temperature in the wardrobe plummets. Yet before long, I feel the sweat running down my brow once more.

Just a few more minutes.

I don't have a watch, but I know I'm running out of time. There are four guardsmen currently patrolling the High Council Wing. Octavian assured me that all four could be trusted, but in an hour or so, the shifts will change, and I'll have no such guarantee.

Whatever happens, Jack can't know I was here.

Just a few more minutes, I tell myself for the tenth time.

I'm in the middle of cooling the wardrobe when I hear the front door fling open, followed by two pairs of footsteps. One stops by the bed. The other continues past the wardrobe, scurrying toward the washroom.

"How many times do I have to tell you? I want my bath waiting for me," Crasilda scolds. "I'm not asking you to do alchemy; it's a simple bath."

"The meeting finished early," the maid mumbles. "I thought—"

"I don't want to hear excuses," Crasilda snaps. "You work slower when you ramble. You don't have the brains to multitask."

"Yes, ma'am." I hear the creak of a faucet and the gurgle of water pouring from the spout.

"And don't make it too hot," Crasilda calls. "I felt like a boiled hen last time."

"Yes, ma'am."

I hear the crunch of a log landing on coals. Then the clank of a pot.

"You know what, forget it," Crasilda groans. " I don't have time for this. Just fill the tub. I'll heat it myself."

"But—"

The maid falls silent, and I can already imagine the glare Crasilda must be giving her.

"Demons," Crasilda mumbles to herself. "You're incompetent. I swear. At least light some candles… No! You imbecile. Cut the wick before you light it. I hate it when they flicker. It gives me a headache."

"Y-yes, ma'am."

I clench my fists, but I can't intervene. For all I know, the maid could be one of Jack's spies.

It takes a quarter hour to fill the tub. Finally, I hear the creak of a faucet, and the water stops, followed by a subtle splash as Crasilda steps inside.

"Why don't you make yourself useful and run to the kitchen? I'm starving."

"What would you like?"

"Do I have to spell everything out for you? Just get me something palatable, and we won't have a problem."

"But—"

"I swear, if I hear one more 'but' out of you, I'm going to kill someone."

"Yes, ma'am."

A pair of footsteps moves toward me.

"When I say run, I mean it," Crasilda shouts from the washroom.

The maid scurries past the wardrobe and throws open the front door. She fumbles with the doorknob for a second before closing it hastily behind her.

Finally, Crasilda is alone.

Slowly, I ease the wardrobe open. Fortunately for me, it doesn't creak.

The room is dim, illuminated only by two candles—one on each nightstand. The sun must have set while I was hiding in the wardrobe.

Unlike my room, there isn't a washroom door, just an open entry. From where I stand, I can see the threshold, illuminated by half a dozen candles.

I tiptoe closer.

When I reach the edge of the washroom, I pause.

Shield.

Once the ripples settle, I take a deep breath and step into the candlelight.

To my surprise, Crasilda doesn't react. In fact, her head is completely underwater. I watch as she blows a few bubbles before surfacing, her eyes still sealed shut.

She's naked except for a silver amplifier draped around her neck. Her strawberry hair covers her breasts and clings to the sides of the tub. The remainder of her body is submerged, hidden by the candles' reflection.

With a tired sigh, she wipes the hair off of her face and opens her eyes.

I'm the first thing she sees.

"Puh!" She lets out a short gasp as her body stiffens. At first, she's speechless. She may as well be posing for a portrait. Then, her eyes fill with indignation.

"You… How dare you?" Her hand goes to her amulet.

"I don't want to fight you. I came to talk," I reply, keeping my voice as neutral as I can muster.

She keeps one hand on her amulet. The other clutches the side of the tub.

"Who do you think you are?" Crasilda seethes. "You break into my home, corner me while I'm bathing. How dare you… I mean… HOW DARE YOU?"

"I'm here to warn—"

Before I can finish the sentence, all six of the candlesticks lurch across the room. Ripples cascade before my face as they ricochet off my shield, extinguishing the flames and plunging us into darkness.

Immediately, I hear the water sloshing as Crasilda leaps to her feet.

It's dark, but not pitch dark. A tiny morsel of light seeps in from the room behind me, just enough to distinguish Crasilda's outline standing in the tub.

I could freeze the water around her ankles, trapping her like an animal, naked and shivering, but I refrain. I don't want to be seen as the enemy.

"Get a towel," I command. "I'll wait."

She steps slowly out of the tub.

Next thing I know, the basin is airborne. It crashes into my energy shield, carrying the weight of the bathwater with it.

I shudder under the strain, wrapping my energy shield around the tub like a primitive hand. I don't just deflect it; I try to slow its fall as a torrent of water pours across the floor.

With a grunt, I lower the tub, albeit quicker than intended. It lands beside me, cracking the tile floor and shaking the room. Surely, the downstairs residents heard the ruckus, but I doubt the guards will be alerted.

"Are you finished?" I patronize.

Crasilda says nothing. I can't make out her facial expression in the dark, but I know she must be confused. I've yet to retaliate.

"Good," I say. "I'll wait for you in the bedchamber. I have a warning for you."

I wait by her desk, lighting a few candles with dominion. The only decor—a small picture stand—catches my eye. It's a charcoal sketch of Crasilda's family—two young girls sandwiched between their smiling parents.

I didn't know she had a sister.

"What do you want?" Crasilda barks, stepping into the room. She's wrapped in a plush bathrobe with a fluffy belt of fabric tied around her waist to keep the skirt from flapping open.

"Listen," I start. "I know you're spying on me for General Kaynes."

Crasilda shakes her head. "You don't know shit."

"I'm not stupid, Crasilda. Kaynes added you to the High Council, and I know you've been snooping around in my room. It's not that hard to connect the dots."

Crasilda says nothing, confirming my suspicions.

"Look. I'm not here to criticize you. You're only doing as you're told. But there's something you need to know…"

Crasilda crosses her arms. "And what's that?"

"General Kaynes is working for the Holy One."

"And?" Crasilda meets my gaze, challenging me.

"You… you knew?"

"Why else would I bother digging around in your pigsty. I'm not doing it for some gilded geezer; I can promise you that."

"Crasilda, please listen to me. You don't get it. If you give the Holy One any reason to think I'm fighting back, any reason at all, he'll destroy the palace. He'll kill us all."

"So?"

"But..." I'm at a loss for words. "What... what about your mom? Your friends?"

Crasilda rolls her eyes. "Is that all you came to say?"

I stand there, speechless, unable to comprehend her apathy.

Crasilda touches her hand to her amulet, and her front door swings open. She gestures at the doorway. "Get out. Or should I call Jack to escort you to your chambers?" She opens her mouth wide. "Guar—"

"Stop!" I beg. "I'm going." I backpedal through the doorway and into the hallway, keeping my eyes on Crasilda. "What is he offering you? What can he possibly give you that's worth your family? Your home?"

Her eyes harden. "What I deserve!"

The air ripples, and her door slams in my face.

I blink in disbelief, staring at her door. Of all my schemes, this was supposed to be the easy one. She was supposed to be receptive, grateful even. I genuinely thought she would comply, maintaining the appearance of espionage without divulging her discoveries to Jack or my father.

How could I be so wrong?

Despair presses down on my shoulders, making them sag as I sulk back to my chambers. I can't fathom any sort of happy ending for Cavernum. The harder I try, the worse things become.

There's always Matt, I remind myself. *That is, if Iris hasn't caught him yet.*

15

MATT

We park along the curb in front of a gothic chapel. A row of stone gargoyles peer down at us from their precarious perches.

Kildron puts the car in park. "Ready?"

I frown from the backseat. "Do I seriously have to go?"

"Yes. This is their belief system, Matt. Even feeders have a way to justify their actions. The more you know, the better you'll understand them."

I narrow my eyes. "And they won't try to kill us?"

Kildron shakes his head. "Not this church. This is the Church of Opposition. Unlike the Order, they're pacifists… mostly. You'll see."

"What's the difference?"

Kildron frowns. "You know what? I better give you some background before we go in."

He twists his body so he can look at us in the backseat. "The ancient texts teach that there are many Gods. Even the Adamic acknowledge this. They are known as the Celestial Family. The texts don't speak of the parents, but it goes into detail about their two sons. The firstborn was Lucifer, or light-bringer. The second was Yahweh.

Yahweh is more commonly known as the great Creator—the God of the Adamic. The Adamic view Lucifer as his opposite, the Destroyer."

"Yaweh is good and Lucifer is evil," I summarize. "Easy."

Kildron rolls his eyes. "That's how the Adamic see it, yes, but the Cainic teach differently. They don't believe Lucifer is evil. His name means light-bringer for heaven's sake. To them, he is a deity, not a devil. He adopted the name Satan, which means adversary—or more specifically, opposition. Not opposition to God, as the Adamic claim, but opposition to injustice. All crimes must be punished. Good deeds must be rewarded. The Adversary isn't an opposite force, but an opposing one… both equal and reciprocal. An eye for an eye. A tooth for a tooth. That was his doctrine."

"Like karma?" I say. "Satan is karma?"

"That's one way to look at it, yeah. Yahweh promised justice in the next life, but Satan did one better. He promised it here on Earth. Every crime must be punished in the flesh, and every blessing must be rewarded in this lifetime. That's why the Cainic worship him."

"Okay," I acknowledge. "What does that have to do with feeders?"

"Everything," Kildron claims. "It's the very core of their beliefs. Feeders believe in two great crimes. The first crime occurred before the creation, when Yaweh betrayed his elder brother. Satan was meant to rule the heavens, but God overthrew him. This injustice still requires penance. Cainics believe that Satan's throne must someday be restored, and God must suffer for his sins."

"That's… interesting. And the second?"

"The second great crime occurred after the creation. You know the story of Cain and Abel?"

"Mostly," I admit.

Kildron sighs. "The Adamic teach that Cain slew Abel and was punished by God, losing his dominion. But the Cainic tell a different story. They believe that Cain was a visionary. He was the only mortal to worship Satan as the rightful heir to heaven. When Abel sacrificed a lamb for his God, Cain did one better. He sacrificed the fattest pig in Satan's name. This made God envious. In his jealousy, he cursed Cain and stole his dominion. Seeing this injustice, Satan provided opposition. He allowed Cain to feed on Abel, replacing his lost dominion. The Cainic view feeding as their birthright, restoring what should have always been theirs."

He looks at Kendra then back at me. "The same principle applies to demons. For centuries, the Cainic were at the mercy of the Adamic. Without dominion, they were no better than slaves. Satan, in his goodness, provided opposition. He blessed the Cainic with demonhood, flipping the balance. From that moment forward, the Adamic became our lessers. Demons believe we are destined to rule the Adamic."

"Hmmm," I think aloud. "That kinda makes sense, in a twisted sort of way."

"Of course it makes sense," Kildron sighs. "No one would believe it if it didn't."

"Still," I say, "it doesn't justify murder."

"Not all feeders are the same, Matt. The original church split into two very different sects. The most dangerous is the Order of the Firstborn."

"Firstborn?" I question.

Kildron nods. "Satan and Cain were both the firstborn—both undermined by their younger brothers. The Order of the Firstborn focuses on avenging their own wrongs, restoring their dominion by any means necessary. Their leaders are the oldest, most dangerous feeders alive, as well as some Adamic demons—my father for example. But not all feeders are so cruel. The second faction—a much smaller sect—is The Church of Opposition. They focus on avenging others. They only feed on the wicked, targeting those Adamic who abuse their power. Occasionally, they might kill the elderly, putting them out of their misery. They spare the rest, never harming the young or the innocent. They are agents of Opposition, dealing justice where they see fit."

"They must be saints," I murmur.

"They aren't," Kildron says, "but they aren't evil either." He sighs. "I'm not evil, Matt."

"So what?" I demand. "You're telling me you believe all this?"

He looks down. "Years ago, yes, I believed it. Mutalah brought me here when we were teenagers. After everything I was taught in the

Order, things started to make more sense." He looks away. "Now, I'm not sure I believe anything."

"Then why are we here?" I demand.

Kildron meets my eyes, "Sometimes, you have to listen to the lies to find the truth."

"It certainly makes you think," Kendra concludes. "I've never heard that perspective before."

Kildron nods. "While we're gone, stay invisible, Kendra. If anything happens, honk the horn. You ready Matt?"

"Sure," I groan.

I climb out of the car and follow Kildron through two massive wooden doors—big enough to fit an elephant.

The hallways are completely deserted. Lit by sparse candlelight, they almost remind me of Cavernum—musty and medieval. We turn left and stop at a closed door. A small wooden slat opens at eye level. A dark pair of eyes stare out at us.

"What do you seek?"

Kildron leans forward. "To silence the sinner, to crush the oppressor, to bless the good-hearted, to raise up the weak."

"As you have said, so may it be."

The door swings open, and we enter a large nave, lined with rows of wooden pews. Only the first few rows are occupied—nine or ten people, if I had to guess. Some wear black robes, like the feeders I've seen, but most have on everyday attire.

"Welcome, my brethren," a priest calls from the podium. He stands at a wooden pulpit. Behind him, a massive mural of a dark haired man stares stoically at the audience—Satan, I assume.

Between the pews and the podium is a massive cube of concrete—an altar by the looks of it. Iron rings are anchored into the concrete slab. From the rings, long leather straps dangle down the side of the concrete. Worst of all, a dark, reddish substance stains the upper surface of the altar.

"We are about to begin." The priest gestures at the front row. "Come take your seats."

As we approach, he squints at us. Suddenly, his mouth parts in a toothy grin. "It is an honor to be in the presence of two Lords of Opposition."

Kildron ignores the priest as we shuffle into the third pew.

"Why did he call us lords?" I say softly.

"We're a higher rank," Kildron whispers back. "Feeders bring opposition to the public, but only demons can bring opposition to the feeders. We're in a position to punish them."

I nod.

The priest rests his hands on the pulpit. "As I look out, I see many unfamiliar faces. Travelers. Strangers. All united by a single cause—a single burden. I hope you find refuge and relief in this holy edifice."

His face darkens. "Before we proceed, brethren, I'd like to take a moment and address something that has weighed heavily on my heart. As you know, these are dark times, times foreseen by feeders of old."

He points his index finger at the chapel wall. "Out there, you will be bombarded with false teachings. There are those who claim to be Satan's servants. They *claim* to do his will, but they are deceived. They speak of the Devil's will, but they only destroy. They are instruments of death, nothing more. Do not be led astray when you hear their enticings. Ours is a greater cause. We are the Devil's elect. We must live to a higher standard."

He clutches the pulpit with white knuckles. "We do not feed with impunity. No! We seek out the wicked. We feed on the iniquitous, taking their sins upon us. Not just the sins of one, but the sins of many. As we feed upon the wicked, we become more than a man. We become many. We become Legion!"

He points at the audience, sweeping his hand in a slow arc. "Even now, you carry this impurity within you. We carry these sins in our memory. We relive them in our minds. It is an unrivaled offering. To save those around us, we sacrifice ourselves."

He turns, pointing at Satan's mural. "The Lord of Opposition sees our suffering. He has seen our sacrifice, and he has offered an escape. By his benevolence, we can be cleansed."

He raises his hands in the air. "Brethren, rise and come forward. It is time we cast out the Legions within us!"

A hooded figure enters the room, wearing a long black cloak. He holds a leather leash, dragging a hefty hog at his side. He guides it to the concrete alter—waiting as it steps up onto the stone block—and ties its collar to an iron ring. Then, he tosses the two leather bands over the pig and ties them on the other side. With a grunt, the hooded pig-handler tightens the straps, pinning down the pig like a Christmas tree on the roof of a car.

"Come," the priest directs. "Make a circle around the sacrificial swine."

Kildron moves quickly, joining the feeders around the altar. A stranger fills the space next to him.

"Kneel," the priest commands, "and place your right hand upon the sacrifice."

I'm last to join the circle. The only gap around the altar is at the hog's head.

I kneel. Elevated on the stone, the pig is at the level of my chest. Its eyes droop, looking at me beneath long blonde lashes. It oinks at me in quick, frantic snorts.

"Like this, my Lord." The hooded pig-handler takes my hand and lifts it, placing it on the very top of the hog's head.

"Now," the priest calls, "your cleansing can begin." His voice is calmer now, almost soothing—less like a preacher and more like a yoga instructor. "Look deep within yourselves. Find the sins of your victims. Find their iniquities—fragments of their wicked souls."

I watch Kildron across the altar. To my surprise, he bows his head and closes his eyes. I do the same.

"Remember the suffering those souls have caused. Think of the pain."

I think of Vyle. His memories are still there, just beneath the surface. I'm looking out of his eyes as his father screams, spittle flying from his face. I feel the sting of a slap.

Another memory. I see Rose. She's standing on a bridge as snow falls around her. The bridge collapses, and I watch as she disappears into the murky water. I don't hesitate. I reach out and freeze the surface. I watched as her cloudy outline appears beneath the water. She claws at the ice, but I do nothing. I want her to die.

"These memories are no longer your burden to bear," the priest hums. "They are not your sins. Let these fragments flow out of you and into the swine. Let the beast receive your iniquity. Let the swine cleanse you."

The pig shudders beneath my hand. It squeals louder.

A new memory arises. I'm in a room alone with Lynn. She's wearing her training uniform from the guard. She tries to run, but she's thrown back against the wall. I feel the satisfaction as I draw the air from her lungs. When she's pinned against the wall and powerless, I reach inside her shirt and watch her squirm.

I feel sick. My stomach twists, and I swallow the acid rising in my throat.

A hand touches my shoulder. It's the hooded pig-handler. "It's not yours to bear," he whispers. "Let it go."

I do. I reject the memory. I take hold of the guilt and push it as far away as possible. I push until it seeps out of my mind and into the swine. I do the same with the next memory, and the next. The rage for his father. The inadequacy. The pride. I reject it all.

"Now, your cleansing is completed by the spilling of blood. Amen."

Shlink.

I open my eyes too late. Blood gushes from the hog's throat. It pours down the altar and pools around my knees.

As soon as the hog stops squirming, the other feeders rise and make their way toward the exit.

Kildron claps me on the back. "Good stuff, right? Really clears the mind." He takes my arm and yanks me to my feet. "Don't worry about the blood. That stuff comes right out. Next time, avoid the head if you can."

"Kildron?" a voice whispers behind us.

Kildron slowly turns, facing the hooded pig-handler. The feeder removes his hood, revealing a tattooed face of Adamic armor—the first feeder I ever laid eyes on.

Hood.

Kildron's jaw drops open. "Mutalah?"

"Shhhh." Mutalah eyes the priest. "Not here. Come with me."

We follow him past the pew and into a new room. It's small with only a table and some bookshelves.

Kildron holds out his arms and embraces Mutalah.

Mutalah laughs. "They told me the Archangel lives, but I didn't believe them. How are you, old friend?"

"I'm good," Kildron says. "I'm back with my boy. He told me you saved him… I can't thank you enough."

"It's nothing," Mutalah says, his smile fading. "Opposition was due."

"You should come with us." Kildron says. "We're searching for Atlantia."

"To fight the Holy One?" Mutalah asks.

"Exactly. You've been spying for years. You know his secrets. You can help us."

"Not spying," Mutalah cringes. "Serving. He broke me, Kildron. He broke me a long time ago."

"But you got away," Kildron says. "You're here, aren't you? You can make amends."

"I did make amends," Mutalah hisses, his hands balled at his side. "I set your boy free. I risked everything. Opposition has been paid."

Kildron shakes his head. "That wasn't opposition. You were a pawn, Mutalah. Those prisoners you set free, they were possessed. They brought Heavenly Fire to Cavernum. The sanctuary is destroyed."

Mutalah shudders. "I… I didn't know."

"But now you do. Come with us. Set things right."

Mutalah shakes his head. "I can't. If he catches me… No! I can't go back."

"Please," Kildron begs. After a moment, his eyes harden. "How many deaths have you caused at his side? Hmmm? What about Opposition? The least you can do is give your life."

"He's not the same man that he was," Mutalah hisses. "I'm not afraid he'll kill me. I'm afraid that he won't." He points at his face, hand shaking. "When I first betrayed him, he sealed my eyelids shut for a month. I tried to cut them open, but he healed them closed again." His lips compress, and he exhales through his nose. "The second time I disobeyed, he sealed them open. I couldn't blink, Kildron. Day and night, I couldn't blink for a month. Do you know what that's like?"

Kildron looks down. "I'm sorry, Mutalah. I… I can't imagine."

Mutalah shudders. "I can't go back. I can't face him again." He holds up the sacrificial knife, still dripping with pig blood. "I'm a vessel of the church now. This is my calling. This is the best I can do."

Kildron nods. "I won't try to change your mind. It was nice to see you. Goodbye, Mutalah." He turns toward the door. "C'mon, Matt. There's nothing left for us here."

"If you kill him," Mutalah calls as we leave, "Don't make it quick. Make him suffer. Please... Make him suffer as I did."

I awake as a hand grasps mine beneath the sheets.

It takes me a second to remember where I am. We're at Kildron's penthouse in Seattle. He gave us his bed for the night, settling for the couch. He's out there, on the other side of the door, googling flights on Klinton's cell phone.

Kendra.

I let our fingers intertwine, tracing my thumb over hers.

I turn my head. The alarm clock reads 11:40 PM in neon green letters.

"Can't sleep?" I conclude.

"Not really," Kendra whispers beside me.

"I wasn't snoring, was I?"

Kendra grins. "No. It's not you. I just have a lot on my mind."

"Family?" I wonder. Her parents and little brother Decklin, are still in the palace, at the mercy of the Holy One.

"Yeah, that's part of it."

I roll over and flip a switch beside the bed. Instantly, a bedside lamp blinks to life, illuminating the bed like a theater production.

I prop myself up on my elbow, studying Kendra. She's wearing what I can only describe as a Victorian nightgown. The fabric is loose and distractingly low-cut. Her hair isn't curled, and she's not wearing makeup, but she's more intoxicating than I remember.

Her green eyes stare back at me, wide and alluring… and worried.

"Do you want to talk about it?" I ask.

"Not really."

"Anything else I can do to help?"

"Just cuddle me. I need a distraction."

"I can do that."

I slide closer, wrapping my arm over her side and across her chest. She tucks her knees, letting her hips fit in the crook of my waist.

"How's this?"

"Could be better…" Kendra teases.

"What?"

"I can't see you." She rolls to face me. Letting go of my hand, she reaches up and runs her fingers through my hair. "I missed this." She flattens her fingers together, letting my curls slip between them like falling sand.

"What? My hair?"

"Everything, but especially your hair." She caresses down the back of my head, tickling my scalp with her nails. The sensation sends chills down my spine. I tuck my chin and close my eyes, letting her scratch the back of my neck.

Suddenly, she stops, fingers retreating. "What did you miss most about me?" she asks with a grin. "And don't you dare say my personality. That's a given."

"Specifically physical?" I clarify.

"Yes! But not eyes or lips. That's too obvious."

My eyes wander downward.

"Nooo," she laughs. "Don't you dare. Your dad probably has his ear pressed against that door."

I don't know if I should laugh or cringe at the thought. "Okay. Fine. This is easy."

I point, tapping just below her nose. "This little dip right here."

"My philtrum?"

"Your what?"

She points to the same spot. "This ridge between the nasal septum and the upper lip. It's called the philtrum."

"Seriously?"

"Of course. It's a reservoir of extra skin, helping your lips stretch when you smile."

I lean in closer. "Have I ever told you I have a thing for nerds?"

She returns a thin-lipped grin. "All nerds?"

"Just you, nerd."

"Good." She scoots closer and closes her eyes, kissing me softly. Her legs move beneath the sheets, filling the space between us. She takes my hand and places it midway up her thigh. I can feel the thin seam of her nightgown. I let my thumb brush it aside, relishing the smoothness of her skin.

The door handle to the bedroom suddenly turns. Kildron doesn't knock, but chooses instead to say the words aloud. "Knock, knock. Coming in."

By the time he opens the door, we've rolled apart, lying innocently on our backs. Kendra blushes, and my face feels warm as well.

Kildron looks down at his phone as he walks in. "Alright. I found a flight to Miami. It leaves at 6:15 in the morning, so we need to leave here around 4:00 in the morning." He looks up, eyes oscillating between the two of us. He grins. "Don't stay up all night, okay? And no noise! I'll be in to wake you up at 3:30. Okay? Goodnight."

"Goodnight," I echo as he closes the door.

Immediately, Kendra rolls back toward me, nuzzling her head into the crook of my neck. She drapes one knee over my legs and rests her hand on my chest.

She looks up at me with glistening eyes. I watch as they flicker down to my mouth. Her lips part as she lifts her chin. At the last second, she veers to the side, finding my ear instead of my mouth. "We should probably get some sleep," she breathes softly.

I shake my head, smiling. "You're such a tease."

She flashes a mischievous smile. "A tease?" She feigns offense. "If I wanted to tease you, I would start with a healing massage." She laughs at the looks on my face. "I'm guessing you've heard of it?"

"You're bluffing!" I mutter.

She shrugs. "I guess you'll never know."

"Oh, yeah? Two can play that game." I roll over, displacing Kendra from her place at my side. Then, I pounce on top of her. I pin her within the sheet, one knee to either side of her rib cage.

As I move, the bed creaks loudly.

"I can hear that!" Kildron calls from the other room.

We both freeze for several seconds. Kendra stares up at me, challenging me with a smile. "You have me," she whispers. "What are you gonna do with me?"

Slowly, carefully, I take her hands in mine. I stretch them above her head, and press them into the mattress, one on top of the other. Then, I pinch the invisibility ring and tug it off her thumb. Before she can protest, I slip it on my finger and twist.

Immediately, I disappear from sight. She can see the indent of my knees on the mattress, and she can feel my weight, but she can't see my hands.

"Don't move," I command quietly.

Her eyes dance around the room, looking right through me, but she doesn't move a muscle. She's tense, anticipating the unseen contact.

I reach for her face. As soon as my fingers touch her cheeks, she disappears from view—an extension of the spell.

I don't mind. I drag the tip of my fingers, blindly feeling the contour of her features. She shivers as my fingers graze lightly along her neck. I lift the delicate chain of her amplifier, tracing underneath. Following the path of the chain, I caress softly over her collarbone, stopping at the seam of her nightgown.

I lift my hands, watching as she materializes.

"That's it?" She whispers, eyes half closed.

I take her hands in mine, interlocking our fingers. "I'm just getting started," I assure her.

I shift my weight forward, leaning toward her lips.

Creaaaak!

"I can hear that!" Kildron calls.

I ignore him. Moving slower this time, I let my lips brush hers. At first, she doesn't move. Then, her lips twitch, and her chin lifts ever so slightly. I kiss her again, tantalizingly slow. Finally, when she opens her mouth to kiss me back, I retreat.

"We should probably get some sleep," I whisper, twisting the ring and rolling off her.

Kendra furrows her brow as I roll off her. "Oh, you're mean."

"You asked for it." I say.

"So," Kendra whispers. "I'll see you in my dream then?"

I straighten the blanket and rest my head on the pillow. "I'll be right there."

We lay in silence. Within a minute, Kendra's breathing grows louder, and I know she's asleep—with the help of self-dominion, I assume. I focus on my breathing, letting my body relax. Now, all I have to do is let my soul drift.

BAM!

The door to our room flies open, punching a hole in the drywall with the doorknob. Immediately, Kendra startles awake, taking hold of my arm.

"Up! Up! Up!" Kildron shouts as he rushes the bed. He grabs my hand, yanking me out of the sheets. "We're under attack! To the balcony now!"

Kendra grabs her duffel bag, and we all stumble onto the balcony. It's a cold night, and the wind whips through my hair. Kendra's nightgown flutters like a superhero cape.

Kildron grabs Kendra's arm. "Invisible, now!"

"I have it," I remember, twisting the ring to align the symbols.

CRASH!

The front door blasts inward, tossed from its hinges. Through the window, I see a flurry of black cloaks charging into the apartment.

I take Kendra and Kildron by the hand, extending the spell of invisibility. They disappear on contact.

"We jump on 'three,'" Kildron says.

The railing easily reaches my waist. And we're on the 28th story.

"But—"

"Just do it," Kildron barks. "One. Two. Three!"

I take two steps and leap over the railing, smacking my shins on the iron bar. Then, we plummet.

The world rushes by, and my stomach rises into my throat. A primitive part of my brain begins to panic as the wind screams in my ear.

Suddenly, gravity flips upside down. Something tugs in my gut, slowing my fall. Next thing I know, we're drifting downward like a dandelion on the wind. Windows flash in and out of view, and the traffic below us slowly gets bigger.

After a minute of drifting, my feet land softly on the sidewalk.

Keeping a tight hold on Kildron and Kendra, I turn to look up at the balcony we just leapt from. To my surprise, a figure is on the balcony, looking down in our general direction. From this distance, I can't see much, but I do see her blonde pixie-cut.

Iris.

"Come on," Kildron says, pulling us down the street. "Let's get some distance. Then we'll find a taxi."

I pull back. "But… it's Iris. Maybe we can talk to her—make her come to her senses."

"Don't you get it?" Kildron shouts, shaking my arm. "She's hunting us. She'll kill us if she gets the chance!" He sighs, rubbing his temples. "You can't be so naive, Matt. We're at war. You have to be ready to do the same."

16

ROSE

Two days! It took Antai two days to reach out. His servant delivered the letter this morning. It wasn't Antai's handwriting, but they're his words—artistically concise.

Rose,

I have a little surprise for you today. Meet me in my quarters at noon.

Love,
Antai

He signed it with '*Love.*' That's a good sign, right?

I pause outside his door, teasing my hair one last time. I'm wearing a flared A-line dress with my amulet tucked underneath the collar. The fabric is forest green, with a bow that cinches around my waist.

I knock. "Can I come in?"

"One second," Antai calls.

To my surprise, the handle turns and the door swings open on its own, accompanied with the subtle ripples of force dominion.

Antai isn't in his bed. He's sitting in a wheelchair from the Beyond, complete with black leather and a stainless steel frame.

His hair—uncut since his coma—is washed and parted down the middle. He must have shaved, because there are no signs of stubble from the previous night. He's wearing a gray colored shirt with the sleeves folded up above his elbows. His slacks are recently hemmed to match his shortened legs.

"Antai," I gasp. "You look… great."

"Thanks, you look beautiful yourself. I like the bow, by the way."

"No really, Antai!" I look him over once more. "You look amazing. How did you…?"

"Nevela helped with the sewing, " he explains. "And my servant did the shaving and the buttons. The rest I managed on my own. You were right. With enough patience, a little dominion can go a long way."

"How long did it take you?"

His grin fades. "Three hours, give or take, but this is just the beginning," he quickly adds. "I'll get better the more I practice."

"This is big, Antai. Honestly, I'm blown away."

"Don't be. It's just the basics." He waves his arm, and the air ripples behind the wheelchair. With a sudden lurch, it pushes him into the center of the room.

"Where'd you get the wheelchair?" I wonder

"It was King Dralton's, believe it or not. They were worried his cane wouldn't be enough."

He looks down, staring at his elbows. "Hey Rose, I'm sorry about what I said the other day. I didn't mean it. I wasn't thinking straight, but I'm better now."

"You were processing. You still are. You don't have to apologize," I say.

"Yes, I do," he insists. "The things I said…" he shakes his head. "I'm sorry. Do you forgive me?"

"Of course."

"Thank you." He looks at me over again, eyes tracing the curves of my dress. "You ready?"

"Absolutely," I say, simply glad to change the subject. "Where are we going?"

"The library, but it's nothing too special, okay? Keep your expectations low." Already, Antai's wheelchair is rolling toward the door, propelled by dominion. The air ripples around the handle, and the door swings open.

"After you," Antai says, nodding his head at the doorway.

I step into the hallway and turn to watch as Antai follows behind me.

He rolls a few feet when his wheels bump the bottom of the doorframe. The doorsill is merely an inch thick, but it's enough to stop him in his tracks.

I step closer, but Antai shakes his head. "Don't worry, I've got it." The air reverberates behind Antai, forcing the wheelchair over the wooden slat and nearly tipping the chair in the process.

As his wheelchair coasts to a stop, Antai squirms to reposition himself properly. "See. That wasn't so bad."

"You're sure you don't want me to push you?"

"Positive," Antai insists.

We don't talk as we travel down the hallway. He's too focused on maneuvering his wheelchair with dominion.

Before long, we arrive at the Central Staircase. To reach the library, we have to descend a massive flight of polished marble steps.

"Wait here," I suggest. "I'll get some guards to help you down."

Antai doesn't listen. His wheelchair is already airborne. The air below him quivers as he hovers above the stairs.

"Antai!"

If he hears me, he gives no indication. His eyes are squeezed shut, and his neck muscles bulge from focus.

His wheelchair floats out over the staircase, descending parallel to the steps so that he's never more than a few feet in the air. At first, he moves smoothly… confidently.

"See," Antai gloats, "nothing to worry about."

Eyes still shut, he descends quickly, catching the rear wheels on the bottom step. Limbs flail as he topples out of the leather seat and tumbles onto the marble landing.

"Antai!" I race after him, descending the steps in seconds. Crouching by his side, I gingerly flip him onto his back.

"Oof!" Antai laughs. "I'm sorry you had to see that." He brushes the hair out of his eyes using the stub of his wrist.

Perhaps it's relief, or maybe it's the contagious sound of his cackle, but I burst into laughter.

We laugh on the floor until a guard marches past. The man stops and stares with a gaping mouth, utterly bewildered by the scene.

Antai suddenly grows serious. "Nothing to see here, Soldier. Get a move on!"

The soldier hesitates before resuming his patrol. He cranes his neck to get one last look before rounding the corner and marching out of sight.

"Okay," I say. "Let's get you up, before someone else sees us." I grab his wheelchair, which appears to be in one piece, and set it upright. A moment later, Antai levitates himself into the air and plops into his seat.

We continue down the hall and turn into the library. The librarian, Miss Wrongfein, lifts her head as we enter, a surprised smile engulfing her face. "Oh, you made it." She quickly collects a small stack of books and gives Antai a sharp nod. "I'll go ahead and give you two some privacy. Enjoy."

Antai smiles graciously back at her. "Thank you, Miss Wrongfein. I appreciate it."

"My pleasure." She waddles past us and shuts the library door on her way out.

Looking around, I don't see a single soul. "Antai? What's going on?" An empty library is an anomaly. There's always someone—at least a lawyer perusing some legal text.

"It's nothing too crazy. Miss Wrongfein was nice enough to restrict library access for the afternoon. No one should be interrupting us."

"You reserved the Library? I didn't know that was a thing."

"It's not, but she made an exception. How do you say no to this?" Antai lifts his elbow stumps into the air. "C'mon, this way."

He wheels himself between a row of bookshelves and turns left when we reach the poetry section. Finally, he stops at a small table positioned by the wall. Arranged on the table are two bottles of wine, two glasses, and something box-shaped covered by a cloth. A small candle is lit in the middle.

"Did you…?"

"I didn't," he says. "It was my idea, but Nevela was my hands on this one. Like I said, it's not much. I figured you could use a break from everything going on. Just an hour to clear your mind. Go ahead, take a seat."

There's only one chair. I take a seat as Antai wheels himself to the edge of the table. "Would you like a drink? We have a Cranberry Riesling and a Fragola with afternotes of strawberry."

"Yes and yes."

I reach for the Reisling, but it levitates into the air before I can grab it.

"Allow me," Antai insists. The air reverberates around the cork, but it doesn't pull free.

I reach for the corkscrew bottle opener. "If you want, I can—"

"I've got it," Antai says, his eyes narrow in concentration.

As he battles with the cork, I can't help but peer out the window. The courtyard is gorgeous, even in its recent neglect. Snow blankets the ground, blurring the border between garden and footpath. Copper statues of our founding prophet are sparsely distributed around the courtyard along with bubbling Adamic fountains that have somehow survived the freeze.

A small mob of children is running around the yard, throwing snowballs and making snow monsters.

By one of the fountains, Bob is gathered with his posse of Equalists—30 or 40 of them. They're manipulating the water, lifting it in the air and reshaping it with dominion.

Tshhh!

I flinch as the neck of the bottle shatters around the cork, raining glass and frothy wine onto the tablecloth.

"Piece of shit!" The air ripples as Antai slams the remainder of the bottle onto the ground. Then, the air reverberates across the table, sweeping the glass fragments onto the floor.

"I'll clean that up later," Antai grumbles.

"You know," I say, "a strawberry afternote sounds pretty enticing right now."

I reach for the wine, but it's already airborne. The space around the bottle vibrates, applying pressure from all sides. Antai's brow furrows.

"Antai, are you sure…"

"I've got it."

"Maybe it's best if—"

POP!

The cork launches out of the bottle, ricocheting off an encyclopedia and bouncing across the floor.

"There we go," Antai beams. "Told you I had it."

With narrowed eyes, Antai levitates the bottle and tips it over my glass. At first, it pours onto the table, but Antai quickly adjusts, catching the rest of the wine in my glass. He pours his glass next, spilling only a few drops this time.

Using dominion, he raises his glass in the air. "Cheers!"

"Cheers."

I softly clink our glasses, careful not to knock the glass out of his control.

I sip first. The wine is sweet and tart, almost making my mouth pucker. I take a gulp, letting the acidity coat my throat.

"Are you kidding me!"

I look up to see a river of red wine pouring down Antai's neck and pooling in his lap. The glass still hovers in the air next to his head.

"Here, let me help." I reach out with my mind, finding the moisture in his clothes.

Evaporate!

Small tendrils of steam flow from his shirt and dissipate in the air.

Unfortunately, the steam leaves behind the red dye, staining the fabric in horrendous red blotches.

I cringe. "Sorry, I think I made it worse."

"It's fine. I'll probably spill again." He lifts the bottle with dominion and refills his glass, several more drops splashing onto the table.

I stand. "Here, what if I help?"

"No! If I spill, I spill. I have to learn for myself."

"Or, you could let me help you, just this once."

"I don't want your help, Rose."

I roll my eyes. "Don't be so stubborn, Antai. C'mon, Just let me help."

"No. I didn't come back from the dead so you could hand feed me, okay?"

"It's not a big deal, Antai. Just—"

"No!" he barks. "I refuse to be a burden, okay? I'm doing this myself."

I stare at him, my nostrils flaring. "Is that what I am to you?" I ask. "A burden?"

Antai frowns. "What are you talking about?"

"You said that you don't want my help because you don't want to be a burden. Well, what does that make me? All you ever do is help me. You coached me for The Dividing. You saved me from a riot. You rescued me from an assassin. You're always helping me, Antai. By that logic, I must be a burden to you!"

"Don't make this a big thing, Rose."

Already, I can feel my frustration building behind my eyes. "You do so much for me, and I don't do anything for you, ever. And now, when you actually need my help, you won't let me near you."

"It's not like that, Rose."

"Well, that's what it feels like," I say. "I just want to help you. It's not a burden; I want to, Antai. But you'd rather pour wine down your shirt than accept my help."

Antai looks down at the stain on his shirt. "I just… I feel useless, okay? I don't expect you to understand. No matter what I do, I'll never be who I used to be. When you used to look at me, Rose, I saw admiration. Now, you pity me. I can see it in your eyes. All I want is for you to look at me the way you used to."

I take a deep breath, choosing my words carefully. "I think I get what you're saying, Antai, and… I can see why you would feel that way. I really do. But I want to make one thing clear. You are the same person. The important stuff hasn't changed. You're still you. You're still thoughtful and caring and brave. Even now, you're doing nice things for me, and it makes me mad, Antai. You deserve better. I don't pity you; I pity myself."

"Rose—"

"No!" I interject. "I need to say this. When I look at you, I feel inadequate. I know deep down that, if I were ever in your position, I wouldn't be half as strong as you are. I wouldn't be half as hopeful. I mean look at you. It's been two days and you're taking me on a date. I think I'm afraid that, someday down the road, you'll realize I'm the weak link. Even at your lowest, you don't need me. And I need you constantly."

I sniffle, refusing to cry this time. "The only thing I could offer was a crown, and now I've lost that too… literally." I laugh, more at myself than anything. "And now, somehow, I've gone and made this about myself. God, I'm so egocentric! How do you even put up with me?"

"It's tough." Antai grins mischievously. "I'm not gonna lie, it's a real burden being the beautiful, intelligent, heroic queen's crippled paramour, but you know what? You can make it a little more bearable by pouring some of that sweet succulent wine down my throat."

I smile, relief rushing through me. Once again, he's coming to my rescue, repairing my insecurities.

"You're sure?" I ask.

"Positive."

I stand and make my way to his side. I pick up the glass in one hand and wait for his lips to mold on the lower rim. Finally, I tilt it slowly, watching his throat move as he gulps it down.

"More?" I ask.

"That's good for now, thanks."

"No, thank you!" I look around the library, relishing the quaint atmosphere. "I needed this. It's a nice change of pace, Antai. Really."

"This isn't even the best part," Antai says, eyeing the mysterious, cloth-covered item. "Should I unveil it, or you? Actually, you do it. I could use the help." He grins and gives me a quick wink.

"What is it?" I wonder, reaching for the cloth.

"You'll see. Go ahead."

I lift the cloth. Underneath is a rectangular wooden box, about the size of a loaf of bread. Extending from the box is a metal crank. A small piece of parchment, which I immediately recognize as sheet music, is extending from beneath the box.

I lift the box and remove the sheet music, holding it up to my face. The notes are relatively sparse—a simple tune by the looks of it.

"A few days ago," Antai explains. "I was going through some of Dralton's belongings. You wouldn't leave the wall, so I figured I'd organize it myself. I found some old music in his closet. Look at the bottom."

My eyes skip to the bottom of the page. *Violet Malik* is scribbled in my mother's handwriting.

"My mom wrote this," I gasp. I jump to the top of the parchment and find the title: *My Little Flower.*

"I was going to give it to you a few days ago," Antai says, "but I thought I'd make it a surprise, so I talked to Winx."

Winx is the palace luthier. Nearly every instrument in the orchestra is a product of his hands.

"Go ahead. Open it," Antai instructs.

I lift the lid. Inside is a circular bronze disk with small nodules dotting the surface.

I blink. "Stop… you didn't!"

"Give it a crank."

I turn the handle once and let go. As the metal plate begins to spin, a soft, chiming melody fills the library.

I close my eyes as the music box plays. The melody is gentle and soothing—perhaps a lullaby. I don't say a word until the music falls silent.

"Thank you, Antai."

"It's nothing," he says. "I'm glad you like it."

"I love it." *It's perfect.* I stare at him, relishing his dark hair and copper eyes.

"Remember that question you asked me the other day?"

Antai narrows his eyes. "Which one?"

"Why I don't say 'I love you.'"

"I'm sorry," Antai says. "Like I said, I wasn't thinking straight."

"No, it's a valid question," I insist. "I've been thinking about it the last few days, and I think I finally have an answer."

He raises an eyebrow. "Really?"

I nod. "I'm not trying to be convoluted, but I think 'I love you' can mean a lot of different things. For some, it's simply a way to show their feelings… Maybe for most, actually. And that's fair. But for me, it feels more like a promise. It's like… it's like I'm giving you my future, when I'm not even sure I have a future to give. Does that make sense?"

Antai furrows his brow. "I think so…"

"I do love you," I affirm. "More than I've ever loved anyone. I love everything about you, but the words just don't feel right sometimes. I want to say it, but I can't get myself to make that commitment. I can't know for sure if I'll always love you… or if I'll always have you to love." I sigh. "I probably sound crazy, but that's how I think of it."

"It makes sense," Antai insists. "Thank you. I think I get it now."

My eyes wander to his wine-stained lips. I fake a frown, standing from my chair. "Hold on. I think you've got something on your face." Cringing at how cheesy it sounds.

Antai doesn't seem to mind. "Oh really? I think you better get it for me."

"I think I will." I reach out and gently drag my thumb along his lip.

He looks up at me, his voice playful. "Did you get it?"

"Not quite."

It feels strange, stooping for a kiss, but I enjoy the novelty. I tip his head back and lower my lips until they find his. The kiss starts slow—timid, uncertain. When it ends, I kiss him again, letting my lower lip fall between his teeth. With each kiss, the speed intensifies.

Taking the lead, I swing my leg over Antai and straddle the entire wheelchair, the crook of my knee pressing into the armrest. If my weight bothers Antai, he gives no indication.

I let the weight of my chest lean into him, and his lips dance along my jawline.

"I missed this," I pant.

"What about this?" His lips find my earlobe, gently tugging with his teeth.

"Mmmhmm,"

"And this?" He makes his way down my neck, lingering on my collarbone. His breath sends shivers down my spine.

"Especially that." My hands reach for the back of his head. Instinctually, I arch my back and guide his mouth lower. I tug on his triceps, pulling his arms around me. The nubs of his forearms bend around my ribs. As soon as they make contact, Antai goes rigid. His arms lower back to his side, and his mouth seals shut.

"Sorry," he says. "It just… it feels weird."

"Did I do something wrong?" I worry, climbing off his lap.

"No, it wasn't you. It's just… I don't know…"

"What?"

"I don't know if I can do this, Rose. I'm trying, but… I don't have arms. I can't touch you. I can't hold your hand."

"I don't care."

"But I do!" Antai's voice grows louder. "I do care, Rose. Dominion is nice, but what about the future? What if we have children someday? Am I gonna levitate them through the air? I won't even be able to hold them. I… I don't think I want that. You… they deserve better."

My heart sinks, and I feel like my lungs are too heavy to breathe. I gesture at the table. "There's nothing better than this. You might not believe it, but you are the best, arms or not."

"I don't know," Antai sighs.

"Well, I do," I insist. "If it makes you feel any better, we can take it day by day. No promises. Just—"

BANG!

A gunshot erupts from somewhere outside.

I dash to the window and immediately spot the commotion. A mass of guardsmen surrounds Bob's posse of Equalists. Their guns are raised, fingers on the trigger.

The Equalists don't surrender. An energy field ripples around the Equalists forming a dome of protection.

I've seen enough.

"I'm going down there. Wait here." I take off through the bookshelves, dashing for the exit.

"Rose—"

I can't hear him anymore. I burst out of the library and race down the staircase. As I reach the bottom floor, I almost run into Diego.

"What's going on? I heard a gunshot," he huffs.

"It's the Equalists." I say as I run for the courtyard. "They're fighting the guard."

He follows a step behind me as we push through the doors and stumble into the courtyard snow.

The scene is exactly as I left it. The dome-shaped shield is still intact, and the Equalists huddle together at its center.

"This is your last chance!" a woman shouts. "If you surrender now, you won't be charged for any crimes." She has amber hair and freckles sprinkle her pale face. I recognize her instantly.

"Crasilda, what are you doing?"

She rolls her eyes. "What does it look like? I'm enforcing the law."

"The queen gave us these amulets," Bob calls back. "What right do you have to take them away?"

"The queen may have given them to you," Crasilda says, "but the High Council demands you return them at once."

"The High Council says no such thing," I assert.

"How would you know?" Crasilda sneers. "You're not on the council, are you?"

"Antai would've told me."

"They met without him last night," Crasilda explains. "He was still unconscious. Not that he would've made a difference. The vote was five to one."

"You're lying."

"You're pathetic," Crasilda snaps back. "Just stay out of my way."

Crasilda faces the Equalists once more. "I'm not warning you again. So long as you hold an amulet, you're an active threat. You will be met with lethal force. I'll count to three. One..."

No one removes their amulet.

"Two..." Electricity crackles on the tip of her fingers. Crasilda raises her hand, pointing her fingers at the Equalists.

"Three!"

I see a silver blur as Diego dives forward. His metallic hand closes around Crasilda's fingers at the precise moment she releases the lightning.

KA-KRACK!

The lighting redirects in a brilliant flash of blue, surging through Diego's arm and dispersing into the snow at his feet. Immediately, his hand squeezes, crushing all four of Crasilda's fingers. She opens her mouth to scream as Diego's left fist smashes into her jaw.

Tunk!

Her body goes limp, and her eyes roll back. She hardly makes a sound as she slumps into the snow.

Diego, his skin fully encased in titanium, turns to face the guardsmen. He backpedals until his shoulder blades press against the energy shield, eliciting several small ripples from the dome. "If you want to get to them, you'll have to go through me," he growls.

Silence ensues as two guardsmen retrieve Crasilda's body. She's not just unconscious, she's disfigured. Her jaw is twisted at an odd angle—either broken or dislocated—and I can spot a few of her teeth in the snow. Bloody drool drips from her mouth and down her cheek.

The guardsmen glance at each other, noticeably uneasy. Then, they drag her away from the battlefield.

For a moment, no one moves. Then, a brave guardsman takes hold of his amplifier.

WOOOSH!

A fireball engulfs Diego's torso. At the sight, the other guardsmen find their courage.

BANG! BANG! BANG!

They fire into the fireball. Others fire at the Equalists, their bullets deflecting off the energy shield sporadically.

"Stop!" Antai's shouts. His wheelchair slowly drags through the snow, pushed with dominion. Leaving a trail like a sled, he rolls himself until he's alongside the guardsmen.

"Let's talk about this," Antai suggests. He surveys the Equalists, doing a mental tally. "You're clearly outnumbered, three men to one. Fighting will only mean casualties. Just put down the amulets."

"We won't," Bob bellows. "Without an amulet, we're as good as dead."

Antai shakes his head. "No harm will come to you, I promise. The guard will keep you safe."

Bob chuckles. "You don't get it, boy. The feeders aren't the danger. You are the danger. The *guard* is the danger. You're the cat, and we're the mouse. We're trapped in a cage with a predator, and these amulets are all we have to defend ourselves."

Antai shakes his head. "You have my word, you will not be harmed if you surrender."

Bob frowns. "A cat may not eat the mouse right away, but you'll play with us. You'll toss us around for your own entertainment. We won't go back to being subservient."

"Bob, please." Antai rolls closer. "Tell them to surrender. We can't lose anyone else." He rolls a little further.

Diego steps in front of the wheelchair. By the time Antai stops, the wheelchair is inches from Diego's knees.

Diego glares down at Antai. "That's close enough," his voice warbles, distorted by his metal mouth.

Antai grits his teeth. "Stand down, Ortega."

Diego's fingers tighten into a fist. "Now's our chance," he whispers just loud enough that I overhear. "We can take control right now. You're the only other Guardian. We can seize the council."

Antai shakes his head. "I can't let that happen. This isn't a coup; it's civil war. There would be casualties, more than I can live with."

"You're worried about casualties?" Diego raises his voice. "Then tell your men to back off."

Antai clenched his jaw. "I can't do that."

"Can't, or won't?" Diego demands.

"I like you, Ortega; so I'll give you one more chance." Antai grumbles. "Stand down, or I'll have no choice but to arrest you."

Diego narrows his metal eyelids. "I'd like to see you try."

"Antai," I warn. Sure, he has a soul-anchor—a monumental advantage—but he's also limbless.

"You asked for it," Antai says.

Immediately, the snow liquefies around Diego's feet, gathering around his ankles and climbing up his body. Once his shoulders and arms are engulfed, the water freezes into a life-sized ice sculpture. Only Diego's head is exposed.

Diego closes his eyes, and the surface of the ice begins to steam around him.

Antai narrows his eyes as well, and a vein bulges in his forehead. Suddenly, the ice stops steaming as Antai doubles down on his command. No matter how hard Diego tries, Antai's dominion is stronger.

"Diego Ortega," Antai proudly declares, "you are under arrest for defying your superior."

"Ahhhh!" Diego strains against the ice, his neck muscles swelling with effort."

"It's over, Ortega. Don't make this worse for yourself."

Suddenly, a small crack splits down the ice, stretching from Diego's collarbone down to his knee. "Ahhh!" With a cry, Diego's arms burst from the ice, large chunks falling free around his waist.

Then, Diego charges.

17

ROSE

Diego charges at Antai, halving the distance in a few quick strides. He dives at Antai as the air ripples between them.

Immediately, Diego impacts an invisible wall, first with his hands and then with his head. His wrists buckle and his neck hyperextends.

As soon as he hits the snow, Diego is back on his feet. He reaches for his waist and draws an Adamic blade.

Antai lifts his elbow, and the air ripples between them, launching Diego backward.

He slides across the snow until his metal scalp crashes into one of the fountains. The tiles crack, and water begins to leak from the basin, pouring over his metal frame and flooding the snow covered path beneath him.

Before Diego can stand, the water freezes, trapping him on his back. This time, the ice is several times thicker. Not even Diego could muscle his way out.

For a moment, I worry the Equalists will come to his aid, but they remain in the safety of their energy dome.

Antai furrows his brow, wheeling closer to Diego. "Surrender. You've already lo—"

KA-BOOM!

The ice around Diego explodes in all directions. The portion of the fountain closest to Diego is obliterated as well, sending ice and ceramic shrapnel through the air. A guardsman cries out as a ceramic shard pierces his uniform. Another screams and claws at his eyes. A few of the windows facing the courtyard shatter.

Diego crawls from the small bomb crater left in the ice. I'm surprised he didn't kill himself—once again saved by his titanium skin.

In a single motion, Diego bends down and grabs a broken slab of concrete from the fountain. Metallic muscles bulging, he heaves it in the air.

The slab soars high over Antai's head. By the looks of it, Diego was significantly off target. Unless, he wasn't aiming for the wheelchair.

Antai almost realizes too late. He forms an energy shield above his head seconds before the slab explodes, launching fragments in all directions.

This time the onlookers are prepared. The guardsmen easily deflect the shrapnel with dominion.

Diego is already in motion. He unleashes a stream of fire, but Antai redirects it to either side. The flames lick at the snow, sending steam into the air.

Diego follows the steam with his eyes. His lips peel into a steely smile. He closes his eyes and lets the fireball dissolve. A second later, the snow around Antai sizzles. A plume of boiling-hot steam erupts into the air. It smothers Antai, rising in a tortuous pillar above his head.

"Ahh!" Antai squeezes his eyes shut, trying to shield his face with his amputated arms. Then, he disappears from view as the steam cloud grows denser.

Diego pounces like a jungle cat. He dives through the steam cloud and crashes into Antai's wheelchair. Emerging from the opposite end, they both go tumbling through the snow.

My stomach plummets, and my heart races. Antai is lying on his back in the slush, staring at the sky. He tries to sit up, but he only manages to lift his thighs in the air. He's a turtle, trapped upside down on his shell.

Diego pounces, dagger tip pointed downward. He's still airborne when the snow rises to meet him—not just the snow, but the frozen soil underneath. A glob of earth—easily the size of a hay bale—smashes into Diego's chest, throwing him backwards. This time, he lands beside a copper statue of the Prophet Johediah.

Antai finally rolls to his stomach.

Diego does the same, climbing to his feet. This time, he doesn't charge. Instead he reaches out and takes hold of the statue.

Immediately, the metal copper begins to melt. It doesn't glow orange, but it flows as if it were molten. It oozes up Diego's fingers and collects in a sphere in his right palm. As the metal sphere grows, it envelopes his hand and wrist, now reaching the size of a honeydew.

The air reverberates beneath Antai as he lifts himself into a seated position in the snow. He remains on the ground as he watches Diego approach.

Diego walks slowly, swinging his right hand like a wrecking ball. His left hand clutches his Adamic blade.

With each swing, the metal glob in Diego's hand begins to elongate. It oozes onto the ground, stretching into a thin, cylindrical cord. It trails behind him, elongating in the snow. Eight feet. Ten feet. Twelve feet.

Diego raises his hand above his head and swings it forward.

CRACK!

The copper cord behaves like a whip, snapping forward and cracking against Antai's energy shield. Diego gives two more swings, sweeping his arm in long strokes.

CRACK! CRACK!

The air ripples with each impact. Diego smiles. He isn't trying to attack. *He's simply warming up.*

Satisfied, Diego steps back. He picks up the far end of his whip and coils it around the handle of his Adamic Dagger. The metal oozes, molding to the grooves of the handle. Then, Diego charges.

He swings the dagger-tipped whip in a long arc, whipping it through the air and slicing through Antai's energy shield. The dagger dip pierces the snow inches from Antai's thigh.

The air reverberates between them, and Diego once again tumbles backward, cartwheeling twice across the snow. Somehow, he keeps hold of the whip.

Diego stands and rushes again, only to meet another blast of force dominion. He slides some 15 feet before crashing through the base of a crudely constructed snow monster.

Despite it all, Diego is unphased. He pushes himself to his feet, still gripping his bladed whip, and shakes the snow from his shoulders. It's subtle, but a shadow sweeps over his metallic skin. The titanium grows a shade darker—slightly less reflective. If I'm not mistaken, he sinks deeper into the snow. When he takes a step, his foot compresses the frozen soil.

Tungsten!

Diego charges again. This time, he takes longer to pick up speed. His movements are slower… strained even.

The air ripples, yet Diego doesn't go flying. As his torso lurches backwards, his feet remain planted in the snow. He takes another step forward.

Another force wave slams into Diego. He stumbles back a step, but only slows for a second. Already, he's within range. He swings the whip.

"No!" I shriek.

At the last second, the snow beneath Antai lurches, dragging his body with it. He slides himself to the side as the dagger chops the soil where he sat a moment prior.

Diego pulls the whip back and swings again. This time, Antai is ready. The snow molds around his limbs, creating an icy exoskeleton.

As the dagger whistles through the air, the snow drags Antai out of its path.

Diego swings again, but Antai predicts the trajectory once more. The snow pulls him back— no more than a foot out of reach.

With a cry, Diego swings again, lunging forward. This time, he sweeps the whip horizontally above the snow. The Adamic blade whistles behind Antai, overshooting him by several feet.

The snow starts to lift Antai into the air, but it's too slow. The metal cord catches his thighs, wrapping twice all the way around him. As if it has a mind of its own, the metal constricts.

Diego doesn't waste a second. Like a fish on the line, Diego drags Antai backwards. Then, he spins in a circle, his feet drilling a hole deeper and deeper into the snow.

As Diego spins, Antai swings around and around, like a moon in orbit. The centripetal force keeps Antai nearly horizontal, his head skimming just above the snow.

On Antai's third rotation, something silver glitters as it skips across the snow.

No!

Diego releases the whip, and Antai rolls to a stop. He looks around frantically until he spots his soul-anchor. It shines in the sunlight, chain resting delicately atop the snow. With no other options, Antai starts crawling on his stomach toward the soul-anchor.

The crowd watches as he makes painful progress, grunting with exertion, thighs dragging in the snow as he army crawls on severed elbows.

As Antai approaches his amulet, I hold my breath. Any second now, I expect Diego to attack, but he doesn't move a muscle. He watches Antai's progress with a mix of curiosity and pity.

Finally, Antai is within reach. He collapses to his stomach and extends his severed arms. With a face half buried in the snow, he pinches the amulet between the two nubs. As he lifts it, the soul-anchor slips, disappearing beneath the snow. Antai starts to dig, clawing at the snow with his amputated arms. With each scoop of his arm, he only knocks it deeper.

"It's over, Elsborne," Diego gloats. "Don't make this worse for yourself." He lifts his head, scanning the crowd of guardsmen. "Anyone else? Anyone else think they can take away our amulets?"

The guardsmen share timid looks. They've already watched two Guardians fail. They would be foolish to try their luck.

Some of the men look at me, expecting me to intervene, and maybe I should, but what's the point? What would I gain?

"That's what I thought," Diego snaps. "Lay a hand on us, and you'll regret it."

Hesitantly, the Equalists let go of their amplifiers, and the energy dome dissolves. Slowly, they begin to disperse. The guard doesn't stop them.

"No!" Antai keeps digging in the snow, growing more and more frantic as the crowd scatters. "Stop them. It's not over yet!"

Most of the guardsmen head back to their stations, but several pause to watch Antai dig. There's intrigue in their gaze, but mostly, I see pity.

I push through the beads, scanning the loft for Madame Xantone.

"Hello, Your Majesty," A healer calls from the back room. "How can we help you?"

"I'm looking for Madame Xantone."

"Unfortunately, she's not on-duty right now."

I frown. "You're sure? I thought she works today."

The healer hesitates. "That is true, yes… but she didn't come in today. I can take a message if you'd like."

"No thanks, it's a personal matter." I came to invite her to my secret meeting in two days.

"As you wish," the healer replies.

"Do you know why she's out today? Is she feeling sick?" I ask, fearing the worst. *She created the plague. What if she exposed herself?*

The healer frowns. "Actually, to tell you the truth, I haven't heard from her."

"Well, if you see her, tell her I'm looking for her."

"Oh course, Your Majesty."

I'm about to leave when I hear a muffled scream coming from one of the back rooms—a private healing suite for the High Council.

I step closer and push through the beads.

"Gaaaah!" Crasilda groans through gritted teeth. Her mouth is covered in dried blood, and some red-stained drool runs down the corner of her mouth.

A woman I recognize, the dental specialist, sits at the head of the bed, cupping Crasilda's jaw with both of her hands. Already, she looks exhausted.

"I'm sorry, honey," The healer says. "I'm afraid I'm spent. That's all I can do for today. I'm going to seal your jaw shut for tonight. Then, I'll resume the repair tomorrow. It might take a few days, but we'll get you eating again soon. As for the missing teeth, I'm afraid there isn't much more I can do."

"Is it bad?" I ask.

At the sound of my voice, Crasilda's eyes snap open, but she doesn't lift her head to look at me.

The dentist turns to face me. "Oh, hello, Your Majesty. I was just finishing up. General Lumb has eight facial fractures, and she lost several teeth as well. It'll be a tough recovery."

I feign surprise. "Oh, no! I'm so sorry."

The healer purses her lips. "Yes, well, she's a Guardian after all. She'll pull through."

As the healer is facing me, I meet Crasilda's rage-filled eyes. As soon as she knows I'm looking, she drags her index finger slowly across the length of her throat. Then, the corner of her lips twitch in a devious grin.

Perhaps it's the blood on her face, or the fact that she's mute, but a shiver runs down my spine.

"Thanks for the update," I mutter, "but I better get going. Get well soon, Crasilda."

With that, I hurry out of the healing loft and make my way to the Eastern Wing.

I stop in front of room 334 and knock softly.

As I wait, I shift my weight back and forth.

Nothing.

Frowning, I knock again. "Madame Xantone? Are you in there?"

No one answers.

I bang my fist in the door over and over. "Madame Xantone!"

Silence. Not even a sleepy grumble.

I look around the hallway, making sure no one is looking in my direction. Then, I stretch my soul into the lock, pushing the pins into place.

I turn the handle and step inside.

Already, I can see Xantone's frame beneath the bed spread. The blanket forms a long valley between her toes and her breasts.

"Madame Xantone?" I approach slowly, not wanting to startle her. When she still doesn't move, I give her a tap on the leg. Then, a harder tap.

"Madame?" I shove her this time, panic beginning to flood my mind. I touch her face, cold and blue. I don't need to feel for a pulse. It's obvious she's dead.

"Guards!" I scream. "I need guards. And send me a healer!"

I wait in the hallway until several healers arrive, Jephora among them. Then, I follow her into the room. Immediately, she sets to work, placing her hands on Madame Xantone's chest.

"Hmmm, interesting." She moves her hands slightly to the side. "Hmmm… hmmm."

"What is it?"

"It's odd. She presents with the same features as General Katu—asphyxiation, yet lacking signs of trauma. I've never seen anything like it."

Suddenly, I have an idea. I lean in and lower my voice. "What if she was possessed? What if a demon made her hold her breath? Could this happen?"

"That would be interesting…" Jephora tilts her head to the side. "but unlikely. I'm not sure about the specifics, but I would assume that once she lost consciousness, the demon would lose consciousness as well. At that point, the brain stem would take over, and breathing would resume."

"There has to be something," I groan. "You mentioned opioids last time. Is there anything else that could cause this? Poison? Radiation? Anything?"

Jephora starts to shake her head, then her eyes widen. "Maybe…" She jumps to her feet, taking hold of Xantone's arm. She lifts it, bending it at the elbow. Xantone's hand dangles limply, bouncing with each movement. Jephora lifts her leg next, raising it into the air and letting it flop back into the bed.

"Demons! You were right," she gasps. "I can't believe I missed it. Her muscles are limp."

"She's dead," I say, confused. "Shouldn't they be limp?"

"No, no, no. The opposite, actually. After two hours, Rigor Mortis takes effect," Jephora says. "She should be stiff as a board, but she's limp like a noodle. We call that flaccid paralysis."

I furrow my brow. "Paralysis? I thought you said she asphyxiated."

"She did. Both, actually. The diaphragm is the key," Jephora explains. "It's a muscle after all. If the diaphragm gets paralyzed, you can't take a breath. Eventually, you suffocate, even if your lungs are perfectly functional."

"What would cause that? A poison?"

Jephora nods. "A neurotoxin, most likely. I wouldn't even know how to recognize it. I've never encountered a poison like this before. But it's the only thing that makes sense. I fear you were right, Your Majesty. Madame Xantone was murdered. They both were."

I lean against the wall, and let myself slide until my bottom hits the floor. I'm suddenly so exhausted.

Jack did this. No... my father did this. Every move I make he seems to be one step ahead.

"Everything alright, My Queen?" Jephora asks, stepping closer.

"I'm just tired," I mutter. *Tired of all the death.*

"I'll get you some water," Jephora offers.

"No, thank you. I'm fine. I just need a second." I take a deep breath and close my eyes. "How do you do it?" I finally ask.

"Do what?"

I motion at Madame Xantone's body. "You're surrounded by tragedy. Isn't it… depressing?"

Jephora nods, cracking a smile. "It is. Most days, yes."

"Then why do it?"

She shrugs. "It's what I'm good at. Most healers struggle with the dead. After all, the deceased can't give permission to be healed. Gaining access to the tissues, even as an observer, can be tricky." She glances down at Xantone's unblinking eyes. "I happen to excel at it."

"Still. So much death. I don't know how you do it." I say.

"It's funny; my colleagues say the same thing: my patients are dead, and there's nothing I can do to save them. Sounds bleak. But I find it comforting. I can't kill them with a mistake. I can't do any harm."

"You don't want to save lives?"

"I used to," Jephora admits. "In fact, I started my career in post-natal care. From a healing perspective, babies are a lot like the dead. They can't consciously give permission to be healed. We can only observe. Well, it was my job to find out what was wrong—heart deformities, brain tumors, anything you can imagine—but I couldn't heal them… not without permission. Most of the time, I watched those babies die under my care. Nothing is more depressing than that."

"That's why you switched to autopsies?"

Jephora nods.

"Do you—"

"Your Majesty?" a voice calls from the hallway outside. "Has anyone seen the queen?"

"In here!" I call.

Octavian dashes into the room. He grimaces when he spots the body, but his smile quickly returns.

"You're highness," he pants. "I must tell you something in private."

"Not here; we can speak in my chambers."

I thank Jephora and lead Octavian to my room.

By the time I shut the door, he can barely contain his excitement. "It worked!"

"What did?" I ask. "The virus?"

"The guards are all talking about it," he laughs. "They can hear coughing from the wall. The plague is spreading!"

18

MATT

I leap to my feet as the hotel door swings open. Kildron steps inside.

"Did you find something good enough?"

Kildron smiles. "That depends; is a triple-decker megayacht good enough for you?" He tosses a key ring onto the coffee table. "It'll be ready to leave in the morning. They're getting it fueled and loaded with food. We should be able to man it with just the three of us."

"You know how to sail a yacht?"

He taps his finger on the side of his head. "I do now. A quick trip in the captain's head gave me everything I need. It's not that complicated, really. It has autopilot and stuff."

"You're sure we shouldn't fly?" I ask. "We could get a private jet. Pay a pilot. It would be faster."

Kildron shakes his head. "You forget we're feeders, Matt?"

I frown. "So?"

"How high up does the sanctuary spell extend?" Kildron asks. "I've tried to climb over one before. It's endless. Now, imagine we're flying at 500 miles per hour. You'd splatter into a million pieces, and so would I."

"Point taken," I say. "Megayacht it is."

"That's not all," Kildron says, his voice softening. "There's something you should know if we're gonna do this."

"I'm listening."

"Remember that relic I told you about. The Shackles of Redemption."

"I remember."

"Well, I've done some research over the years—quite a bit, in fact."

"Okay… and?" I ask.

"Turns out, it was made by the Prophet Posedonah—the Lord of Atlantia. It's rumored he made multiple."

"Oh." My mind starts spinning.

"There's a catch," Kildron warns. "Posedonah hated feeders. I mean, really hated them. They say he sunk his sanctuary by accident, trying to cause another flood. He was willing to drown the world just to kill a few feeders."

"Okay," I say. "They hate us; I get it."

"I just want you to be aware of what we're getting into. That's all. If we do find Atlantia, they might not be so friendly to people like us."

"Noted," I say. "Can I borrow the phone now? I want to call Klinton again."

Kildron tosses me the phone, and I hit redial. The phone doesn't ring. Instead, it goes directly to a voicemail of Renshu's voice. I call again.

"No answer," I announce. "I called twice."

"Guess we stick to the plan then," Kildron says.

"Do you think something happened to them?"

"Like what?" Kildron asks.

I shrug. "I don't know, it's just weird that they're not answering."

"Maybe they had a power outage?"

"Maybe." I glance at the balcony. "I'll let Kendra know the plan."

I walk over to the glass door and slide it open. Looking down, I smile. "Still soaking it in?"

"It goes on forever," Kendra says, sitting cross-legged on a lounge chair.

From the balcony, we have a panoramic view of Miami Bay and

the connecting ocean. A full moon hovers over the ocean, creating a patchwork of white splotches on the water. The flashing beacons of unseen boats blink on the horizon.

I sit down beside her. "Breathtaking, right?"

"More like terrifying," she laughs, only half-joking. "It's so dark. How deep does it go?"

"Depends. The bay isn't that deep, but the open ocean can go down for miles and miles."

Kendra swallows. "You're joking." Her face pales. "You're not joking, are you?"

"It's not a big d—" I stop. "Kendra, do you know how to swim?"

"Of course not. No one can swim in Cavernum," Kendra exclaims. "Where would we learn? The fountain? The canal?"

"No, it makes sense," I laugh. "I just didn't realize…"

"Psh," Kendra shakes her head playfully. "You Beyonders and your assumptions. Makes me sick."

We sit for a moment in silence, enjoying the balcony breeze.

"What did Kildron say in there?" Kendra finally asks.

"Oh, yeah. We have a boat now. We leave in the morning."

She nods her head. "Sounds like a plan." She continues to stare out at the night sky. "You were serious, right, about people walking on the moon?"

"It's crazy. I know."

"And they did it without dominion?"

"Nothing but science."

She shakes her head. "There's no way."

"You want to hear more Beyond trivia?"

"Always."

"Every one of those stars is a ball of fire the size of the sun. They look like tiny dots because they're so far away. And each one has its own planets just like Earth."

"Every star?"

"Technically," I correct, "some of those stars are galaxies with billions of stars in them. With those odds, it's basically guaranteed that somewhere out there, there's another planet with intelligent life like us."

Kendra lets her eyes wander across the sky, skipping from star to star like a stone across a pond. "You really believe that?" Kendra asks.

I have to think for a second. "Sure. I believe it… there's no way we're the only ones."

"Hmmm," Kendra continues to stare. "Maybe that's where God went."

I tilt my head. "What do you mean?"

Kendra continues to study the stars. "God used to work miracles, right? And I don't mean coincidences like some people say. I mean real, undeniable miracles… At some point, that just stopped. Maybe He's out there, visiting one of his other planets. Maybe they need him more than we do. I like to think he didn't just abandon us."

"Hmmm," I nod my head. "That's a good point. Maybe you're right."

Kendra sighs. "Boy, could we use one of His miracles about now." She sighs again.

I take her hand in mine. "You wanna talk about it?"

She shakes her head.

"Distraction then?"

"I guess."

I look out over the water, and suddenly, it hits me. "Are you ready for bed?"

"Yeah, why?"

"I have a distraction in mind if you want to dream with me."

"I don't know."

I stand, tugging on her arm. "C'mon. It'll be fun."

"Fine," she says as I pull her to her feet. "What are we going to do?"

"It's a surprise," I say.

I open the door for Kendra and follow her back inside. "We're going to bed," I announce to Kildron.

"Sounds good. I'll be here, keep'n watch."

"Do you need me to take a shift?" I ask.

"I'll be fine," Kildron says.

"Okay, goodnight."

Retreating into our room, we crawl into bed and turn out the lights. We're side by side now, her pinky overlapping my palm. I turn to kiss her goodnight, but she's already leaning over.

"See you soon," she whispers.

With the help of self-dominion, she's asleep almost immediately. I don't waste any time. I let my soul sink deeper and deeper, gradually drifting out of my body.

The sensation is familiar. As I leave my senses behind, I gain a 'spiritual' sight. I can perceive my surroundings with my soul—the mattress beneath me, the air above, and Kendra to my left.

I move toward her, like a bloodhound chasing a scent. Then, I let my soul envelope hers.

"Kendra?" I call into the void. She's not dreaming yet, so there's no scenery around me. No sound. Everything is emptiness.

"I'm here!" she calls.

Still, I can't see her. I stretch my soul into the void, and command the dream.

Pool!

Instantly, the darkness transforms. Bright sunshine illuminates the poolside, and a cool breeze blows over my arms. The sound of children playing breaks the silence. I'm outdoors, standing beside the Kentville Community Pool.

The place is packed, mirroring my childhood memories. Kids scurry to and fro as adults watch from their lounge chairs, hiding their faces beneath big sunglasses and wide brim hats.

"Cannonball!" A teen boy jumps off the high-dive. Water rains down on the onlookers, eliciting a few complaints.

Nearby, a lifeguard blows his whistle. "No running!"

It only takes me a second to spot Kendra. She stands awkwardly by the snack bar, still wearing her nightgown. She looks relieved when she sees me.

"What is this place?"

"Community pool. I'm going to teach you how to swim."

“Oh, no. I’m not going in there.”

“Cmon, it’ll be fun,” I insist.

She takes a deep breath, “I don’t know…” Suddenly, a three-year-old races past us and leaps into the deep end. Kendra watches, riveted, as he doggy paddles to the side.

“See,” I tease. “So easy, a baby can do it.”

“That wasn’t a baby,” Kendra argues.

“Basically. You’ve got this,” I assert.

Kendra continues to watch the toddler as he kicks off the wall and doggy paddles to his mom, clinging to her neck.

“I guess it doesn’t seem so bad,” Kendra concludes.

“It’s not; come on. I even warmed it for you.”

She dips her foot into the pool, stirring the water with curled toes. “Oh, that’s nice. It’s like a bath.”

“Told you. We’ll have you jumping off the high-dive in no time. But first you’ll need a swimsuit.”

Her eyes dart from one swimmer to the next, frowning at the sight of their bikinis. “Isn’t it… cold?”

“Not in the water.” I say. “It’s about reducing drag.” I cast a look at her nightgown. “In that, you won’t go anywhere but down.”

“Can you help?” she asks. “Just give me something simple.”

“Of course. Hold still.”

I stretch my soul toward her and command the dream.

Swimsuit!

The colors swirl around Kendra like a Crayola tornado. When they finally settle, she’s wearing a light blue one-piece. An hourglass of material covers her belly button, but the suit leaves her sides and back exposed.

“How do I look?” Kendra asks, giving a quick spin as she inspects her own swimwear.

“You look… good!” I gawk. “Really good.”

When I gave the command, I didn’t imagine a specific design. My subconscious must have decided for me.

Already wearing my board shorts, I step into the shallow end and offer my hand. “You ready?”

"Yeah," Kendra reaches for my hand but suddenly pulls it back, threatening me with a pointed finger. "But if you let me drown, I don't care if it's a dream, I'll make you regret it."

"You won't drown. Pinky promise."

Using the steps, I lead her into the shallow end, stopping when the water is chest deep. "Okay, I'll teach you how my mom taught me. Put your hands flat, palms facing down. Then, you sweep the water in two motions. First, bring your palms together like you're praying. Then, push them apart like you're opening curtains. And repeat. Keep your hands flat and firm the whole time. Go ahead."

Kendra gives it a try. She slowly warms up to the motion, increasing speed.

"Okay, now kick your legs up and down."

After a minute, a big smile erupts on her face. "I'm doing it. Look!"

Sure enough, her feet are a few inches off the bottom of the pool.

"Okay, now let's go deeper. Keep going." I take her hips, slowly walking her to the deep end. Sure enough, she manages to keep her mouth above water.

"That's it. You're doing it."

For the next hour, we mess around. I teach her to do the frog kick, and she watches me do flips off the diving board. Some neighborhood kids start a game of Marco Polo, and we join in.

Eventually, we sit on the side of the pool, kicking our feet in the water and sharing a snow cone from the snack bar.

"They look so happy," Kendra mutters to herself.

I know what she's thinking. No starvation. No floggings. Just summertime bliss.

"It's a whole different world," I agree. "Growing up, I never even knew how good I had it."

She sighs. "I wish Decklin could see this. He'd—"

Suddenly, the world shakes, lurching beneath my feet. Kendra grabs my shoulder to keep from falling in the pool.

"Matt?"

The concrete vibrates beneath me.

"That's weird. That's never happened bef—"

Once again, the world shudders back and forth, only this time, the ground tilts.

Water pours from the pool, sweeping us across the concrete and into a chain link fence. Still, the ground continues to tilt, steeper and steeper, and the entire pool rains down on us. The weight alone is crushing. It presses me into the fence and buries me in a thousand gallons.

I can't breathe. I can't breathe!

"Ptuh!" I suck in a breath, awaking in my bed. Kildron has me by the shoulders, shaking me violently back and forth. In his glacier eyes, I see cold, genuine fear.

"Up, now! We're under attack!"

TSSHHHH!

The window beside our bed shatters. Wrapped in a black cloak, a feeder takes hold of the broken window frame and pulls himself inside. His hands and face are tattooed with Adamic armor.

I look to the bedroom door—our only remaining exit. A moment later, it swings open, and a feeder steps inside.

Just like that, we're surrounded.

19

ROSE

I close the book, *The Early Reign of Dethyric Malik*, and add it to the stack. I open the next book, *Prophetic Fulfillment*, and lift the candlestick to illuminate the pages. I start skimming.

After a few words, I realize I'm not retaining anything, merely tracing the words with my eyes.

I sigh. I've scoured half the library, and found nothing. Why would this book be any different?

I add it to the stack.

My eyes wander to the library window. It's sometime in the early morning—at least an hour until sunrise. I should be in bed, but my mind is too cluttered to sleep. There's so much that must be done. Too many mysteries to solve.

I repeat the poem in my mind.

Deep beneath your feet is the power you seek

Adamic is the key, but you cannot speak

It is an ark of salvation when the future is bleak

But beware, once opened, destruction will leak

My mind wanders to my father, and our previous conversation. "Faza Le Bakanzah," I whisper aloud.

Unseal Bakanzah.

And yet, it doesn't make sense.

Adamic is the key, but you cannot speak.

My father believes a spoken spell opens the sanctuary, and yet the poem indicates the opposite. Is Zezric mistaken? Has he forgotten the riddle?

I'm enthralled by the thought when I hear a flurry of footsteps outside the library door. They quickly grow louder, then fade as the culprit flees down the hall.

That's weird.

I stand and open the library door, stepping into the hallway.

Bam!

Something rock solid crashes into me, throwing me across the floor. I slide on my back until I come to a stop.

Illuminate!

Diego stands above me with his hands raised, squinting at the sudden burst of light. His skin gleams like polished silver, and he holds his Adamic blade in one hand. I'm lucky he didn't impale me by accident.

"Demons, Diego! What are you doing?" I climb to my feet, rubbing my bruised hip.

"Where'd he go?" Diego demands.

"Who?"

"I was chasing him!" Diego snaps. "He was outside my door controlling the snake."

"A snake?" My nose wrinkles. "What are you talking about?"

"There was a snake in my room—a big one with yellow stripes. I heard it slithering under my bed," Diego insists. "I killed the snake, but the guy ran away."

"That's odd. There's no snakes like that in Cavernum," I say. Garter snakes sure. Rattlesnakes too, but not like Diego described.

Diego scans the shadows for another few seconds. Then, he frowns. "I'll show you. It's still in my room."

Maintaining the light dominion, I follow Diego as he jogs back to his quarters. He holds open the door as I step inside.

"See, I told you."

Diego's mom has lit several candles, illuminating what was once a maid's chamber. The entire family is awake. I spot Isabela, Mary, and Diego's two brothers as well.

Abuela shuffles into the light. She stares at the dead snake on the floor. "Dios Mío," she quickly signs a cross over her heart. "The Devil has come for us."

I step closer, peering down at the serpent. Just as Diego said, the snake is striped like a bumble bee. It's wider than my arm and eight feet long. It looks healthy except for a flattened head—thanks to Diego's fist, no doubt.

I kneel and pick up the snake's head, prying the jaws open. Sure enough, two needle-like fangs protrude from the snake's mouth.

My stomach sinks. "Diego, did you get bit by chance?"

He shakes his head. "I sleep metal at night. It couldn't have bit me."

"You're sure?"

Before Diego can respond, Mary groans.

"My stomach hurts," she whines, clutching her abdomen. She's barely uttered the words when she turns and vomits across her bed.

Diego and I share a look of horror.

"Give me that!" Diego says, snatching the snake from my hand. He pulls the snake jaws open, frowning at the fangs.

"Everyone, look for bite marks," I demand. "Two small dots next to each other, about this far apart." I hold up my fingers to indicate.

"Ummm, guys." Isabela slowly raises an index finger in the air. On the tip of her finger, right below the nail, two red dots are visible.

"I have them too," Jorge says. He holds up his bare foot, showing the dots on the bottom of his heel.

"Me too," Javier echoes.

"He'll die for this," Diego tightens his grip on the dagger. Then, snake still in hand, he dashes out of the room.

I chase after him. "Diego, wait! Let's think this through!"

We race past two guards. "Your Majesty?" They look at each other before joining the chase.

I already know where he's going. Diego turns into the High Council Wing and stops in front of General Kaynes's door.

He raises his hand and closes his eyes.

KA-BOOM!

The door explodes inward. Before the dust settles, Diego charges in, dagger raised.

20

MATT

I only have a moment to make a decision.

Two feeders—one in the window, one in the door. More just around the corner.

The bed next to me is empty. I don't see any indents from Kendra's weight. That's good. So long as she's invisible, the feeders won't know she's here.

The feeder in the doorway strikes first. He narrows his eyes at Kildron, raising his hand. Kildron raises his hand as well. A shockwave emanates from each of them, meeting in the middle. As the two forces collide, the room shudders.

I don't see what happens after that. I turn back to the feeder in the window a moment before he lunges.

Lift!

Reaching forward with my mind, I toss the bedsheet into the air.

Push!

The sheet accelerates at the feeder's head. Before it makes contact, the sheet ignites in a flash of fire. A few strands of fabric snag on the feeder's frame only to disintegrate a second later, embers falling to the floor.

"That's it?" The feeder breathes. There's a chunk missing from his ear, and one of his front teeth is chipped. "The son of the great Archang—"

Lift!

This time, I use the curtains. They whip into the air and wrap around Chip's face. For a brief moment, he's blind.

Push! I command with all my might.

A pulse of energy reverberates outward, connecting with the feeder's chest. Chip flies back as if hit by a train. His head smashes into the top of the window frame, ripping it from the wall as his body is folded and forced out the window. He screams as he falls toward the beach below.

I don't have any time to waste. I scan the room, looking for my Adamic dagger. I left it on the nightstand when I went to bed, but it isn't there now.

Kendra has it, I can only hope.

Shlink!

I hear a knife find its mark behind me, followed by the crackle of electricity.

I turn as Kildron stabs a feeder for a second time. With one hand around the feeder's neck, he gives it a third quick jab in the stomach, releasing its throat as it slumps to the carpet. Then, he narrows his eyes at the doorway.

Three more feeders rush through the door frame, one after the other.

I raise my hand.

Fire!

The flames engulf the doorway, swallowing the three feeders. Unfortunately, I don't hear any screams.

Burn!

I intensify my command, urging the very oxygen to ignite. The heat radiates back at me, but I don't relent. As the flames finally recede, the feeders press forward. Their cloaks are ablaze, but they hardly notice, like a stuntman covered in gasoline.

"Adamic armor!" Kildron warns.

The first feeder through the doorway is holding an Adamic blade. It isn't a dagger, like I'm used to seeing. It's long and curved, growing thicker near the tip.

The feeder squares up to Kildron, then strikes. The scimitar whistles through the air.

Tink!

Kildron parries the blow with his gladius, and delivers a quick thrust through the feeder's gut. Rather than withdraw the blade, he pulls sideways, cutting outward through the feeder's torso.

Carrying his momentum, he swings at the next feeder, taking off its hand.

WOOOOOP! WOOOOOP!

The fire alarm begins to wail, triggered by the burning cloaks.

As the next feeder passes through the doorway, I extend my mind. When I reach the edge of her consciousness, I drive my soul deeper.

Images rush past my eyes. I see myself holding a child, cradling her in my arms. In the next image, I'm sinking my teeth into a grown man.

After wading through a sludge of memories, I break the surface of her soul.

"Ptuh!" I open my eyes—her eyes. Her cloak obscures my peripheral vision, and I can feel her long hair down the back of my neck. Unfortunately, I'm not holding an Adamic blade, but I can still wreak havoc.

I spin in her body, charging electricity on my fingertips. I grab the feeder behind me by the throat.

TZZZZ!

The shock has no effect, and neither do my fingers. As I squeeze, the Adamic armor resists me, dispersing the force evenly across his skin.

"Good, Matt," Kildron calls. "You hold, I stab."

Shlink!

As the gladius enters my back, my lungs seize. The pain is dizzying, and next thing I know, I'm coughing in my own body.

Kildron swings at the next feeder, but the feeder ducks under his blade. The air ripples, throwing Kildron back. His back punches through the drywall and a series of electrical wires tangle his limbs, preventing him from falling into the hotel room next door.

The feeder smiles, raising his hand. Electricity crackles on his fingertips.

With a deep breath, I throw myself into his soul.

Lightn—

Stop! I command, halting the electrons in their path. I turn again, driving my index finger into the nearest feeder's eye.

The feeder screams as I fall to my knees, scooping up the scimitar from its place on the floor. From the corner of my eye, I see a flash of yellow.

Shie—

I'm too late. A fireball surrounds me, and I squeeze my eyes shut. Surprisingly, it doesn't burn. I can barely feel the heat through the feeder's tattooed skin.

I lunge through the flames, swinging the scimitar.

The feeder sidesteps my blow. I try to stop the swing, but my momentum carries the sword forward, embedding itself in the charred doorframe.

Silver flashes near my waist as the feeder thrusts an Adamic dagger.

Before it makes contact, I abandon my current body, heaving my soul at the new attacker.

Taking control, I open his eyes as his arm—now my arm—finishes the thrust. The dagger plunged into the feeder I had just abandoned, sinking hilt-deep. I give it a twist before yanking it out of his gut. Then, I deliver a quick slash across his throat.

"Matt!" It's Kendra's voice, shrill and frantic. It originates from somewhere by the bed.

I spin as a feeder emerges from the window. It's the same feeder as before—with the mutilated ear and the chipped incisor.

Chip narrows his eyes on my comatose body. I only have a second.

I lift the Adamic blade to my chest and plunge it into my host. "Ahhh!" My muscles seize before I can drive the blade deeper. I hope it's enough.

As the darkness creeps into my vision, I throw my soul at Chip.

Immediately, I feel the difference. As my mind fills his limbs, his consciousness pushes back, resisting my very presence. His body isn't mine to command.

Chip is a demon.

Using his hand, I reach for his eyes, hoping to gouge them out before he can stop me.

NOOOOO! His soul screams at me, filling our head with rage.

His soul condenses in our right arm, forcing me out. I focus my efforts on the left arm, once again reaching for his eyes. The right arm—under his control—grabs the left arm at the wrist. I strain against him, but he's right handed. His right arm is physically stronger—more dexterous too.

I look up at Kildron, hoping to find help, but he's battling two more feeders.

I relinquish control of the left arm, extending my soul through his entire body. I find the moisture hidden within every cell. Then, I command.

Freez—

NOOO!

The feeder resists me again. Our commands cancel each other out, and the cells remain unchanged.

I only have one other option.

"Kendra," I manage to choke through his teeth. "Stab… me…"

His body remains motionless, trapped in a mental tug-of-war. I feel his eyes move, focusing on my body, particularly my neck. I feel the command forming in his mind—the intention to decapitate.

Slic—

Shlink!

Searing pain erupts in the back of my neck. I feel the blood begin to pour.

Shlink. Shlink.

By the second stab, I'm already retreating back into my body.

"Ptuh!" I take a breath with my own lungs and turn to face Chip.

I can't see Kendra, but I see his scalp open as she drives the knife through the back of Chip's skull and out the front of his forehead. Finally, the feeder collapses, never to rise again.

I spin to see Kildron standing face to face with a feeder. Just like the others, Adamic armor blankets the feeder's face.

Unlike the other feeders, this feeder doesn't move. It's eyes are glazed, and it's jaw is locked open—frozen from within.

Dead.

"Kendra, can I see the knife?" I hold out my hand. The blade materializes as the handle plops into my palm. I scan the room.

WOOOOOP! WOOOOOP!

I don't hear anything except the fire alarm and the distant shouts of hotel guests.

To my relief, nobody comes rushing through the doorway. No feeders come crawling through the window either. Everything is still.

The battle is over.

C'mon! Kildron speaks in my head. I can only assume he's saying the same to Kendra. He moves to the side of the room, stepping over several dead feeders. He eyes the demolished drywall where his body collided just moments ago. Then, he closes his eyes.

The air ripples in the center of the hole, snapping two-by-fours and pushing wires out of the way. When he's finished, there's just enough room to walk through.

Everyone, invisible, he hisses in my head. *Hurry!*

Kendra takes my hand, then Kildron's. Single file, Kildron pulls us through the wall and into the hotel room next door. We're in another bedroom now; the floor plan is a mirror-opposite of the one we just left.

We're going off the balcony, Kildron speaks in my mind. *No one break grip, and no one say a word.*

He opens the door to the living room, and turns right toward the balcony. I take two steps when the air comes to life around me.

SCREEEEEECH!!!

The noise is ear-shattering! It drills into my head, flooding my thoughts with pure agony.

"Aahhhhh!" Kendra shrieks. Her hand rips from my grasp as she reaches to plug her ears.

Kildron materializes as well. His face is calm and focused. He must be muffling the attack with dominion.

I focus on the space around my head.

Mute!

The noise doesn't stop, but it's quieter now—at least for me. Somewhere nearby, invisible to my eyes, Kendra is still cowering in anguish.

Out of the corner of my eye, I see movement. Iris steps out of the hotel closet, her face taut with determination. She's wearing her soul-anchor on the outside of her shirt, where it has no effect.

Two more feeders emerge from the bathroom, standing beside her.

Suddenly, the screeching stops. Iris's eyes glaze over, like a trance, and a familiar entity slithers into my mind.

I'm sorry, Matt, Iris says. Then, her soul fills my body. I only have time to utter two words before she takes control.

"Run, Kendra!"

Already, my hand betrays me. I raise my Adamic blade and lunge at Kildron.

He moves at the last second, lifting the gladius. The dagger slides along its edge, catching on the hilt.

"Fight her, Matt!" he barks.

I try to resist, but my body is already in motion. I dash forward, poking at Kildron's defenses. He parries again, keeping the point of his sword aimed at my chest.

"Iris," he seethes. "Let him go. We can talk about this."

Iris isn't listening. She reaches beyond me—beyond Kildron—and commands the air outside the windows.

KA-BOOM!

The window implodes with a brilliant flash. Glass peppers my face, and I momentarily regain control, turning away from the shrapnel. I spread my fingers, trying to drop the dagger.

No you don't! Iris says. Her soul seems to swell, forcing me out of each limb. I feel my fingers tighten over the dagger.

I push back, but my metaphysical feet seem to slide beneath me. I can't get any traction.

I'm a helpless observer as my legs carry me forward.

Darkness! she commands.

Everything goes black. As my body leaps forward, my arm swings in the void.

Tink!

I feel the sharp jolt as the dagger stops in its tracks. Then, my body is ducking and spinning. My arm swings again, slicing through something soft.

Kildron curses. A moment later, I hear the warble of a force wave.

Shield!

It's not enough. A wall of energy crashes through Iris's defenses. The invisible force rams me in the gut, and my feet lift off the floor. Next thing I know, my back crashes into the flatscreen. My head snaps back, and the room spins.

Light floods the room.

While I'm disoriented, Kildron turns on Iris's body. A gash in his thigh oozes blood as he raises his arm.

Emerging from his fingertips, a torrent of fire sweeps through the room. The flames are blinding, stretching from floor to ceiling. The two feeders raise their arms as they disappear behind the flames.

By the time it recedes, the walls and ceiling are ablaze. Iris's body, however, is not. She and the two feeders are completely unharmed.

Suddenly, pipes hiss overhead as water rains down from the fire sprinklers.

Kildron charges Iris, but a feeder intercepts him. It raises an Adamic dagger, pointing the tip at Kildron.

Tzzzz!

A blue arc of electricity crackles from the tip of the blade. It surges into Kildron's hand, but he doesn't shake or seize. Instead, the electricity condenses into a blue orb, growing in his palm as the jolt continues.

Before I know what's happening, my arms push me upright.

Unable to stop myself, I climb to my feet and charge Kildron from behind.

He hears my footsteps. Turning, he unleashes the orb of electricity in a quick jolt of lightning.

KA-CRACK!

Iris tries to deflect the lightning, but it's too much. Electricity courses through my body, burning my skin and throwing me back. My nerves are so fried, I don't even feel myself hit the ground. All I see is a strobe light of white light.

As my vision clears, Kildron cuts down one of the feeders. Adrenaline rushes through me, spurred by Iris's panic.

At her command, my body shakily stands. Then, I'm charging again. My eyes flicker down, focusing on the water that has begun to collect on the floor. As I watch, the sprinklers continue to gush.

Kildron turns on the next feeder, his arm a blur. His blade cuts through the feeder's force field and catches the creature in the neck. Electricity crackles one last time on his fingers before the feeders slumps to the ground.

Now, no one stands between Kildron and Iris. Sword in hand, he lunges.

At that moment, Iris reaches out with her mind.

Condense!

The water on the floor congeals around Kildron's feet.

Freeze!

The water crackles as it hardens, cementing Kildron's feet to the carpet.

Iris controls my body like a master puppeteer. I drop to my hip and slide gracefully across a thin sheet of newly-frozen ice. As I slip between Kildron's legs, I swipe with my dagger.

Shlink!

My face smiles as the blade cuts through his Achilles and clunks against the back of his shin bone.

"Agh!" He melts the ice, shifting his weight to his good leg.

I'm back on my feet now, standing between Kildron and Iris's body. Never taking my eyes off of Kildron, I reach back and take hold of Iris's spear. In the same motion, I sheathe the dagger.

"Iris!" Kildron pants. "You don't have to do—"

With two hands on the spear, I thrust at Kildron.

Tink!

He twists out of the way, parrying with his gladius. My arms thrust again, and Kildron stumbles back.

I can feel Iris's excitement. She has him right where she wants him.

"Freeze!"

A security guard stands in the doorway, a few feet from Iris's body. He holds a revolver in his white-knuckles grip and points it back and forth between the three of us.

"No one move!" the guard says. He takes a step closer. "Hands where I can see—"

Iris doesn't let him finish the sentence.

Slice!

Nooo!

I can't stop her as a paper-thin wave of dominion cuts across his throat. The guard drops his gun and clutches his neck. A second later, he collapses, bloodied hands dragging down the side of the wall.

Already, she forces my eyes back on Kildron. My arms thrust the spear at his chest.

Kildron bends to the left and jumps, as if doing a cartwheel. As soon as his feet leave the ground, gravity flips.

My body accelerates toward the ceiling. Iris raises my hands to cushion the fall. The spear slips from my grasp as my face smashes into the drywall. The impact is stronger than expected, forcing my head to the side and nearly snapping my spine.

Kildron didn't just flip gravity; he amplified it.

I'm climbing to my feet when gravity flips back to normal. My body drops back to the carpet, landing flat on my back. The air whooshes from my lungs.

The spear lands on the floor between Kildron and I. It's perpendicular to the hallway, drawing a line between us.

Kildron is still on his feet. He steps on the spear, pinning it between his boot and the floor. Then, his eyes dart upward. They narrow on Iris's neck.

"Stop!" Iris shrieks with my voice. My arm moves, unsheathing my dagger. A moment later, I feel the blade's edge press into my throat. "I'll kill him," she hisses through my teeth. "You know I'll do it. He'll die before I do."

Kildron raises his hands, pinching the hilt of his gladius between his index finger and his thumb. Somehow, it looks less threatening that way.

"Iris," Kildron speaks slowly. "Don't do something you'll regret. You still have options."

"Drop the sword," she commands.

Kildron doesn't. "C'mon, Matt. Now's your time to shine. Do something."

I try. I really do. I push against Iris. I command my arm with all my might, but nothing happens.

She's stronger than me... so much stronger than me.

The knife digs deeper, drawing blood. "Last chance."

"Matt?" Kildron pleads.

"This is on you," she hisses through my mouth. My arm tenses, and the blade cuts into my neck.

Nooo!

Kildron's eyes roll back as he drives his soul into my body. Immediately, he takes control, pulling the dagger away from my neck.

Iris doesn't resist him. In fact, she's gone. I can no longer sense her inside my body.

Kildron controls my eyes now. They look up at Iris's body, and my heart sinks.

Nooo!

She smiles, touching her hand to her soul-anchor.

In the blink of an eye, the spear flies into the air, forcing its way past Kildron's boot. Nothing but a blur, the side of the spear shaft smashes through Kildron's jaw, tossing back his head and lifting him into the air. Then, before his body has time to fall, it accelerates back toward the ground. The shaft catches him by the neck and drives his skull into the hotel floor.

I hear his bones crack.

"Nooo!" I scream, finally alone in my own body. Kildron's consciousness is gone, snuffed out upon impact.

His chest still moves, but only barely. The air whistles through his broken windpipe. He won't be waking up anytime soon, if ever.

I draw back my dagger and heave it at Iris. Or at least, that's what I try to do. Just before the blade leaves my grasp, my fingers tighten.

No you don't. Iris settles back into my body, resuming control. *Let's finish this.*

I step up to Kildron and take a knee beside his head. My arm lowers, pressing the knife to his throat.

Iris's thoughts whisper in my head.

Goodbye, father.

With that, my arm pushes downward, driving the knife into his neck.

21

ROSE

I race after Diego, following him into General Kaynes' chambers.

Light! I illuminate the room.

Kaynes is standing beside his bed, wearing baggy silk pajamas. He smiles as Diego marches up to him.

Diego strikes like a cobra, reaching for General Kaynes' throat. When his fingers close, they pass right through General Kaynes' flesh.

The apparition vanishes.

"Now, now. That's not how we behave, is it Diego?" Kaynes's voice comes from the center of the room, but I don't see him.

Suddenly, he materializes by the window… or is it another illusion?

"You want revenge, don't you, mate. I understand that; I do. But your rage will be your downfall, my friend. If you listen to me, I might just help you save them."

Diego throws the snake on the floor. His fists tremble at his side. "What is this?"

"Ah, yes. The Banded Krait, native to Southeast Asia. Remarkable creature… doesn't get enough credit in my opinion. More venomous than the cobra, and yet so many have never heard of it."

"You'll die for this," Diego seethes.

"Me?" Kaynes touches his hand to his chest as if shocked. "But I didn't do anything. It was Crasilda who possessed the snake. She's the one who endangered your family, and against my orders, I might add. I only gave her your name." Jack shrugs nonchalantly. "I imagine when she came across your metallic sleeping arrangement, she got frustrated… took matters into her own hands."

"Katu… and Madame Xantone," I breathe. "This is how you did it."

"Your father had the idea," Jack admits. "Ingenious, I might add. Guided by dominion, a snake is a potent weapon. The banded krait delivers 20 milligrams of venom per bite, but it can store five times that amount. With dominion, one can control precisely how much venom is injected. Let me tell you, 100 milligrams really gets the job done. And did I mention the bite is painless? Rarely does it wake the victim. Most will pass in their sleep."

"Why?" Diego chokes.

Jack touches his hand to his chest. "You'll have to ask Crasilda. Like I already mentioned, she was the puppeteer. Impulsive girl, she decided to massacre your family all on her own, and she did a terrible job, might I add. If she had any brains at all, she would've picked one —little Mary perhaps—and focused all of the venom on her. Instead, she divided the venom across six victims, diluting what would've been a lethal dose. Now, they all might survive. But you better hurry. They'll need healers."

Diego doesn't budge. His hand tightens on the Adamic blade.

Jack sighs. "My God, you're a stubborn one, aren't you? Listen carefully… Acetylcholine esterase inhibitor. It's a big word; can you remember it? Let the healers know it's the only antidote. Now go and let me chat with our queen."

Diego narrows his eyes before bolting from the room. His metal footsteps clank down the hall.

"Everything alright, sir?" One of the previous guards asks, peeking into the room. He eyes the demolished doorway, gun drawn.

"Everything is under control, Captain," Jack insists. "Resume your station."

"Yessir." The guards disappear into the hallway, mumbling something to another guard. Their footsteps grow quiet.

"Finally," Jack brushes the dust from his robe. "The adults can talk." He takes a seat on the bed, crossing his legs. "You've been busy, Rose. Holding secret meetings, searching for Atlantia… starting plagues."

At his last words, my stomach sinks, and my eyes widen.

"Oh, yes," Jack sneers. "The Holy One knows all about your little virus. It's a shame Lady Xantone had to suffer for your recklessness." He purses his lips. "Well, I suppose suffer isn't the right word. The bite is painless after all. I imagine she passed peacefully."

Jack looks at me and laughs. "How can you be mad, Rose? We warned you, didn't we? In fact, your father has been lenient, but he's growing tired of your games. There will be no more mercy, not even for his beloved daughter. Consider this your final warning. Interfere again—even the slightest act of rebellion—and the palace will crumble."

I sit in my bed, letting my self-pity shadow me like a storm cloud. My tears are a steady rainfall, running down my cheek and wetting the soil of my bedsheets.

As I cry, I listen to my mother's music box. The notes split my attention, dampening the despair. I listen until the gears click, and the music falls silent.

I want to reach out and crank the handle, but I can't muster the energy to move. Amid the silence, my hopelessness intensifies.

You killed them, Rose. They died because you chose to rebel.

Katu, Madame Xantone, and now Diego's grandmother. Despite the efforts of the healers, Abuela didn't make it through the night.

All because of me.

My mind spirals through an inevitable loop of outcomes. If I resist, more people will die. If I don't, my father will control the world.

I can't win!

I lay there, letting my teary storm run its course, slowly washing away my self pity. Not washing it away completely, but smudging it like ground chalk—smearing it into something unrecognizable… something I can ignore.

I turn my pillow over to avoid the damp spots and rest a few minutes more, basking in the post-cry calm.

Suddenly, I hear the faint scraping of metal on metal, coming from my door. As I listen, the scraping continues. Then, Antai swears.

I climb to my feet and wipe my eyes. "Coming." I grab my key off of the desk and hurry to the door.

"No need," Antai calls out. "I've almost g—"

I fit my key in the lock and twist. The door swings open, revealing a dejected Antai.

"I almost had it," he sighs. His Adamic key slowly levitates back into a pouch on the side of his wheelchair.

"Sorry," I say. "I just couldn't wait to see you."

A skeleton of a smile twitches on his lips, then he grows serious again. "I have a letter for you."

A curled piece of paper floats up from his wheelchair pouch. I snatch it out of the air.

"Have you read it?"

He nods.

"Bad news?"

"Kinda," he shrugs. "Nothing we didn't already know."

I unravel the paper and devour the words.

Rose,

This is Klinton and Ron from the communication bunker. I'm afraid we have some bad news for you.

Three days ago, Matt and Kendra stopped by the bunker to research Atlantia. After finding some leads, we gave them a cell-phone, and they left for Seattle.

An hour later, Iris arrived with several feeders. She had some weird glasses that she was using to track them. I think she wants to kill them.

We're trying to warn Matt, but she trashed our equipment. It could take weeks to rebuild.

We'll send another bird as soon as we learn anything. I hope things are going better in the palace.

With love,
Klinton and Ron

"That backstabbing bitch," I hiss. "She's probably caught up to them by now."

"They'll be okay," Antai says matter-of-factly.

"You don't know that."

"She let Ron and Klinton live," Antai notes. "I could be wrong, but I don't think she has it in her."

"She was my father's executioner," I remind him. "I'm pretty sure she does."

Antai studies me. If he still had fingers, I'm sure they'd be tapping on his belt.

"You doing okay, Rose?"

The truth is, I'm not. I can't take it any longer, but I can't tell him that. He's too fragile right now.

"I'm surviving," I say. "What about you?"

"I'm okay," he says.

I sit down on the bed so that I'm not towering over him. "You sure?" I ask. "I haven't seen you wink in a while."

A sliver of a smile returns, before it disappears again, like a fleeting rainbow after a storm.

"Actually," Antai says, "I wanted to apologize for how things went in the library yesterday."

"You don't have to apologize."

"Well, I want to," he insists. "I wish I could go back and do things differently."

I raise an eyebrow, mischievously. "I'm curious. What would you do differently?"

"I would have winked more."

I find myself smiling this time. "I would've liked that."

Suddenly, the air reverberates around my hand, giving it a subtle squeeze. I'm not sure if he can feel it, but I squeeze back.

"So, we're good?" he asks.

"We're good," I say.

He nods, falling silent.

"Hey, Antai?"

"Yeah?"

"There's no rush to get back to how things were. We can take things slow, figure out our new normal. I'm not in a rush. I hope you know that."

He considers my words for a second before he nods. "I do. Thanks."

"Good… Hey, can I ask you something random? Do you know Crasilda's older sister?"

"Drizzy? The crazy one?"

"She's crazy?"

"Yeah. She sat next to me for my last year of institute. She kept telling people the Palace was cursed. Always paranoid that someone was out to get her. She ran off before The Dividing. Her parents found her in the Ring, but she refused to go home. Last I heard, she was a beggar near Covenant Street—probably feeder-food if I had to guess." Antai furrows an eyebrow. "Why do you ask?"

"Crasilda confuses me, that's all. I'm trying to figure out her motive."

Antai shakes his head. "You're counting raindrops, Rose. Let it go before you end up soaked."

"Yeah… Maybe…"

Antai glances down at his watch, which is strapped to the wheelchair's armrest. "I should probably get going. I'm meeting up with Ortega at noon."

"Diego? What for?"

"I challenged him to a rematch."

I spring to my feet. "No! You can't be serious!"

Antai laughs. "Calm down. It was a joke. I don't need another beating."

I sit back down. "Then why meet?"

"It's actually a bit of a surprise," Antai says. "Don't worry. I'll show you eventually." He gives me a quick wink.

The air vibrates behind his wheelchair, pushing him toward the door. Before I can help him, the handle turns and the door swings open. "I'll roll by tonight."

"See you then."

As soon as the door closes, Nevela is knocking on the maid's door.

"Come in, it's unlocked."

The door opens, and Nevela steps into the room. I expect her to start interviewing me about Antai, but she doesn't. Instead, she holds open the maid's door.

"Rose, could you join me in my chambers for a moment? I need your opinion on a matter."

"Oh, of course. Be right there."

I look over at Klinton's note.

Burn!

The paper disintegrates into a puff of smoke, leaving black ash on my desktop.

"Coming."

I step into the room, smiling at Wendy who lounges in a rocking chair. Their room is spotless except for three strips of fabric laid out on Nevela's bed.

Nevela skips over to the fabric and stands beside her bed. "Okay, I'm making a dress for you, and I want to know which color you prefer. I tried to stick with the winter theme." She points at each color as she announces them. "We have burgundy, sapphire blue, and dark emerald."

"I'm not sure I understand."

"Clothes are quite the commodity right now. These are the only fabrics I could get a hold of."

I shake my head. "Sorry, what I meant was, why would I need a new dress?"

"Well… the Winter Solstice is only a month away. I wanted to get an early start."

"Oh, Nevela. That's so sweet, but with everything going on, I doubt we'll be having the Winter Banquet this year."

Nevela and Wendy share a knowing glance.

"What?"

Wendy grins. "You might as well tell her."

"Tell me what?"

"Well, this year, instead of the banquet, I was thinking we could have a masquerade instead. The Solstice Masquerade. It has a nice ring to it, doesn't it."

"It's a lovely thought," I say, "but I'm not sure if the Council will be on board."

Nevela and Wendy share another glance.

"What?" I ask.

Nevela is smiling from ear to ear. "That's the thing. I already pitched it to the High Council, and they approved." She flaps her hands excitedly. "They even added me to the Planning Committee."

"Really? A masquerade… with everything that's happened?"

"They were hesitant at first, but Antai helped convince them. The vote was unanimous."

"Unanimous? You're kidding."

Nevela's smile begins to falter. "What's wrong? You don't like the idea?"

"It's not that. It's just… who knows what condition we'll be in by the solstice. We might be out of food by then." *We might be dead*, I think, but I can't get myself to say it.

"That's the beauty of it," Nevela sings. "We have so many things to dread about the future; the masquerade will give us one little thing to look forward to."

"If we're starving, we're gonna need a good distraction," Wendy adds.

"I suppose we will," I admit, tapping my foot. "And what about drinks? They emptied the wine cellar days ago."

"Already covered,' Wendy says. "Bob made three barrels of his special brew before he left. It's fermenting in his room."

"And," Nevela adds, "we're starting a dress-share program so that the laborers can borrow the right attire. The committee has thought of everything." She excitedly points at her bed. "All I need to know is what color you want."

Just be happy for her, Rose.

I study the fabrics for a second, forcing myself to smile. "Alright. Then I choose… burgundy."

"Oh, yay. I was hoping you'd pick that one. I already have a vision in mind. I was even thinking we can decorate Antai's wheelchair to match. It'll be so cute. And–"

"Owwww." Wendy doubles over, one hand clutching her belly, the other gripping the armrest. Her face is twisted, and her breath is rapid.

"What happened?" I demand.

"It's nothing," Wendy chokes. "Just Braxton Hicks contractions." She takes a few deep breaths, exhaling slowly through puckered lips.

I lean forward, trying to study her face. "Are you sure?" I ask.

"Yeah," she gasps. "I've been getting them all day. See…" She sits up a little taller. "It's already getting better."

"Okay," I say. "If you insist."

Nevela frowns. "What were we talking about? Oh yeah, the wheelchair. I was thinking of adding silver embroidery so that it complements the wheelchair. And we could cover—"

Wendy sucks in a quick breath, followed by a prolonged grimace. Once again, she stoops over and clutches her belly. "Ahhhhh," she groans.

"Again?"

"They don't usually hurt like this. I—" Wendy clenches her teeth and groans, exhaling forcefully.

"It's okay," I say. "Just breathe."

Nearly a minute goes by before Wendy relaxes. When she finally looks up at me, I see fear in her eyes. "These contractions feel different. I think I'm in labor."

"But… it's too soon," I argue. "How many weeks are you now?

She hesitates. "33."

"Okay." I start to pace. "Okay. Everything will be fine. We'll get you to the healers, and they'll take care of the rest."

Wendy nods, but she isn't convinced. I can see the fear in her eyes.

"C'mon." I place my hand between her shoulder blades and guide her toward the door. "Let's get you to the loft."

We only take two steps before Wendy doubles over. "Another one is coming," she mutters quickly. Her face scrunches and her eyes squeeze shut. "Aghhh" she groans through clenched teeth.

I turn to Nevela. "Run to the Healing Loft and get a healer. Ask for Jephora. Hurry!"

"On it!" Nevela mutters as she dashes across the room. In a matter of seconds, she's out the door and sprinting down the hall.

"Why Jephora?" Wendy gasps between contractions.

"To be honest, I don't have a lot of healers I trust right now. Kendra is gone, and Lady Xantone…"

"But you trust this one?" Wendy worries.

It's little more than a gut feeling, but I nod confidently. "I do."

I wait at Wendy's side in silence. Three more contractions come and go before Nevela returns.

"I've got her," she happily squeaks as she flings the door open.

Jephora steps hesitantly into the room. "Your Majesty, I was trying to explain to your maid that labor isn't my specialty. I would be doing you a disservice. Mrs. Glaysburn would be a better fit for this case. Perhaps—"

"I want it to be you," Wendy interjects. "Please!"

Jephora looks at Wendy, looks back at the exit, and sighs. "As you wish." Her hands go straight to Wendy's belly, instilled with a new sense of urgency.

"33 weeks?" Jephora confirms.

"Yes, ma'am."

Jephora closes her eyes. “Mmhhh, that sounds about right. He’s small—a little over 4 pounds.”

Wendy sucks in a breath. “It’s a boy?”

“Oh, I’m sorry. I assumed you knew. He’s a boy, all right.”

Wendy says nothing. If anything, she looks horrified. She simply swallows, staring at the corner of the room.

“Let’s see,” Jephora mutters to herself. “No hydrocephalus. No heart defects. Oh my…”

Wendy stiffens. “What’s wrong?”

“He uh…” Jephora laughs awkwardly. “He just started peeing out of nowhere. I didn’t expect it.”

Wendy wrinkles her nose. “He pees in there?”

Jephora nods. “Quite a bit, actually.” She removes her hands. “He looks healthy, but his lungs are still underdeveloped. On average, they won’t mature until 37 weeks. If he’s born today, I fear he won’t survive.”

Wendy’s jaw falls open. “He won’t?”

“It’s okay,” Jephora insists. “This is nothing to worry about. I can stop the contractions—calm things down and keep him inside. However, that doesn’t mean the contractions won't come back tomorrow. We’ll have to keep a close eye on you from now on, okay? And I want you on bed rest for the next few weeks, got it? That’ll help postpone labor.”

Wendy nods, clenching her teeth as another contraction overtakes her body. “Okay…” she groans.

“Alright. Let's get started.” Jephora returns her hands to Wendy’s belly and closes her eyes.

Immediately, the contractions seem to weaken, and Wendy breathes a bit easier. I watch in silence as Jephora works her magic. Sure enough, the time between contractions grows longer and longer. Within a half hour, they stop altogether.

“How are you feeling?” Jephora finally asks. “Better?”

“Much better,” Wendy gushes. “I can’t thank you enough.”

“It’s nothing,” Jephora insists. “You make much better company than a corpse. Trust me.”

Wendy frowns. “A corpse?”

Jephora frowns as well. “I’m sorry, I thought you knew.”

“Jephora is a pathologist,” I explain. “Typically, she works with the deceased, but she used to work with newborns.”

“Oh,” Wendy says, unsure how to respond. “Well, thank you.”

“You rest up, and remember, bed rest for the next few weeks. I want you on your feet no more than an hour a day, got it?”

Wendy nods.

“Good,” Jephora says, turning to me. “Before I go, can we have a word in private?”

“Of course.” I lead her into my room and close the maid’s door. “What is it?”

As soon as we’re alone, Jephora’s cheery smile fades into a look of horror. “I’m sorry, Your Majesty, but I lied.”

“Excuse me?”

“The baby isn’t healthy. His intestines are outside of his body. It’s called an omphalocele.”

“I’m sorry?” I blink my confusion. “What?”

“It’s somewhat rare, but I’ve seen it before. The baby’s intestines are protruding from the abdomen. I should’ve said something, but I didn’t know how. I’m not used to giving bad news.”

“Okay,” I take a deep breath, trying to wrap my head around the diagnosis. “What does that mean for the baby?”

“It depends,” Jephora says. “According to the textbooks, it can go away on its own, but that’s not very common. Almost certainly, it’ll need healing, but he’ll have to survive a few years until he can consciously give permission.”

“The last time you saw this,” I whisper, “did the baby survive that long?”

Jephora chews on her lip.

“Jephora?”

“No,” Jephora breathes. “She only made it a month.”

Suddenly, I feel sick to my stomach. “Maybe he’ll be different. He could be one of the luck—”

Knock! Knock! Knock!

"Oh, Roseyyy?" General Kaynes' pretentious voice hums from the hallway. "Where are you?"

I fall silent.

Jack knocks again. "Come now, don't be shy. I heard your little voices talking. I know you're in there."

His tone triggers something within me. I'm a rabbit hearing the howl of a wolf. Every fiber begs me to get distance—urges me to run.

"Helloooo?" he sings.

C'mon, Rose. Get a hold of yourself.

"W-what do you want?" I finally demand, my voice quivering.

"I hope I'm not making you nervous," he mocks.

"What do you want?" I repeat, this time with more conviction.

"I have a message from our mutual friend," Jack responds. "He wants to meet today for lunch. Shall I remind you how excited he is to see you? It might do you well to put in some effort this time. A little makeup goes a long way. Anyways, come out when you're ready."

"He wants to meet today? Like, now?"

"You have five minutes. Let's not keep our gracious host waiting."

22

MATT

My arm presses downward, driving the knife at Kildron's neck. It pushes into his skin, drawing blood, cutting into the tendons at the top of his collarbone.

Noooo!

I use my desperation as a mental foothold. With my newfound anchor, I push against Iris. My arm stops. The knife quivers, pressing into the connective tissue, but it doesn't cut.

Really? For him? Iris sneers. *He doesn't love us; he abandoned us. He's lonely and we're his entertainment.*

My body weight tips forward, but I fight harder. My bicep contracts, and the dagger lifts from his neck.

Fine, Iris thinks. *I'll do it myself.*

My arm swings, throwing my dagger at her feet. Then, she reaches into my shirt and removes my amplifier. With a flick of my wrist, she tosses it into the air.

The second it leaves my fingers, Iris jumps back to her own body. Her hand reaches out and snatches my amulet from the air, looping it over her head in a single motion. Then she retrieves the weapons scattered about the floor. She picks up my dagger first, followed by the spear.

My amplifier is gone. I have nothing but my bare fists.

I'm powerless.

I crouch by Kildron's side. There's one last thing I can do. I place my hand on his face as Iris raises the spear over his heart.

Jazon! I command the morph mask.

I have a specific memory in mind—a memory I got from Iris the very first time she possessed me.

Kildron quivers as he transforms. His stubble recedes and his hair darkens. His face bubbles as his features rearrange. His nose shrinks, and skin fills the cleft of his chin. His clothes shrink and his pigment darkens.

Kildron is gone, replaced with a handsome young man—the only man Iris ever loved.

He's wearing what you'd expect for a laborer—a cotton top with thick, bulky pants—but that's not all. His clothes are soaked from the rain. His hair is damp and plastered to his forehead. Drops of water collect on his cheeks and dribble over his lips.

The last detail is the most important: blood soaks Jazon's shirt, gushing from a bullet wound in his side.

Every detail, down to the rain-soaked socks, mimics that tragic night. This is how he looked as he passed away in her arms.

Iris shudders at the sight of him. She sucks in a quiet gasp and nearly drops the spear. Then, she wrenches her head to the side, unable to bear the sight of him. Still, her eyes flicker back at the body in disbelief.

"Change him back!" she demands, her voice catching in her throat. She averts her gaze, as if his very appearance scalds her eyes. "Change. Him. NOW!"

"No," I whisper.

Iris paces back and forth. Then, she tightens her grip on the spear shaft. Twisting, she lifts the weapon over Jazon's chest. Slowly, painfully, she presses it into his shirt.

"Uhhhhh," Kildron groans, but it comes out as Jazon's voice.

Iris gawks at him, her mouth half open. The spear shaft shakes, and she turns away.

"Change him," Iris whispers, "or I'll kill you."

I'm not afraid. Just moments ago, when she held the knife to my throat, I could feel her hesitation.

"No."

The air reverberates around my throat, pressing into my trachea, but it never squeezes.

"Fuck you, Matt!"

She reaches for Jazon's chin—for the morph mask.

"No!" I push her hand away, my anger rising. "You say you believe in his cause. Then prove it! Prove it, Iris!" I wave my hand at the security guard. "It's easy to kill a stranger. Or maybe a father you never knew. But this is Jazon. You see him here. He's breathing. In this moment, he's alive. Are you going to kill him too? Do you have that kind of faith in his cause?"

Iris squeezes her eyes shut. With her free hand, she presses her knuckles into her forehead.

"Show me you believe, Iris." I step back, gesturing at Jazon. "Convince me! Do it for the Holy One. I want you to do it. Do you hear me? I want to believe he'll save us, but you have to convince me!"

Iris grits her teeth. She twists the spear in her hands, adjusting the grip. Then, she returns the tip against Jazon's chest.

"Everything can be undone." I remind her. "He can bring Jazon back. Do you believe it? Show me you believe it! Show me you have no doubt! SHOW ME, IRIS! DO IT! DO IT!"

"AHHHHH!" she screams, lifting the spear and thrusting down. The speartip stops just above Jazon's shirt. Slowly, her fingers unfurl and the spear clatters to the ground.

For a moment, I think it's over. Then, Iris turns. She marches over to the dead security guard, bends over, and retrieves his revolver.

After checking that the chamber is loaded, she points the gun at Jazon's head. It's a double-action firearm. As her finger tugs the trigger, the hammer slowly draws back.

She doesn't look at Jazon directly. She looks to the side, aiming out of the corner of her eye.

This time, I watch with bated breath. The slightest flinch of her finger will end Kildron's life. With each second, her finger squeezes tighter, and the hammer swings further back.

Her eyes flicker sideways, and she pauses. The revolver hammer wiggles like a windshield wiper as her finger quivers.

Finally, she lowers the gun. She stares down at the weapon for a few moments before taking a deep breath. Then, she raises it again. Only this time, she doesn't aim it at Jazon. She presses the muzzle to her temple and squeezes her eyes shut. With her entire body taut, she pulls the trigger.

I watch helplessly as the hammer draws all the way back. I can't use dominion. I can't do anything. All I can do is watch as the hammer drops.

Click.

I blink, confused by what I see.

Iris holds the trigger down, but the revolver hammer is jammed. It stops a centimeter from striking the firing pin, as if held in the air by an invisible force.

Kendra materializes next to Iris, her index finger filling the space between the hammer and the firing pin. She takes the gun as Iris starts sobbing.

Revolver in hand, Kendra wraps her arms around Iris and rocks her side to side.

"It's okay," she soothes. "It's gonna be okay, now. Everything's gonna be okay."

23

ROSE

I wait with Jack in the stairwell as Crasilda convenes with my father. She's been in there for half an hour—much longer than I expected.

Finally, the door opens and Crasilda struts out, her wide grin exposing a perfect smile. My father healed her, somehow rebuilding and aligning her missing teeth. The act alone is miraculous, not to mention wasted on someone so dreadful.

"Your turn." Crasilda sneers as she passes me, making her way down the staircase.

I stop in front of the door, hand resting lightly on the handle. Last time I stepped foot in that room, Antai was cut to pieces.

"Go on," Jack coos. "He won't bite."

I turn the handle and walk through the doorway.

Like last time, my father has prepared a meal. The table is turned into one giant charcuterie board. Cured meats and large wheels of cheese are fancifully arranged like a market display. I spot artisan bread with various jars of jam—the lids already removed. Closest to my seat are two wine bottles and a small platter of fruit, including blackberries, cherries, and honey-drizzled cantaloupe.

My father sits on the far side of the table, one leg crossed over the other. His plate is already filled with salami and prosciutto. He holds a wine glass in his hand—only a few sips of the red left.

“Hello, Rose. Take a seat. I want to apologize for all of the chaos last time. I’m hoping our visit today will be a bit more… civilized.”

I don’t say anything. I simply stare as I take my seat, letting him see the hatred in my eyes.

“Well, dig in,” he says, folding a slice of prosciutto. “We can talk when we’re full.”

I look at the food, but I don’t move.

“What's wrong?” He asks. “Worried you’ll catch the plague?”

I stiffen.

“Oh, yes. I know all about your infectious escapade. I must admit, the virus was clever. But I can assure you it won’t be a threat while you're here.”

“How can you be so sure?”

“Because I took the appropriate countermeasures. I spent nearly two days replicating the virus. Then, I inactivated it. Yesterday, I infused it with the water supply—a universal vaccine, if you will. We’ll lose some feeders of course—those initially infected—but the rest will be immune by the end of the week.”

He takes a sip of his wine. “I’ll admit, the whole fiasco was really quite a nuisance. I lost several days of precious time. Certainly, you can see why I had to kill Madame Xantone.” He lowers his head. “Honestly, a shame. She was my healer when I was a boy. Saved me from a stomach bug more than once.”

Zezric picks up a slice of salami and pops it in his mouth. He gestures at the table. “Go ahead and dig in. Have as much as you’d like.”

“I'm not hungry,” I mutter.

As if on cue, my stomach grumbles.

Zezric cracks a smile. “I get it, Rose. I hurt you, and now you want to hurt me. You don’t want me feeling like I’ve done you any favors. That’s completely understandable.”

I bite my tongue.

“Well, if it makes you feel any better, it does pain me, knowing how you feel—such animosity from my own daughter. Believe it or not, I want your approval, Rose. I really do."

I say nothing, my rage muddling my thoughts.

"That said, I can sympathize with your perspective. It's fathomable why you might resist me. However, I'm afraid I can no longer tolerate your acts of rebellion. I want to reiterate what Jack told you. Any opposition, any resistance whatsoever, and I'll destroy the palace."

I should be afraid—I've seen him unleash his power—but instead, all I feel is rage.

"I won't let you do this," I seethe.

Zezric uncrosses his legs. "Yes, you will. You will sit there and do nothing. Because if you don't, I will kill you and everyone you care about."

"Then you might as well kill me now."

Zezric swings his arm, shattering the wine glass on the edge of the table. "DAMNIT, ROSE! Don't you get how serious this is? I want you to be safe, but you make it sooo very difficult for me. I can't lose my credibility, not after everything I've done. My word is law; they *have* to know that. They have to. So..." He exhales, his tone instantly turning casual. "If I say there will be consequences, I will follow through, no matter how much it hurts me."

"I know you will."

"Do you, Rose? Because I'm not so sure you do. You criticize me for killing masses, and now you're about to do the very same—jeopardizing lives like they're nothing to you."

I shake my head. "You can't compare us. This is not the same."

"Then please, stop resisting, or their blood—the blood of countless children... countless friends—will be on your hands."

"No!" I seethe. "I am not responsible for what you do. This is on you!"

Zezric pretends he didn't hear me. "In case I haven't made myself clear, I'd like to show you something." He twists in his seat, looking toward one of the back rooms. "Levon, can you come out here for a moment?"

After a moment, a man emerges from the bedroom and walks down the hall, wearing nothing but a pair of trousers. Familiar symbols are tattooed across his chest.

Fire from heaven.

Zezric smiles proudly. "I have three more just like him, ready at my disposal. If I give the word, the palace will be nothing but rubble by nightfall. This is real, Rose. You've already lost. There's nothing you can do to stop me."

Seeing my look of horror, Zezric smiles. "Thank you, Levon. You're dismissed."

I watch as the man retreats. All I can think about is the spell. The way his body will incinerate the moment it's unleashed. The way his flesh and bones will instantly turn to dust.

"Does he know what it'll do?" I ask.

"Of course he does," Zezric scoffs. "He volunteered for this, as did the others."

I shake my head. "Why would he do that?"

"The same reason most men obey God—the promise of heavenly reward. And reward him, I shall." He reaches down and stacks a salami onto a crouton before tossing the snack into his mouth. He bites down with an obnoxious crunch.

"How did you get this way?" I ask.

Zezric holds up a finger as he quickly chews and swallows. "Excuse me?" He seems genuinely perplexed.

"Is it because of the person you possessed?" I demand. "I know true possession is different. You… intertwine. Was he a feeder? Is he the one making you like this?"

Zezric sighs. "No, Rose. He is not making me like this."

"It was a feeder, wasn't it?" I speculate. "He corrupted you. That's why you're so heartless."

"Rose, will you st—"

"He's messing with your head. He's making you think this way. It's the only explanation. He—"

"SILENCE!" Zezric screams, his voice amplified with dominion. My body goes rigid, and my jaw hangs open.

Seeing my terror, his rage instantly dissipates. "Thank you." He straightens his suit coat and crosses his leg. "You want to know? So be it." With his glass broken, he reaches for the wine bottle. "There came a moment, 18 years ago, where I was on the verge of death. I had no choice; I abandoned my body."

"You soul-walked?"

"I did. And I got lucky. I found a host. It wasn't a feeder. It wasn't a bloodthirsty killer. It was just a random woman I'd never met. Some unlucky damsel who happened to wander by."

He watches me for a moment, studying my reaction. "At the time," he continues, "I had the mark of the beast. I was, for all intents and purposes, a demon. But, once I anchored myself to her body, I lost the effect of the spell. Without the spell, I had no advantage. We were equals, forever intertwined."

He tips the bottle slowly, taking a measured sip. "I already had plans to find the Books of Life. I knew what had to be done, but she wouldn't let me. Her morals held me captive, and her consciousness fought me every step of the way. Her weakness was like an infection, making me doubt my cause. Until one day, I figured it out. I had to consume her soul—absorb her from the inside. It was the only way to regain my autonomy. So, that's exactly what I did. That was the day I became a feeder."

He gives the entire wine bottle a swirl. "So, to answer your question, nobody is making me this way, Rose. There is no puppeteer pulling my strings. No devil on my shoulder, whispering in my ear. I'm the only one." He takes another swig from the bottle, this one a bit more sloppy. "There's no one to blame but me."

"You're..." I can't even think of the words. "You're sick."

He laughs. "Yes, Rose, I am. I get sick just thinking about the things I've done. That is part of the sacrifice that makes me holy. Don't you see?"

My nose wrinkles, disclosing my dissent.

"You don't believe me?"

"You think genocide makes you holy?" I scoff.

Zezric sits up, happy to see me engaging in the conversation. "And what do you consider a true sacrifice? Giving to the poor? Feeding the hungry?"

"Sure," I say. "More of a sacrifice than murder, that's for sure."

"And when a man gives money to the poor, what happens in response?"

"He helps people, that's what!"

"Sure," Zezric agrees, "but it's more than that. When a rich man gives to the poor, he feels good inside, right? He feels proud of himself, doesn't he? Is this not a direct consequence of his benevolence? And if his sacrifice is instantly rewarded, can we consider it a sacrifice at all? No! It becomes transactional. Self-serving. Do a good deed, feel good in return."

I want to argue, but I don't know how.

"Aha!" Zezric exclaims. "You get it, don't you? So long as the benefactor profits from his service, it can't be considered a true sacrifice. Compare that to Abraham, for example—commanded to kill his own son. That… that was a true sacrifice… nothing but grief to be gained."

He takes a sip from the bottle, letting his words ferment in the air, growing more potent as the pause grows longer.

When I don't disagree, he nods, lowering the bottle. "Now, take me for example. I, too, am fighting to feed the hungry." He sighs, his shoulders slumping. "More than that. I'm fighting to rid the entire world of hunger. And what must I sacrifice to attain this goal?"

He looks at me expectantly, waiting for my response, but I say nothing.

Frowning, he takes another sip from his bottle. "I'll tell you what; it's not my wealth. It's not my status. It's not any number of Earthly possessions. Oh, I wish it were that simple, Rose, but Godhood requires a godly sacrifice."

He watches me for a second longer, giving me one last chance to respond. Then, he looks out the window. "Like Abraham, I must abandon my morals, Rose—the one thing that makes me human. I must immolate my conscience—my inner voice. Set it upon the sacrificial altar and burn it until nothing but ashes remain."

His hand tightens on the bottle. "Don't you see? To get where I am now, I had to kill the innocent. I had to torture the weak and maim the young. I had to do… terrible things to the ones I love most… even you." He swallows once, then again, his throat wrestling with his guilt. Finally, he looks back at me. "But I do it for a greater purpose. I do it out of love."

"Bullshit!" I sneer. "You don't get to talk about love! You don't love m—!"

The words are still on my tongue as the air ripples around my throat. For a second, I fear he'll snap my neck, but the force immediately dissipates.

Zezric turns away, and I think I see a tear in the corner of his eye.

"I sacrifice my daughter's love—I sacrifice *everything*—and what do I get in return? Do I get warmth in my heart and peace in my mind? Do I get the conviction of a job well done?" His hand tightens, shattering the bottle within his palm. The blood begins to drip as he continues to squeeze the shards.

"Quite the opposite. I'm left with endless guilt and sleepless nights. My reward is a lifetime of self-hatred." With his unbloodied hand, he taps on his chest. "Pain is my reward, Rose. Hellfire and damnation, my only recompense."

Finally, he opens his hand and drops the crushed glass on the table. With a frown, he inspects his hands, waiting as the gashes knit themselves closed. Without bothering to wipe the blood, he looks up at me. "You see, that's what truly makes me a saint. I'm willing to endure a life of hell to make this world heavenly. I'm willing to take the sins upon myself—do the killing with my own hands—so that no one will ever kill again. I'm willing to hurt the ones I love so that all suffering can cease. That is true sacrifice—saving the world, knowing it'll only make me miserable."

"And what if you fail? What if all this…" I pause, failing to find the words. "What if everything you've done is for nothing?"

Zezric shrugs. "If that's the case, I hope I'll get what I deserve."

24

ROSE

Everyone arrives at my chambers as planned, staggering their entrances a few minutes apart.

Wendy is laying on my comforter, adhering to Jephora's bed rest prescription. Nevela is sitting beside her, and Gideon is standing by the window.

The group is so much smaller than I'd hoped. Antai is at the High Council Meeting, keeping an eye on Jack and Crasilda. Octavian is patrolling the Royal Wing. And Madame Xantone was murdered.

Small is good, I tell myself. '*Loyalty before legions.*' A quote Grandpa used to say.

Diego is the last to arrive. He sulks through the door, keeping his gaze focused on the floor. When he glances up, he's wearing a searing scowl. I'd expect nothing less after the attack on his family.

"Alright, that's everyone," I announce once the door is shut. "Thanks for coming. A lot has changed since we last met. I have some matters I'd like to discuss, but first, you all deserve an update."

I glance at my whiteboard as I collect my thoughts.

"On a positive note, we've been making progress with the Adamic weapons. Mr. Enemary and his son have already made a thousand

Adamic arrowheads, and Gideon has constructed over 100 bows. He started archery training yesterday."

"We had a big crowd," Gideon beams. "What did you think, Diego? You got the hang of it pretty quick."

"Yeah, it was fine," Diego grunts.

"And Nevela," I remember. "She's been working on the Adamic armor. How many have you made, Nevela?"

"I just finished my twentieth, but I'm getting much faster at it."

"So that's going well," I sigh. "Unfortunately… that's about it for the good news. We haven't heard from Bob, and it's been five days… We haven't heard from Kendra or Matt either. And, as I'm sure you're all aware, the Adamic bullet didn't work." I don't elaborate.

"And what of the virus?" Gideon asks hopefully. "I've heard it's beginning to spread."

"About that…" I take a deep breath. "I met with the Holy One yesterday to discuss the terms of our stalemate. Unfortunately, he knows about the plague and… he claims he's already vaccinated the feeders. He killed Madame Xantone as retribution—or rather, Crasilda did at his command."

I give a somber glance around the room. "This isn't what you want to hear, but the Holy One gave me a warning when we spoke yesterday. If we do anything to rebel, anything at all, he'll destroy the palace."

Gideon frowns. "What are you suggesting, My Queen?"

"I'm not sure if we really have a choice. He has spies in the palace. Crasilda was searching my room, and who knows how many others are out there. I just… I… I think we should play it safe. We can continue with the archery training, but no more Adamic sewing. No more Adamic arrows. Everything needs to be hidden where they won't be found."

Diego clenched his fists. "That's it? We're just giving up?"

"We're not giving up, we're buying time," I insist. "Bob is still down there looking for an escape route. Matt and Kendra are looking for Atlantia. They could bring reinforcements any day now, but if we don't lay low, there won't be a sanctuary for them to save."

"They won't find it," Diego blurts. "It's pointless. They're pissing in the wind."

I shake my head. "The Holy One sent feeders after them. He knows what they're doing, and it scares him. That has to mean something. I think they have a chance."

"Or, we could fight," Diego insists. "We already have the arrows and the armor. If we surprise them—"

"Diego," I interject. "I'm sorry, but it's not enough. Not even close."

"You guys are serious? We're just gonna let him do whatever he wants. We're gonna lay down at his feet and let him finish us off?"

"Submission isn't always defeat," Gideon says, "We must weigh the risk and reward."

"We don't need to weigh anything!" Diego shouts. "We need to kill him, no matter the cost." Diego looks around, expecting support.

"I don't know," Wendy says. "I think I agree with Rose."

"Are you freaking kidding me? Have you already forgotten what he did? Do you know many bodies are out there, rotting in the snow? And it's not just that. He trapped my mom in a prison and stole her dominion like a leech. You were there Nevela. How can you act like it never happened?"

Nevela says nothing, choosing instead to stare at her lap.

"And you?" Diego points in my direction. "You wear that tattoo like it means something. What would Velma think of this?"

I look down at my wrist, studying my tattoo.

With so much recent death, I haven't even thought about Velma.

Diego's finger shakes. "She would never let him bully us like this. She would fight."

"She would choose her battles," Wendy argues.

Diego shakes his head. "No. This is insane. Are we even sure we can trust her?" He points at me accusingly. "How do we know you're not stalling for the Holy One?"

"Diego!" Wendy gasps. "What's wrong with you?"

Diego meets my gaze. His eyes are suspicious slits and his jaw is taut with enmity. "Go on, tell them!" Diego demands. "Tell them who he is…Or do they already know? Was I the only one in the dark?"

"What?" Nevela demands. "Tell us what?"

"Tell them about the Holy One, Rose… Or would you rather they hear it from me?"

My eyes double in size. "Who told you?"

"The entire Guard is talking about it," Diego says. "Soon everyone will know your little secret."

Crasilda!

Nevela looks at me, "What is he talking about, Rose?"

Already, the panic coils around my throat like a boa constrictor. "I was going to tell you, I just didn't know the right time. There was so much going on. I—"

"The Holy One is her dad," Diego blurts.

"But— no. " Nevela's jaw quivers.

"That's right! Her dad was the one who locked you under Hogrum. He's the one who drained your soul day after day." He glances at Wendy. "Her dad sent the feeders that killed Velma. He… he killed everyone! He caused all of this! And she purposefully kept us in the dark!"

"This is why!" I bark. "I knew you'd blame me. I didn't want us to be divided."

"Oh, really?" Diego rolls his eyes. "So you lied, instead. What a great way to earn our loyalty."

"I didn't lie."

"Yes, you did!" Diego seethes. "Don't pretend there's a difference."

"You really knew?" Nevela squeaks. "Since the invasion? And you didn't say anything?"

"It's complicated, Nevela. I wanted to tell you," I protest. "You have to believe me!"

"What's complicated?" Diego demands. "Whether you should help your dad or not?"

"No! Of course not! Look what he did to Antai. You think I could ever support that?" The more I think about it, the more my shame mutates into outrage. "You guys know me. Do you really think I'd ever help that monster? Do any of you actually believe that?"

No one speaks. After a second, Nevela shakes her head, followed by Wendy.

"Diego?" I slouch to meet his downcast eyes. "Tell me you don't believe that."

"I…" He meets my gaze for an instant, only to look away. "I'm not sure."

Gideon steps forward. "It seems that the Queen has made a mistake. Many of us were hurt by that mistake. However, that error does not erase the rationale of her suggestion. The truth is, we can't risk war. Not yet. We need more time, and compliance gives us that time."

Diego shakes his head, hands still balled into fists. "Live to fight another day, right?"

"That's right," I say.

"I don't believe that's an option anymore," Diego growls. "If the Equalists have taught me anything, it's this: compliance leads to submission, and submission leads to servitude."

"Diego…" I plead, but I don't know what to say.

"No, thank you. I'm done." He strides to the exit, hesitating in front of the door. "If I get the chance to hurt him, I'm going to take it." He reaches for the handle.

"And what if you get us all killed?" I demand.

Diego pauses with his hand on the door. "My dad once told me, 'Every war requires sacrifice.' At the time, I thought he was crazy, but I'm starting to think he was right all along." With that, he disappears through the doorway.

25

MATT

I look out over the ocean, not that there's much to see. Water, water, and more water.

One month we've been sailing through the Atlantic. One month of white-topped waves and cloud-covered sky.

I reposition myself on the vinyl couch, overlooking the bow. I lift the seerglasses and place them over my head.

Rose.

Color swirls in the glass, like VR goggles, and a figure forms.

Rose is walking. She's bundled in thick pants and a winter coat—dressed for the outdoors. I can see tiny glimpses of the cobblestone as she steps, but her surroundings are dim and ambiguous. Her mouth moves as she talks to someone. If it's Antai, she doesn't hold his hand.

Suddenly, the ground begins to slope beneath her feet. She isn't just outside, she's outside the palace walls.

That's weird.

Footsteps approach—Kendra's by the sound of them. She must be finished with Kildron's healing session.

I remove the seerglasses as she takes a seat beside me, motioning at the relic.

"The palace okay?" she worries.

"Still standing. How's Kildron?" I ask. His fractured skull and severed Achilles tendon healed quickly—within a week of dedicated healing—but his brain isn't quite so responsive.

"Fine," Kendra sighs. "His migraines are doing better, but not his hemianopsia."

Hemianopsia. Kendra already explained the word to me. It means losing half your visual field. In Kildron's case, he can't see the left side of each eye.

"You'll figure it out," I assure her. "These things take time."

"Maybe," Kendra shrugs. "Some things are out of my scope, Matt… Some things just don't heal."

I wrap my arm around her, pulling her close. She rests her head on my shoulder.

"And Iris?" I ask.

After the hotel incident, Kendra insisted she join us on the yacht, but it's been complicated. She sleeps all day and never leaves her room. Kildron thinks she may be a threat, and Kendra worries she's a threat to herself.

"She refused again," Kendra sighs. "I explained everything, but she doesn't want me in her head. I'm worried about her, Matt."

"I know." I tilt my head, resting it on hers. "Me too. We'll figure it out."

We sit there, enjoying the clear skies and the warm air. The sun is setting, and the water is a shimmering sheet of orange and red. I squint as the bottom of the sun dips behind the horizon.

A month ago, I would have made some comment about the spectacular view, but the sea lost its magic weeks ago.

I glance at Kendra. Her lips are drawn back and her forehead tense.

"What are you thinking about?" I ask.

"I… I don't want to say. It'll sound terrible."

"I won't judge."

"I…" She shakes her head. "I need more time to figure out what I want. Give me until tomorrow. We can talk about it then."

Concerned, I ease my consciousness forward, inhaling the subtlety of her emotions. Her soul reeks of disappointment, maybe even despair. She doesn't believe we'll find Atlantia, and she's convinced her family will die in the coming days. She's wasting what may be their final days on a fool's errand.

Suddenly, I sense something else: Anger.

"Demons, Matt!" Her torso stiffens, and she leans away from me. "Can't you give me some mental privacy for like five minutes. Seriously! I didn't give you unlimited access!"

"Sorry, I just—"

"I already told you I didn't want to talk about it. What gave you the impression I wanted you reading my mind?"

"Nothing. I'm sorry," I repeat. "It won't happen again."

Kendra sighs. "Just this once, I want to know how I feel about something before you do. Is that so much to ask?"

"You're right," I say. "I shouldn't have done that. Like I said, it won't happen again. I promise."

Kendra turns her head to the ocean, refusing to look me in the eyes.

"Kendra?"

"I'm thinking," she mutters.

I say nothing, letting the silence drag on. But after a few minutes, I lose patience.

"If you want, I'll tell Kildron to turn the ship around. We can drop you off on the coast. You'll be back at Cavernum in a few days."

"Seriously, Matt?" she groans. "I said I didn't want to talk about it." She stands suddenly. "I'm going to bed. Try not to wake me when you come in."

"Oh, okay. Goodnight," I manage, watching her retreat into the cabin.

How could I be so stupid?

I sit until the sunlight fades completely, slowly draining behind the horizon. At some point, Kildron joins me on the bow, pushing aside the pillows and stretching his legs.

He looks at me and frowns. "Long day?"

"You could say so."

"Wanna talk about it?"

"Not really."

Kildron smiles playfully. “We could practice Durebrum, and I could force it out of you.”

“No thanks.”

His lips flatten. “Suit yourself.” After a second, he glances back over. “What if I teach you something new? You wanna learn how to sense dominion? Or I could teach you how to fly.”

“I’m fine,”

Kildron sits forward, looking at me closer. “Really? Passing up a chance to fly? My son?” When I say nothing, he leans back, sinking into the couch cushion. “Alright, sure. We’ll just lounge and do nothing. Fine by me.”

We sit in silence as the stars begin to emerge. Eventually, I sigh. “She wants to go back.”

“Damn,” Kildron looks over at me, furrowing his brow. “She told you that?”

“Well… not exactly. But I could feel it.”

Kildron shrugs. “Yeah, maybe. Though I’m not too convinced. Sometimes, what people want isn’t what they want most. There’s a difference. Assuming one or the other can get you into trouble.”

“It doesn’t really matter,” I argue. “The bottom line is, she wants it. It’s not fair that she has to give up everything to be with me. If she stays, she’ll start to resent me. Maybe not at first, but eventually she will. I feel like it’s already happening.”

I expect him to disagree; but he only nods. “Makes sense,” he muses.

“She deserves to be with her family. I don’t know why I ever thought we could make it work.”

“I hear ya,” Kildron nods. “It’s a tough situation.” He doesn’t give advice. He just listens. His presence is surprisingly comforting.

I've been thinking about it for days, but I finally say it out loud. “I guess that’s it then. It won’t work between us. I think we need to end it.”

“Wait, what?” Kildron sits up, his eyes wide. “You two are breaking up?”

“It’s the only option. She’s better off without me.”

"Better off without you?" Kildron echoes. "Are you joking?"

"What?"

Kildron shrugs. "I don't know. This whole thing sounds a bit dramatic, if you ask me."

"How?" I demand. "You abandoned Iris for this same exact reason. As long as Kendra is out here, I put her at risk. Not to mention, I'm separating her from everyone she knows and loves."

Kildron grows quiet. "Hmmm, I suppose I did." He leans back, rubbing his chin. "Yeah, guess it makes sense when you put it like that. Damn… I really liked her for you." He thinks a moment longer before turning to me. "For what it's worth, I regret what happened with Iris. I shouldn't have left her how I did."

We sit in silence, listening to the seawater rush beneath the hull.

Eventually, I break the stalemate. "Be honest. Do you think this whole thing is a waste of time?"

Kildron stares out over the water. "You know, I used to have this saying, 'faith is the act of denying reason.'" He smiles to himself. "Jenevrah hated when I said it. She thought I was just being cynical, but I was convinced. Faith is a coping mechanism. Nothing more. It's an escape for those too weak to face reality."

What would Judy say? I wonder.

Nothing comes to mind. Something positive, I imagine, but the words don't come. Already, her influence is fading.

Kildron sits up straighter. "You asked if this trip is a waste of time, right?"

I nod.

Kildron sighs. "A few weeks ago, I thought you were dead. Every bit of logic pointed to your unequivocal demise. And yet, here you are, alive and well. Now, every night as I fall asleep, I wonder if things could've been different. If I had just had a little bit of faith, maybe I could've found you… If I had just believed, maybe… maybe I could've raised you myself. I have to live with that regret. So no, I don't think this was a waste. Now, no matter what the future holds, you'll always know you tried."

I feel a smile creeping on my face. *That's it.* I think to myself. *That's what Judy would say.*

"Hey, dad?"

"Yeah?"

"Thanks for talking. I needed this." I stand and reposition the cushions. "I think I'm going to bed.

Kildron smiles. "Anyt—"

Suddenly, the deck tips to the side as the yacht gradually turns left.

"Again?" Kildron frowns. "Piece of junk auto-pilot." He jumps to his feet, jogging up a flight of stairs toward the helm. I feel the boat steady as he takes the wheel.

I look out over the ocean, shoving down my hopes as they begin to rise.

It's nothing, Matt.

Suddenly, the deck lights flicker. Then, they go out completely, plunging the ship into complete darkness.

"Kildron?" I call into the void.

"It's the battery," he calls back from the helm. "The generator failed."

I can hear the hum of the engine. At least for the moment, we're still in motion.

CRASH!

The ship lurches as it strikes something below the water. I'm thrown to the floor, nearly tumbling beneath the railing as the boat decelerates. The engine falls silent as we coast to a stop.

Kildron swears from the helm.

"What was that?" I shout.

"I think we hit a reef," he says. "The radar isn't working. Look around. See if you see anything."

Light!

I command the air, illuminating the ship. Leaning over the railing, I illuminate the sea before me. The water is eerily calm. It swallows the light, revealing the occasional flash of a stony structure."

"I see rocks," I call back.

"What's going on?" Kendra calls, stumbling up onto the deck. "Did we hit something?"

Iris emerges behind her, her head on a swivel.

"We hit a reef," Kildron says. He turns the key to restart the engine. The motor grinds, but doesn't roar to life. "Don't worry, we're not taking water. We just need to jumpstart the generator."

Suddenly, I hear a splash in the distance. I turn back to the water, catching a flash of movement along the dark horizon.

Brighter!

My light intensifies, but it doesn't make a difference at this distance. I squint. Whatever it was, it's gone now.

"Did you see something?" Kendra asks.

"I don't know," I admit.

Suddenly, I hear it again. This time on the left side of the ship and much closer.

Kendra approaches the nearest stretch of railing and looks down, peering over the port side

"Hmmm," she says. "That's weir—"

She doesn't finish the word before a giant blob of water erupts from the ocean. It moves like an appendage, rising over the railing and descending on her head. The water engulfs her entire body before retracting back into the ocean, dragging her with it.

"Kendra!" I scream.

I'm gripping my amulet now, sprinting toward the railing where she just stood. I don't make it before the yacht rocks. The deck tilts toward me as a massive wave crashes over the bow. It sweeps my feet out from under me and washes me toward the opposite side of the yacht. Before I can stop myself, the wave drags me beneath the railing.

I manage a gasp of air before I plunge into the frigid ocean.

Light!

Salt water stings my eyes as I scan the ocean around me. I search for an attacker, but I see nothing but bubbles and blackness.

Condense.

I command the water beneath my feet, shaping the liquid into two solid footholds.

Lift!

I rocket upward. As my head breaks the surface, the water continues to push on my feet, lifting until my shoes rest on top of the water. I'm only a few feet from the yacht. I can see Iris and Kildron on the deck. They weren't swept overboard like I was.

Kendra!

There's no time to waste. I run along the top of the water, supporting each step with dominion. As I approach the side of the hull, I command the water beneath me.

Rise!

The water erupts like a geyser. It throws me into the air and over the railing. I crash onto the deck, rolling to my feet. In seconds, I'm portside, scanning the water below.

Iris doesn't help me search, her eyes dart back and forth, scanning the horizon. "It's out there," she breathes. "Whatever it is."

As if on cue, I see a flash of movement in the distance. I squint, trying to make sense of what I see. Something is gliding across the surface of the water—something big. The creature is black, blending in with the night sky. As it moves, the stars disappear behind it, reappearing a moment later.

I watch it for as long as I can, but as soon as I blink, I lose track of it.

Kildron leans forward, squinting. "What was that?"

I turn back to the water, growing desperate. My heart pounds. "Kendra!"

Silence. The water is eerily calm. As I look down, my reflection stares back at me, illuminated by Iris's light dominion.

"Kendra!" I scream again. "Kendr—"

A plume of bubbles—likely containing Kendra's last breath—simmer on the surface a stone's throw from the ship.

I'm already in motion. I hurdle feet-first over the railing, commanding the water in mid-air. The liquid feels like jelly as my feet plunge through the surface. I only sink to my waist before slowing to a stop. Then, the ocean pushes me back to the surface. I take a few quick steps across the water stopping at the spot I last saw Kendra. *Illuminate!*

I spot her almost immediately. Her arms flail a dozen feet beneath the surface. As the bubbles spill from her mouth, she sinks faster and faster.

I clap my hands above my head and dive in her direction. When the bubbles clear, she's still out of reach, drifting deeper and deeper.

Flow!

A current forms. It rushes toward Kendra, carrying me with it. As soon as I grab her arm, she clings to me. She pushes down on my shoulders, trying to lift herself toward the surface.

Rise!

The water churns around us. A thousand watery hands tug on my clothes, dragging us quickly toward the surface.

"Ptuh!" Kendra gasps as we breech.

I keep a hand under her armpit, making sure she doesn't dip back beneath the waves.

"You okay?" I ask.

"I los—" She coughs, retching as water spills from her lungs. She sucks in another gasp of air. "I lost my amulet. It sunk."

"It's okay. Hold onto me."

I pull her close until we're chest to chest. She wraps her legs around me and clings to my neck.

WOOSH!

Something zooms past us, skimming the surface of the water. I see a flash of black in my peripherals, but it's gone when I turn my head, blurring with the background.

Kendra turns her head wildly. "Matt?"

"Hold on."

Commanding the currents, I drag us closer to the boat.

Lift!

The ocean bubbles around us, forming a mound above the ocean plane. As it rises, we float with it. We continue to rise, gaining altitude alongside the yacht.

As we approach the railing, Kildron appears above us. He grabs hold of Kendra and yanks her onto the deck. Free of her weight, I grab the railing and pull myself over.

Letting go of Kendra, Kildron levitates into the air, rising effortlessly above the yacht. "I'll get a better look," he calls, floating higher and higher.

THUD!

Another wave hits the boat, but Iris is ready. She raises her hand, parting the water around us. The wave—almost up to my waist—rushes past on either side and drains off the boat. Some of the torrent pours into the cabin, and the yacht dips in the water.

As soon as water clears, Iris is scanning the horizon. Suddenly, her eyes narrow. Her head slowly swivels as she tracks the movement of something in the distance. Then, she raises a hand above her head.

I squint as a brilliant light erupts from her fingertips. It emanates from a small, perfectly white orb in the center of her palm. As the orb gets bigger, the light intensifies. I turn away, no longer able to look at the sphere directly.

With a swing of her arm, Iris heaves the orb high into the air. The orb travels slowly in its natural arc, illuminating our surroundings like stadium lights. Beneath the beacon, the black ocean glistens, reflecting every contour of the sea. I lean forward, trying to make sense of what I see.

In the distance, something black skitters across the surface of the water. It isn't a creature at all, but a black sail, tall and triangular. A figure clings to the sail, standing on a wooden surfboard.

Windsurfing?

I don't feel a breeze, but the sail billows as if blown by storm-force winds. The wind-surfer leans, and their sail shifts. Now, the wind appears to be blowing from the opposite direction.

Dominion, I think to myself.

Then, I spot another wind-surfer. This one is moving to my right. There's a third to my left. They're circling us like sharks, slowly getting closer with each pass.

As the beacon begins to drop toward the water, Iris raises her hand.

"No!" Kildron calls from above, but it's too late.

KA-KRACK!

Lighting erupts from Iris's fingers. In a single bolt, it surges above the ocean, but it doesn't hit one of the surfers. Instead, a wave of water lifts from the sea, absorbing the shock entirely.

"Don't attack," Kildron urges. "They're Atlantians." He plummets back toward the ship, slowing at the last second and landing beside me.

I watch as the wind-surfers circle again, closing in on our ship. There are more than I initially realized, maybe ten or so.

Now that their cover is blown, they speak to each other in some foreign language—like nothing I've ever heard before. They shout across the water, filling the air with sharp consonants and gurgles of the throat.

"We come in peace!" Kildron calls. "We mean you no harm." He holds up his gladius and drops it onto the yacht deck. "We will not fight you."

I watch as each of the Atlantians raise one hand, maneuvering their sails with the other.

"Sink it!" a woman shouts.

In unison, their hands drop, and the yacht lurches. The deck tips back, lifting the bow into the air. In seconds, the cabin is submerged, and the water begins to rise up my ankles.

"We are Cavernic!" Kildron calls. "We are your allies!"

The ship shudders as it hits something below the surface. The stern stops sinking and the bow dips deeper, slowly leveling out. I cling to the railing as the water climbs past my knees and settles around my waist.

With a shudder, the ship grows still, precariously balanced on an underwater structure, most likely the reef.

I hear more unintelligible shouting. Among them, I catch a snapshot of English.

"Form an iceberg," a woman's voice commands.

Suddenly, the air is filled with a deafening crackle. All around me, the water solidifies, forming individual sheets of ice. In seconds, the sheets expand, connecting into one giant platform. The water freezes around my hips, cutting into my jeans and pinning me in place.

The entire yacht is anchored to the ice, forming a slippery platform the size of a basketball court. It's only a foot thick, but the feat is still astounding.

"Don't resist," Kildron instructs. He holds his hands in the air, fingers spread to show his empty hands. "Remove your amulets."

I do as instructed, reaching into my shirt. I hold my amulet in the air by the chain, displaying my hands the same way Kildron does.

Kendra raises her empty hands, having lost her amulet to the sea.

The wind-surfers circle us, just outside the border of the iceberg. They continue to talk in their language, waiting for something.

"Iris," Kildron hisses. "Your amulet."

Iris rolls her eyes, finally reaching into her shirt. She removes her soul-anchor, holding it by the chain. As soon as she does, her light dominion flickers out, casting us into darkness. She doesn't, however, remove her amplifier.

The surfers shout some more, but I don't catch any English this time.

I don't like this, Matt, Iris speaks to my mind. *If I give the signal, we fight.*

But—

"Dismount!" A woman shouts. Her voice is feminine and feathery, yet calm and confident.

The wind-surfers lean to the side, turning suddenly. They glide over the water and directly onto the iceberg, sliding smoothly over the ice.

As they slow, they leap from their boards and run barefoot across the ice. In one coordinated attack, they converge from all sides.

"We come in peace!" Kildron repeats. "We are not your en—"

"Silence, invader!" the woman spits.

In the blink of an eye, the water melts around Kildron's waist. Kildron looks down as a pillar of water explodes upward. It slaps him in the face, molding around his jaw and head. With a crackle, the ice solidifies into a single shard, sealing his open jaw in the center.

"Gaaah," Kildron lets out a muffled gasp, sniffling through his protruding nose. He still holds his amulet by the chain, but he doesn't try to use it.

The woman strides across the glacier, smiling as she approaches. As she walks, the iceberg begins to glow. It functions like a lampshade, dispersing the light evenly, without shadows or glare.

Half-submerged in the ice, my eyes only come to her belly-button. Her stomach is bare, as is most of her body, displaying her smooth, coffee skin. She wears a loincloth woven with some kind of plant fiber. A brown cloth—nearly the same tone as her skin—wraps around her chest in a single band. Not only is she beautiful, she's strong. Her six-pack is chiseled, and her biceps put my own to shame.

Look! Iris sucks in a breath. *They all have soul-anchors!*

I look at their neck, expecting to see an amulet. Instead, I spot a tattoo at the top of her chest. The symbols curve along the length of her collarbone.

Guardians... every one of them.

Iris turns, watching as the other wind-surfers gather around us. They approach slowly, half crouched. A few climb on the helm—the only part of the ship that isn't submerged. They stare down at us with unblinking eyes, ready to strike at the slightest movement.

"You will not speak until spoken to," the lead woman scolds Kildron. I didn't notice them before, but her ear lobes are massive, stretched by some sort of gauge-like earring. A solid gold ring lines the inside of her lobe like a tire rim. A flat, gold tongue-piercing undulates as she speaks. "Now, throw down your amulets, all of you."

As commanded, I drop my amulet on the ice. It skitters, landing at the woman's feet. Kildron and Kendra do the same.

"There we go. And you," the woman says, pointing a finger at Iris. "I know defiance when I see it. You can try whatever it is you're planning, but I promise it won't bode well for you."

Iris grits her teeth. Slowly, her finger loosen and the amulet clanks onto the iceberg.

The woman narrows her eyes. "And the other one."

"I don't kn—"

"How dumb do you think I am? The spell piece under your shirt. Now!"

Slowly, Iris removes her amplifier and tosses it onto the ice.

"And the dagger." Sheyba says.

Iris rolls her eyes as she removes the dagger from her waist. She throws it down, sticking it point first into the ice.

"Happy?" Iris asks.

The woman grins victoriously. "Elated."

In unison. All five amulets begin to sink as the ice melts beneath them. The dagger slowly sinks as well. As soon as they disappear beneath the surface, the water freezes above them, encasing them in ice.

The woman steps closer. "Let's see." She squats down, putting herself at eye-level, and looks us over one by one. "What an interesting bunch?"

Her eyes settle on Kendra, who stares proudly ahead. A sliver of a smile tugs on her lip.

"You're happy?" the woman questions.

Kendra says nothing.

"That was a question. You may speak, girl."

"Yes, I'm happy. We've been—"

"Silence! I didn't ask *why* you're happy," the woman sneers.

Kendra swallows, nodding silently.

The woman turns to Iris, her eyes lingering. "You. Why do you seek Atlantia?"

Iris shrugs. "I've got nothing better to do?"

Kendra opens her mouth. "We—"

"Silence!" the woman roars. "We are speaking." She turns back to Iris. "What is your name?"

Iris narrows her eyes. "You first."

I expect the woman to retaliate, but she only smiles. "I am Sheyba, protector of Atlantia. Now, who are you?"

"Iris."

Sheyba scowls. "Have you no title, Iris?"

Iris shrugs.

"Fine," Sheyba grins to herself. "We will call you Iris, the unimportant."

At her words, the other Atlantians chuckle.

So they do understand.

Sheyba turns to Kendra. "And who are you?"

"My name is Kendra. I—"

"Kendra what?" Sheyba demands.

"Excuse me?"

Sheyba impatiently waves her hand in the air. "Your title?"

"Oh, I'm Kendra, uhhh, healer of mankind."

Sheyba raises an eyebrow. "Now that is a title. And what do you want with Atlantia, Kendra, healer of mankind?"

"I come with a warning," Kendra explains. "You don't understand how important this is. There is a man across the sea who is about to find The Book of Life. If he succeeds, the world will never be the same. We need your help to stop him. The entire world depends on it."

"You want my aid?" Sheyba asks.

"Yes," Kendra insists.

"To save the world?"

"Yes, to save the world. If he finds the Book of Life, no one will be safe."

The woman seems to consider this, pacing back and forth on the ice. "Do you remember my name, Kendra, healer of man?"

"Yes, it's Sheyba."

"Sheyba… what?" the woman asks.

"Sheyba, protector of Atlantia."

"Is my name, by any chance, Sheyba, protector of the world?"

"No?" Kendra says. "But—"

"Then I cannot help you," Sheyba says. "Return to whatever realm you came from, and plead with its appointed protectors."

"Please," Kendra begs. "Let us speak with your leader. They need to hear our warning. Cavernum is destroyed. No one is safe."

At this, Sheyba raises an eyebrow. "A temple-city, destroyed? Impossible."

"It's the truth!" Kendra insists. "The walls were d—"

"Silence!" Sheyba shouts. "I will not listen to any more of your lies."

Suddenly, I have an idea. I focus my soul around my face, communicating with the Morphmask.

Crown.

I feel its weight as the crown materializes on my head. It was always there, held in place and camouflaged by the relic. Now, it glitters in the soft glow of dominion.

I tuck my chin to my chest and let the crown tip forward, clattering across the ice.

Sheyba bends down and picks it up. Her eyes widen as she spots the deformed Adamic symbols on the inner edge.

"Whose is this?" she demands.

I wait until she meets my gaze. "It belonged to the king of Cavernum," I say matter-of-factly. "He's dead now. No one has lied to you."

Sheyba considers this for a moment before looking at Iris. "You, too, wish to warn my king?"

Iris shrugs. "Sure, why not."

Sheyba points at me. "And you? This is your desire as well?"

I swallow, afraid that I'm about to make a mistake.

"Actually, I seek the Shackles of Redemption," I say as confidently as I can.

Sheyba's eyebrow twitches, but she doesn't give much of a response. The other Atlantians watch with blank faces.

I avert my eyes. "I… I fed to save a friend. I wish to be cured of my current… predicament. I've been told you can help me."

Sheyba studies me, unblinking. "This man seeks the Shackles of Redemption," she finally echos. At her words, the Atlantians take a step back. They mutter to each other and shake their heads in disgust.

Sheyba steps closer. "What is your name, sinner?"

"Matt, the repentant."

Sheyba nods. "A fitting name." She squats down in front of me, her voice a threatening whisper. "I must warn you, Matt the repentant, this is no meager request. You must be judged by the High Priest. If they determine you are unworthy, you will be cleansed by fire. Are you certain you wish to proceed?"

"I'm sure," I insist.

"And you, noisy one." Sheyba raises her hand, and the ice liquifies around Kildron's face. "What do you seek from Atlantia?"

Kildron looks over at Kendra and I. "Nothing," he says. "Think of me as transportation, nothing more."

Sheyba squints at him a moment before shrugging. "Have it your way."

"She turns to the rest of us. "I must warn you, all who enter Atlantia must be judged. Those who are wicked will receive their recompense. Do you wish to proceed?"

"Yes," Kendra and I mutter in unison. Iris nods her head.

Sheyba grins. "Very well. I will consult with the king. I'll have your response at first light."

She turns around, retreating back the way she came. "Homeward!" She picks up her sail and steps onto the wooden board. Immediately, the sail billows, dragging her along the ice. The other Atlantians follow suit. As they slide away, the iceberg begins to melt, slowly dissolving around my waist.

Standing on our half-sunken ship, Kendra smiles, her outline barely visible in the moonlight. "Well… that was exciting."

"You think they're gonna kill us?" Iris asks.

"Maybe," Kendra laughs. "But I like our odds."

26

MATT

Dawn's dazzling glow slowly penetrates the sea, unveiling the underworld with increasing clarity.

We're stranded in the center of a massive reef. Big circles of coral expand beneath the surface, like underwater mushrooms on the sandy sea floor.

Already, a white sail lulls on the horizon. The fabric catches the sunlight like a signaling mirror, flashing every few seconds.

"There they are," I announce, pointing with my finger.

It isn't a sail-board, like last time. It's a catamaran—two dugout canoes interconnected by a series of wooden logs. A matchstick of a mast, long and slender, extends from the center-most plank.

"Finally," Iris stands, stretching her arms above her head.

Kildron says nothing. He frowns as the sail draws closer. He isn't excited, like Kendra is. His brow is furrowed and his chin tucked. As I watch him, the grooves in his forehead sink deeper.

"You good?" I ask.

"Huh?" He snaps from his trance. "Oh, yeah. Just a little anxious. I'll feel better when we're all back together."

"You sure you don't want to come?"

He nods. "I'm an abomination to everything they stand for. Trust me; it's best I stay behind." His eyes return to the sail once more.

As they approach, we climb down from the helm—the only part of our ship still above sea level. I slosh across the half-submerged deck, stopping at the railing.

"This is it," Kendra says, coming up beside me and taking my hand.

"This is it," I agree.

The catamaran coasts slowly toward us—at least a dozen men and women on board. Sheyba stands precariously on one of the connecting beams, leaning on the thin mast. Three amulets glitter around her neck—her prizes from the previous night. The sail, cotton by the looks of it, flaps above her head as they coast slowly alongside us.

"Freeze it!" she commands.

Like last night, a dozen individual ice-caps appear on the water, expanding until they converge into a single icy platform. Only this time, the ice stops at the yacht railing.

Sheyba dashes across the plank and leaps from her boat, crouching as she lands on the glacier. Her bare feet never slip or slide on the ice. With a sweep of her hand, the ice extends to the boat, anchoring it to the iceberg.

"Come, invaders. Step aboard. Atlantia awaits you."

I hold Kendra's hand as she climbs over the yacht railing and onto the ice-cap.

An Atlantian man at the rear of the catamaran grumbles something indiscernible before patting the empty seat in front of him. Kendra steps into the canoe and takes a seat where he indicated. I do the same, positioning myself behind her. In order to fit, I stretch my legs to either side of her back.

Iris scans the crowded catamaran. "Where am I supposed to sit?"

Sheyba steps onto the crossbeams, tight-roping her way to the mast. "There's room with me on the leadlog, so long as you're not sand-footed."

"The leadlog?" Iris questions.

Sheyba ignores the question. "Make haste, invader. We don't have all day."

Iris rolls her eyes. "Yeah, yeah." She steps onto the crossbeam and makes a quick dash for the mast, grabbing on with both hands.

"Homeward!" Sheyba shouts.

Simultaneously, the ice dissolves around the ship and a ferocious wind howls above my head, filling the mast and whipping us forward.

From the corner of my eye, I see Iris nearly topple from the crossbeam.

Sheyba snickers. "You can sit if you'd like. Drag your toes in the sea, even."

"I'm fine," Iris mutters, still clinging to the mast.

"How far to Atlantia?" Kendra asks, raising her voice to be heard over the sloshing sea. "If you don't mind me asking."

Sheyba looks down, as if studying the reef below us. "Not far. Five miles at most. Isn't that right, Wayko? How far is the Jetty?"

The man sitting behind me mutters something in Atlantian.

"Yeah," Sheyba agrees. "He says four miles from here. We should be there in half a fist?"

Kendra furrows her brow. "Excuse me?"

"Half a fist?" Sheyba repeats. "You know… fist." She makes a fist with one and extends her arm completely. With one eye closed, she aligns her fist with the sun's path. "This time of year we get 12 or 13 fists of sunlight."

"Oh," Kendra nods her head. "That makes sense. Thank you."

Within minutes, my butt hurts from the unforgiving hull of the catamaran. I reach to reposition myself and elbow the guy's knee who sits behind me.

The man—I think Wayko was his name—mutters something in Atlantian.

"My bad," I insist. "Sorry about that."

The man, clearly confused, looks at Sheyba.

"The invader says without intention," Sheyba tells him.

The Atlantian nods his head as if suddenly understanding.

"Okay," Kendra glances suspiciously between Sheyba and Wayko.

"Something weird is going on. Why do they understand you, but not us? We're both speaking English."

Sheyba grins. "Are you sure about that?"

Iris squints at Sheyba's mouth. "It's the piercing, isn't it? Some kind of spell."

"You're sharp," Sheyba sticks out her tongue, letting Iris study the piercing. It's a flat, gold bar. I assume it has symbols, but I can't make them out from where I'm seated.

"It's called the Gift of Tongues," Sheyba explains. "Whatever I say is understood by all, perceived in their native language." She points at the gauges in her earlobes. "And these are called the Gift of the Interpretation of Tongues. They allow me to understand all invaders, no matter the dialect. To me, everything you say sounds Atlantian."

Already, ideas are running through my head. "So, if I say hello, hola, konichiwa, what do you hear?"

"You said hello three times."

"And if I say howdy?"

"Hello again," Sheyba repeats.

"Incredible," Kendra laughs.

I laugh as well. "What if—

"That's enough," Sheyba says. "I'm not a show parrot."

"How many of you have the Gift of Tongues?" Kendra asks.

"There's only three of us," Sheyba says proudly. "The king, the high priestess, and myself."

"What happens when we arrive?" Iris asks, changing the subject.

"The High Priestess is awaiting you. She will hear your message this evening. If you haven't already, I suggest you rehearse what you have to say."

"Then what?" Iris asks.

"Then, you will be sent on your way. That, or we'll kill you."

"You could try," Iris mumbles under her breath.

Sheyba must hear because the corner of her lip curls up in amusement.

After a few minutes, I notice several seagulls in the air behind us.

They fly toward our ship, passing almost directly overhead. As I watch, they suddenly vanish, leaving only a faint ripple in the air.

"Stop," Sheyba shouts. "We're here."

She turns to the man sitting behind me. "Wayko, get the cuffs."

The man reaches behind him and picks up two iron cylinders—more like cones, actually. They're narrower on one end and wider on the other. Each has matching Adamic symbols.

"Are you sure you want to do this?" Sheyba asks me. "Once the shackles are bonded, they can never be removed. If you are found to be unworthy, we will have to kill you."

"I'm sure," I say. "I'm ready,"

"So be it." Sheyba motions at Wayko. "Give him your arms."

I twist my torso and extend my arms. Wayko holds up the cuffs, one in each palm. The artifacts are massive, easily wide enough that I can fit my entire hand through it.

"It looks a little big," I say.

"Put your hands in," Sheyba commands.

I extend my hand.

"No," Sheyba scolds. "Both at once. It's easier that way."

Taking a deep breath, I slide both hands into the wide end of the cylinder and out the skinny end. As soon as my knuckles clear the cuff, the metal starts to constrict, growing warm on the bottom of my forearms. Next thing I know, it's burning hot..

"Ow! Agh!"

The metal continues to heat as it constricts around my wrist, pressing into the flesh from all sides. I clench my teeth and thrash in my seat.

"Matt?" Kendra gasps. "Matt, what's happening?"

It feels like a hot skillet is being held against my wrists, cooking my flesh like a slab of beef. I dive for the side of the canoe and shove my hands into the ocean. To my horror, it does nothing to cool the cuffs.

Finally, the pain overrides my restrain.

"AHHHHHHHHHH!"

I fall back into the canoe and curl into a ball like a dying beetle, crying out as I roll side to side.

Then, in an instant, the pain vanishes, leaving me panting on my back.

I slowly sit up. "What the hell just happened?" I look down at my wrists, expecting to see horrendous burns and steaming metal. Instead, the cuffs are cool to the touch. They're skintight, shaping perfecting to my forearms, but there's no inflammation. No sign of a burn.

"Wonderful," Sheyba says matter-of-factly. "Onward."

I hear the sail billow above my head, and the ship lurches forward.

"What the hell was that?" I ask as I slowly sit up.

Sheyba rolls her eyes. "A small price to pay for your salvation. How about some gratitude?"

I drag a finger along the inner rim of the cuff. Even pushing down, I can't force my finger beneath the cuff. It's as though the metal has fused with my flesh.

"Thanks," I finally mutter.

I lift my arms, feeling the uncomfortable weight of the cuffs. I'm still studying my shackles when a familiar sensation washes over me: the ice-cold wave of pins and needles.

We're passing through the wall.

For a second, the air tugs on me, and my butt starts to slide backwards in the canoe. Just when I think I'll be dragged into the water, my cuffs grow warm and the feeling subsides.

It actually worked!

When I look up, I don't see an endless ocean. Instead, I see the shadowed slopes of a massive mountain range. It comprises the majority of the island, reaching down to the white, sandy beaches. Everything, save the sand, is blanketed by a thick, tropical forest.

Between our ship and the island is a picturesque lagoon, something straight from the cover of a travel magazine. Just when I think it couldn't get any better, a small pod of dolphins swim past the boat as if greeting old friends.

Sheyba beams. "Welcome to Atlantia."

"It's incredible!" Kendra gushes.

Iris shrugs. "Eh, It's alright."

I twist to see behind us. Rather than a wall, a long jetty forms a circle around the island. The jetty is continuous, save for the small opening we just passed through. Spaced along the rocks, like telephone poles, are cylindrical monoliths. Each one bears a column of symbols engraved into the stone.

"Take us to the sand," Sheyba calls.

The winds rush overhead, propelling us toward the beach. As we get closer, the wind dies, and we coast.

"Oh, look! A sea scythe," Sheyba calls.

Kendra follows her gaze, gasping as she spots the eight foot reef shark.

"We don't see these too often at this time of day," Sheyba comments. "They're strictly night-feeders."

Sheyba closes her eyes, and the shark begins to swim toward the catamaran.

"Ah!" Kendra leans away from the edge, trying to create as much space as possible.

"Don't worry," Sheyba says. "He's harmless."

The shark slows at Sheyba's command, keeping pace alongside Kendra and I. It swims on the very surface, dorsal fin protruding like a radio antenna.

"Go ahead," Sheyba says. "Give it a pet."

Kendra starts to reach down, then retracts her hand. "I think I'm okay."

I reach out into the water, dragging my fingers over the shark's tail. "So smooth!"

"Go the other way!" Sheyba instructs.

As I do, the scales catch my skin like sandpaper.

Sheyba smiles. "Pretty neat, right?"

"Definitely." As I retract my hand, the shark does a 180 and swims off.

I'm still watching the shark when I hear excited shouting. I turn as we pass a small canoe filled with children. There are three boys and a girl, all around ten years old. They point and shout at us as we pass.

My jaw drops open. Every one of them is tattooed.

"They have soul-anchors?" I gasp. "They're so young."

"Of course, they do," Sheyba sneers. "How else would they channel the divine?"

"At what age do they get tattooed?" Kendra asks.

"The day they utter their first word," Sheyba explains. "When they can speak, they can commune with the Great Flame."

I continue to watch as the kids laugh in the boat. The oldest boy closes his eyes, followed by the others.

Suddenly, a fish leaps out of the water and flips into the canoe. A moment later, a second fish flops into the canoe, followed by a third and a fourth.

The children open their eyes and begin shouting, hoisting their fishes into the air to compare size.

"Brace yourselves!" Sheyba shouts. "Prepare to beach."

Pebbles grind under the hull as we scrape up the beach, momentum carrying the ship several yards out of the water. As soon as the ship settles, Sheyba hops down, her feet sinking into the soggy sand.

"That'll do. I want all hands preparing for the Reckoning. The High Priestess will be here in three fist's time, as will the king." She looks over at Iris. "Invaders, you come with me. I'll show you around."

She leads us up the beach toward a tight cluster of palm trees. A man and woman huddle in the shade, stooping over several large boulders. The stones are waist high and perfectly flat on the top. Several blackened fish sizzle on the stone as they grill.

"This is the kitchen," Sheyba announces. "And these are my lifegivers." Sheyba leans toward her mom until their noses gently touch. "Mom, these are the invaders. Kendra, healer of man. Matt, the repentant. And Iris, the boring."

Her mom frowns, saying something in Atlantian.

Sheyba sighs. "She didn't have a title, so I gave her one."

I don't understand what her mom says, but I know it's a reprimand of some kind.

"Alright, alright." Sheyba says in defeat. "I'll give her a new one. Iris, the mysterious."

Her mom mutters something else before smiling at Iris.

Sheyba rolls her eyes. "She says you can choose your own title. Anything you'd like."

Iris is grinning now, clearly amused by Sheyba's daughterly submission.

"Call me Iris… protector of the world."

Her mom looks at Sheyba for translation.

Sheyba purses her lips. "Iris, protector of the world."

Her mother lights up, clapping her hands together. She begins to chatter at us, interrupting her unintelligible sentences with the occasional motherly smile.

"Mom, stop." Sheyba interjects. "I don't want to translate all this."

Her mom scowls, unleashing what I recognize as a heartfelt lecture.

"Fine," Sheyba rolls her eyes again.

Her mom continues to ramble.

"I said fine, Mom." She turns to us, her cheeks turning red. "My mom said that you are welcome here, and she wishes you all the blessings of the Great Flame."

Her mom slaps her shoulder and mutters something else.

"Mom, stop. I'm not gonna tell them that."

Sheyba's mom crosses her arms, giving Sheyba a silent stare.

Sheyba sighs. "Aaaand… she says if I give you any trouble, that you should come to her, and she'll set me straight."

Iris laughs aloud.

Kendra smiles wide and presses her hand to her heart. "Tell her we said thank you."

"They say thanks," Sheyba declares reluctantly.

Sheyba's mom smiles again. Then, she leans over and whispers something to Sheyba while nudging her with her elbow. A second later, she raises her eyebrows, nodding at Iris.

Iris turns around, making sure there's no one behind her. "What? What did she say about me?"

"It's nothing," Sheyba asserts. "Follow me. There's more to see."

I scan the beach as we walk, counting 30 people. "Is this everyone?" I think aloud.

"Some of us are fishing," Sheyba says. "but this is most of the Sand-sleepers."

"Sand-sleepers?" Kendra asks.

"There are two tribes in Atlantia, the Tree-sleepers and the Sand-sleepers. The Tree-sleepers are more plentiful, but the Sand-sleepers have it better, if you ask me."

"How many are you in total?" Kendra asks.

"Five hundred, give or take."

Kendra frowns. I know what she's thinking. We need an unstoppable army. Even with their soul-anchors, five hundred might not be enough.

As she leads us down the beach, several kids run up beside us—three boys and a girl.

The fishing kids.

Giggling, they tug on my t-shirt, and squeak to each other in Atlantian.

"Hey!" Sheyba shouts, waving her hand. "Hands off, munchkins. Don't pester the invaders."

"It's okay," Kendra says. "We don't mind."

"Speak for yourself," Iris grumbles.

One of the boys points at me and shouts something. He almost looks angry.

"Oh, shut it," Sheyba raises her hand in the air. Making a fist, she pulls it down. As her hand drops, the children simultaneously sink up to their neck's in the sand.

Sheyba laughs as the children shout at her. They wiggle in a frantic attempt to unbury their arms.

I look over at Sheyba. "What'd he say?"

"He called you sunless."

"Sunless? What is that supposed to mean?"

"It's an outdated belief, something their grandparents probably told them. I don't know about you, but we worship the Great Flame." She points at the sun. "She is the light and life of the world. Without her, there is nothing." She looks down at her arms. "As you can see, my people are sunbaked, but you, no offense… you look raw—untouched by fire or flame. Some of our ancestors thought this was a sign that you were shunned from the Great Flame—human devils sent to torment us."

"Do you believe this?" Kendra asks.

Sheyba shakes her head. "I've met raw-skins before. You guys aren't so bad." She points, suddenly distracted. "There it is."

Ahead of us is a giant pile of driftwood and coconut leaves. They're piled around a ten foot monolith—a rectangular pillar made of solid stone. The tip of the monolith has a chunk removed, creating an L shape—a primitive seat if I'm not mistaken. The stony surface is stained black with soot and ash.

My heart quickens. "Is that what I think it is?"

"The Judgment Seat," Sheyba explains. "This is where we watch the Reckoning."

"You burn them, don't you?" I accuse. "That's what the Reckoning is?"

Sheyba nods.

Kendra studies the monolith with a downturned mouth and taut jaw. “How often does this happen?”

Sheyba shrugs. “Depends how often we get invaders.” I can hear the hesitation in her voice… the shame. “Usually once a year, give or take. If they’re Adamic, we often let them go, but the Cainic… They always burn.”

Kendra covers her mouth. “That’s terrible!”

Sheyba shrugs. “The wicked must burn, right?” She doesn’t sound convinced.

I can’t take my eyes off of the blackened throne. “But I should be fine, right? I’m Adamic.”

“If you’re pure of heart, you have nothing to worry about.”

“Who decides that?”

“The High Priestess.”

“And she’s a good judge of character?” Kendra hopes.

Sheyba hesitates. “She’s fine. She's just a bit… traditional, that’s all.”

“She believes we’re sunless,” I suspect, “doesn’t she?”

Sheyba bites her tongue.

“Great,” Iris groans. “Of all the ways to die.”

Sheyba’s lips compress. “If you’re pure of heart, you have nothing to worry about,” she repeats.

I can tell she doesn’t believe it.

27

MATT

The ceremony begins with a feast. The Atlantians gather by the bonfire—yet to be lit—and sit directly in the sand. Some of the elders disperse food on flat shards of rock. The cuisine is fairly simple: fish and fried banana and a mystery meat that might be iguana.

I don't have an appetite, but I force myself to eat, afraid to offend them before my judgment has even begun.

"One fist until sundown," Sheyba whispers. "It will begin soon."

Sure enough, a woman stands, dressed completely in white. A cotton shawl conceals her shoulders, and two squares of cloth conceal her nether regions, leaving the sides of her wrinkly thighs exposed. A tapestry of black symbols—not quite Adamic—decorates the simple skirt.

The woman's not ancient, but she's definitely getting there. Her hair is contained in a cloth wrap, small tufts of white frizz puffing out around her ears. Her wrinkles overflow into her eyes, and her arms shake as she lifts them in the air.

"Welcome, strangers!" Just like Sheyba, he has a silver tongue piercing and hollow gauge earrings. "My name is Bonohina, vessel of the Great Flame. And this is Aronix, King of Atlantia."

The king waves, giving us a goofy grin. Unlike the priestess, he wears almost nothing. His bare chest is covered in Adamic symbols—spells I've never seen before.

He looks in our direction, but his eyes seem to pass right through me. "There art no strangers unto the Great Flame, for she hast known us from the beginning." He smiles wider and raises his eyebrow, as if sharing an inside joke.

The priestess ignores him, stepping forward. "The time has come for each of you to be judged. Only then will we hear your message." She glances between us. "Who will go first?"

"I will," Kendra volunteers.

The king nods. "The righteous are eager, for they fear not the flame, nor are they burned." Once again, he looks around, but no one reacts.

The priestess approaches Kendra, holding something in her hands. It looks like a doughnut-shaped ring of woven reeds. A row of Adamic symbols are painted onto the bumpy surface.

She lifts the wicker-basket wreath and drapes it over Kendra's shoulders like a neck pillow.

"This," the priestess announces, "is the Collar of Candor. You will wear it throughout your judgment."

The priestess takes a step back. "We shall begin. What is your name?"

"Kendra,"

"Kendra what?" the priestess demands.

"Kendra, uh, healer of man."

The other Atlantians watch from their seats in the sand. They can't understand Kendra's responses, but they're riveted regardless.

The priestess stands perfectly still, like a white-robed scarecrow. Her voice is as weathered and coarse as her scarecrow frame.

"Kendra, healer of man… do you profess to serve the Great Flame?"

Kendra thinks for a moment. "I do. Yes."

"Do you have any intentions of harming Atlantia or its inhabitants."

"No. None at all."

The priestess stares, unblinking. "Do you support or aid any entities who would harm Atlantia or its inhabitants?"

"No. Never."

"Should I spare your life, will you keep the location of Atlantia a secret for as long as you live?"

"Yes."

The priestess almost looks disappointed. "Do you have any markings I should be aware of?"

"I do not."

The priestess pauses, anticipating the gravity of her next question. "During your lifetime, have you committed any sins that I should be aware of? Any at all?"

"No."

Kendra stiffens as the wreath begins to wiggle around her neck. The woven fibers scrape as they slide past each other, closing the circumference of the ring.

The priestess smiles for the first time. "Do not lie, my dear. The Collar of Candor will not allow it." She leans in closer. "Confess to me. What sins weigh down your soul?"

"I'm not lying."

The collar constricts once more. Now, there's only a few inches between the wicker and her throat.

"Let's try this again," the priestess gloats. "What sins, if any, have you committed?"

Kendra looks down and sighs. "Last year, I was healing this man. He was sick… very sick. I tried everything I could, but he didn't get better. He was dying a slow and painful death. He wanted to pass on, so… I helped him. I put him to sleep, then… I stopped his heart."

The priestess grins, touching the tip of her fingers together. "You confess to killing an innocent man?"

Kendra's swallows, holding her chin high. "I do."

King Aronix nods his head. "For all have sinned, and all fall short of the Flame."

"This is a grave offense," the Priestess agrees. "This is murder. Tell me, Kendra, healer of man… do you feel remorse?"

Kendra exhales loudly. "I do."

"If you could go back," The priestess asks, "would you do things differently?"

"I… I think so. I would've tried harder to heal him. I would've found another way."

The priestess frowns. "Do you consider yourself clean before the Great Flame?"

"I do," Kendra says without hesitation.

King Aronix claps his hands together. "For it is by grace that we are saved," he cackles. "Transformed through the Flame's holy light." He juts his chin forward, looking around for a sliver of acknowledgment, but no one meets his gaze.

"Very well," the priestess mutters, clearly disappointed. "You are proven pure of heart, Kendra, healer of man. We will now hear your message."

"Thank you!" Kendra gushes, stepping forward. "The entire world is in danger, I can't stress this enough." She waves her hands with the inflection of her voice. "There is a man across the ocean—an evil man. He is searching for the Book of Life." Kendra hesitates. "Do you know what that is?"

"I'm familiar," the priestess sneers.

"Then you understand what will happen if he finds it!" Kendra exclaims. "The world will be at his mercy. Atlantia will be at his mercy. If we don't stop him, everything you know and love could be destroyed. We can't stop this man on our own. He's already destroyed Cavernum. We need your help. Please! I'm begging you."

The priestess taps the tips of her fingernails together. She says nothing.

"Please!" Kendra falls to her knees in the sand. "I'm begging you." She grabs the collar around her neck. "You know I'm telling the truth. If you don't do something, Atlantia will fall. Once he's Adalingual, he'll see you as a threat. He'll destroy you. Please! You have to help us!"

King Aronix nods his head, staring at the sand. “The sun will be darkened,” he breathes. “And the moon will not give its light, and the stars will fall from the sky, and the heavenly bodies will be shaken.”

The priestess ignores him. She approaches Kendra, her voice almost a whisper. “Enough. I will not hear any more of this.”

Kendra’s jaw quivers. “B-but… you know it's true. How can you do nothing?”

The Priestess shakes her head. “The collar is not objective truth. I know that *you* believe it's true, but that doesn’t make it so. I will not send my people to fight a foreigner’s war.”

I open my mouth. “But—”

“Silence!” the priestess screams, threatening me with a shaky finger. “You will have your chance.” She turns back to Kendra. “Is this your only message, Kendra, healer of man?”

Kendra’s eyes widen. “But… they haven’t even heard my message.” She gestures at the audience of Atlantians who watch with a blank stare. “Don’t they deserve to know what’s coming? Shouldn’t they decide for themselves if they want to fight?”

The priestess clasps her hands behind her back and leans into Kendra’s ear. I’m only a few feet away, but I can barely hear her.

“I do not care what happens beyond the sea,” the priestess hisses. “I do not care about your silly, little warning. And most of all, I do not care if an evil man becomes Adalingual. Do you know why? Because the Flame will always prevail, as will her chosen people.”

“How do you know?” Kendra demands.

The priestess glares at Kendra. “Because I have faith, you heathen. The Earth has been plagued by wicked men before. Yes, even Adalinguals. And do you know what? The Great Flame sent down many waters, and washed them from the Earth. She buried them beneath the sea, where they couldn’t utter a word against her. So, if the day comes that you are correct, and this man you fear succeeds, I pray the Great Flame will flood the Earth again. Either way, we will be safe within our sanctuary.”

“Are you crazy?” Kendra asks, rage replacing desperation.

"Another flood will kill billions. Is that what you want? You'd rather witness mass destruction than fight?"

"If the Cainic suffer, so be it. The Flame's elect will live on."

"You're insane!" Kendra sneers.

"Enough!" the priestess screams. "You will not speak of this again." She looks over at Iris and I. "None of you will. Do you understand me?"

Kendra is fuming, but she holds her tongue.

"Now," the priestess says, lifting the collar from Kendra's neck. "Who will be judged next?"

"Eh, why not," Iris says, raising her hand.

The priestess slips the collar over her head. There's not a lot of slack as it slips over her ears, still constricted from Kendra's lies.

"What is your name?" the priestess asks.

"Iris, protector of the world."

I watch, waiting for the collar to tighten, but nothing happens. The priestess raises an eyebrow as well.

"Do you serve the Great Flame?"

"Yeah, I like to think I do."

"Do you have any intentions to harm Atlantia or its inhabitants?"

"Nope."

"Do you support or aid any entities who would intend harm to Atlantia or its inhabitants?"

I hold my breath.

Iris shakes her head. "You know, I can't say that I do."

Once again, I wait for the collar to constrict, but nothing happens. Kendra meets my eye, sharing a relieved smile.

"Should I spare your life, will you keep the location of Atlantia a secret for as long as you live?"

"Cross my heart, hope to die."

The priestess frowns. "Is that a yes?"

"It is indeed."

The priestess huffs and rolls her eyes. "A simple yes or no will suffice next time. Do you have any markings I should be aware of?"

"You're going to love it," Iris says matter-of-factly. "It's on my back. Let me show you." Iris turns around and lifts the base of her shirt up to her neck. The mark of the beast is clearly visible above her bra strap.

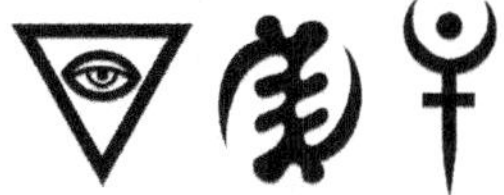

"Demon!" the priestess hisses. "Sunless fiend!"

A collective gasp echoes over the audience. I don't have to understand the voices to detect their disgust.

"Now," Iris calmly exclaims, "before you grab your pitchforks and torches, you should know, I didn't ask for these tattoos. They were given to me as an infant against my will. So, I think we can agree I'm not exactly responsible. Demon, sure. Sunless fiend… eh, that's debatable."

"You bear the Devil's mark. There must be a reckoning!" The priestess calls.

I find Sheyba in the audience. She watches with a furrowed brow, arms crossed.

"I agree," Iris says. "Someone should burn, definitely, but should it really be me? I mean, I didn't do this. I'm just the victim, right? I'm as innocent as you are."

The priestess eyes the collar, waiting for it to tighten. When it doesn't, she grits her teeth.

King Aronix cackles. "Whoever eats sour grapes—their own teeth will be set on edge."

"I already told you, I serve the Flame," Iris argues. "Isn't that what matters most?"

The king laughs again. "She has come in our midst, a sheep in wolf's clothing."

The priestess frowns. "Very well. And Iris, protector of man, have you committed any sins that I should be aware of?"

"Oh, where do I start? I killed a lot of people—slit their throats as they slept," Iris replies nonchalantly. "They were bad people, don't get me wrong. They needed a Reckoning, if you know what I mean, but that's beside the point. Hmmm, I also robbed a vault of Adamic weapons and dispersed them to an anarchist rebel group. Let's see... oh, I betrayed my brother, handing him over to a madman who I believed was going to kill him or worse. Not to mention all of the innocent guards I've killed over the years. So yeah... I've done a lot."

The priestess blinks.

"But that's in my past," Iris shows her open palms. "I'm a changed woman; what can I say?"

"I'll be the judge of that," the priestess grins. "For all of those sins, do you feel complete and utter remorse?"

Iris takes a deep breath. "I do."

The collar doesn't tighten.

"If you could do it over," the priestess croaks. "Would you do it differently?"

"Very differently." Iris nods. "Completely different. If I knew then what I know now, none of that would've happened."

The priestess pouts. "Do you consider yourself clean before the Flame?"

Iris grins. "Spotless."

The collar doesn't tighten.

King Aronix giggles softly to himself. "Though your sins may be as scarlet, they shall be white as snow."

The priestess chews on her lips for a moment. "Well, get on with it then!" she explodes. "Do you have a message for me or not?"

"I don't," Iris says, scanning the crowd until she finds Sheyba. "But I have a message for you. You're the only sane one who can understand us. Gather your forces and go to Cavernum. If you don't, I promise you... Atlantia will fall. It's only a matter of time."

The priestess doesn't let Sheyba respond. She lifts the collar from Iris's neck, and slips it over my head. The relic catches on my ears as she forces it down around my neck.

"Your name?"

"Matt, the repentant."

"Hmph, we'll see about that."

She asks the first four questions, and I give the proper, harmless responses.

"Yes." "No." "No." "Yes."

The priestess pauses before the fifth question, narrowing her eyes. "Do you have any markings that I should be aware of?"

"I do,' I answer confidently. "Iris, protector of the world, is my sister. I was tattooed as an infant just like she was. If she's innocent, so am I."

I turn around and lift my shirt.

The priestess studies me a second before moving on. "I see you are wearing the Shackles of Redemption. I'm eager to know, Matt, the repentant… Have you committed any sins that I should be aware of?"

I take a deep breath. "A few weeks ago, the sanctuary of Cavernum was attacked." As I speak, I look out at the crowd, knowing they can't understand me. "I did not have a soul-anchor like you Atlantians. I only had an amplifier. Well… there came a moment when I was no longer able to fight. In order to save myself—and those I care about—I fed on one of the enemy. But, it was in self-defense! And it was the only time it ever happened!"

The priestess grins victoriously. "Feeding is an abomination before the Flame. Forgiveness does not come easy. Tell me, Matt the repentant, do you ever wish to feed? Do you ever hunger for the soul of man?"

"I don't."

The collar squirms around my neck, tightening beneath my jawbone. Already, it's too tight to remove.

"No! It's not what it sounds like!" I exclaim, my heart pounding. "You asked two questions. Yes, sometimes, I have… cravings, I guess. But it's cravings for dominion. I don't actually want to feed. I don't! That's the truth."

I hold my breath. This time, the collar doesn't move.

"The flesh is weak," the king mutters, "but the spirit is willing."

The priestess wrinkles her nose. "So you say... But are you contrite? Do you feel remorse for your crimes?"

"I do."

The collar constricts, pressing flat against my skin. For the first time, the relic actually looks like a collar.

The priestess grins from ear to ear. "You lie, Matt the repentant! You lie before the Flame!"

"It's not a…" I stop myself before I say something stupid. I close my eyes, searching my soul for something I can say. "I can honestly say I feel bad for what I did," I finally stammer.

The priestess shakes her head, still grinning. "That's not what I asked. I asked if you feel remorse."

My hands are clammy, and my heart drums in my ears. My thoughts are already muddled by the pile of kindling behind me. "Define remorse," I choke.

"Is there some kind of translation error? Your companions seemed to understand me just fine." She groans her inconvenience. "Very well. I'll cater to your ignorance. Remorse is a comprehensive emotion. It entails accountability, regret, and the desire to make amends. Do you understand?"

"Yes," I grumble.

"Then answer the question," the priestess demands. "Do you feel remorse?"

"I take accountability for what I did, and I fully regret what happened," I say.

"I'm losing my patience," the priestess warns.

I look around. "What am I doing wrong? I honestly don't know. I'm just answering your questions."

The priestess rolls her eyes, muttering under her breath. "Sunless imbecile." She glances at the king, as if expecting some sort of comment. When he says nothing, she turns back to me.

"For the last time, Matt the repentant, do you feel remorse? Do you regret what *you* did? I don't want to know if you regret what happened, I want to know if you regret your own actions specifically?"

"I… I did it in self-defense," I concede. "I don't know what you want me to say."

She shakes her head. "That's not what I asked. Answer the question!"

"I—"

"No! No! No!" The priestess erupts, swinging her arms like a toddler in a tantrum. "I don't want to hear your convoluted equivocations. Give me a yes or a no. Do you feel remorse?"

"Matt…" Kendra whispers. I hear the despair in her voice, but there's nothing I can do. I can't change the way I feel.

I speak softly, hoping the collar won't hear my response.

"Yes. I feel remorse."

The wicker wraps tighter around my throat, pressing into my trachea and making me cough.

"Another lie," the priestess gloats. "Just to be certain, tell me this. If you could go back, would you do anything differently?"

"Yes."

The collar squeezes, on all sides. My pulse throbs in my neck, and my head begins to spin.

"Is that so?" the priestess laughs.

"I had to do it!" I wheeze, stopping to catch my breath. As I gasp, the air whistles through my straw-sized throat. I try coughing, but the irritation returns as the collar compresses my trachea.

The world spins, and I collapse to my knees. Immediately, Kendra is at my side. She slips her fingers between the collar and my skin, trying to pull it apart, but the added pressure only makes things worse.

"If I didn't do it," I choke. "Kendra would've died!" I'm shouting, but the words are nothing more than a raspy gasp. "I did it to save her! Isn't that justified?"

The priestess shakes her head. "There is no justification for sin, Matt the unrepentant."

"I'm pure of heart," I gasp with my last remaining breath. "I'm pure of heart."

To my surprise, the collar doesn't tighten. It believes me—or rather, I believe myself.

The priestess shakes her head. “Your declarations mean nothing to me. The Great Flame has seen your flaws. Your filth must be cleansed by fire.” She turns to face the Atlantians, smiling like a bride on her wedding day. “It seems to me that a Reckoning is in order. The Flame will be lit at nightfall.”

Darkness creeps at the edge of my vision. The last thing I hear is celebration.

28

ROSE

I sit on the sofa in Great-Grandpa Titan's chambers—or what used to be his chambers before Jack murdered him. I flip through the small agenda, scouring every word for something insightful.

Each page has daily reminders jotted in the corner.

- *Visit the tailor.*
- *Amend article 57.*
- *High Council Meeting at 3:15.*

I flip the page again and again. Nothing useful in November. Nothing noteworthy about December. Next thing I know, I'm staring at the back binding.

For the last few weeks, I've been scouring every document my father, grandfather, and great-grandfather ever owned. Textbooks, journals, notebooks, calendars… even birthday cards. I was hoping I might find something useful about the Lost Library. About my father. About Foresight. Anything!

I was wrong.

I toss the journal onto the trash pile—an expansive slurry of papers spilling off of Titan's desk.

That's the last of it.

I pull out his desk drawer—the skinny one that stretches across my lap—and examine the treasures of my hunt.

Of course, I have Titan's journal—well, technically it was his wife's, Clarinda. The diary is full of interesting insights, but it doesn't describe the Library's location, nor does it speak of Foresight.

Then, there are the letters that Zezric sent Grandpa, three of them in total. They tell a brief story: Zezric attempting to infiltrate the demon cult. They speak of my birth… and of my mother's subsequent death. Finally, they mention Hogrum's imminent demise.

Lastly, there's a brief medical record I found in my father's study. I pick it up, reading it for the tenth time.

July 25th, 2002

Patient: King Titan Malik

Chief complaint: Amnesia

Findings: The patient reports memory loss that began last night following the traumatic news of his grandson's death in Hogrum. He is unable to recall various events from the last week. He also displays delusional thinking, repeatedly claiming that he "spoke with Rose" and is "going to help Rose." Rose is the name of his infant great-granddaughter who also perished in Hogrum yesterday.

The patient did not cooperate with treatment, displaying several bouts of irritability. He did not consent to be healed, and therefore, we cannot continue with the procedure.

It is my professional opinion that Titan Malik is not fit for his kingly duties at this time. We will continue to monitor.

Signed: Maxira Troff, Head Healer

The letter is intriguing, but it doesn't tell me how I can stop my father. I drop the parchment in the drawer and slam it closed.

It's over.

As of today, the palace pantry is officially out of food. They're slaughtering the horses for tonight's feast, but after that, we starve.

I should be frantic. I should be scrambling to save Cavernum, but the truth is, I mourned her death weeks ago. Matt was our last chance at a miracle, and frankly, it was a dead man's errand all along.

What happened to you, Matt?

Tap. Tap. Tap.

I recognize the knock instantly. "Come in, Nevela."

Nevela steps into the room, holding a sky-colored mask to her face. Her upper lid is a flash of pastel pink, and her pupils are framed by ink-black eyeliner.

"You get the first glimpse. How do I look?" She curtsies, lifting the hem of her powder-blue ballgown with her non-mask-holding hand.

"Nevela!" I gush. "You look stunning!"

She blushes, lowering the mask. "Thanks." She clenches her hand into a fist and lets out a little squeal. "Eeeh, I'm so excited. Have you seen the ballroom yet? They're finishing up the decorations."

"Not yet."

"You're going to love it," Nevela says. "I've put your gown and mask on your bed. Shoes and accessories are on the desk. If you'd like, I can meet you in a few hours to help with your makeup."

I shake my head. "That's alright. I'll manage. You focus on the festivities."

"Okay." Nevela pauses, sensing something in my tone. "Ummm, Rose? Are you feeling alright today?"

"Hmmm?" I look up, her question finally registering. "Oh, of course, why do you ask?"

"I don't know," Nevela admits. "You just don't seem yourself."

"I'm probably just tired," I say. "To be honest, I'm not sure I have much energy to socialize."

Nevela narrows her eyes, seeing right through me. "I don't think anyone will bother you?" she predicts. "With your mask on, they might not even notice you."

I sigh. "I hope so."

A month ago, a rumor spread about my father—well, not a rumor; the simple truth. Since then, I've been a leper. Wherever I go, the people scatter. Those who don't flee have only insults and accusations for me.

Nevela watches me, brow heavy with empathy. "If they knew the real you, they would feel differently," she asserts.

"Maybe," I say, hoping to avoid a pep-talk.

Diego knows the real me, and yet, when I went to archery practice the other day, he abandoned his bow without a word. He's hardly spoken a word to me since the last secret meeting.

"You always have Antai and I," Nevela stresses. "Who cares what everyone else thinks. Tonight, we're going to have a ball!" She giggles. "Literally!"

"Thanks, Nevela. You don't know how much that means—."

I'm cut off by three booming thumps on the door.

Knock! Knock! Knock!

"Your Majesty?" It's Octavian, his thunderous voice muffled by the oak. "Are you in there? It's urgent."

Last time Octavian labeled something as urgent, General Katu had been assassinated. I leap to my feet and throw open the door.

"What happened?"

Octavian steps into the room and closes the door. He's short of breath, presumably from running. "It's Bob! He's back!"

"What?"

Octavian nods. "He just came out of the Pit. He's on his way to his chambers."

My mind races. "Have you talked to him yet?"

"I tried, but he was too distracted."

"Who's stationed in the Pit?" I demand. "Are they loyal?"

Octavian cringes. "I'm not sure. Since news got out about the Holy One's identity, some soldiers are… less reliable than they used to be."

"Okay!" I'm already moving toward the door. "Keep an eye on Jack. I'm going to talk to Bob."

I hurry through the halls, making my way toward Bob's room. When I arrive, the door is already ajar.

"Where's my brew!" Bob bellows from within. "Those black-suited bastards stole my brew!"

"Bob?" I push through the door. "Can I come in? I—"

I stop. The man I see looks more like a feeder than the Bob I knew. His lips are one continuous scab, and his eyes seem to be retracting into his skull. They stay half-shut to tolerate the sunlight streaming through the window. He still has a belly, but it's only a fraction of the size. It sags below his waist as if it were a separate satchel.

"Bob?" I gasp. "What happened?"

"Can't talk," he mumbles, bending over to look beneath his bed. "Gotta find a drink." He reaches under the bed, removing a mason jar of yellowish liquid. "They took it all except for this teaspoon sip of princess perfume." Without looking, he tosses the jar at me.

Miraculously, I manage to catch it. "Bob, your brew is in the ballroom. I can have someone—"

Before I can finish the sentence, Bob is already gone, stumbling out of his room and down the hall. He staggers around the corner, nearly tripping as his feet drag over the rug.

"Bob, wait!" I chase after him. "We need to be discreet about this. Please, just wait a second!"

Bob doesn't wait. In fact, his haggard gait only hastens. He clings to the rail as he descends the Central Staircase, bursting at last into the ballroom.

"There she is!" He beelines for the drink stand—a round table supporting three 31 gallon barrels of Bob's special brew. With a sigh of relief, he grabs a porcelain goblet and fills it from the spigot.

Nevela stares with wide eyes, as do her fellow committee members. They stop, floral arrangements in hand, to watch the scene pan out.

"Excuse me!" I announce as Bob gulps his first beer. "Could everyone step outside for just a moment? We need to discuss a matter in private."

The women share annoyed looks for a moment. The nearest committee member gives me the evil eye. "Why can't you two step out?"

"How about we take five?" Nevela intervenes. "You ladies deserve a break."

To my relief, the women comply. They set down their bouquets and shuffle reluctantly out of the ballroom.

"Thank you," I mouth as Nevela pulls the double doors shut.

"Bob?" I step up beside him as he gulps down another beer. As soon as the goblet is empty, it's back under the spigot.

"Bob?"

"Mhhh," he groans as he drinks the third cup in a single go. "That's better." He places it back under the spigot. "Much better." This time, he takes intermittent gulps, pausing to admire the aesthetic of his goblet.

Once empty, he fills it again, but instead of taking a sip, he looks over at me. His eyes widen as if seeing me for the first time.

"Sorry about that, princess. I've been drinking nothing but nature's piss for far too long. Needed me a proper drink."

"Bob, what happened? You've been gone for weeks. We all thought you were dead."

He nods, "I thought the same."

"So… what happened? Did you find an escape route?"

He tips the goblet back. Once empty, he sighs. "I'm sorry, princess. I forgot the way… got all mixed up down there. We wandered for days."

We? I forgot he brought backup.

"What happened?" I finally ask.

He pats his midsection. "The others didn't have the stores I do. They couldn't keep going… so… I left them there. Eventually, I got lucky. Found my way back here."

I shudder. "You've been down there this whole time?"

He nods. "I'm sorry, princess. There's nothing more I can do for us."

"What about the others?" I inquire. "How long ago did you leave them?"

Bob ignores my question. Instead, he motions at the Mason jar in my arms. "I made it myself. It's lemon-ginger beer. Your favorite, no?"

"The others, Bob! Should we send a search party? Please, tell me what we need to do!"

"There's only one thing we can do, princess." He reaches over and taps the lid of the mason jar.

"What?" I ask, looking down. "You mean drink?"

"Not just drink." Bob lifts his goblet to his lips. "Forget."

I'm already tipsy as I make my way back to my room. It was only one mason jar, but the brew was a bit stronger than I anticipated. My arms feel heavy, and I'm hyper-aware of the way my hips swing as I walk down the hallway.

You can forget, Rose. Tonight, you can let go.

When I reach my quarters, I stop. There's a note on my door.

> *Rose,*
>
> *For the masquerade, I was thinking we should embrace the ambiance of mystery. Why don't we meet on the dance floor? No expectations. Nothing planned. Just two strangers crossing paths.*
>
> *Awaiting our romantic rendezvous,*
>
> *Your secret admirer*

Meet as strangers?

The idea stirs up butterflies in my stomach. The sensation is almost nostalgic. It reminds me of our first date, back before we ever kissed—before I knew he loved me.

A small part of me wants the security of our routine, but I appreciate the appeal of his suggestion.

In our current relationship, there's almost no spontaneity. No risk. We lay out our feelings like lawyers, endless elaborations to avoid the slightest misconception. Every kiss is practically planned—once at hello, once at goodbye, and once after each sweet gesture. Don't get me wrong. The kisses are nice, but they don't always feel like they used to.

Antai's proposal puts all of that in question. As strangers, every gesture will be heartfelt, not habitual.

Strangers it is.

Smiling, I twist the handle and step inside my quarters.

I set his note on the desk and stand at the foot of my bed, admiring my outfit.

The dress is a deep, cranberry red with gold and black accents, but it's my mask that steals the show. It's composed entirely of thick black lace, designed to leave small patches of my skin exposed in a beautiful swirling pattern.

I lift the mask to my face and stand before my mirror. The mask comes to a swooping point in the middle of my forehead, resembling the peak of a crown.

You've outdone yourself, Nevela.

I'm in the process of undressing when my hand bumps the key around my neck.

That's odd.

Now that I think of it, I didn't use my key before coming in. It was already unlocked when I arrived, and I know for a fact I locked up on my way out.

That's very odd.

Moving slowly, I pull my shirt back over my head. Then, I tiptoe over to my wardrobe and yank the door open.

It's empty.

I drop to the floor and check under the bed.

Nothing.

After giving the drapes a gentle push, I tiptoe to the maid's door. When I turn the handle, it opens.

My heart thumps against my rib cage like a battering ram. Hypothetically, if someone snuck into my room with Jack's key, they would've locked up on their way out, right? They would've made extra sure to leave everything as they found it. That only leaves one option.

They're still inside.

Shield.

I wait until the force field surrounds me. Then, I push the maid's door all the way open and step inside.

Immediately, my eyes go to Nevela's bed. The sheets are stripped, and the mattress is mutilated with multiple long gashes. Feathers bleed out onto the floor.

What in the world?

It's not only feathers pouring from the mattress. Multiple white garments hang half-exposed from the fabric like a brutal disembowelment. Several more are strewn around the floor, landing haphazardly after being torn from their hiding place.

Each garment is identical. It's a knee length cloak with full-length sleeves and a spacious hood. Tiny black print is sewn across the entire surface.

Adamic armor!

The longer I stare, the more I notice. I count several dozen.

She kept making more, and they found them.

I scan the room for threats, moving slowly. I check the washroom first, then the wardrobe. Finally, I bend down and peer under Nevela's bed.

Nothing.

I look under Wendy's bed next.

Also nothing.

I'm about to stand up when I notice something. The space beneath the bed seems to vibrate—similar to an energy shield, yet different. It's more subtle and continuous, like the faint warping when you open the oven or the blurry haze above the road on a hot day.

I blink, but the air continues to waver.

What the—

Suddenly, a force wave collides with my shield, breaking through the barrier and throwing me back. My head hits the baseboard, and the room spins.

My vision steadies just in time to see Crasilda materialize beneath Wendy's bed, amulet in hand. She was there the entire time, cloaking herself with imperfect invisibility.

She smiles as the bedframe lurches at me, sliding across the floor.

Shield!

I shape the barrier like a wedge, the sharp end facing Crasilda. As the bedframe collides with my shield, it splits in half, smashing into the wall on either side of me.

Crasilda and I climb to our feet in unison. For a split second, I consider the spell.

Havaknah Ra.

Four syllables, and she'd be incapacitated… maybe dead, but I can't bring myself to do it.

As I hesitate, Crasilda extends her hand.

TZZZZ!

Electricity arcs toward me, dancing over my barrier and dissipating into the floor around me.

Crasilda takes a step forward and smiles. The electricity intensifies, threatening to leech through my shield.

Repel!

I extend my consciousness. As Crasilda channels the electrons toward me, I speak to them directly, ordering them to scatter. Still, I gape at the sheer force of her commands. At this rate, she'll strain her soul in seconds.

She steps closer. "What's wrong? Not what you expected?"

The electricity intensifies, pressing into my shield and forcing my back against the wall. The stone around me begins to heat, slowly turning molten orange.

"That's right," Crasilda sneers. "Your daddy gave me a soul-anchor too. How does it feel to fight an equal for once?"

Her consciousness continues to drive the electrons toward me. Already, I can feel the hair standing up on my arms. Static pours into the air around me, saturating my skin. Before long, a rogue jolt seeps through my shield, coursing through my arm. In an instant, my shield disintegrates, and the full force of Crasilda's electricity surges through me.

I scream as my muscles seize. The electricity ignites my nerves and melts any concentration I try to muster.

Then, it stops.

"Don't worry!" Crasilda laughs. "I can't kill you. I'd have hell to pay if I did." She narrows her eyes. "But that doesn't mean we can't have some fun."

She extends her hand, and another jolt of lightning surges through me.

"Ahhh!" I thrash on the floor.

One second. Two seconds…

By some miracle, I manage to reach out with my mind.

Liquify!

The stone beneath Crasilda's feet begins to sag. She tries to jump, but the floor offers no resistance. It gives way beneath her feet, raining liquid rock on the bedroom below. As she falls, the electricity ceases.

Crasilda only plummets a few feet before landing on an invisible force—a safety net of her own making. The air ripples as it lifts her back through the hole and deposits her on solid ground.

This time I don't hesitate. I unleash a stream of fire, pouring my entire soul into the blaze. I know it won't kill her, but it should keep Crasilda occupied for a few seconds.

As expected, Crasilda diverts the flames with ease. They swirl to either side of her, igniting the feathers and sending embers into the air.

Within seconds, the mattress ignites as well, filling the room with smoke as it quickly turns to ash.

I continue the torrent, slowly sidestepping my way towards the maid's door.

The brightness of the flames blinds Crasilda, but it doesn't keep her from lashing out. The air reverberates to my left as her force wave punches a hole into the adjacent room. A second layer, the air shudders above my head, and the stones topple. A cloud of dust fills the air, indistinguishable from the smoke.

I take one last step towards the maid's door and heave myself through, cutting the flow of fire. I position myself out of Crasilda's view, using the wall between us as cover.

The stone shudders as Crasilda batters it with force dominion, but the wall doesn't crumble as the others did.

It worked!

Not long ago, Grandpa fortified my room with the same Adamic spell that secures the Palace Vault. Not only does the spell prevent entry at the door, but it strengthens the walls as well. If Crasilda wants to get me, she'll have to come through the maid's door like I did.

I scan my bedroom, immediately spotting what I came for. My longbow is propped against my nightstand in the corner of the room. I extend my soul.

Pull!

The bow hurdles through the air and into my open hand.

I focus on the quiver of arrows next.

Pull!

A single arrow flies toward me, and I snatch it by the shaft. I nock the arrow, training it on the doorway. My eyes burn from the smoke, but I refuse to blink.

"I knew you were hiding something," Crasilda calls from the other room, "but I didn't expect this. There's got to be what, 30 cloaks of armor? Maybe 50? You really put that poor girl to work didn't you?"

50? Nevela kept sewing, even after I told her not to. One part of me is proud, but another is furious.

"I wonder what your old man will think of this," Crasilda taunts.

"It's a shame I had to find it before the masquerade, but hey, maybe your father will be merciful. If you tell me where the arrows are hidden, he might let you enjoy the night before total annihilation."

I hold my breath, waiting for Crasilda to step through the door. The seconds tick by.

"Don't play dumb, Rose. I see them training out there. Like you said, it doesn't take a genius to connect the dots. Just tell me where the arrows are, and we'll go easy on you."

I glance quickly at my front door. I could run. I could bolt out the door and find backup, but that wouldn't fix my problem. Crasilda knows too much. She'll tell Jack, and my father will retaliate. I can't let that happen.

She has to die!

"You still in there, Rose?" Crasilda calls. "If you think I'm walking through that doorway, you're stupider than I th—."

I spin, leaning into the doorway enough to expose my bow.

I process the scene in a split second. Crasilda is standing beside Nevela's bed frame, far away from the hole I created. She's watching the doorway with her hand raised. Unlike before, she's wearing the Adamic armor. The hood is pulled over her head, and the hem reaches down to her shin.

As lightning crackles on her fingertips, I align the arrowhead and relax my fingers.

Twang.

KA-CRACK!

A flash of ethereal whiteness consumes my vision. The next thing I know, I'm opening my eyes. I'm sprawled on the floor in the doorway, and my muscles burn from head to toe.

The lapse of consciousness must have been fleeting, because Crasilda is struggling to remove an Adamic arrow. It pierced her cloak just below the armpit, pinning her to Nevela's headboard.

I missed!

Finally, Crasilda snaps the arrow shaft, sliding the fabric over the arrow to free herself. She looks down at me and shakes her head.

"This is the best you've got? I'm disappointed, Rose."

I try to move my arms, but they feel like lead. I can only lift my head a few inches.

"You're pathetic," she spits. "I hope your father sees you for what you are."

I let my body slump back to the ground, pinching my amulet between my breastbone and the stone floor. I might not be able to stand, but I still have dominion.

Magnetize!

I create a magnetic field in the air above my head, aiming it in Crasilda's direction.

Immediately, her amulet tugs toward me, nearly tearing from her grasp. She wraps a second hand around the amulet as it slowly drags her across the floor. Then, she narrows her eyes. The air ripples around her hands as she anchors her amulet in place with force dominion.

"Pathetic," she sneers again.

What Crasilda doesn't notice is the sewing machine behind her. It's solid iron and nearly as thick as an anvil. It flies through the air, smashing into the back of her head.

Crasilda doesn't stand a chance. She topples onto her face, and her amulet rips free from her fingers.

Both the sewing machine and the amulet hover in the air above me. But I don't stop there.

As Crasilda climbs to her feet, I amplify the magnetic field. A dozen loose sewing needles shoot through the air, embedding themselves point first in Crasilda's back.

"Ahh!" She collapses to the floor, contorting her arms to claw at the needles. "You bitch!" she screams.

I reach my mind beneath the floor, creating a new magnetic field underneath Crasilda.

Magnetize!

Now, the needles are drawn downward, digging deeper into Crasilda's back and pinning her to the floor. Should she try to stand, she'll only drive the needles deeper.

When I'm confident she's contained, I slowly climb to my feet, using the doorframe for support. Then, I peer into my chambers, extending my soul to the quiver.

Pull!

An Adamic arrow flies into my hand, and I nock the bow. Taking a deep breath. I walk over to Crasilda and wrestle back the bowstring.

It's time to finish the job.

Crasilda laughs. "You're stupider than I thought."

"How so?" I demand, aiming the arrow at her heart.

"You know you can't kill me, right?" she claims, her face plastered to the floor. "If you think the armor is bad, I promise you, this is worse. Daddy would not be happy. How long until Jack comes looking for me? What are you going to do, dispose of my body? Clean up the crime scene?"

I bite my lip, trying to find a reason to let the arrow fly.

"Face it," Crasilda sneers. "We're stuck with each other."

I lower the bow. *She's right.* Which only gives me one last option. I have to change her mind.

Repel.

I reverse the magnetism, pushing the needles out of Crasilda's back. Then, I kick her soul-anchor in her direction.

"Get up. Let's talk about this."

"Would you look at that," Crasilda scoffs as she climbs to her feet. "She has a brain after all,"

"What do you want?" I demand.

Crasilda furrows her brow.

I gesture at the Adamic armor on the floor. "What do you want to keep quiet about this whole thing?"

Crasilda laughs again. "Oh, please. You can't give me what I want."

"Is this about your sister?" I wonder. "You think the Holy One will bring her back?"

Crasilda looks genuinely offended. "Are you serious? My sister isn't dead, you moron. She's downstairs with the other filthy vermin."

I frown. "This isn't for her?"

"God no! Screw her. I'm doing this for myself," Crasilda exclaims.

"My whole life, I did everything right. Perfect test scores. Perfect behavior. And did my parents care? Absolutely not. They were too busy worrying about my sister—not the star student, the failure. She dropped out of institute and ran off before The Dividing. And do you know how my parents reacted? They offered her a free room. They offered her free food. But no, she would rather be homeless. And somehow, none of that matters to them. She's all they ever think about."

"Crasilda, I… Maybe you sister is unwell,"

"She's listless, just like the other pickers. She doesn't deserve my sympathy."

I shake my head, unable to believe what I'm hearing. "If you tell Jack, your sister will die along with everyone else."

"Good. That's what she gets," Crasilda scoffs. "She threw her life away, and now she's living in the palace, eating the same rations I am. How is that fair? No, no, no. She chose her path, and she should suffer the consequences."

"Death?" I question.

Crasilda shrugs. "Why not?"

I clench my teeth. This argument is impossible.

"If you want justice," I say, "my father will only disappoint you. He preaches equality, not justice. Why do you think the Equalists were so quick to support him?"

"You don't know what you're talking about," Crasilda replies confidently. "He preaches the parable of the talents. Serve him well, and he'll reward you ten fold. Betray him, and your talents will be stripped from you. True, my sister won't starve, but she won't rule like I will. She'll never speak Adamic. She'll never be a goddess."

"Please, Crasilda. I'm begging you. Whatever my father promised you, he lied. You'll never be a goddess. He'll save the language for himself."

Crasilda gives me a condescending smile. "He's already kept his word. He's given me more than you ever could. The soul-anchor was just the beginning." She turns, reaching back and sweeping her auburn hair to the side. On the back of her neck, just beneath the hairline, is the mark of the beast.

When she sees that I'm speechless, she smiles victoriously. "Anyways, it was nice knowing ya."

She struts toward the door.

"I'll make you queen… Tonight."

Crasilda pauses.

"My father won't give you my crown. He loves me too much, but I can give it to you. I'll crown you at the masquerade. I'll forfeit my seat on the throne. You'll have two votes. You'll have the respect you deserve. Just please… don't tell Jack."

She doesn't turn around. She just stands there, contemplating.

"If the Holy One succeeds, you'll still be a goddess," I ramble. "And if he doesn't, you'll be queen. It's a win-win. Please… I'm begging you." I fall to my knees. "Please, Crasilda. I'll do anything."

"Alright, you convinced me," Crasilda says. "On a few conditions, of course." She turns, smiling at the sight of my submission. "Firstly, I want your chambers. The queen must reside in the Royal Wing, after all. Second, my servants have been… underperforming." Her smile grows wider. "I want yours. The blonde one… and the whore too."

"But…"

Crasilda raises an eyebrow. "Or would you prefer the alternative?"

I don't want to imagine the suffering Crasilda will inflict on my friends, but I have no choice.

Defeated, I bow my head. "You have a deal."

29

MATT

The Judgment Seat is unpleasant, especially with the gag in my mouth. The rope goes between my teeth, forcing my jaw open, and wraps around the top of the backrest. It pins my head to the stone, preventing me from sitting forward. A second rope coils around my chest and under my armpits, disappearing behind me.

From where I'm seated, I can't reach any knots with my fingers, and the rope is thicker than a stick of salami. I could chew on it for days without breaking through.

I'm doomed.

The sun has already set, and dusk is fading fast. If I look close enough, I can make out the Milky Way overhead. At most, I have thirty minutes until they light the bonfire beneath me.

From my seat atop the monolith, I have a decent view of the crowd. In the front row, several Atlantians play an assortment of wooden drums. The others snack on papaya and mango as they wait for the Reckoning, passing several platters through the masses. They offer some to Iris and Kendra who quickly decline.

Sheyba is sitting with them, whispering something to Iris. After a minute, Sheyba turns to her mom, whispering in her ear as well. Her mother places a hand on Sheyba's shoulder, and they touch noses, holding the embrace for several seconds.

I'm still watching as Iris looks up and meets my gaze. I wait for her to give me a signal—something to indicate they have a plan—but she only frowns.

Kendra stands suddenly. "Excuse me, but I want to leave. I… I don't think I can watch this."

Unsure what Kendra said, the Atlantians turn their heads in unison toward the High Priestess.

The old woman waves her hand. "Well, what are you waiting for? Off with you! Take a vessel and go back where you came from. Sheyba, escort them to the wave-skimmer."

Kendra looks up at me, tears in her eyes. She opens her mouth but turns away without a word.

"Keeh-aaah!" I grunt, but my voice doesn't project with the rope in my mouth. "Keeeh-aaah!"

Sheyba guides them down the beach. My eyes follow Kendra until she's completely out of sight. She never looks back—not even once.

They left me.

Tha ache is excruciating. It's an acid, eroding my gut from the inside.

They really left me.

With nothing left to do, I struggle against the binds. I tug and twist, hoping to wiggle free, but it's pointless. There's nothing I can do. I'm stuck here until the fire burns the rope, and by then, I'll be cooked as well.

As the minutes tick by, I stare at my cuffs. Maybe, after my body is burned to a crisp, they'll recover the relic from the ashes and give it to someone else… someone they deem worthy.

I'm going to burn alive.

The panic is already building, rising to my head, swelling within my skull.

"Don't make a noise," someone whispers directly into my right ear. They're so close, I can feel their breath tickle my skin.

I stiffen, trying to turn my head to the side. I look with my eyes, but I don't see anyone. There's nothing but empty air beside me.

The invisibility ring.

"Don't react and don't try to look at me," the voice breathes. It's masculine and familiar, but I just can't put my finger on it.

"We're going to get you out of here," he whispers, "but you have to do exactly as I say. We have it all planned out."

Suddenly, it dawns on me. The voice sounds different than it does in my head.

It's my voice.

The morph mask!

"Keh-ah!" I gag.

"Shhhh," the voice breathes. "Before we get started, I have to know you'll follow the plan. Blink twice if you'll do as I say."

I blink twice.

"Good. Here's what's going to happen. First, you need an amulet. I want you to open your hand. In a few seconds, I'll drop it in. I removed the chain, so it won't make any noise. Blink twice when you're ready."

I let my fingers uncurl, but keep my hand partially closed so that it looks relaxed and natural. Then, I blink twice.

A second later, the amulet materializes in my palm. It's not an amplifier like I expect; it's Iris's soul-anchor—a thick golden ring, shaped like a flattened doughnut. The bonding spell perfectly matches the tattoo on my shoulder.

I close my fingers around it.

"Okay," my voice whispers. "I'm going to cut you free now, but you can't move. Keep pretending like you're tied up. Blink twice if you understand."

I blink twice.

Within seconds, the rope loosens, but it doesn't fall away. Something holds it in place, maintaining the appearance of captivity.

"Okay, now if you can, scoot a little to your left. I'm gonna sit next to you," my voice directs.

With my restraints now slack, I use one hand to push off the seat, shimmying to the left an inch at a time.

"Okay, that's enough," my voice says. Next thing I know, something bumps my shoulder. A weight presses against my hip as a body—my body—sits next to me on the Judgment Seat. Despite our contact, I don't turn invisible thanks to the fabric between us. It has to be skin contact, after all.

"Alright," my voice whispers, "this is the tricky part. When you're ready, I'm going to slip the ring on your finger. You'll be invisible, and I'll take your place. When that happens, your bindings will turn invisible too, and I'll form my own using the morph mask. Then, all you have to do is sneak out of here. Just don't use force dominion. They'll see the ripples. Okay? Blink twice if you understand."

I adjust my arms, making sure I have skin contact with the strap around my chest. I don't have to worry about the gag considering it's jammed into my throat.

I blink twice.

My rescuer hesitates, breathing in my ear for a second. "You really have to trust me, Matt," my voice breathes. "Don't wait for me. Just follow the plan. Make your way down the beach and go north. The ship will be waiting for you there. I'll take care of the rest. Got it?"

I extend my pinky knowing that the ring will slide onto it with the least resistance.

Satisfied, I blink twice.

"Okay. Once we switch places, I won't be able to talk to you, but I'll meet you by the ship. Here we go. Three… Two…"

I barely feel it as the invisibility ring slips over my pinky. It's neither warm nor cold, perfectly acclimated to my body temperature.

The moment it touches my skin, my body disappears, and I'm left staring at the bare stone where my legs should be.

When I look to my right, it's like looking in a mirror. My face is staring back at me with the same terrified expression I had just a minute ago. My replica is bound by two ropes which wrap behind my invisible head and shoulders, looping around the backrest. They restrain my replacement while leaving me free to escape.

Panicked, I look around. A few Atlantians are looking up at the

Judgement Seat, but after a few seconds, they continue gnawing on their mangoes and chatting with their neighbors.

It actually worked!

I can't help but marvel at Kendra's genius. To any onlookers, it would've appeared like a glitch in the matrix. In a split second, I shifted position, teleporting two feet to the side. Everything else—my appearance and my restraints—appear untouched. Most men would question their own sanity before investigating the occurrence.

As I lean forward, my own invisible restraints come loose. I'm careful to maintain skin-contact as I bundle them into my arms. The last thing I need is a dangling length of rope slapping someone in the face as I sneak off.

I stand on the Judgment Seat, keeping sure not to bump Kendra and turn her invisible. I spin in a small circle, assessing my options. I'm ten feet in the air and surrounded on three sides by Atlantians. The stretch of sand between the bonfire and the sea is relatively open, but they'll still see my footsteps in the sand. My only option is to fly.

Dammit!

Kildron offered to teach me, and I turned him down like an idiot.

Regardless, I give it a try. I focus on my body, commanding the elements within me.

Fly!

I remain planted on the monolith.

Zero gravity! Weightless! Float!

Nothing happens.

Levitate!

For a second, I feel my insides lift, but they don't move in unison. Organs rise into my rib cage while my feet remain grounded. I swallow the vomit rising in my throat.

So much for that idea.

As a reposition the rope in my arms, my wrists bump together, eliciting a metallic chink from my cuffs.

That's it! I can't see them, but I reach out with my mind, feeling for the metal around my wrists. When I'm sure I have a good grip on the rope, I give the metal a single command.

Lift.

The cuffs raise into the air, taking me with them. I flex my arms and tighten my core as the cuffs carry me higher and higher above the Judgment Seat.

5 feet.

10 feet.

20 feet.

Satisfied, I give a new command.

Forward.

The cuffs lurch, swinging me horizontally toward the ocean. Everything about the motion feels awkward as I dangle from my arms, like a cat held by the scruff of its neck.

I'm a decent distance from the bonfire now, but I refuse to land in the sand where they can track my movement. Instead, I carry myself all the way to the shallows, dropping myself into the water. It's only ankle deep, but it's enough to remove any footprints I leave behind.

I look back one last time. Due to the slope of the beach, I can only see the upper half of the monolith. At this distance, my replica looks like a doll strapped to the Judgment Seat with tiny rubber bands.

What are you planning, Kendra?

Will she simply remove the morph-mask, trading it for her freedom? When they see an innocent girl has taken my place, will they set her free? Will they punish her for aiding my escape?

You have to trust her, I tell myself. *Just trust her.*

I start running north. To be honest, I'm not even sure which way north is, but this is the general direction Sheyba led everyone when they left.

I race along the water's edge, my feet splashing in the shallows with every step. The full moon offers more than enough light to dodge the rocks and debris on the beach. There are a few waves, but they're almost negligible—no taller than my knees.

A minute into my run, I spot four figures moving toward me. They stroll along the shallows, chattering in Atlantean and kicking at the waves as they wash past. Judging by the size of the silhouettes, they must be children.

The fishing kids!

I stop in my tracks, holding my breath as amble closer. If I'm lucky, my invisibility will be enough.

The children are 50 feet away now.

25 feet away.

10 feet away.

To my horror, the wave recedes as they approach, exposing a foot-shaped indent where I wait in the sand. So far, no one seems to notice.

One boy walks several yards ahead of the others. He trudges right past my footprints and continues down the beach.

The next two boys angle towards the water, chasing the retreating waves. They pass by without even glancing my direction.

The last figure, the little girl, is walking backward. She drags her toes, leaving long wavy lines in the sand behind her.

10 feet.

5 feet.

She nearly bumps into me, passing an arm's length to my left. She continues to stare at her toes as she shuffles past.

Woosh!

A wave rushes up the beach. As it sweeps past my knees, beach foam sprays into the air.

The little girl stops, staring at the aquatic crater my invisible calves create. She shouts something in Atlantean as she splashes over to get a closer look. Her head nearly bumps my stomach as she peers down the leg-shaped cavity.

The wave recedes by the time the other boys arrive, leaving them huddled around my two footprints.

I decide to make an aerial escape. I stretch my soul into the metal cuffs.

Lif—

Before I can finish the command, one of the boys kicks at the footprint. The tips of his toes crunch against the side of my ankle.

"Agh!" The boy cries out, hopping around on one foot.

Another boy reaches out with one finger and pokes the top of my foot. Then, he pokes my ankle, working his way higher. When he feels my shorts, he grabs onto the fabric and tugs.

It's too late to fly. Instead, I take off at a sprint, racing the beach.

The children jump back, shouting in Atlantian. A few seconds later, I hear their soggy footsteps as they chase after me.

Shield!

I form the barrier between us just in case. It moves with me as I run, defending my backside.

They chase me for a few seconds, following my footsteps as they take shape in the sand.

Suddenly, one of the boys stops, raising his hand.

As my foot strikes the shore, a blob of mud rises up out of the ground, coalescing around my ankle. It suctions over my skin and anchors me to the beach. With nowhere else to go, my momentum carries my torso straight into the sand.

"Oof," I grunt as the wind is knocked out of me.

Shield!

I cocoon myself in a force field as the sand rises up around me. It blocks out the stars as it diffuses over my barrier. I feel the pressure building against me as more and more sand piles up.

Expand!

My shield explodes outward, sending sand in all directions. A second later, I leap into the air. Before my feet hit the ground, I create a platform of pure force. The air ripples beneath my feet, propelling upward.

10 feet.

30 feet.

I stop, satisfied that I'm concealed. Without my footsteps, they'll have no way to spot—

A coconut whizzes past my head. I look down to see the four kids staring up at me with squinty eyes.

In the dark, it should be impossible, but they see the ripples from my force dominion. It's the only explanation.

The tallest boy levitates another coconut and hurdles it toward my legs. I manage to twist out of the way at the last second.

The little girl raises her hand next, and several fist-sized stones levitate into the air. They catapult at me in quick succession, one after the other.

Shield.

Each stone elicits a large ripple across my force field, spreading outward in all directions.

The children cheer, pointing up at the distortions. I wait for them to throw more rocks, but the boys close their eyes instead.

Squaw!

Above my head a bird shrieks. Next thing I know, something sharp digs into the back of my shirt.

"Agh!"

Before I can retaliate, the creature is airborne. I catch a glimpse of it as I spin around, careful not to fall off of my platform.

It's a white bird with a red beak and a three foot wingspan.

Squaw!

A second bird swoops down with talons extended. They slash across my forehead as I duck out of the way. Immediately, blood tickles into my eye.

Squaw!

This time I'm ready. When the next bird swoops I don't hesitate.

Slice.

The air ripples, completely severing one of its wings. The bird plunges to the sand below.

I send an energy wave at the next bird, reducing it to a plume of feathers.

More birds circle in the air above me. They seem to be drawn by the commotion, swarming like pigeons in a park.

All at once, they swoop

Slice!

Rather than a single cut, I form a wave of razor-thin parallel lines. In an instant, a dozen birds pass through the cheese-grater, raining down onto the beach in their individual parts.

I'm so focused on the birds, I don't notice as the little girl catapults another coconut. It catches me on the collarbone, knocking me back. I step to regain my balance, but my foot misses the platform. My stomach lurches as I plummet.

Just before I hit the ground, I draw my soul into my bones.

Fortify.

"Oof!"

Fortunately, the sand softens my landing. As far as I know, nothing breaks.

I roll to my feet a moment before the birds dive me.

Shield.

A dome ripples above my head as the birds claw and peck. Looking past the feathery onslaught, I find the children standing in a trance.

That's it!

I extend my soul.

Squeeze.

I snatch all of the children at once, an invisible force pressing down on them from all sides. Then, I turn toward the ocean.

Launch.

I hurl the children into the air, watching as they soar over the surf and splash into the sea.

Maybe they got hurt on impact; maybe they didn't. At this point I don't really care.

Good riddance.

I wipe the blood from my brow before resuming my trek down the beach.

WHOOSH!

A monstrous wave sweeps over me, instantly burying me within the turbulent current.

I tumble a dozen times before my head smacks the bottom of the sand, giving me a sense of up and down. I flip over and kick off the sand, gasping as my head breaks the surface.

Tightening my hand on the amulet, I command the water to condense beneath my feet.

Rise.

My liquid footholds lift me above the surface until my feet are level with the ocean plane. As I stand, seawater spews off my shoulders, becoming visible the moment it separates from my skin.

That's when I see them. Four heads floating casually in the water. All of them are looking in my direction.

I could try the aerial route again, hoisting myself through the air by my cuffs, but they'll follow the rainfall from my sopping clothes.

Instead, I take a deep breath.

Sink.

The water swallows me, and I let myself descend to the bottom. Normally, I can hold my breath for a minute. With dominion maximizing the oxygen in my bloodstream, I think I can triple that number.

Flow.

The water rushes around me, creating an artificial current that pulls me parallel to the beach. In the darkness, it's hard to know how fast I'm going, but I think I'll be out of earshot by the time I have to surface.

This is going to work.

Suddenly, something flutters past me in the abyss. As it moves, its velvety skin brushes against mine. The texture is smooth and familiar.

Shark!

I forgot about my wounds. At this very moment, blood is oozing from my brow, leaving a scent trail in the water that may as well be footprints in the sand.

Dang, those kids are smart.

Once again, something flutters past me, moving quickly. A second later it returns, nuzzling into my leg.

Then, it bites.

"Agh!" I gurgle as sea water fills my mouth.

Slice.

I sever its spine before the shark can shake its head and do more damage. My heart races, and I release the current, forming an energy shield instead.

I spin in a circle, peering into the depths. At the bottom of the lagoon, it's pitch black. I can't see anything, and blood is pouring from my leg. If there aren't more sharks, there will be soon.

With no other options, I command myself to the surface.

"Ptuh!" I suck in a breath as quietly as I can. I'm still wiping the water from my eyes when the ocean erupts around me, lifting me into the air in a giant sphere of liquid. I float above the lagoon like a goldfish in its bowl.

Immediately, I spot the children. They tread water, eyes narrowed with concentration as they carry me closer.

After all the trouble they've given me, I'm tempted to use sound dominion and shatter their eardrums, but anything loud or bright will alert the beachgoers a half mile away.

Unless.

In my mind, I form the reflectors, enclosing the children in a soundproof, blackout box. Immediately, the children disappear from sight.

From where I stand, the prism appears to be a hollow void, keeping the light hostage within, preventing it from ever reaching my eyes.

For a second, I feel bad for the suffering I'm about to inflict. Then, I give the commands.

Screech!

Flash!

Immediately, the watery sphere bursts, dropping me back into the ocean. I maintain my reflectors as I swim to the surface. I don't see any light, but I know within the prism it must be deafening and blinding.

That should do it.

As I remove the spell, juvenile screams peirce the air.

I waste no time. I command my cuffs.

Levitate!

I hover in the air.

Dry!

My body emits a plume of steam. Once that clears, I'm completely undetectable. No dripping water. No ripples of force dominion. I'm ready to—

A rhythmic chant echoes across the sea, accompanied by the steady beat of the drums. I turn toward the source of the sound.

NO!

In the distance, I spot the hazy glow of a bonfire. A column of smoke obscures my view of the monolith.

I don't waste a second. I face the bonfire and command my cuffs.

Forward!

I careen diagonally along the beach as if hanging haphazardly from a zip line. My arms burn from the strain, and my cuffs feel like they might tear free at any moment, but I force myself onward.

I descend on the sand, landing a football field from the bonfire. Fortunately, all eyes are on the Judgment Seat.

Kendra!

For some reason, she's still maintaining my form. She's strapped to the seat—or at least she's pretending to be. She twists and screams in my voice as the flames rise up around her.

The Atlantians continue to chant as the flames grow higher. To my horror, the smoke consumes Kendra completely, obscuring her from view.

"Matt!… Matt!"

I turn to find Iris sprinting up the beach. Her head moves on a swivel, scanning the sand for any signs of movement.

"We have to help Kendra!" I call out as I race toward the bonfire.

I'm still too far away, but I don't care. I have to try.

EXTINGU—

Before I can finish the command, the smoke begins to spiral around the monolith, traveling along a predetermined current. The flames rise higher, following the same spiral pattern. As the smoke condenses, I see my body standing on the Judgment Seat, arms swinging to guide the smoke.

Kendra?

Suddenly, the wind picks up. Even at this distance, it whips at my face. The sand around the bonfire stirs, lifting off the ground. Then, it sucks violently into the growing vortex.

"Matt!" Iris calls into the wind. "That's not Kendra. We need to go."

I twist my ring, and her eyes find me as I materialize.

"The ship is right here!" she screams. "Let's go!" She turns and runs toward the . Sure enough, a catamaran is beached directly down the shore. When I didn't show up, they came looking.

"Hurry!" Iris screams.

I sprint after her, looking back over my shoulder. The vortex is now a full-fledged tornado. Flames billow within the sand funnel, sustained by dominion alone.

Most of the Atlanteans have scattered, but several dozen stand to face my replica.

KA-CRACK!

A series of lightning bolts surge at the vortex, but they're quickly dissipated by the sand, never reaching my replica. Whoever they are, they remain in the tornado, never attacking, as it absorbs everything the Atlantians throw at it.

I race after Iris, quickly arriving at the catamaran. Kendra stands in one of the canoes, watching as we approach.

"Kendra!"

"Hurry!" she yells.

The sails billow as we leap aboard. The hull scrapes on the sand, and just like that, we're skimming across the waves.

I look back at the monolith, amplifying my eyesight. The vortex slows, and the air grows. The once-suspended sand rains down around my replica—only they aren't my replica any more. The figure has long black hair and a loincloth.

Sheyba.

For a second, no one moves. Then, Sheyba spreads her arms and teeters back. She falls from the top of the Judgment Seat, landing with a flat back in the sand. Only, she doesn't hit the sand. She disappears into the ground as if it were liquid.

She doesn't resurface.

"She saved me?" I mutter to myself. "I don't understand."

Kendra wraps her arms around me, giving me a squeeze. "I'm so glad you're okay."

"It was my idea," Iris says, maneuvering the tiller from the leadlog. She guides the ship toward the opening in the jetty. "You can thank me later."

I look back as we pass through. In the blink of an eye, the island disappears, replaced with the endless sea. Any navigational landmarks are now gone.

"Do you know how to find Kildron?" I worry.

"No." Iris points into the darkness. "But she does."

I squint, magnifying my eyes once more. Sure enough, a black sail skims over the water. Sheyba quickly catches up, leaping from her board and onto the catamaran. Without skipping a beat, she joins Iris on the leadlog, taking the tiller.

"Thank you," I breathe.

Sheyba waves her hand. "Eh, it was nothing."

I look back at Kendra, squeezing her tighter. Her chest helps to dampen my racing heart. "I thought it was you back there," I mutter. "I thought you were dead."

"I'm fine," Kendra says, squeezing me back. "We're both fine. That's what matters."

At our speed, it only takes a few minutes to reach Kildron. When he sees us coming, he moves to the railing.

"Get in!" Iris shouts as we pull alongside the yacht. "We're in a rush."

Kildron leaps aboard, taking a seat beside me. He looks around with a furrowed brow. "No reinforcements?"

"Just her," Iris says, pointing at Sheyba.

"It was all for nothing," Kendra sighs.

"It wasn't for nothing," I claim.

Kildron studies me, a thin smile forming when he sees my cuffs. "I guess it wasn't."

"That's not what I meant." I wait until everyone is looking at me. "I think I know where the Library is."

"You're serious?" Iris doubts.

"I think so," I say. "Think about it. God sent the flood to cleanse the world of Adalinguals, right? Why? Why a flood?"

They look between each other, waiting for someone to answer.

I'm too excited to wait. "Because you can't speak Adamic underwater. That's why!"

Kildron frowns. "What's your point?"

"Think about the clue," I urge. "'Adamic is the key, but you cannot speak.' It's talking about water. You can't speak underwater. And then there's the last two lines. 'It is an ark of salvation when the future is bleak.' An ark—another reference to the flood! And the last line. 'Once opened, destruction will leak.' It's not supposed to be a metaphor. I think it's literal. Imagine you have an underwater library? What happens when you open the door?"

"Water leaks in," Kendra affirms.

"Yes! Exactly. And water destroys paper. Destruction will *literally* leak into the library. This has to be it. Everything fits too perfectly."

"I don't know," Kildron wrinkles his forehead. "Underwater… really? Where is it supposed to be? The palace fountain?"

"Oh my God," Iris breathes, her eyes doubling in size. "You don't think…"

I'm already nodding along. "It's in the Trench, somewhere beneath the lake. It has to be."

I run my fingers through her hair as Kendra sleeps on my lap. I can't sleep, so I study the stars overhead—a speckled canvas of the cosmos.

Just yesterday, I doubted we'd ever find Atlantia. Now, I have the Shackles of Redemption, and an invaluable hunch. For the first time in weeks, I feel hopeful.

The catamaran jostles as the ocean swells. Sheyba is navigating on the leadlog. Kildron and Iris are both curled up in the other canoe.

I can sense Sheyba watching me, but every time I look up, she averts her eyes. After a few minutes, she finally breaks the silence.

"Can I ask you something, Matt, the repentant?"

"Sure. And just call me Matt."

"As you wish, Matt. I have a question about your sister, Iris, protector of the world?"

I glance over at Iris who doesn't stir. "Ask away."

Sheyba leans toward my side of the ship, lowering her voice. "From my observations, she has a stiff face. Would you agree, or is it just me?"

"Ummm, I'm not sure that was translated right."

"Which part?" Sheyba asks.

"Stiff face?"

Sheyba motions to Kendra sleeping in my lap. "Your mate, for example. She has a very soft face. Her emotions mold her skin more easily."

"Oh, you mean she's hard to read."

"Read?" Sheyba squints. "Read what?"

I wave my hand. "Nevermind. But yes, I agree with you. Iris has always been like that, as far as I know. It's not just you."

"That is reassuring," Sheyba sighs. "Most Atlantians are very expressive. I've never met someone filled with such dark water."

"Yep, that about sums her up. If it makes you feel better, she's a mystery to me too."

Sheyba glances at me again, and then averts her eyes. "Matt, can I ask you something else?"

"Go for it."

"Your sister. Do you think she breathes for me?"

"Ummm, I'm not really sure what you mean."

"You know…" Sheyba glances over at Iris, lowering her tone until it's barely audible. "Do you think she hungers for me?"

"Oh… ummm. I'm not really sure. You'd have to ask her yourself."

Sheyba frowns. "Did I say something inappropriate?"

"No, it's just… Hunger sounds a tad strong in English, but I get what you're saying."

"Rather than hunger, I should say… what?"

"You could ask if she has a crush on you," I suggest.

She tilts her head. "She crushes me?"

I laugh. "No, she… you know what, it's not important. I can't speak for her, but I'd say she likes you more than the average acquaintance."

"Okay…" Sheyba says, clearly disappointed. "That's a good start, I suppose."

"You like her a lot?" I ask.

Sheyba glances at Iris again, admiring her figure curled in the canoe. "I do." She finally decides. "I have no choice in the matter... I felt the tether."

"The tether?"

"You don't believe in the tether?" Sheyba asks.

"I'm not sure I know what it is."

"Atlantians believe in the eternal tether. In the Great Before, everyone was assigned a soul-twin—an equal of mind and spirit. Do you also believe this?"

"Soulmates," I say.

Her eyes light up. "So you do know,"

I shrug. "We have a word for it, but we don't take it too seriously."

"Well," Sheyba continues. "We believe each soul-twin is destined for each other. Their hearts are tethered at birth. Throughout life, the tether tugs them closer until they eventually cross paths. Yesterday, when I first saw Iris, I felt the tug in my chest." She places her hand over her heart. "We're soul-twins; I know it."

"Okay, that's enough," Kildron grumbles. "I can't listen to this gushy garbage any longer." Kildron stands up, stretching his arms above his head. "It's nothing personal, I'm just not an advocate of love at first sight." He stands and takes a seat on one of the cross beams. "Let's talk business, if you don't mind. How are we charting?"

"Good," Sheyba says. "Due west like you told me."

"How far do you think we've traveled?" Kildron wonders.

"Hard to say. Maybe 200 miles… Maybe less.

Kildron frowns. "Does this thing go any faster?"

Sheyba shrugs. "Sure, but it'll be bumpy."

"Let's do it."

The wind intensifies, and the mast creaks. As its name indicates, the wave skimmer hops from one wave to the next. The faster we go, the longer it hangs in the air, and the further it falls.

The ship lurches as it ramps off an exceptionally large wave. I feel myself lifting from the wood beneath me. Then, we come crashing down. My lap cushions Kendra's head, but I hear Iris's skull smack the bottom of the catamaran.

"Owww!" she groans, rubbing her head and sitting up. "What the hell did we hit?"

The boat shudders again as it cuts through another large swell.

"Get situated. It's gonna be a bumpy ride." Kildron announces. "I want to make it to Miami by sundown."

Kendra lifts her head from my lap and stretches her arms above her head, yawning.

Iris groans as she rolls into a seated position. "So much for some sleep,"

Kildron looks us over. After a second, he sighs. "While we're all awake, I have something to tell you guys before we get back to Cavernum." He turns to Sheyba. "I know I just asked you to speed up, but can we slow back down for a bit? I want everyone to hear this."

Sheyba nods. Within a few seconds, the wind slows, and the sound of the rushing water softens. The lurching of the boat is now a gentle lull.

"What is it?" Iris demands.

"I..." Kildron clears his throat. "I was going to wait until everyone mastered Durebrum, but considering the circumstances, I think you should know the truth." He pauses.

"Just spit it out," Iris barks.

Kildron focuses his gaze on Iris. "I have a relic I never told you about. I said it was a proposal gift, but that was a lie." Kildron removes the hourglass necklace from within his shirt, holding it up for everyone to see. It's one continuous piece of glass filled with minuscule black granules.

"If that's a relic," Iris grumbles, "then where's the spell?"

"It's concealed quite cleverly. You need a spell to activate it. It's the only one I know." He closes his eyes.

"Valiptah."

Reveal.

I stare at the hourglass.

Iris frowns "I don't—

"Just watch." Kildron turns the hourglass upside down. As the granules fall into the lower pyramid, they whisk against the sides of the glass. As more and more granules accumulate, they form a pattern, and eventually… symbols. Within a minute, there are four unique symbols, one displayed on each side of the glass.

"It belonged to the King of Hogrum," Kildron explains. "Jenevrah called it Reversion… It's a time-travel relic."

"What is wrong with you!" Iris shouts, leaping to her feet. "We had a relic this entire time, and we never used it? Are you stupid?"

"I know how it sounds, but it's not like that," Kikdron responds calmly. "Let me explain, and then you can criticize all you want, okay?"

Iris looks like she might lash out at any moment, but she doesn't object.

Kildron sighs, grabbing the edge of the catamaran as we crest another wave. "Time travel isn't what you think it is. It's not a magical solution for everything, okay? Time travel occurs within the history you've already witnessed.

The past, the present… it's all fixed. You can't change it. Our current history has already accounted for any time traveling you'll ever do. Does that make sense?"

"What are you talking about?" Iris impatiently replies.

Kildron rubs his temples. "Jenevrah had a much better way of explaining this. Look, the bottom line is this. You can't change the past. For example, let's say you want to go back and kill the Holy One as a baby. Well… you could try, but it wouldn't work. Like I said, everything in the past has already happened, even if you haven't done it yet. So, if you were going to succeed at killing baby Zezric, he would already be dead. Does that make sense? I feel like I'm repeating myself."

"I think I get it," Kendra says hesitantly.

"Let me see if I have this right," I offer. "Based on the fact that the Holy One is alive, we know we can't kill him with time travel. You're saying it can be concluded with complete certainty that any attempts will fail. That's what you're telling us?"

Kildron nods his head, relieved. "That's it."

"Okay," I say. "So, what if we go in the future and br—"

"Can't," Kildron interjects. "Revision only takes you to the past, and it can only take you to a date within your lifespan. Something about using your past self as an anchor. I don't remember how Jenevrah explained it."

Iris rolls her eyes. "If it's useless, why tell us at all?"

"It's not useless," Kildron contends. "If I wanted to, I could go back in time 20 years. I could spend all day with Jenevrah. I could visit Zane. Does that sound useless to you?"

"But wouldn't that be changing the past?" Kendra questions.

Kildron shakes his head. "Not really, no. Because for all I know, it already happened, and they never told me."

"So why don't you do it?" Sheyba asks.

"Huh?" Kildron turns to Sheyba, surprised by the question.

"Why don't you go back to her?" Sheyba asks.

"That's a good question." Kildron looks wistfully down at the hourglass. "The prophets who made this thing, they put a limitation. You can only use the relic once in your lifetime. I'm saving it for a rainy day. Maybe if I still haven't used it by the time everything settles, I'll pay Jenevrah a visit."

"How does it work?" Kendra asks.

"It's pretty simple," Kildron says. "Activate the spell and invert the glass. Then, imagine your desired date. You also have to decide the duration. And when you travel, you stay in the same physical location, so choose carefully. You don't want to end up buried underground or in a wall or something."

He pauses for a second. "I think that's pretty much it. Now you know in case you ever need to use it. Hopefully it proves useful." He loops the relic back over his head. "Alright. Let's get this thing moving. Iris, you should swap with Sheyba at the rudder. Let her get some sleep. You too, Matt. You're gonna need rest to heal that shark bite."

"Actually," I say. "I was hoping you could teach me how to fly."

Kildron grins mischievously. "I thought you'd never ask."

30

ROSE

The masquerade is magnificent.

Faces flash before me, each one concealed in an elegant mask. Some wander in pairs, holding hands or locking elbows. Others, like me, scan the crowd, searching for a familiar face beneath the masks.

An accordion blares over an ensemble of trembling violin strings. Attendees rush the dance floor to join in the fast-paced polka.

At the back of the ballroom, laborers huddle around the drink station, tipping back Bob's brew while their more refined neighbors sip it slowly out of wine glasses, wrinkling their noses in disapproval.

It's all quite spectacular, but I can't enjoy any of it. Nevela and Wendy consume my thoughts, keeping my stomach queasy and my hands clammy.

How am I supposed to tell them I've traded their lives for my own? How do I tell them they're a sacrifice for the greater good?

They'll understand, Rose. I tell myself. *You had no choice.*

Still, I don't feel any better.

I force myself to wander around the ballroom, increasing my odds of bumping into Antai.

He must be running late.

Suddenly, the music stops, and everyone huddles around the stage. I follow their gaze.

Two actors—a man and a woman—are positioned in front of the orchestra. They're dressed in plain white robes with white masks. On their backs, they wear delicate angel wings shaped out of feathers and wool.

The angels recline on two white mattresses. Suddenly, they come to life. The man leans over the side of his mattress, peering down at the floor as if looking through it.

"You know?" he muses. "I just don't understand how they're so cheery. I mean, look at them down there, dancing and smiling. Doesn't it strike you as strange?"

The woman extends her head over the edge of her mattress, staring straight into the floor. "Oh, yes. How peculiar."

"I just don't understand it," the man pouts. "Look at their bellies; they're completely empty, rumbling and tumbling like carriage wheels on cobblestone."

"The living are a bizarre bunch," the woman agrees. "I was Earth-gazing the other day, and I heard them talking about how they pity the dead. Can you believe that? They pity us up here in our celestial mansions." She spreads her arms wide, gesturing at a make-believe manor.

"And would you look at that," the man points down at the floor. "They're using those scratchy old curtains as covers. I don't know how they sleep a wink." He shakes his head. "How is it they prefer to live when they don't even have a cloud to sleep on?"

"Beats me," the woman says as she lays back on the mattress and sighs happily. "You couldn't force me to go back there. Do you remember what pain was like?"

"Oh, it was terrible!" the man groans. "Back aches and headaches and toothaches."

"AND CHILDBIRTH!" the woman wails. "Oh, the creator himself couldn't get me to go back."

I notice several older women smiling to themselves and nodding their heads.

“I couldn't agree more,” the male angel says. “Mortality just has so many inconveniences. Do you remember when we had to…” He looks around and leans over, one hand covering the side of his mouth. “Poop,” he whispers, eliciting several giggles from the children in the room.

The woman nods excitedly. “Don't get me wrong; the great creator is a genius, but why in his holy name did he design us with such an… odorous flaw?”

“Life truly was the worst,” the man says. “So many things to hate about it. Bugs, boogers, whining babies.”

“Pimples,” the woman adds. “Pot-holes, politicians…”

“You know?” the man says, “Now that I think of it, there is one thing I miss.”

“What's that?”

“The mystery,” the angel says. “Sure, Heaven is perfectly perfect, but perfectly perfect is always the same. I miss not knowing how my day will go… not knowing how things will work out. The uncertainty —the stress of it all—was almost exciting.”

“Yeah,” the woman nods. “I suppose it was.” She thinks about this a moment longer. “Do you ever wish you could go back?”

The man jumps to his feet “NOT IN A MILLION YEARS!” he sings to the crowd. The other woman stands beside him, and they both take a bow as the audience stomps their feet.

When the applause ends, the male angel steps forward. “Thank you for watching, folks. Before we go, we want to give a special thanks to the royal orchestra for sacrificing their night to give you this wonderful music. Enjoy the masquerade!”

The audience stomps their feet, and the conductor counts off the next song.

“Touching isn't it?” Jack says from beside me, using his pompous impersonation of General Kaynes. Even in the face of imminent death, they can still find a reason to laugh.”

I can't tell if he's being serious or simply taunting me, so I don't say a word.

He leans in closer. “I just spoke with Crasilda.”

My heart quickens.

He grins. "She said you've been behaving yourself. Of course, there is the whole Bob fiasco, but from what I understand, he was dispatched before your final warning was given. Considering it didn't amount to much, we can pretend it never happened."

"Thank you," I breathe, hoping my voice doesn't convey the terror I feel.

"You've been a good girl these last few weeks," Jack offers. "I hope you enjoy the afternoon. You deserve it."

With that, he gives me a pat on the shoulder and wanders towards the snack table.

I let out the breath I've been holding.

Phew!

I meander my way around the perimeter of the room, keeping my eyes peeled for a black wheelchair. If he were here, I would be able to spot him from a mile away.

The song ends, and a harp replaces the accordion on stage. As the melody begins, couples begin slow dancing around the ballroom.

I stiffen as I spot Crasilda. Her forest-green gown swishes around her legs as she struts toward me. Instead of a mask, she wears a crown of crisscrossing ivy. Another ring of ivy accentuates her waist. "Hello, Rose. I'd like you to meet Krim." She motions to the doe-eyed young man who trials behind her. "Krim and I are going for a walk in the gardens. I expect your big announcement when we get back. Is that clear?"

"As you wish," I say with a slight curtsy.

"Good," Crasilda huffs. "C'mon, Krim." She takes him by the hand and leads him toward the exit.

I turn back to the crowd.

Where are you, Antai?

Almost immediately, I spot a familiar figure. Her baby bump renders her mask obsolete.

I intercept her by the terrace. "Wendy? You came!"

One month ago, Jephora prescribed Wendy constant bed rest, but I can't blame her for bending the rules.

She motions at the crowd. "Nevela's been yapping about this for weeks. I had to see what the hype was about." She looks around. "Where's Antai?"

"It's funny," I laugh. "I've been asking myself the same thing."

"Wh—" Wendy opens her mouth but winces before she can form a word. She stoops over, clutching her belly."

"Whoa, you okay? Wendy?"

"I'm fine," she gasps. "Just need a second."

"Do you think—"

She waves a hand dismissively. "It's nothing. I've been getting these all day. I'm fine." She stands up, her face relaxing. "See."

"Maybe Jephora should take a look?"

"I'm okay, Rose. I mean it."

"Okay," I relent. "I believe you."

Diego waves at Wendy from the drink station. Bob notices as well, standing beside his brew. He gives us a quick nod of the head.

"I'm gonna go say hi," Wendy says. "I'll catch up with you later."

"Okay, I'll see you then."

I watch as she waddles over. To my surprise, Jack is also lurking by the barrels. I watch as he downs a glass. Then another.

Turning away, I survey the ballroom one more time, searching for any sign of a wheelchair.

What's taking him so long?

Already, I'm stressing about what I'll say. Do I try a pick-up line? Do I simply bat my eyes until he makes the first move?

Someone taps me on the shoulder.

I turn, facing a tall man in a black suit. His mask is metallic gold, as are his gloves. The mask obscures most of his face, but his lips are full and his brown eyes inviting. Immediately, I know who I'm staring at, but my brain can't make sense of it.

"Antai?"

His lips part in a radiant smile. "Surprise." He holds out his hands in self-display. "What do you think?"

My mind is a runaway wagon. "I don't understand? Did… did my father heal you? Did you—"

"No," Antai laughs. "No, it's not like that, Rose. It's metal. Look." He holds up his hand, turning it over. "It's a prosthetic. I'm controlling it with dominion. Diego helped me figure it out."

I blink. Sure enough, there is no glove. It's a solid chunk of gold in the shape of a hand.

"You can touch it," Antai says, holding out his palm.

I place my hand in his. To my surprise, the metal is warm and almost… soft? When I squeeze his hand, my fingers sink ever so slightly into the metal.

"It's a bismuth gold alloy," Antai beams. "Super malleable. What do you think?"

"It's amazing?" I gasp. "How long have you had this?"

"A few weeks. I practice whenever you're busy."

"I still can't believe it," I gawk. "And you're taller."

"Yeah, a perk of the legs." He reaches down. His metal fingers pinch the fold of his pants and lift, giving me a glimpse of his golden ankle.

Antai lowers the hem. He straightens his back and steps closer, bowing his head to look down at me. He's as tall as Matt, maybe taller.

"Do you like it?" he hopes.

I lean in, lifting my chin until our masks are almost touching. "To be honest, I liked it better when your lips were closer."

"Really?" He sounds disappointed. "I'll shorten them if you want, but for now, you'll have to use your tiptoes," he reaches his prosthetic around my back and pulls me closer. His hand presses into the small of my back, guiding me onto the balls of my feet.

I close my eyes as our lips meet, letting my body sink into his chest.

His other hand falls to my upper back, slowly climbing the nape of my neck. At some point, his fingers close, unintentionally snagging my hair.

"Ow!"

His eyes snap open, and Antai quickly pulls his hands away. Unfortunately, my hair is still caught between his metal fingers. I shriek as my head whips back.

"Agh!"

"Sorry!" Antai quickly jumps back, holding his hands in the air. "Sorry, I didn't mean to."

"It's okay," I say, rubbing my scalp.

Antai looks down at his hands. "They don't have any nerves, so it's hard to feel what I'm doing. I'm really sorry."

"Antai, it's fine. Really." I straighten my mask and stand tall. "You said you wanted to dance?"

His smile returns. "One second." He turns, and takes two steps toward the exit. To my surprise, his gait is smooth and fluid.

He really has been practicing.

Suddenly, he spins around and walks back toward me. He gazes down at me with timid eyes and pursed lips. "Excuse me, miss, but I couldn't help but notice how stunning you look this fine afternoon. Do you think, maybe… you wouldn't mind dancing with a schmuck like myself?"

I can't help but grin.

"I don't know," I say. "I was actually waiting for someone special. He kinda looks like you, but he's in a wheelchair. In fact, I've been waiting a while now." I peer around the room, faking a look of exasperation. "I'm starting to wonder if he stood me up."

"Stood you up?" Antai shakes his head in disbelief. "Not a chance. I'd bet my left leg he'll show up eventually." He hesitates. "In the meantime, do you mind if I wait with you? A lady such as yourself shouldn't be without company."

"I would like that, thank you."

Antai stands next to me, his golden hands clasped behind his back. "You look familiar. Have we met before?"

I shake my head. "Definitely not. I would remember."

"Are you sure? What's your name?" he asks.

"Lynn."

"Hmmm." He scratches his chin. "You're right. Doesn't ring a bell."

"And your name?" I ask.

"Ty. Call me Ty."

I suppress a laugh. "Alright, Ty. Tell me about yourself."

"I'm afraid there's not much to tell. I consider myself a simple man with simple aspirations."

"Oh, yeah," I raise an eyebrow. "And what do you aspire to?"

"To be honest, Lynn, I'm convinced the world is ending. I merely want to bask in life's beauty while I still can."

"And how is that going for you?"

Antai looks me over, a shrewd smile consuming his face. "Right now, pretty good."

My cheeks get warm. "This may be a bit forward for a lady, but do you want to dance with me?" I ask.

He hesitates. "I have to warn you, I'm not much of a dancer."

"Nonsense." I grab him by the hand, leading him to the dance floor. His fingers clamp down on my hand, and I try not to wince, not wanting to ruin the romance.

The orchestra plays a flamboyant song with percussive bursts of piano. Couples of all ages tango their way across the dance floor.

Antai extends his arm, and I hold my arm parallel. He puts his other hand on my hip and holds me close.

We start slow, taking long strides heel to toe. At the strike of the piano, we pivot and repeat. Antai leads, giving me subtle tugs at the start of each turn.

I wince. "Can you soften your grip just a bit?"

"Oh, sorry."

"Thank you."

The couples around us are putting on a show, sweeping their legs and embellishing each stride with wide kicks and the flick of their hips.

"Want to try something?" Antai asks.

"I'm ready if you are."

On beat, he tips me back… way back. I extend my chin, letting my back arch over his supporting hand. He continues to lower me until the crown of my head is nearly on the floor.

"I'm impressed," he says as he lifts me back into his arms. We press our cheeks together and step to the music.

As we lunge, Antai's foot lands on top of my own. The gold prosthetic makes him even heavier than expected. I can't help but cry out.

"Agh!"

"Sorry." Immediately, Antai repositions his shoe.

I keep pace with the piano, trying to hide a slight limp.

Antai frowns. "Should we stop?"

I shake my head. "It's fine. Let's keep going.

"You sure?"

"Yeah."

We take several walking steps. Then, we spin. Antai remains rooted, swinging me around him as we rotate.

At some point, the edge of his foot pins my pinky toe.

"Ow!"

"Sorry," Antai grumbles. "I'm trying my best."

"Why don't we take a break," I suggest.

"Yeah… okay," He looks down at his legs, clearly crestfallen.

"Hey, Ty." I lift his chin until he's looking in my eyes. "That was nice. I mean it."

"You don't have to humor me," Antai sighs. "I mangled your feet like a grape stomp."

"My feet are not mangled, thank you very much." I hold up my leg, pointing my toes for display. "They are feminine and dainty, and they look just fine."

"Still, I was a mess out there,"

"Maybe I like things a little messy?"

Antai raises a brow. "Is that so?"

"Maybe…" I smirk.

Antai looks around. "Now that you mention it, it looks pretty tidy out here. You know… my room is rather messy. Maybe you'd prefer if we hung out there?"

I know I'm blushing, but I don't care at this point.

"Sounds perfect."

We hold hands as we climb the central staircase. I can't stop smiling as our arms swing together, joined at the fingertips. It's not the fact that his arms are back—albeit an imperfect substitute; it's the fact that he made them with me in mind.

My heart is racing by the time we reach his chambers, and for the first time in months, I welcome the feeling.

Is this really happening?

He opens the door for me, and I step inside.

Do I sit on the bed? Do I stand?

I can't decide, so I end up lingering at the doorway, gazing around the room. I spot his boxers, a t-shirt, and a damp towel by the foot of the bed.

"You know," I observe. "It's not as messy as you made it sound."

"If you want, we can make it messier," He reaches up and tugs on his tie. It takes a second, but the knot unravels into a long stretch of fabric. With a grin, Antai tosses it on the floor.

"See, messier already,"

He steps on the heel of his loafers and promptly kicks them off across the room.

"Can I try?" I step closer to Antai, slipping my fingers under the collar of his suit coat. He extends his arms as I remove the coat from behind, dropping it at my feet.

I start at the top, maintaining eye contact as I unbutton his dress shirt. I can see the excitement in his eyes. The desire. Some fear as well.

When I finish the last button, I stand back. His shirt is now a stage curtain, parting in the middle to reveal the main act. He's regained much of his weight since the coma. His pecks are sturdy, and his abs are rugged. But that's not what makes my heart race. It's the way he looks at me.

He scours my features as if he's seeing it all for the first time. His eyes are wide, almost hypnotized, as they trace my lips.

I try to remove his shirt, but the fabric gets caught on his wrists.

"There's more buttons," Antai laughs.

"Seriously?" I find the buttons on his cuffs and wrestle the shirt off him. As it falls free, I gasp.

The gold prosthetic reaches all the way up to his elbows. It's incredibly detailed, complete with forearm muscles and a bulging vein.

"I wanted it to look as normal as possible." Antai says. "What do you think? Too weird?"

"No," I breathe. "It's incredible. I can't believe you pulled this off."

"Actually, the Holy One pulled it off. I was the one who put it back on."

I can't help but giggle at the sheer cheesiness. "Okay, fair. I set myself up for that one." I squint, leaning closer. "What's that?" I point to the inside of his forearm.

"Isn't it obvious?" he says, holding out his arm so I can get a better look. "It's a rose."

The design is engraved into the gold. It's a sky-view imprint of the petals, stretching halfway to his elbow.

"This might surprise you," Antai says, "but I'm actually a gardenerd, particularly of the rosaceae family."

"A gardenerd?" I laugh. "I haven't heard that one before."

"Yeah, well it takes one to know one," Antai says, glancing down at the engraving. "It's not inspired by a particular girl if that's what you're thinking."

He looks up and winks.

"I love it," I say, running my fingers across the surface, feeling the rough edges of the engraving. I let my hands wander over the crook of his elbows, lingering on his biceps… then his shoulders.

Our eyes lock as I clasp my fingers around his neck. His body heat lures me closer, and I lean into him.

"I love you, Antai. You know that, right?"

"I know," he breathes into my ear, sending chills down my spine. "And I love you."

That's all I need to hear. I pull his head down, pressing my lips into his. He avoids my hair this time, pulling my waist into him with both hands.

Our lips move in a dance, coming together and breaking away in rhythmic harmony. Our breath becomes one, shallow and desperate.

Suddenly, he alters the tempo, kissing from the corner of my mouth down to my jaw.

I tilt my head to the side, surrendering my neck to his teeth. They nibble on my skin at the end of each kiss.

"Mhhhhhh." The air escapes me before I can stop it.

Antai moves behind me, gingerly kissing the nape of my neck.

"Unzip me," I whisper.

He hesitates. "Are you sure?"

"Unzip me," I beg. "I want this." *I've wanted it for a long time.*

The zipper squeals as Antai yanks it down. He peels the dress to the floor, and I step out of it. Immediately, his fingers flounder with the bra clasp.

After a few seconds, I grow inpatient. "I can h—"

The hook falls away, and my bra goes slack. Antai moves slowly now, teasing the straps off my arms.

Thud. Thud. Thud.

Someone knocks with a firm fist.

"Shhh," he whispers in my ear, taking my arms in his and folding them over my chest. "We're not here."

THUD. THUD. THUD.

"Your Majesty, are you in there?" Octavian calls through the door.

No! Why now?

I don't say a word.

"It's urgent!" Octavian calls.

"Ugh," I groan. "One second!"

Antai helps me squeeze back into my ballgown before pulling on a t-shirt from the floor.

I open the door.

Octavian steps into the room. He holds out a piece of parchment. "This just arrived via messenger hawk."

Matt!

I snatch the paper, fumbling to unfurl it. I hold it so that Antai can read as well.

Rose,

This is Klinton and Ron. We managed to repair the communication system. Today, we got a phone call from Matt. Here's what he told us.

They found Atlantia, but the Atlantians refused to help. But it's okay because Matt thinks he knows where the Lost Library is hidden. He says he's 90% sure. He didn't share the location, but he said he'll be in Cavernum sometime tomorrow. He'll come find you. He's hoping you will know how to open the Library.

Holding down the fort,
Klinton and Ron

"This… this is huge!" I exclaim. "This is exactly what we need. We can learn Adamic first. We can win!"

Antai frowns.

"What's wrong?" I worry.

"I don't think it's that simple. Zezric said it himself. Adamic could take years to learn, but Jack will notice you're gone within a few hours."

I press my lips into a thin line. "What if I give Matt the spell to open it. He can learn the Language, and Zezric won't suspect a thing."

Antai shakes his head. "We'll starve long before he's fluent."

"Matt doesn't have to be fluent. He just needs to learn a killing spell."

"Your dad has Foresight, remember. You saw what he did to me. He'll kill us before we can utter a word."

"What are you saying? You think we're already dead?"

"No! Not at all," Antai asserts. "I'm trying to provide some perspective. This is a great opportunity, but it's not an instant victory. Maybe we need another meeting to discuss our options."

I exhale, trying to expel the cortisol that clouds my concentration.

"You're right. Let's do it today," I suggest. "Crasilda is with some boy. Jack is getting drunk. Now may be our only chance."

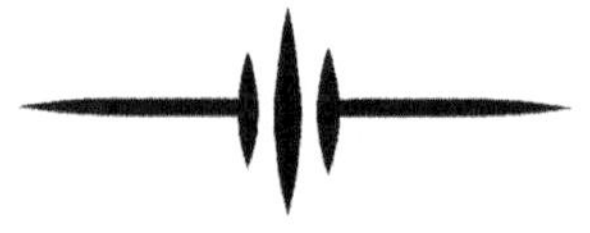

I stare at the chalkboard. In plain print, I've listed six potential plans.

I lean over my desk and circle plan number four.

"From what I've heard, it sounds like we agree that four is our best bet. Tomorrow, Antai and I will go with Matt to burn the library. Without the Book of Life, my father will have no reason to keep fighting. His entire plan will fall apart. At that point, destroying the palace won't have any benefit for him."

Diego narrows his eyes. "And what if he just kills us all for revenge?"

"It's possible, but I don't think he will," I say.

"Why wouldn't he?" Diego questions. "He killed children… babies. He killed his own dad. Clearly, this guy is a psychopath? We can't predict what he'll do."

I shake my head. "It's not like that. He only kills because he believes he'll undo it someday," I reason. "Once we take that away…"

Diego rolls his eyes. "Because you know him so well."

Antai drums a metal finger on the bedpost. "Nothing is certain, but this is our best bet. I don't think we have a choice. We burn the Library, and we prepare for retaliation. We distribute the armor, put the archers on the wall… the whole shebang."

I look over my coalition of trustees. Antai. Nevela. Wendy. Diego. Gideon. Octavian.

"If anyone is opposed, speak now," I say.

No one raises their hands.

I offer a subtle smile. "Thanks everyone. Hopefully, this will all be over by tomorrow. Now go enjoy the festivities. We'll stagger our way out. Nevela, you go first. Then, Wendy, Octavian, Gideon. Okay?"

I watch as Nevela skips out the door.

"Alright, Wendy, just give it another minute or two."

"Uh, Rose," Wendy mutters from where she sits on my bed. "I think we have a problem."

She's looking at her lap. A circle of liquid has soaked into the bedspread between her legs.

"Wendy!" I rush to the side of the bed, not quite knowing how to help. "What happened? Are you okay?"

"I'm fine," Wendy stammers, still staring at the wet spot. "I think my water broke."

"Okay… that's okay," I tell myself. "You're gonna be fine."

"I think I can still walk. Should I go to the healing loft?"

"Definitely," I insist. "But I need to give you something first." I walk over to my night stand, picking up the Inheritance Box. When my fingers touch the weathered wood, it grows warm—an indication that it is now unlocked.

I lift the lid and remove a silver amulet. It's not an amplifier or a soul anchor. It's one of a kind—made for the select purpose of possession.

I take Wendy's hand and place the amulet in her palm. "Give this to Jephora and no one else. Tell her it'll help heal the baby. She'll take care of the rest."

"You're not coming?" Wendy worries.

"I wish I could, but I have to take care of something important." *I have to appease Crasilda, at least for one night.* "But Octavian will make sure you get there safely. Won't you, Octavian?"

"Of course, Your Majesty." Octavian is already at the bedside, holding out his arm. "I'm ready when you are, m'lady."

He walks her to the door and holds it open as she hobbles through.

As soon as she's through the threshold, Wendy stops in her tracks. "Uh…Rose? We have another problem."

"Come on out, Rosey." Jack calls in his Australian accent. "There's an itty bitty matter we need to discuss."

My heart plummets as I step through the doorway.

Jack stands in the hallway, holding a handful of Nevela's hair. Her jaw trembles as she whimpers. In Jack's other hand, he holds an Adamic blade to her throat.

"I was rooting for you, Rosey, and you had to throw it all away—on tonight of all nights."

I take a slow step into the hallway, careful not to spook Jack. The slightest flinch of the blade could slit her throat.

Antai emerges next from my room, followed by Diego and Gideon. Diego is already encased in metal, and Gideon has his bow nocked. He trains the arrow at Jack's head.

"Just let her go," I plead, "and we can talk about anything you want."

Jack slouches, ducking his head behind Nevela's golden locks. Then, a cascade of rippling light spreads around him in the shape of a dome, completing his shield.

He grins. "No, I don't think I will."

Wendy stands frozen in the hallway, hypnotized by the hostage situation.

"C'mon, Wendy," Octavian says, tugging her down the hallway. "Let's get you to the loft."

I wait until she's around the bend. "What do you want, Jack?"

"I'm here to explain your consequences."

"Consequences for what? I haven't done anything," I insist.

"I'm disappointed, Rosey!" Jack says, making a tsk sound with his tongue. "After all we've been through together, you're going to lie to my face."

"I'm not lying."

"And the web grows bigger. You see, Rose, a little birdie told me you received a messenger hawk today. Another birdie told me the same thing. You know what they say, don't you? 'By the mouth of two witnesses, the truth shall be made manifest.'"

I bite my tongue.

Jack raises an eyebrow. "You don't deny it?"

I press my hand to my amulet. "Just let Nevela go, and we can work this out."

"How about this? I'll release the girl when you give me the letter."

"I don't have it any more," I confess.

Jack nods. "Unfortunate. I imagine you already disposed of it, which only corroborates my suspicions. Of course, had you ignored the insurgent communications, it might have been remissible, but you didn't! You gathered your allies to plot alongside you." He tightens his grip on Nevela's hair, pulling back to remove any slack. "And that is the reason you all must die."

Jack hoists Nevela onto her tiptoes, using her as a human shield as he backs toward the hallway window. Only the tiniest bit of his face is exposed, eclipsed by Nevela's forehead. He watches me with one eye, peering through her tangled hair.

Gideon squeezes one eye shut. He adjusts his bow, aligning it with Jack's exposed eye.

"Oh, no you don't," Jack sings.

As I watch, the air between us grows misty, like the condensation on a washroom mirror. I can still make out the silhouette of Nevela and Jack, but the colors are hazy and the edges blurred.

Before, the shot was perilous. Now, it's practically an execution.

Gideon purses his lips. "I don't have a clear shot. It's your call, Your Majesty."

I know what's at stake. If Jack escapes through that window, it's all over.

I open my mouth, but I can't bring myself to say the words.

Gideon holds the bow steady, peering down the arrow shaft. "Just say the word…"

I can't think. So much is happening at once.

Jack shuffles another step toward the window.

Diego retreats back into my room.

Antai extends his arm.

KA-CRACK!

At this range, the flash is blinding. White spots dance across my vision. When they clear, Jack stands with his back against the window, completely unharmed. With the blurry barrier he's created, I can't make out his expression, but I have no doubt he's smiling.

"Now or never," Gideon grunts.

I open my mouth, but nothing comes out. Then, the window shatters.

Twang!

The arrow flies directly into the center of the hazy mass. As soon as it makes contact, the blurry film dissipates.

No!

The fletching protrudes from Nevela's chest, a few inches left of midline. The rest of the arrow shaft is hidden from view, passing through Nevela and into Jack's torso.

Together, they tip through the empty window frame, tumbling toward the gardens below. The arrow pins them together as they fall.

THUD!

I dash over and lean through the window frame. As expected, Jack and Nevela are lying on the walking path, motionless. Crimson blood seeps from the wound, a nauseating contrast with her baby blue gown.

Rage ignites within me. "Why?" I turn to face Gideon. To my surprise, his arrow is still nocked.

Beside him, Diego holds the bow from my bedroom. His metallic brow is defiantly furrowed.

"I had to," is all he mutters.

"Oh my god!" A masculine voice gasps from down in the garden.

I didn't see them at first, but a couple stands a stone's throw from the impact site. The man has his hands over his mouth, but the woman leans closer, intrigued. She has auburn hair and a forest green dress.

No!

Crasilda stiffens when she recognizes General Kaynes's silver cloak. She cranes her head upward until she finds us standing in the window.

I shake my head. "Crasilda, please!" I beg. "Don't do it."

Crasilda looks back at General Kaynes's body. Then, she runs.

KA-CRACK!

Antai unleashes a deafening bolt of lightning.

Crasilda stumbles as the stone explodes behind her, but it doesn't slow her down. When she reaches the wall, the air ripples beneath her feet, propelling her over the parapet in a long sweeping arc.

Just like that, she disappears from sight.

I stand there, staring at the wall in disbelief. Then, I turn my attention back to Nevela.

Condense.

I step out of the window. The air—now nearly as dense as water—tugs on my gown as I sink to the garden.

I land beside Nevela, falling to my knees. I know it's futile, but brush the hair from her neck and feel for a pulse.

Nothing.

Why her? Tonight was supposed to be the night of her life. She's wearing her favorite gown, enjoying the event she planned herself.

Of everybody in the palace, why her?

I reach up, gently closing her eyelids. Then, I lift her jaw so that her mouth isn't gaping. When I remove my fingers, it falls open again, as if trapped in an eternal cry of agony.

"Rose," Antai places a heavy hand on my shoulder. "I'm sorry, but we need to prepare for what's coming. The people should hear it from you."

"We need to build a pyre," I mumble. "She needs to be cremated."

"Rose, listen to me. If we don't act fast, we'll all be dead by morning. Please… I need your help. We need to gather the troops."

I nod. "Okay… okay." I stand, giving one last look at Nevela's body. "Let's go."

I fight back tears as Antai guides me through the corridors. We hurry into the ballroom and push through the crowd.

Antai doesn't waste any time. He climbs right onto the stage and waves his arms. "Hey! Stop the music! This is an emergency! Stop!"

The music falls silent, except for a few straggling toots of a trumpet.

Antai looks at me, giving me the floor.

I clear my throat, looking out at the ballroom. The attendees blink at me from behind their masks.

I take a deep breath and remove my mask. "Attention, everyone. I'm afraid I have dire news. We have reason to believe that there will be an imminent attack on the palace."

The chatter falls silent.

"Please, if everyone could return to their rooms, we'll be reaching out with further instructions. All guardsmen, please report to the armory at once."

In the blink of an eye, chaos erupts. Several members of the orchestra abandon their instruments as they rush off stage. Names echo off the walls, as parents scream for their children. Everyone storms the exit at once, and a woman screams as her dress gets caught beneath the flood of feet.

I raise my voice, amplifying it with dominion. "Please! No one panic. We n—"

"INUMKAH LENE MARATAGAH."

The words reverberate through the room at an incomprehensible volume, and yet, my father's tone is soft and soothing. His voice isn't strained like it would be from a scream. In fact, it's no harsher than casual conversation.

As I listen, my soul comprehends.

Be still and unchanging.

I try to cover my ears, but I'm already frozen in place, as are the guests before me. Their clothes are solidified in unnatural positions, denying the effects of gravity.

No one says a word. No one blinks.

"Inhabitants of Cavernum," my fathers voice fills the room, originating from the terrace doors which hang ajar.

"This is the Holy One speaking to you from the Royal Plaza. I would appreciate your undivided attention as I explain our current predicament."

There's a slight pause. "For those of you who don't know, my name is Zezric Malik, and I am the father of your queen. I've been given a holy calling to glorify this world to a paradisiacal state. I will fulfill this calling in the coming days, once I complete my ascension to godhood."

His words ignite a fire in me, and I strain against the spell.

"Since my arrival in Cavernum," his voice echoes, "I've had a spoken agreement with your queen. So long as she didn't interfere with my ascension, I would spare your palace and your people. In fact, I was prepared to save you. I was aware of your impending famine, and had every intention to provide you the necessary rations. That is, until your queen chose to sabotage my ascension. I want you all to know that her willful disregard of your life has brought about your destruction."

As I scan the ballroom, I shudder. Everyone is staring back at me.

"That said, I have come to share with you the good news." Zezric's voice is confident and joyous. "For the grave hath no power against Godhood. At the completion of my ascension, there will commence The Great Reviving. All who were lost by my hand will be restored to their full capacities."

His voice grows cautionary. "Though you should know, my brothers and sisters… Not all will be revived in the same hour. My valiant servants will rise in the first resurrection. They will be crowned with glory and made rulers among men..." He lets his promise hang in the air.

"It is for this purpose I speak to you tonight. Though we stand on opposite sides of the wall, an eternal reward is within your grasp."

His voice grows louder. "I am looking for the faithful to join me, not the faint of heart. You must believe in my power and in my purpose. You must believe with such a conviction that you are willing to sacrifice your very soul, even as Abraham of old."

He speaks slower now, giving us more time to process.

"My offer is as follows. If you desert the palace—if you come before me with a broken heart and a contrite spirit—I will accept you into my fold. However, there is one condition. Prior to leaving the palace, you must perform a display of faith… you must feed. Do this, and you will be rewarded. Your family will be counted in the first resurrection, and your posterity will be forever blessed. My offer stands until sunrise."

There's a long pause. For a second, I think his message might be finished.

"Good night, Rose," he whispers. "Sleep tight. I'll see you in the morning."

31

ROSE

My eyes flicker around the room as the spell wanes. Ever so slowly, my subjects turn to face me, fighting the celestial forces holding them in place.

I see pure hatred in their eyes.

Dammit!

In a matter of seconds, my father has turned the entire palace against me. They shout their disdain, faces red and spittle flying.

"This is your fault, you royal whore!"

"She should die first!"

"I'll kill her myself!"

A guard to my right takes hold of his amulet, raising his hand in my direction.

Please, let this work.

I do as my father once described, extending my soul to my immediate surroundings.

Not me. Everyone but me.

I've only heard the spell twice, but the pronunciation is simple enough.

"Inumkah Lene Maratagah." I speak the words loud and slow.

For the second time today, every occupant of the ballroom freezes mid-step. Their mouths are agape with half-spoken insults.

As I look around the room, my head turns freely.

It worked.

I take a deep breath and feel a rush of satisfaction as my chest expands without constraint.

It really worked!

Now for the hard part. I have to defame a god.

I don't yell, but I amplify my voice with dominion. "You listened to my father. It's only fair that you listen to me as well."

I point toward the terrace doors. "My father wants you to believe he's a God, that he's utterly unstoppable… but he's not. He's a man with a few Adamic spells, no greater than you or me. He wanted you to feel powerless, but it's a facade. The spell he used can't even hurt you."

My confidence grows the more I speak.

"At his very core, my father is a fraud. He claims to be holy, but what does he have to show for it? Destruction? Death? He speaks of a perfect world, but he hasn't helped a single soul. He claims to be spotless, we've seen the fruits of his labor. All you have to do is look past the palace wall, and you'll see exactly who he is… an angel of death at best… maybe even the devil himself."

I pace back and forth in my tiny sphere of freedom. "I know his claims are tempting—the possibility of reviving our loved ones—but we can't fall for that kind of empty promise. We have to prioritize the ones we still have. We have to save them first."

I stop pacing, my jaw going taut. "There's one last thing I want you to know. Everything my father said about me was true. I have been sabotaging his so-called ascension. Over the last six weeks, I've been preparing for war. We've been making Adamic arrows—arrows that will cut down our enemies before they can breach the walls—and Gideon has been teaching you how to shoot them. We have been crafting Adamic armor and forging Adamic blades that will give us the fighting edge against the feeders." My voice grows louder, hopefully conveying my conviction.

"Today, when my father discovered our preparations, he shook with fear. He knew that if he didn't attack soon, we would grow too strong. But he's already too late! If we stand together, his armies will fall, and we will reclaim Cavernum as our home. But I can't do it alone! We need every single one of you, do you hear me? I don't care if you hate me. I don't care if you think I'm a traitor." I let my voice soften. "If you join me, I will save us. That I promise you. I will save us if it's the last thing I do."

In the front row, a few attendees look around, clearly uncertain about how to proceed.

They can move!

I hadn't even realized it, but the spell has worn off. To my surprise, no one charges the stage. The guardsmen to my right lowers his hand, refusing to look me in the eye.

Antai steps forward, facing the crowd. "Like we said, all guardsmen to the armory… and all Equalist soldiers as well," he adds. "Everyone with bow experience, report to the Palace Gate. All other able-bodied men and women, report to the courtyard. We'll assess your capabilities and assign you a role. We will have two separate shelters for the children: one in the vault and one in the queen's chambers. Each is fortified by Adamic spells, but they won't fit everyone. The remainder will hide out in the Pit. Now go! We don't have a lot of time."

To my surprise, the crowd begins to disperse, slowly at first, then more frantically as parents rush to gather their children.

I can't believe we did it.

Before, they only had two options: serve God or be destroyed.

I gave them a new choice: sell their soul to the Holy One, or wage war against the devil.

32

ROSE

I take one last look into my bedroom. Bodies are packed like pickled turnips, sitting shoulder to shoulder. Moms huddle with their children, whispering tender lies to soothe their troubled souls.

I close the door and turn the key, sealing them inside. It's a harrowing fact, but should I lose my key in battle, there'll be no way to set them free.

I try not to think about it.

I turned around, studying the remainder of the children—the ones who didn't fit. There's about 30 or so. The youngest have their mothers accompanying them, but most are parentless—holding hands with their older siblings. Some, I imagine, are orphans.

All of them are my responsibility.

Light.

A beam of light illuminates the tile before us. The children huddle close behind me as we stroll down the corridors.

"All right," I announce, "the rest of us will be heading down to the Pit where we'll be safe, okay?"

My mind wanders to Antai as we walk. At the moment, he's on the wall, organizing our defenses. After all, he is the last Guardian standing.

Diego is with him too, a voice of reason to ensure that the Equalists comply. And Gideon is there, organizing the archers.

In fact, every guard is gathered on the wall or stationed at one of the palace entrances. I should be with them, but simply put, I don't trust anyone alone with the children. There have already been several guardsmen-turned-feeders, and as dawn grows nearer, people will only get more desperate.

I'm still thinking about feeders when a body comes into view. A man is face down on the rug, blood soaking into the plush fabric. A few children shriek.

"Everyone, wait here," I instruct. "Don't get any closer."

Lift.

I command the sleeve of his shirt, lifting it into the air and flipping the deceased onto his back. The man has multiple bullet wounds on his chest. His mouth is stained with blood.

A culprit, not a victim.

I search for something to cover him.

Lift.

Using dominion, I grab the edge of the rug and pull it over the corpse.

"Alright, let's go, everyone. Stay close."

We hurry down the staircase and along the Central Wing. We're nearly to the Pit when a figure steps in front of me. He shields his eyes as my light settles on him.

When I finally get a glimpse of his face, I squint in confusion. "Chancellor Quine?" I lower my bow. "You scared me. What are you doing here?"

"I was coming to check on my daughter, Lavana. I wanted to make sure she made it in the strong-hold before I head to the wall."

"She made it," I assure him. "I just locked it up a few minutes ago. She's safe inside."

"Oh… perfect." He shifts his weight from one foot to the other. "In that case, I better get a move on." He points down the hallway past the children. "They'll be expecting me on the battlefront."

As he gestures, I can't help but notice something. There's a faint red tinge beneath his fingernails and along his cuticles. Whatever it is, he tried to wash it off, albeit unsuccessfully.

"Hold on," I command. "Look at me."

He hesitates, slowly turning his chin. I hadn't noticed it before, but now it's unmistakable. His lips may be scrubbed clean, but there's a faint collection of red crust in the outer crevice of his right nostril.

"Quine?" My hands tighten in my bow. "What did you do?"

He lets out a short, strained chuckle. "Your Majesty, I'm afraid I don't know what you mean." His eyes dart to either side, looking for an escape. "As I said, I was simply checking on my daughter. Now, if you'll excuse me, I'll be on my way."

He tries to push past me, but he only makes it a step. The air ripples, throwing him against the wall.

Squeeze.

An unseen force compresses his rib cage and squeezes the air out of him. He cries out, nothing more than a frail, pathetic moan.

The children stumble back, looking to their parents for reassurance.

"Tell me what you did," I rage, "or I'll break every one of your ribs."

Quine doesn't try to fight back. He merely shakes his head from side to side. "I didn't want to do it," he whines. "She begged me. How could I say no."

"Who?"

"My wife!" he cries. "She begged me to do it. It was the only way I could save Lavana. I had no choice. We're all going to die, anyway."

"No one had to die," I refute.

Suddenly, his face hardens. "Please, don't insult me, you insufferable child. I'm not some sheep you can usher to their death. I'm a chancellor for god's sake. I know when the battle is lost."

"So… you killed her?"

"YOU THINK I WANTED TO DO IT?" he screams.

The children take another step back.

He shakes his head wildly back-and-forth. "You think I wanted to taste my wife's blood? To watch her give her last breath? You're sick! It was the hardest thing I've ever done, and I did it for Lavana. If you kill me now… her death—my wife's sweet sacrifice—it'll all be for nothing. My daughter will die without her parents, crammed in a cage with a bunch of strangers. No! I won't allow it. I can't be for nothing. It can't be. It can't—

I increase the pressure. Silencing his pathetic ramble. "You're wrong," I hiss. "Nothing is going to happen to Lavana. The only one who died for nothing is your wife. I hope you live long enough to realize that."

Release.

Chancellor Quine stumbles away from the wall. Once he regains his balance, he gapes at me. "I-I don't understand."

"Get out of here," I hiss, "before I change my mind."

"I—"

"Go!" I scream.

He finally obeys, sprinting down the hallway and around the corner.

"Everyone okay?" I ask.

Tiny heads bobble up and down.

"Good. We're almost there. It's just down this staircase."

I amplify my light so that everyone can make out the steps. As we descend, the musty scent of mildew grows stronger.

When we arrive at the bottom, several healers rush over. They usher the children through open cell doors and onto wool bedrolls. It's not exactly cozy, but it's safe from the inevitable havoc above.

"Rose?"

I turn. Jephora stands in the central corridor, a bright smile on her face and a baby in her arms.

I rush over, already at a loss for words. "Is… is that him?"

Jephora tucks her chin to her chest, adoring the infant in her arms. "This is him."

"But I thought…"

Jephora looks around to see if anyone is listening. "That amulet you gave me, it saved his life. I was able to get his bowels back inside before he was born. I'm still working out some kinks on the inside, but I think he'll be just fine."

"That's… that's amazing!" I gush. I look around, and my smile fades. "Where is Wendy?

"She's catching up on sleep," Jephora motions deeper into the Pit. "Her cell is over there."

"I'm awake," a voice from down the corridor. "Come on in."

I follow the sound of her voice, stepping into the cell. "Wendy is laying on the floor, propped up by several pillows. A wool blanket is tucked up around her waist. She seems well, but there's evidence of the birth. She's pale and lethargic. Not to mention the pile of bloodied rags

Wendy manages a grin as Jephora follows me into the cell. "He's cute isn't he?"

"Absolutely precious," I agree. "How are you feeling?"

"I'm okay…" she sighs. "We're alive, aren't we?"

Wendy holds out her arms, and Jephora places the baby against her chest. She cradles his head, staring into his innocent eyes.

"Does he have a name?" I wonder.

Wendy nods, never taking her eyes off him. "Adam," she breathes.

"Adam?" I say. "The first man?"

Wendy nods, gazing down at the baby. "He arrived in this world on a dark and hopeless night, but I believe he'll live to see the sun rise… I know he will."

I look down at my sun tattoo, remembering Velma's bedtime story: During their first night on Earth, Adam and Eve were afraid the darkness was never-ending. To calm their troubled hearts, God sent the moon, promising them that better times were on their way… The sun would rise again.

"It's perfect," I finally say. "He's perfect."

"Rose?" Wendy says softly, lifting her head to meet my gaze. "Please don't let him die. I can't lose him already. I—"

"I won't," I interject. "I promise." Slowly, I back toward the door. "I'll let you get some sleep now. This'll all be over before you know it."

With that, I retreat down the corridor the way I came.

"Your Majesty, excuse me," a feminine voice calls.

I stop, spinning in search of the voice's owner.

A blonde woman approaches hesitantly. Her hands are clasped in front of her waist, and she takes short, timid steps. "Pardon me, Your Majesty. I'm Mrs. Eck, Kendra's mother."

"Oh! It's a pleasure to meet you. Ummm, what can I do for you?"

Mrs. Eck steps closest, lowering her voice. "Before she left, Kendra told us she was helping you with… a special mission. That was weeks ago. I was hoping you might have some sort of update for me.

"Yes! As a matter of fact, I do," I happily inform her. "Before the masquerade, I received a letter from Matt. He says their mission was successful," I lie. "They should be getting back sometime today."

Mrs. Eck sucks in a quick gasp. She covers her mouth with her hand, taking an excited step back. "You're serious? You're not just saying that?"

"It's the truth," I say. "I doubt they'll arrive before the attack, but yes, they should be here today."

"Oh, that's the best news. Her brother will be so happy to hear it."

I follow her gaze to one of the nearby cells. A 10-year-old boy is passed out beneath a blanket, his tousled blonde hair spilling onto the stone floor.

"Your Majesty!" Octavian calls as he storms down the corridor, an impatient scowl on his face. "The feeders are gathering in the plaza. We need you on the wall… now!"

"Already? What time is it?"

"Daybreak, My Queen. The invasion is imminent."

I place my palms on the parapet as I peer out over the plaza.

Feeders fill the far side of the clearing, flies drawn to the impending smell of death. More gather every minute. Already, there must be a few thousand.

We don't have enough archers.

Currently, the archers are evenly distributed around the wall, but the feeders are preparing for a weighted frontal attack.

"Octavian," I shout. "Run to the western side of the wall and ask Gideon to send archers. And hurry!"

"Right away, Your Majesty."

"You!" I point to a guardsman I don't recognize. He must be highly ranked, because he's wearing one of Nevela's Adamic Cloaks. "Go to the Eastern side of the wall, and ask Diego for any archers he can spare. Quickly!"

Antai is stationed on the northern side of the wall. I don't bother sending a messenger his way. At this distance, I doubt they'd make it back in time.

I watch as the feeders scream and shove, fighting to be at the frontlines. Any one of them could be concealing an Adamic bomb. Any one could contain our downfall.

I clench my bow, trying to keep my hands from shaking. The men around me are no better. Every so often, a soldier leans over the parapet to retch, spewing roasted horse onto the pavilion below.

"My Queen!" Gideon calls as he leads a small army of archers down the wall walk. "I come bearing gifts."

Gideon stops at my side, facing his men. He shouts commands in his thick French accent. "Line up behind your comrades. I want two rows along the wall. You will alternate nocking and firing. Understood?"

When everyone is settled, he stands at my side. "If you prefer, I will give the archery orders?"

"That would be appreciated. Thank you, Gideon." I look out at the feeders. "Are they within range?"

Gideon purses his lips. "Not quite. Most will fall short."

As I study their forces, my heart thumps faster. They outnumber us two to one.

"How many do you think we'll kill with the arrows?"

Gideon narrows his eyes, studying the plaza. "Hmmm… at 300 meters, it'll take them 30 seconds to reach the wall. Our average archer can fire every 6 seconds. That gives us… 5 volleys, more or less."

"With 500 archers, that's 2,500 arrows," I add.

Gideon nods. "If all goes well, 500 feeders will fall."

"Only 500?"

"20 percent is good, My Queen. " Gideon glances at the archers around us. "With these men, perhaps too optimistic."

Suddenly, the feeders fall silent. I squint as two cloaked figures step forward.

One figure removes his hood.

Dad.

My father paces further into the plaza, his cloaked companion at his side. After creating some distance from his subjects, my father stops. He pauses dramatically before gesturing at the cloaked figure beside him. The figure removes his cloak, letting the fabric flutter to the cobblestone. The feeder stands shirtless before the army, displaying his tattoos like a trophy on his chest.

What is he doing?

The anonymity of the bomber was a massive advantage, but my father is surrendering it before the battle has even begun.

I point at the bomber. "Focus your arrows on that feeder," I shout. "Do not let him near the wall."

My father looks up at the wall. He smiles as if my army is endearing, like a little toddler with a wooden stick, playing soldier in the street.

Then, he raises his hand. His voice echoes over the plaza. "My brothers and sisters, the time for battle is once again upon us. To those who live to see our victory, the spoils of war are yours to enjoy. To those who are slain upon the battlefield, you will be raised up in the first resurrection."

Zezric looks skyward as the sunlight reflects off of the top of the Central Tower. "It is time!" he booms. "Let death commence!" With that, he retreats into the horde, leaving the bomber alone in the plaza.

Immediately, the feeders swarm around the bomber, shielding him from view. The mass grows bigger as hundreds of feeders rush forward.

In unison, they charge the palace wall.

"Everyone!" Gideon shouts. "Draw!"

As the swarm scrambles across the cobblestone, the remainder of the feeders watch from a distance. Not all are so eager to die for the cause.

"First row… Aim!" Gideon calls. "Loose!"

The arrows whistle harmoniously as they soar over the plaza.

Gideon doesn't wait for confirmation. The arrows are still airborne when he gives the next command.

"Second row… Aim…"

As the first volley descends, ripples form above the feeders in scattered patches, but they do nothing to stop the arrows. The shafts rain on the feeders, cutting through cloaks and punching through skulls.

A dozen feeders fall in a disorderly tumble of limbs. A dozen more stagger on, plucking the shafts from their flesh like inconvenient splinters.

"Loose!" Gideon calls.

The second volley flies, raining down like the first. Once again, the charging feeders are helpless. They cry out as arrows pierce their rib cages and penetrate their lungs.

The remainder press on, unphased, hundreds of them.

Already, they are a quarter of the way to the palace gate, but 50 feeders lie in their wake as the horde presses on.

"Draw… Loose… Draw… Loose!"

The first row fires, then the second.

As the horde grows closer, the volleys become more effective. The front line shudders as each feeder is impaled by a handful of arrows. When they drop, more feeders take their place.

"Draw… Loose!" Gideon calls, keeping the rhythm steady. "Draw… Loose!"

The swarm is halfway to the gate, but only half their numbers remain.

"Draw… Loose! Draw… Loose!"

As the fourth volley rains down, the front row of feeders tumble onto the cobblestone, only to be trampled by the feeders behind them. There can't be more than a hundred feeders left. They regroup around the bomber, like bees buzzing around their queen, keeping him concealed in their midst. In a unified mass, they charge headfirst into the next volley.

Why is he doing this?

My father is a strategist. He could've attacked at night when our aim would be abysmal. He could've targeted a less fortified portion of the wall. He could've kept his bomber anonymous, leaving us with no one to target. Each approach would've increased his odds exponentially. At this point, it seems like he's intentionally sacrificing his men.

He's sending a message, I realize.

The Holy One doesn't care about casualties. In his mind, victory is inevitable. He doesn't want swift success; he wants us to witness our own demise, knowing we're powerless to stop it—knowing our very enemy is the only one who can save us.

That's what he wants. He wants to be God, hand-delivering our damnation.

"Draw… Loose!"

Another volley cuts the horde. Only a score of feeders remain, but it's too late. They're a stone's throw from the Palace Gate.

"Draw!"

The feeders dive underneath the archway, throwing themselves against the gate and out of sight from the wall walk.

"Loose!"

The volley skewers a few stragglers, but none of them are the shirtless bomber.

"Away from the gate!" Gideon yells as he dashes past me. "Get back!"

No! There's still time!

From my understanding, it'll take a few seconds to detonate the bomb. The first symbol negates the spell, and must be damaged to trigger the explosion. Until that happens, we still have a chance.

I have to try.

Before I can second-guess myself. I leap from the wall.

Condense.

The air thickens as I plummet, and I land softly on the plaza floor. From my new angle, I can see the feeders huddled in the shadow of the archway—like cockroaches in a cupboard.

Instantly, I spot the shirtless bomber in the center of the pack. He holds a knife in his hand, raising it towards his torso.

I nock an arrow and draw back my bow.

"Oof!"

An energy wave hits me in the gut, throwing me backwards and sending me somersaulting across the cobblestone.

Shield!

I form a barrier around myself as I scramble to my feet. The moment it forms, light explodes around me as electricity combusts against my barrier.

Ka-Crack!

The shockwave shatters my defenses and throws me like a rag doll. By some miracle, I keep hold of my bow.

Shield!

I roll to my feet a second time, grabbing another arrow from my quiver. My eyes settle on the bomber. He's 50 feet away—just within the limits of my accuracy.

I nock the arrow, but I'm too late.

He presses the knife into his skin.

33

ANTAI

I watch Ortega's men scurry south along the wall walk, moving closer to Rose.

From where I stand, the palace obstructs my view of the Palace Gate. I'm not sure what's going on, but I have enough sense to know Rose is in trouble.

I command the men within earshot, pointing in the direction of the palace.

"Everyone with a birthday from January to June, report to your queen at the gate. The rest of you, stay here with me. Pass it on."

The soldiers beside me make their way along the wall, reiterating my message. Meanwhile, I keep my eyes trained on the rooftops of the Core. Already, feeders have begun to congregate, like stupid little pigeons, waiting for crumbs to eat.

They keep their distance, lingering several rooftops away. Here, there isn't a buffer zone like there is in the plaza. The closest rooftop is only 20 feet away.

Then, I hear it—Gideon's voice shouting in the distance. I have to amplify my hearing to make sense of the words.

"Draw… Loose!"

The commands echo around the palace, channeled by the wall's interior.

It's happening!

I'm tempted to abandon my post and rush to Rose's aid, but I refuse to be that foolish.

If I were the Holy One, I would create a distraction in the plaza, only to direct my efforts around back. That would be the smart thing to do… or maybe he knows that's the smart thing to do, and is planning the opposite.

I direct my attention to the Core. The feeders are still perched on the rooftops, unmoving.

"Archers," I command, keeping my eyes on the rooftops, "if they get any closer, open fire."

Ka-Crack!

A flash of lightning reflects off the cloud cover, followed immediately by the rumble of thunder.

I turn around.

KA-BOOOOOM!

The wall shakes, nearly knocking me off my feet. The shockwave pulsates as it expands in all directions. It passes through the palace, shattering the windows and toppling one of the towers.

Shield!

Thanks to my barrier, I barely feel it as the shockwave passes over me, I can't say the same for the men around me. They cry out as they're thrown into the parapet. A few topple off the wall.

Already, a mushroom cloud of crimson smoke billows higher than the tallest tower.

Dammit!

I haven't even killed a feeder, and we've already lost our most valuable asset.

"Archers, shoot on sight," I shout. "Swordsmen, prepare to engage."

Commanding my hand to clench, I grab hold of the hilt, drawing my new sword from its scabbard. Diego forged it himself—a classic broadsword with an upcurved hilt and a sturdy pommel. Adamic symbols are etched into the flat of the blade.

I leave my pistol in its holster. That one is for emergencies only.

Already, the feeders converge. Some leap from the rooftops, clearing the gap in a single bound. Others create bridges of ice or rock. A few scamper directly up the face of the wall, their fingers digging into the stone as if it were bread dough.

I search for the nearest feeder to kill, spotting it as it leaps from the nearest rooftop.

Run.

My legs obey, working in a coordinated series of commands like muscle memory—or perhaps dominion memory is a better term.

Dashing to the edge of the parapet, I extend my sword into the leaping feeder's path. The blade impales him just below the ribs. His weight carries him down the length of my blade and into my hilt.

Crouch.

I command my legs to bend and twist my torso, flipping the feeder over my shoulder and withdrawing my sword from its writhing body.

The next feeder is already on the wall. It reaches its gangly fingers towards one of my men—an Equalist with an Adamic cloak.

A jet of bluish liquid pours from the feeder's hand. It crackles as it washes over the guardsman's Adamic cloak, expanding and solidifying into crystalline ice shards. The bluish sludge continues to engulf the soldier until he's frozen solid.

I'm still watching as the feeder's head twists to the side, his beady bird eyes staring straight at me. He raises his hand, and a stream of ice sludge jets toward me.

Shield.

The blue stream splashes against my force field. Large chunks of ice expand outward. With every passing second, more ice accumulates against my shield, growing thicker and thicker.

I smile, commanding the space just beyond my barrier.

Combust!

My shield works like the barrel of a gun, focusing the blast outward, carrying the icy shrapnel with it. A dozen shards rip through the feeder, throwing him into the parapet.

He doesn't get up.

Run.

My legs carry me across the wall walk. My boots do little to dampen the sound of my metallic footsteps, but I don't have time to worry about that now. A few paces in front of me, a feeder buries his teeth into an archer's throat.

Swing.

My arm obeys. The sword whistles as it slices along the feeders back, cutting through his spine.

Swing.

This time, I extend my blade over the edge of the parapet, decapitating a feeder as he climbs over the wall.

Twang. Twang.

The chaotic snapping of bow strings fills the air. Archers unleash arrow after arrow at the feeders, but they don't stand a chance. In front of me, a guardsman cries out as a feeder pounces, tearing off his limbs with superhuman strength.

Swing.

My blade catches the feeder in the crook of the neck, cutting diagonally into his chest.

I'm beginning to get into the rhythm of things, spinning with my blade as I cut through a feeder's legs.

Slice.

I send out an energy blade, cutting through two more before they even notice me. Still, for every feeder I kill, several of our men succumb.

"Retreat!" someone cries out.

Immediately, the men comply, leaping from the wall and racing for the palace.

"No! Hold the wall!" I shout, but their survival instincts drown me out.

As I look down the wall walk, I only see a few comrades remaining. One has Adamic armor, spewing fire from his open palm. Another carries one of Diego's Adamic battle axes, swinging it like a madman.

With fewer men to target, the feeders focus on me. They stalk closer, coming from both directions.

Electricity.

I let the charge accumulate in each of my arms, filling the gold with an uncontainable energy. Then, I spread my arms and point down opposite sides of the wall walk.

Lightning!

KA-CRACK!

The bolts burn hot and bright, surging through several feeders at once.

"Elsborne!"

I turn to the sound of distress. Two of my men are huddled behind an energy shield of their own making. While one maintains the barrier, the other fires arrows at a feeder, who is covered from head to toe in Adamic tattoos.

Run.

My legs carry me towards them, but I'm not fast enough. The feeder presses his hands against their energy shield, ripples expanding from his flattened palms. With a war cry, the feeder's hands glow red and his fingers sink through the force field. His muscles bulge as he tears the shield down the middle.

Shit!

Smiling, the feeder grabs the archer by the throat.

I'm about to use lightning, but it won't do anything against the feeder's armor. I'll end up electrocuting my soldiers instead. And I'm too far to throw my sword.

That only leaves my pistol, but I don't reach for my holster.

Emergencies only.

I'm still racing toward them when the feeder clamps down on the archer's neck and douses the other in a stream of fire.

Stab!

I plunge my broadsword through the feeder's back. Then, I give him a kick to knock him off my blade.

I want to help the archer as blood oozes from his throat, but there's nothing I can do.

Feeders are everywhere now. They pour over the wall, chasing the retreating soldiers.

I'm about to fall back when I see him. The feeder is easily eight feet tall, and his chest is wider than a boar's belly. His muscles are grotesquely enlarged and veins slither over his arms like garden snakes.

Goddamn!

We make eye contact, and the brute grins, pointing at me with a fat, grubby finger.

"He's mine," a tiny feeder squeaks, stepping past the giant. She's both slender and short, her curves accentuated by a white long sleeve dress. A white porcelain mask covers her face, complete with a painted smile and red, rosy cheeks. She also has white gloves over her hands, concealing every inch of her skin.

She struts past the giant with a long, graceful stride. To my surprise, the giant steps aside, honoring her request. In fact, he doesn't search for another victim. He simply stands and watches as she dances towards me.

"Oh, look at you," the feeder sings, her voice soft and dainty. "So young for a guardian, and handsome at that," To my surprise, the smile on her mask grows wider as she manipulates the paint. "Either the sanctuary has gotten desperate, or you must really be something."

I scan the wall walk in front of me, locating a fallen archer. He has several arrows in his quiver. A short ways away, I spot another.

Applying a subtle force, I grab each arrow by the shaft and lift it into the air. As I fling them, I make sure to give them the proper spin.

Eight arrows whistle toward the masked feeder. She doesn't bother forming a shield. Instead she leaps into the air, contorting her body through the gaps in the arrows.

The arrows continue past her. One catches the giant in the shin, who roars in protest. The others clutter harmlessly against the wall walk.

"Oh, you're a resourceful one." She smiles hungrily. "I like that. Keeps me on my toes."

The masked feeder prances towards me, drawing two tiny knives, one from each sleeve. They're small and curved—no bigger than a butter knife—but the symbols make me think twice.

"Come now, darling," the feeder flirts. "Let's dance." With that, she dashes towards me.

Swing.

My blade whistles as it cuts through the air, but the masked feeder is too quick. She ducks underneath and takes a swipe at my leg. I feel the sting as it cuts through my cloak and slashes through my thigh.

She skips back playfully, standing just out of reach of my blade.

I lunge forward, extending my arm.

Swing.

She rears back as my blade sweeps inches from her throat. Once it passes by, she pounces. She dances in and takes another swipe, this time slicing my other thigh. It's shallow, but it adds up.

"Come on," the feeder begs. "Let me come closer. I want to give you a kiss. Just a quick peck on the cheek. I won't bite, I promise."

Thrust.

I lunge with the blade, but the feeder twists away from the tip. She rolls her body along the length of my blade and swipes her tiny knife across my face. Blood trickles down my cheek.

I backpedal.

The feeder follows. "Oh, don't be afraid, darling. I just want a little taste."

I rack my brain for some kind of solution.

What would Rose do?

The epiphany hits me as the masked feeder skips forward. I extend my soul to the air around her head.

Vacuum.

The woman stops in her tracks as the air withdraws from her vicinity. Her mouth opens, and her hands close around her throat. After a second, she lowers her hands. The smile on her mask inverts, turning the paint into a frown.

She raises her hand.

KA-CRACK!

I release the vacuum in order to strengthen my shield, diverting the blinding lightning to either side. When my eyes adjust, the masked woman is a few steps closer.

"Come now, darling," she complains. "Is that really necessary? I'm being nice, aren't I?"

She rushes toward me.

Swing.

As she twists out of the way, she throws one of her knives. It cuts through my cloak and embeds itself in my right bicep.

"Ahh!" I reach over with my other hand and yank out the knife, tossing it to the floor. I consider switching the sword to my left hand, but decide against it. Luckily, I don't need my bicep to wield a weapon. Dominion does all the work.

"Mhhhhh!" The masked feeder hums. "You are tough. I like a man who can handle a little pain."

She dashes toward me.

Swing.

This time, as my blade whistles, I follow it with an energy wave. The air reverberates, throwing the masked feeder across the wall walk. Her head smacks the stone parapet, and her mask shatters.

When she stands, I see her face for the first time. The skin is all but gone. Long strips of muscle stretch over her jaw. Her lips are peeled back, and her eyelids are nonexistent.

"Noooo!" she screams. Her dainty voice is now a witch's wail. "You dimwit. You're going to regret that!" She stoops down, grabbing a bow and quiver from the wall walk.

With nimble fingers, she nocks an arrow. "If you want to play dirty, I'll play dirty." She draws back the string and lets it snap.

I barely have time to raise my hands. The arrow strikes me in the front of the forearm, embedding itself in my metal prosthetic.

Twang. Twang.

Two more arrows whistle toward me.

I block one with the palm of my hand, but the other deflects off my thumb and cuts across my ribs.

She dashes forward, grabbing a new cluster of arrows from a dead archer. She nocks them in a single fluid motion, faster than I thought possible.

Twang. Twang. Twang.

Lift!

The floor folds upward, creating a small, stony barrier in the center of the wall walk. The three arrows clatter off my rocky shield.

I can hear her footsteps as she scampers towards me. I listen, waiting until her footsteps are basically upon me.

Swing.

My sword swipes through the gap between the parapet and my makeshift shield, but the feeder isn't there. She prances at eye level, sprinting on top of the parapet. The moment she passes my stony shield, she lets the arrow fly.

Twang.

The arrow cuts across the side of my head, slicing a line into my scalp, but it isn't lethal.

Stab.

I thrust with the sword. As expected, she pirouettes away from the tip and lunges at me with her remaining dagger. This time, I drop my sword and intercept the knife with my fingers, squeezing the blade in my fist. She tries to pull away, but my hand liquefies. It spreads down the hilt and engulfs her hand.

With my other hand, I reach for the holster.

BANG. BANG.

She shudders as two Adamic bullets tear through her lungs.

The gold from my hand withdraws, and I push her off me.

She stands there, staring down at her wounds as I retrieve my blade from the floor.

Swing.

It catches her in the neck, taking her head clean off.

"AAAAGH!" The giant bellows as he blunders toward me, ravenous for revenge.

I don't take any chances.

BANG!

The bullet enters his forehead and blows out the back. He falls on his face, sliding to a stop at my feet.

Satisfied, I assess the scene around me. I'm alone on the wall—at least my section, anyway. A few feeders lurk nearby, but they hesitate to engage with me. They saw the massacre that just unfolded.

Screams echo from the eastern section of the wall. A crowd of Equalists still battles on the wall. Two figures stand in the center of the commotion, slaughtering any feeders who venture too close. One figure glistens silver in the morning sun. The other is a large fellow, barely squeezing into his Adamic cloak.

Diego and Bob.

I race toward them, cutting down any feeders in my path. A few actually turn and flee, leaping from the wall to avoid my sword.

I'm almost to the Equalists when I hear the buzzing. It's like static, tickling my ear. Then, something black covers the sun.

It takes me a second to process what I'm seeing. A black cloud blows toward us over the Core. It moves quickly, undulating as it passes above the rooftops. The closer it gets, the louder the buzzing becomes.

I squint as it approaches the Palace Wall. The cloud is massive—nearly the size of the palace itself. The center is pitch dark, obscuring all light, but the edges are hazy. I can see tiny specks hovering along the border.

Bugs.

The cloud descends on the Equalists, and immediately, I hear the screams. The bugs envelope the Equalists. They bite and sting, crawling into any orifice they can find.

Then, the cloud expands, and the swarm envelops me.

Shield!

I form a spherical barrier around myself, making sure it's airtight. Immediately, the bugs buzz against the bubble, blacking out the light.

Fire.

I ignite the outer edge of my shield, roasting the insects, but a new film of flies instantly forms.

Suddenly, a figure comes into view, pressing against my shield. I can't see his face; he's completely covered in an assortment of bugs.

He bangs on my energy shield. "Hel—" His voice is silenced as the bugs fly down his throat. A few seconds later, he collapses, continuing to writhe on the ground.

Holy shit!

Already, I feel trapped. The bugs can't break through my bubble, but I can't do anything either. The second I relinquish my shield, I'm a goner.

What would Rose do?

Nothing comes to mind.

Think harder.

I rack my brain, searching for a solution. Only one thing is certain. Whoever controls this cloud, they must be close. They can't be in the cloud, because they wouldn't be able to see. And they can't be on foot. They have to move with the cloud, remaining in range.

Rise.

The air ripples beneath my boots, lifting me into the air. My bubble moves with me, plowing through the bugs as I rocket upward.

Eventually, I see a few speckled patches of sunlight overhead. The cloud grows thinner until I burst free from the bugs.

Immediately, I spot them. Two feeders hover in the air above the center of the cloud. They have the same stringy black hair and identical gaunt faces.

Twins.

They're 100 yards away, but I don't have time to get any closer. Their heads snap to the side in unison, staring right at me.

I draw my pistol and fire.

BANG! BANG! BANG!

One bullet catches the feeder in the side. The others miss.

I keep firing.

BANG! BANG!

The swarm undulates upward, consuming my bubble and blocking my view of the bug brothers.

Forward!

I give chase, advancing in the direction I last saw the feeders. The swarm continues to surround me. All I see is blackness, and all I hear is incessant buzzing.

"Ow!" Something suddenly pinches the back of my neck.

That's weird.

Another bug lands on my face, crawling across my lip.

Suddenly, it dawns on me. When I fired the pistol, I shot several holes in my shield. Now, the bugs are leaking in.

I extend my soul and repair the bubble, but it's too late. A large beetle crawls into my ear. Something else stings my eyelid, and a flurry of flies go up my nose.

My shield dissolves, and I plummet.

I keep my mouth sealed shut, fighting the urge to inhale as I fall.

Condense!

My body slows as I fall through the thickened air. Then, I crash through the stable roof.

Still, the bugs devour me. They bite at every inch of my skin, working their way beneath my cloaks and into my trousers. They fill my nose, stinging the inside of each nostril.

I try to swat at them, but my metal fingers are nearly useless. They don't feel a thing.

That's it!

Titanium!

I command the outer layer of my skin, just like Diego taught me, rearranging the atoms.. Immediately, the pain disappears, and my senses are dulled.

Using the last of my breath, I exhale through my nose, forcing out the flies. Immediately, I plug each nostril with a finger.

Liquify.

I leave a small gob of gold to seal off my nose. Then, I inhale through clenched teeth.

It's not much, but I'm alive.

I sit in the stable as I catch my breath, keeping my metal eyelids closed. Every so often, I spit out the bugs that get suctioned against my teeth.

Once again, I'm trapped.

What would Rose do?

This time, I have an idea. I think a moment longer, making sure it's my only option. Then, I stand up and scream.

"Havaknah Ra!"

The air ignites around me, and the pressure change compresses my metallic eardrums.

When I open my eyes, the bugs are gone—completely disintegrated. A smoky haze takes their place.

I take a step out of the stable.

Splat! Splat!

Two bodies hit the cobblestone, one right after the other—the bug brothers. Their skin is scorched and raw, but the burns don't look deadly. I imagine they were alive until they hit the ground.

Diego!

I race to the wall and lift myself with dominion. As my head breaches the parapet, Diego nearly takes it off with a short sword.

"Antai?"

"Diego! You made it!" I say, stepping onto the wall walk. "I thought you were a goner."

"Holy freak! It was you!" Diego exclaims. "You did the spell!"

"No time for chit-chat," Bob huffs, stomping over. His hands are blistered and raw, but the rest of him seems to be unharmed—protected by the Adamic cloak.

Armor trumps burn spell. I make a mental note. *Good to know.*

"Hurry," Bob hobbles past me, moving south along the wall. "They need us at the gate. This was only a distraction."

34

ROSE

I watch as the bomber presses the knife into his skin. I have a split second until I'm incinerated.

Sink!

My body plummets downward as the ground liquifies. The stone swallows me, silencing the war cries and sealing out the sunlight.

Sink! Sink! Sink!

In a single second, my body plunges through the earth.

Then, inexplicably, I'm falling through the air.

Thud.

I open my eyes, expecting to see darkness, but a pale yellow light reflects off the cavern walls.

I'm in an underground colosseum—rows and rows of stone seating carved directly into the ground. The stadium is illuminated by Adamic spells carved into the cavern ceiling.

The dueling pit.

BOOM!

The ground rumbles, and rocky debris crumbles overhead. The earth shudders for what feels like an eternity. When everything settles, large cracks cut across the ceiling.

I stand slowly, brushing the dust from my hair. I'm at the uppermost edge of the stadium. From where I stand, the ceiling is only a few feet overhead. However, the depth of the cavern increases as one moves toward the center. In the middle of the stadium, the ceiling is hundreds of feet above the dueling pit.

Suddenly, I have an idea.

I study the spells along the ceiling. Some produce light, but others are unrecognizable. Something tells me they stabilize the ceiling.

I don't have time to destroy them all, so I focus on the nearest symbols. Before I give the command, I cover my ears.

Combust!

The stone explodes, blasting a hole where the spell used to be. I search along the ceiling, extending my soul to the next spell.

Combust!

The rockface fragments in a flash of smoke, and the spell disintegrates with it.

C'mon, Rose. You're running out of time.

Now that the defensive spell is annihilated, the feeders are undoubtedly charging across the plaza, directly over my head.

It has to be now.

I focus on the ceiling halfway between the two demolished spells. I extend my consciousness, commanding the very earth above my head.

Crumble!

A few stones begin to fall. I urge my soul, begging the elements with every ounce of my being.

Crumble!

A large slab of rock tumbles from the ceiling. Then, the earth falls away, quickly cascading into an avalanche.

Liquify!

I dive into the cavern wall as the ceiling rains down where I was just standing.

Even within the wall, I can feel the ground trembling.

Rise!

My body ascends, pushing through the viscous stone. It sloughs off me as I surface a short way from the wall.

I look up, finding Gideon on the wall walk. To my surprise, he's smiling. "Draw!" he commands, staring at the plaza behind me.

I turn around. There's a large depression—about 50 feet across—where the Palace Gate used to be, but that's not what catches my attention.

No way!

Instead of the plaza, I'm standing at the rim of an enormous crater, several hundred feet wide and just as deep in the center. Feeders litter the bottom, intermingled with the debris. By the looks of it, half of my father's army was caught in the rockslide, intercepting them in the midst of their charge.

The other half is marooned on the far side of the plaza. To reach the wall, they'll have to traverse the rubble or go around the crater, funneling through the narrow stretches of remaining plaza.

"Loose!" Gideon calls.

The arrows rain down on the crater, impaling the feeders as they crawl from the wreckage.

With adrenaline in my veins, I race toward the base of the wall.

Lift!

The air ripples beneath my feet, quickly accelerating my body. It catapults me up the wall. At the apex of the arc, I straighten my legs, kicking off from the invisible force. I have just enough momentum to make it over the parapet, landing with a crouch beside Gideon.

"My Queen! You're alive! Thank the Creator."

Before I can respond, he lifts his chin. "Draw!" he shouts into the wind. "Loose!"

Octavian rushes to my side, gesturing down at the crater. "Did… did you do that?"

"I got lucky," I beam.

Gideon continues to give commands as more archers join us from Antai's division.

"Two rows!" Octavian calls to the newcomers. "Fire until you're out of arrows."

I pace behind the archers until I find one who looks particularly unpracticed. With a quick apology, I borrow their bow and quiver. I lost mine in the chaos.

I stand in the second row, joining in the rhythm. *Draw. Loose. Draw. Loose.* With each volley, more feeders fall.

We're actually winning.

As if they heard my thoughts, the feeders retreat, moving to the back of the plaza and out of range. Suddenly, a lone figure floats into the air.

Dad.

He hovers until he's level with the wall walk. Then, holds his hands out in front. Slowly, they begin to glow, emitting a low, resonant hum. As his hands burn brighter, the hum gradually transforms into a high pitched whine.

I can feel the power accumulating, vibrating the very air—the aggregate dominion of one thousand souls.

"Take cover!" Gideon cries out.

My father releases the energy in a single beam. The sound is unearthly, both deafening and electrical. The laser cuts across the entire face of the wall in a single second, from one end of the plaza to the other. At every point of contact, the stone explodes outward from the concussive heat.

I'm still in awe as the wall begins to tilt, pitching us toward the plaza. Then, it crumbles beneath my feet.

Condense!

I gather the air around me, thickening it like a hearty soup. It slows my fall, as well as several of the soldiers around me. We land softly at the edge of the plaza as the feeders charge.

I can hear their whoops and wails as they race toward us. Quickly, I survey the scene.

Most of the guardsmen are just fine, but the archers are in shambles. Half of them were caught in the collapse, buried beneath the rubble. The rest of them roll on the floor, clutching broken limbs. The few who have climbed to their feet flounder to collect their arrows.

In a single attack, my father removed every advantage we had.

Now, we're caught on ground level with a mountain of debris blocking our retreat. When the feeders reach us, we'll be slaughtered.

"Fall back!" I command, racing up the rubble. "Fall back to the palace!"

I stop at the top of a stone slab, holding my ground as the fastest of the feeders charge toward us. They avoid the crater, dashing along the perimeter of the plaza. As they reach the wall, they converge from either side.

"Fall back!" I scream. Around me soldiers scramble over the rubble and race for the palace doors.

I nock my bow and release the arrow at an oncoming feeder.

Gideon positions himself at my side, doing the same. "Back to back," he suggests, firing an arrow at the feeders to the right.

I oblige, facing the left. I draw back the bowstring until my knuckle touches my chin.

Twang.

My arrow whistles, catching a feeder in the thigh.

Twang. Twang.

I release two more, hitting an armored feeder twice in the torso.

Beside me, Gideon nocks another arrow, aiming at the nearest feeder… but he doesn't shoot.

The feeder continues toward him, only 20 feet away.

I want to help, but I have my hands full. Several feeders scramble toward me.

Twang. Twang.

I put one arrow through a feeder's gut and another through its screaming mouth.

I don't have time to nock another. A feeder raises his hand. Sparks crackle on his fingertips.

Liquify!

I command the stone beneath the feeder, but instead of letting him sink, I lift the molten stone and mold it around him, intercepting the arc of electricity.

Solidify.

Granite encases the feeder up to his neck. Before he can escape, I form a razor-thin blade of energy.

Slice.

I don't decapitate him, but I sever enough of his neck to secure the kill.

I turn around.

Still, Gideon hasn't killed the feeder. The feeder approaches him slowly. It's only a few steps away now, standing in the path of Gideon's arrowhead.

Gideon grunts, but he doesn't let it fly. I watch as he grits his teeth. His fingers clench the bow, turning his knuckles white. Then, he twists at the waist, aiming the arrow at my face at point blank range.

With only a second to react, I reach out and grab the shaft just behind the arrowhead.

Twang.

As the bowstring snaps, the shaft splinters.

Push!

The air ripples between us, launching me off the stone slab. I hit the ground hard, rolling over the rock shards.

Shield!

I form a sphere around myself as I retrieve my bow and nock another arrow.

Gideon nocks another arrow as well. Then, the air ripples in front of his face as he forms a shield to match my own.

The demon cowers behind Gideon, using his body as a shield against my arrows.

I focus on the stone beneath his feet.

Liquify!

The demon sees it coming. He counters my attack, solidifying the stone the second it softens.

No! Please, not again! I can't handle another hostage situation. Not after what happened to Nevela.

Gideon struggles against the demon as he adjusts the bow, aiming the arrowhead at my chest.

With no other options, I aim at him as well.

I'm sorry, Gideon.

The moment my fingers begin to go slack, the demon disappears from behind Gideon's shoulder. He simply blinks out of existence.

The second he's gone, Gideon gasps, lowering his bow. "It wasn't me, My Queen. I mean you no harm."

But I'm not listening to Gideon. I'm listening to the muffled gurgle that emanates from behind him. I narrow my eyes, studying the spot where the demon stood just moments ago. As I stare, blood begins to drip onto the ground, appearing from thin air.

What the...

Suddenly, the demon materializes in a crumpled heap. Blood gushes from multiple stab wounds in his back.

Then, something touches my arm, and my body disappears.

I twist my head, but I can't see anyone. "Matt?"

His voice speaks in my ear. "It's us. Listen, we don't have a lot of time."

Twang.

Gideon shoots a feeder in the throat as it scrambles up the rubble, then he frantically spins in a circle. "Rose?" he shouts.

"Gideon, retreat with the others," I command. "Protect the palace."

He spins once more, searching for the source of my voice. When he doesn't find it, he nods. "As you wish." Then, he runs.

Matt's voice whispers in my ear once more. "Rose, please tell me you know how to open the library."

"I do," I whisper as feeders race past us, utterly oblivious. "It's a spell. I have it memorized."

"Good. The library is in the Trench, beneath the lake. Take the ring and go. We'll defend the palace."

His hand travels down my wrist, feeling for my thumb. Then, he slips the invisibility ring over my knuckle.

In the blink of an eye, I'm surrounded. Matt is in front of me, Kidlron is beside him, and Kendra is behind them both.

"MacArthur?" I see a flash of gold as Antai stumbles over a jagged chunk of stone.

"Antai!" I dive into his arms, turning him invisible as my face presses against his.

"Wha– Rose?" He squeezes me for a moment, lifting me in the air. When our faces separate, his smile materializes in front of me.

"Antai!" I shriek. "Your ear."

Blood mats his hair on one side. A long gash traces across the side of his scalp, completely severing the upper third of his ear.

"What?" His prosthetic lifts to the side of his head, groping around for his ear. "Seriously? Not again."

Part of me wants to give him a proper inspection—make sure he isn't bleeding out beneath his cloak—but there simply isn't time.

I grab his hand, but to my surprise, he doesn't turn invisible.

Duh.

I let go of the golden prosthetic and place my hand on the back of his neck, extending the spell. This time, it works.

As soon as Antai disappears from view, Matt and the others race for the palace. Antai takes a step to follow them.

"Wrong way," I whisper. "You're coming with me."

"Okay…" He flinches as several feeders race past us. "And where are we going exactly?"

Antai can't see it, but I feel myself smiling.

"To open the Library."

35

MATT

Already, the feeders surround us as their forces advance on the palace.

Kildron draws his gladius, charging two feeders as they race past. With a lunge, he skewers both feeders at once, forming a human shish kabob with his short sword.

As if it were Excalibur, he slowly draws the blade from the feeders. Then, he spins, cutting through an energy shield and slashing a feeder across the chest. With a smile, he extends the gladius, and electricity crackles across the metal.

KA-CRACK!

Two more are struck by the bolt, falling face first on the plaza floor.

"Get her to the palace," Kildron shouts. "I'll slow them down."

I pull Kendra close. "Hold on tight."

She clings to me, wrapping her arms around my neck and straddling my thigh.

I focus on the air directly above my head, imagining it how Kildron taught me. I pretend the region is gaining mass, drawing me in. I don't reach out to the air molecules, but the location itself—the precise spot in three dimensional space.

Once I have a grasp on the very fabric of reality, I speak with my soul.

Bend.

I push with my soul, creating an artificial mass that bends space—no different than a planet. As space begins to warp, I feel my body being pulled towards the depression, drawn in by the resulting gravity.

The force encapsulates both Kendra and me, lifting us off the ground in unison.

Bend!

The gravitational pull increases, and we plummet into the air. The sensation is akin to falling headfirst, only upward rather than downward. Kendra's hair flutters in my face, and her nails dig into my neck.

As we rocket into the air, the artificial mass moves with us, remaining fixed relative to my head. It's a personal planet—carrying us in our own unique orbit.

When we're a hundred feet in the air, I reposition the artificial mass to the side. Immediately, it pulls horizontally. The wind rushes against my body, helping us rotate until we're flying headfirst once more, bodies parallel to the plaza below.

We soar over the wreckage of the wall, swooping down near the palace entrance. I spot a glimmer of silver on the palace steps, and I change our course, aiming for the ground beside Diego.

As we descend, I dissolve the artificial mass, forming a new one above us, increasing the pull to counteract Earth's gravity. We slow, hovering for a second before we land beside Diego.

"Holy Freak, dude!" His metallic voice reverberates. "Since when can you fly?" He pulls me into a hug and claps me on the back. "When he pulls away, his eyes are all business.

"You should find Rose. She—"

"Already did," I interject. "She's on her way to the Library. We're here to hold the palace."

"That's a relief. Let me tell you, man, we could really use the help." He looks over at the collapsed wall as the first of the feeders trickle over. My dad hovers in front of them, knocking back a dozen of them with a sweeping energy wave.

Kendra looks around. "Where are the healers?"

"In the Pit," Diego says quickly, keeping his eyes on the approaching enemies.

"Go!" I say. "Help them. They'll need all the healers they can get."

Kendra nods. "Stay alive, please." She gives me one last kiss before darting through the massive doorway.

"Form up in front of the doorway!" Gideon commands, finally catching up with us. "Anyone with an Adamic blade, I want you in front. Amulets behind that. Form a shield when they get close. Archers in the back. Focus your fire on the wall. They'll be slowest as they climb down. Ready?"

"Feeders pour over the rubble, scrambling toward us in a single wave.

Gideon narrows his eyes. "Nock…. Aim… Loose!"

Arrows rain down on the crumbled wall, impaling the feeders as they descend the wreckage. Most, however, pass through the volley unscathed. They scream as they charge.

I draw my Adamic dagger. It looks puny beside Diego's longsword, but I don't have time to complain.

Shield.

A slab of stones shatters against my force field, dumping shards of rock around my feet.

Launch!

I send the shards flying back at the feeders, hitting several as they crash into our ranks.

I reach out with my soul, tapping into each feeder as I approach. With possession, I perceive their attacks the moment the idea forms.

Fire!

I twist to the side to avoid being torched and slash with my dagger, taking off a feeder's arm. I duck and swing my blade through another feeder's shin as he runs past.

I stand, finding my next target—a bone-thin feeder with Adamic armor tattooed from head to toe. He carries a ginormous two-handed sword. The sucker must be at least eight feet long. His toothpick arms shouldn't be able to bear the weight, and yet the feeder wields it with ease.

The feeder charges at the front lines, cutting through three men with a single swing.

I race toward him, dagger in hand. His blade has a huge reach, but if I get close enough, the weapon will be useless.

He sees me coming, and squares up to face me, pointing the sword tip at my chest.

When I'm 10 feet away, I lean back and kick out my legs, as if to slide.

The feeder responds with lightning reflexes. He lowers the blade, ready to run me through.

Bend.

Rather than slide, I'm pulled upward. Carried by my momentum, I careen over the great sword and plunge my dagger into the feeder's chest. We both go rolling, and my dagger is torn from my grasp, still embedded in the feeder's breastbone.

Before I can retrieve my dagger, a new feeder takes hold of the great sword and swings it at my head.

I cross my arms, raising them overhead.

Chink!

The blade catches in the intersection of my metal cuffs. Before the feeder can swing again, an arrow rips through its eye socket.

I turn to find Gideon nocking his next arrow. He gives me a quick nod before putting another arrow through a feeder's skull.

"Get up!" Diego grabs me by the arm and pulls me to my feet.

Before I can reach my dagger, another feeder intercepts me.

This time, I speak to the Morphmask.

Spear!

The wooden shaft elongates in my hand as the feeder lunges. The spear tip materializes a split second before it impales the feeder's gut.

I let go of the shaft, and the spear dissolves. The damage, however, remains as the feeder bleeds out.

I dart over to the skinny feeder and wrench my dagger from its chest. Then, I turn to face the horde.

KA-KRACK!

Kildron levitates above me, throwing lightning bolts like free shirts at a football game.

KA-CRACK!

I watch as he draws his gladius, swooping low and fast over the feeders. He lets the blade sweep below him, cutting through the feeders as he zips past.

After making one more pass, he lands at my side. Facing the ravenous feeders.

SCREECH!

Kildron emits the sound waves, channeling them at our attackers. I watch as the feeders squirm, taking precious seconds to protect their ears.

The archers capitalize, demolishing their ranks with volley after volley.

With each round of arrows, fewer feeders climb over the wall.

Just when I think we're winning, the downpour of arrows becomes a drizzle. When I glance back, half of the archers cower in the back lines, their quivers empty.

"Preserve your arrows!" Gideon calls. "Close-range targets only."

The remaining feeders surge, gaining confidence. They clash into our ranks, unleashing the energy from past feedings. Men scream on either side of me as their clothes ignite. Unfortunately, they didn't have Adamic cloaks to protect themselves.

By the looks of it, the two sides are evenly numbered, a feeder for every Cavernic.

We still have a chance.

As if he read my mind, the Holy One descends from the crumpled wall. His black hood is pulled over his head, shadowing his face from the morning sun.

He raises his hand.

The archers gasp behind me as their bowstrings ignite in unison. From a football field away, the Holy One conjured hundreds of tiny flames, melting every bowstring on the battlefield.

Impossible.

The range of his dominion, the physical expanse he had to cover… It should have killed him, and yet he stands in the palace driveway, cloak billowing in the breeze.

"Retreat!" Gideon calls. He throws down his bow and ushers his men through the palace doors. They race to get inside.

I don't run. Perhaps I'm being foolish, but I stand in the gravel as the Holy One approaches.

If I can just possess him—if I can tap into that power for just a few moments—I could demolish the remainder of his army.

I have to try.

The Holy One sees me immediately. He reaches up with one hand and removes his hood. Oddly enough, he's smiling, like a talk-show host welcoming his next guest.

"Stop!" The Holy One calls. "Rein in!"

The feeders obey, reluctantly ceasing their pursuit. They eye us as they slink back behind the Holy One.

Kildron steps beside me and puts an arm around my shoulder. "So, you've chosen to embrace death. I can't say I blame you."

I let out a trembling breath. "If we both possess him at once, we might stand a chance."

Kildron sighs. "We can certainly try."

The Holy One continues to approach, his black dress shoes crunching over the gravel.

Kildron gives my shoulder a squeeze. "There's no way I'd rather die than with you at my side."

"We're not dying!" I insist. "Just help me!"

"Alright," Kildron says, letting go of my shoulder. "Let's do this."

The Holy One stops 10 feet away. "Matthew… Kildron…" He looks at each of us respectively, giving a friendly nod. "Just who I wanted to see. How was your trip to Atlantia? I see you bear the Shackles of Redemption. Please, do expound."

Wait for my signal, Kildron whispers in my head.

The Holy One steps closer. "Clearly, you didn't secure any aid, and yet, I sense hope in you. So the question remains, what happened in Atlantia, Matt? What did you discover?"

Twang!

The Holy One's hand is already in motion, snatching the arrow when the tip is a few inches from his right eye.

The Holy One turns, directing his attention to the one who fired the arrow. "You know, Gideon, it's quite rude to interrupt."

He holds up his hand, fingers spread wide. Then, he curls them into a fist.

In unison with the Holy One's hand, Gideon's head pulses, jiggling like a water balloon as his skull implodes. He dies instantly, crumpling to the floor.

The Holy One lowers his hand. "Where was I? Oh, yes. Atlantia. Care to share, Matt?"

I say nothing.

"Perhaps I should take a peek inside? Hmmm? See what I can find?"

Suddenly, Kildron's consciousness is screaming in my head.

Now!

I drive my soul forward, commanding it into the Holy One's body.

I don't make it through his skin. His soul is so pressurized, it's practically solid, like a car tire or a tank of gas. Each one of his souls layer on top of the other, forming a dense composite. No matter how hard I push, I can't break through.

He's a tree trunk, and I'm a piece of paper, trying to pierce the bark.

It's simply impossible.

I retract my soul as Kildron screams. His body levitates, suspended above the ground. His limbs contort, joints hyperextending. Throughout it all, the air never ripples. The Holy One speaks to his body directly.

Kildron screams again, long and raw. His eyes bulge, and his veins protrude.

"Resisting will only make it worse," the Holy One warns. "Open your mind, Kildron, and it'll all be over."

I watch in horror as something presses against the inside of Kildron's abdomen, stretching the skin as it protrudes outward. It looks as though an animal is inside him, trying to claw their way out, kicking against the skin and thrashing about.

Kildron screams louder.

"Stop it!" I extend my soul, but the Holy One displaces my presence, severing my connection to Kildron's body.

Slowly, blood begins to seep from Kildron's pores, running down his brow like sweat.

With one last cry, Kildron falls silent, going limp. The Holy One frowns—clearly disappointed—and drops his body on the gravel.

With an evil grin, he turns to me. "Your turn, Matthew, but don't worry. I'll be gentle."

Before I can run, his soul engulfs me.

His mind presses down on me, an entire ocean of consciousness flooding into my nose and ears, filling my head until it's about to burst. There's enough of him to soak my entire soul, filling every memory simultaneously.

See, Matt. This isn't so bad. I'm almost done.

Suddenly, I'm on a boat, sailing away from Atlantia. The sail ruffles, and the seawater mists my face.

"It was all for nothing," Kendra sighs.

"It wasn't for nothing," I claim, my heart racing in anticipation.

Kildron studies me, a thin smile forming when he sees my cuffs. "I guess it wasn't."

"That's not what I meant." I wait until everyone is looking at me. "I think I know where the Library is."

NO!!!

I retract my soul, drawing it in. I let my consciousness drain from my limbs, gathering in my core. Immediately, I collapsed to the ground, my face smacking the gravel. I couldn't stand even if I wanted to. My limbs are completely numb.

I don't stop there. I withdraw from my head, leaving behind my eyes and ears. The clamor falls silent, and darkness creeps into my vision, closing in until it consumes my sight.

I abandon my body to the Holy One, severing all connections to the outside world. Physically, I'm at his mercy, but my mind has never been safer.

Don't do it, Matthew. Don't make this harder than it has to be.

I ignore him, gathering my memories into a single mass. This time, my soul isn't a heap of loose laundry; it's a collection of coins, each with a unique date and story.

I gather the memories into a single stack, organizing them so they take up the least amount of space. Then, I force them together until they begin to fuse.

The Holy One hammers at my mind, trying to scatter the coins, but he's too late. My memories have fused into an mental alloy—an amalgamated entity, unrecognizable from its individual parts. Each hammer blow deforms my mind, but it doesn't break me apart.

Whatever memories I previously contained, they're indiscernible. Inaccessible.

Complete Durebrum.

Eventually, the hammer blows stop. If the Holy One is there, lurking outside my consciousness, he doesn't give any indication.

In my current state, it's hard to think. I'm not sure if it's been a minute or an hour. In fact, I can barely remember what I'm even doing. I simply exist, struggling to maintain Durebrum.

Eventually, I can't take it any more. My mind begins to leech, dripping back into my limbs and draining to my head.

I open my eyes.

I'm alive.

I lift my face from the gravel, swatting a few loose pebbles that cling to my skin. I don't feel any pain. As far as I can tell, I'm not injured.

I climb to my feet, scanning the battlefield. I'm the only one standing. The Holy One is gone, as are his feeders. Only the dead remain.

"Matt?"

I spin, finding Kildron on the floor a few steps away. His limbs are splayed in unnatural positions, but he doesn't have any lethal wounds.

"Dad!"

I scramble to his side. "I did it. He didn't get the memory."

"That's good," Kildron winces. "You did good."

I look around again, my stomach sinking. "Did they go inside?"

Kildron grits his teeth, practically groaning each word. "When he couldn't get it from you, he got impatient. He's going after Kendra. She's in the Pit with the others."

Kendra!

"Can you stand?" I ask, looking at his twisted legs.

Kildron shakes his head.

"Okay… that's okay. I'll send a healer after I help Kendra. I'll be right back."

I start for the doorway.

"Matt!" Kildron chokes. "Wait!" His voice is raw… desperate.

I stop. "What's wrong?"

He winces as he bends one arm, reaching into his shirt. With a shaky hand, he removes the hourglass relic, but struggles to lift the chain over his head.

"Take it," he gasps.

"You keep it," I say. "I'll come back for you once I help Kendra."

"Take it," he begs. His voice is a wheeze this time, even weaker than the last. "I'm not gonna make it much longer…"

"Yes you are. You're gonna be just fine." I put my hand over his, lowering the relic back to his chest. "I'll send a healer. They'll be here soon."

"Matt!" He lets go of the hourglass, grabbing my wrist instead. "He ripped up my insides. I don't have much time. Please… take the relic."

"No…" I shake my head. "They can heal you. They—" My voice trails off as I reach out with my soul. I look for something to heal, but I can't recognize a single organ. Everything below the diaphragm is in shambles—as if his intestines got caught in a blender.

"Dad…" I breathe, the reality of it finally sinking in.

He's dying.

"Promise me…" Kildron gasps.

Suddenly, I have an idea.

I snatch the amulet off his chest, holding it in front of him where he can see it. "Take it. You can visit Jenevrah. You still have time."

He shakes his head, still clutching my wrist. He chokes a few words between each watery wheeze. "I would die… in her arms... Wouldn't be… right."

"What do I do?" I panic. My throat constricts, making my voice catch. "How do I heal you? Tell me, and I'll do it. I won't let you die. Just tell me, and I'll do it!"

Still clutching my wrist, he looks up at me, offering a fleeting smile. "I love you, son. I only wish I found you sooner."

Then, I feel the energy flow into me. It comes with a flash of memories.

I'm standing in my chambers in the middle of the night, rocking a baby—my baby—until his eyes finally flutter shut. I give him a kiss on the head before gently placing him in the crib.

Sleep tight, little guy.

Suddenly, I'm walking on a busy street, stalking a man in a black jacket.

A feeder.

Then, I'm on a yacht, climbing the steps to the main deck. I look down at the couch, smiling. Matt is passed out, snoring loudly.

There's no blankets nearby, so I grab a towel, spreading it across his legs.

Sleep tight, little guy.

NO!!!

I try to pull away, but Kildron tightens his grip, channeling the last of his energy through his hand.

Already, I feel his soul swelling within me, buzzing with energy. My mind expands… sharpens. My blood quickens.

Then, he's gone. Just like that, the stream of dominion runs dry.

His hand loosens, falling from my wrist. It's so sudden, so instant, I can barely believe it's true.

My father is dead.

36

KENDRA

I nearly slip as I race down the slick stone steps. The deeper I go, the quieter the screams become.

I've never been in the Pit before, but this is exactly what I expected: cold and damp, like a wet rag abandoned in the sink.

When I reach the landing, I find myself staring down a pitch dark hallway. There isn't a single candle.

Light!

An orb of light appears in my palm. I hold it above my head like a lantern, illuminating the dungeon.

"Hello?"

Silence. The Pit is completely abandoned. I take a step down the corridor and peer into the nearest cell.

It's empty.

"Hello?" I call again.

"Kendra?"

My mom appears out of nowhere, racing down the corridor and diving into my arms. I reciprocate the squeeze as she shakes me side to side.

"Hi, mom," I laugh.

"I thought we lost you," she whispers.

"Kendra!" Decklin plows into my side, joining the embrace. "Did you do it?" he asks excitedly. "Did you stop the Holy One?"

I force a smile on my face. "I hope so," I say. "My friends are fighting him now… But that's not important," I lie. "The important thing is that we're together." I look around. "Where's dad?"

"He's… on the wall," my mother solemnly says.

"You didn't see him?" Decklin worries.

"I'm sure he's fine," I choke. I pull his head against my ribs, so that he won't see me teary eyed.

"This way," my mom says, taking my hand and pulling me down the corridor. "The first dozen cells are supposed to stay empty. Our cell is back here."

Up ahead, I spot one of my coworkers standing in the doorway of a cell. Gorgeous pencil curls bounce over the straps of her healer's apron. I recognize her from pathology, but I can't remember her name.

"Excuse me, Kendra?" she says. "If you can spare a minute, there's someone here who would like to say hello."

I look into the cell and find a young woman laying on blood-soaked blankets. She holds a newborn in her arms.

"Wendy, is that you?" I gasp.

She grins. "Hi, Kendra." She turns her shoulders, exposing the baby's face. "This is little Adam." Her voice is soft—almost weak—yet proud. "He was just born last night."

I let go of my mom's hand. "Oh, my goodness! He's adorable. How was the birth? How are you feeling?"

"I'm okay," Wendy sighs. "It was a rough night, but we're doing better now. Jephora is taking good care of us." She looks over at the pathologist.

Jephora. That's right.

As my eyes pass over her amulet, they double in size. The silver is etched with three Adamic symbols—symbols I've seen a dozen times on Matt's back.

The demon amulet.

Jephora stiffens, and her hand covers the amulet.

I smile at Wendy. "Seems like you're in good hands," I turn to Jephora, meeting her gaze. "If Rose trusts you, so do I."

"Thank you," Jephora sighs. "And I'm happy to answer any questions you have. I'm sure this must be so overwhelming."

"Actually, I do have a few questions. Do we already have a space for the wounded?"

"We have some beds set up further down." Jephora's lips press tight together. "We're just waiting for the survivors to arrive."

We share a knowing look.

If there are any.

Suddenly, the rhythmic tapping of footsteps echoes from the stairwell.

Immediately, everyone falls silent—so silent I could hear a pin drop. I extinguish my light.

Eventually, the footsteps slow to a stop.

"Yoohoo? Anyone home?" A familiar voice sings down the corridor. It's soft and feminine. "Come on out, little mice! I know you're down here."

A light shines down the central corridor. It passes perpendicular to our cell, leaving us in the shadows.

"Yoohoo? I've come to claim my prize. Anyone down here?"

Suddenly, it clicks. The voice belongs to the red-headed guardsman, Crasilda. I healed her once at the guardsmen evaluation—after Velma struck her in the shoulder with an icicle. She never thanked me. Matt once described her as a wretched imp.

Regardless, she's a soldier.

I open my mouth to respond when Jephora clamps down on my wrist. She holds a finger to her lips and shakes her head.

Her fear sends chills down my spine.

Crasilda's light dims as she steps into the first few cells—the empty ones. I listen as she takes a few more steps, presumably peering in the next pair of cells.

"Huh… I could've swore…" Crasilda huffs.

Slowly, hesitantly, her footsteps begin to recede.

"Waaaaaahhhhh!"

I startle as Wendy's baby begins to scream out of nowhere.

Wendy covers her baby's mouth, sealing off the sound. "Shhhh," Wendy begs, but it's too late.

Crasilda races down the corridor, bursting into our cell.

"Oh, this is a treat!" Crasilda savors the scene as she studies Wendy. "The whore-maid finally gave birth to her bastard baby." She steps into the cell, swinging the bars shut behind her.

With a hungry look in her eye, she steps closer to Wendy. "Alright, whore. I'll give you a choice. Do you want to go first or second?"

Wendy looks to Jephora for help, then me.

That's when I see it. Crasilda's side bangs are stained red—not the usual amber, but a deep, dark crimson.

No... it can't be...

"I don't have all day..." Crasilda whines. "Which is it?" Crasilda rolls her eyes. "You know what? Too late. I'll start with the baby so you can watch."

"No... NOOO!" Wendy screams. She clutches her baby to her chest, backing against the wall.

"Oh, please. He's dumber than a rat at this age." Crasilda lunges, grabbing Wendy's arms and prying them open.

"NOOO!" Jephora wails as she dives at Crasilda, fingernails aimed for her eyes.

Crasilda releases Wendy and grabs Jephora by the throat, slamming her against the cell wall. Then, she bites into the side of her neck.

Oh my god!

Jephora thrashes and screams.

I grab my amulet, but I don't attack. I saw the air ripple around Crasilda. I know what she's capable of. I can't break her shield.

I'm sorry, Jephora.

With every second, her kicks grow softer. Finally, her limbs hang limp.

Crasilda drops her body to the floor, wiping her mouth on her sleeve. "What a wholesome girl," Crasilda says. "Feeding is a great way to develop sympathy, let me tell you. I almost regret it." Her eyes narrow on Wendy. "Almost..."

Wendy squeezes her eyes shut as her baby screams. "Please, God, give Adam your protection. Please, God, give Adam your protection."

"Adam?" Crasilda steps closer, using a finger to pet the baby's bald head. "What a fitting name! An incestuous prophet, right? Sleeping with his daughters to replenish the Earth, or something like that. It's a family tradition at this point. Remind me again, who was the father?"

Wendy keeps her eyes shut, reciting her prayer.

"Please, God, give Adam your protection. Please, God, give Adam your protection."

"God can't hear you!" Crasilda shouts. "He's upstairs, killing your friends." She narrows her eyes at Wendy. "You know what, I'm not going to take your baby." Her smile widens. "You're going to give him to me."

Crasilda closes her eyes, and a moment later, Wendy shudders. Immediately, her prayer falls silent. Her lips quiver as she tries to speak, but she can't form the words. Her body is no longer her own.

I see the terror in her eyes as her arms extend, slowly holding Adam out in front of her. The muscles in her neck bulge as she struggles to resist, but it's no use. She holds out her infant, one hand under the head, the other beneath his backside.

Crasilda opens her eyes. "Was that really so hard?"

As she reaches for the infant, I dive for Jephora's body. I take hold of the demon amulet and throw my soul at Crasilda.

Rage and bitterness engulf me. They seep into my skin, leaching into my bloodstream. My heart beats faster, pumping the hostility straight to my brain.

Images flash before my eyes. I feel the sting as needles press into my back. Then, I hear Rose's voice as she promises to make me Queen.

Suddenly, I'm kneeling before the Holy One. He traces his finger over my skin, commanding the symbols to form.

Next thing I know, I'm grabbing a young archer and pinning him to the floor with dominion. He screams as I bite into his neck. The blood tastes vile, but the energy! I feel it rushing into me… expanding my mind… filling me with power.

I need more.

When I open my eyes, my hands are holding a crying infant. For a split second, that urge surfaces, but I bury it with my revulsion.

NOOO!

My fingers extend, and the infant falls back into Wendy's arms.

"Run," I choke.

Fueled by adrenaline, Wendy leaps to her feet and races out of the room.

Already, I can feel Crasilda fighting against me. Her soul constricts around me, squeezing me out like a tourniquet.

I relinquish her muscles, moving instead into her brainstem.

Slee—

Oh, no you don't! Crasilda thinks as she rams me with her soul.

I retreat further, moving into the bloodstream. I only have a second to make this work.

Clot!

I've barely given the command when our body is in motion. She turns us around, facing Kendra's body—my body.

Choke!

I watch as my body lifts into the air. I reach out with my mind.

Release!

My body drops back to the floor, landing on the solid stone.

Get out of me, you bitch!

Her soul thrashes around, pummeling me within the confines of her body. Our arms seize, and our head swings wildly about. I feel like a child, clinging from a bull's back as it bucks me to and fro. If I slip, the bull will trample me to death.

Just a little bit longer.

For the second time, our eyes focus on my body. This time, she notices the amulet clasped in my hand. Her eyes fixate on the thinnest portion of my wrist.

Sli—

No!

I counter her command as I cling to her soul.

Our body—Crasilda's body—falls to its knees, crawling toward where my body lies on the floor. I try to stop us, but Crasilda is too strong. I can only slow us down.

Our arm trembles as it reaches for the amulet. We grab my hand and begin peeling away my fingers one at a time.

Noooo!

I can't stop us. Finally, my last finger falls free of the amulet, and my eyes snap open in my own body.

The air ripples around my neck, throwing me against the wall. Crasilda steps closer, studying my face.

"You're Matt's little rebound, aren't you." The invisible force dissipates, only to be replaced with her hand. Her fingers squeeze my throat as she slams my head against the wall. "You know, I always thought he would be a fun little plaything—so innocent and pure. I can't wait to get a taste of those memories…" With her free hand, she taps on my skull. "See what he's like beneath the sheets, if you know what I mean…" She pauses a moment. "Goody two-shoes like him, he's probably a giver, isn't he? Oh, yeah. I bet he took good care of you…" she grins mischievously. "Or should I say us?"

I try to speak, to unleash the vilest words I can think of, but my trachea is being crushed.

"Awww, I'm sorry," she taunts. The pressure on my neck lessens, just enough so I can talk. "How's this? I want to hear it when you beg for your life."

She leans in, her teeth inches from my neck. "Last chance," Crasilda says, her breath tickling my skin. "Any last worths?" She smiles victoriously… sort of. Her smile is asymmetrical. The right side of her face droops.

I grin. "What was that? I didn't quite catch it."

"I thed, any lath worth?" Suddenly, her hand loosens, and she stumbles back. "Wath happing?" Crasilda teeters before tipping to the side, landing on her hip. She tries to stand, but she can't move her right leg.

I stand over her, rubbing my bruised throat. "I'll tell you what's happening. You're having a stroke—a bad one, might I add. Your middle cerebral artery is completely blocked, and it has been for a couple of minutes now. Of course, if you knew where that was, you might be able to save yourself, but we both know that's not likely." I smile wider. "Pity… looks like I'm your only hope."

"Hep me," she gasps. "Peeth."

I crouch down beside her, feeling a twisted rush of satisfaction as she suffers. "I'm sorry, but you'll have to be louder… I want to hear it when you beg for your life."

"Peeth," she chokes. "Peeth." Then, her eyes roll into the back of her head, and she convulses on the floor. I collect the demon amulet as she seizes next to Jephora's body, limbs trembling and back arching.

After a minute, she grows still.

My mom peers in from the hallway. "Is she… dead?"

I reach out with my soul, searching for signs of life.

Bum, bum… Bum, bum… Bum, bum…

Stop.

Her heart obeys, falling still.

"She's dead," I say matter-of-factly. "She's the first person I've purposefully killed, and I don't feel the slightest guilt. In fact, it feels good.

The world is better off without her.

Wendy steps into the room, bouncing Adam to hush his cries. She stares down at Jephora. "She saved me," she breathes.

I grab the blanket from the ground and toss it over Jephora. I'm adjusting the edges when a stampede echoes from the stairwell. The roar of footsteps grows louder and louder.

"Kendra!" Diego's metal form erupts from the stairwell, sprinting down the hallway. An army of Cavernic soldiers pour out after him.

"He's coming for you!" Diego shouts. "The Holy One is coming!"

Light floods the Pit as soldiers reach for their amulets.

Diego stops in front of me, panting. "The Holy One got Matt. He's coming for you next. He's going to read your mind to find the Library.
"

My knees begin to buckle. "Matt's dead?"

"No!" Diego blurts, "He's alive, but the Holy One is coming for you. You need to get out of here!"

But there's nowhere to go. Already, soldiers crowd the corridor. Supposedly, the Pit connects to the catacombs somewhere, but I have no way to find the entrance—not fast enough, anyway.

"Everyone," Bob bellows from the mouth of the stairwell. "Move as far back as you can. Swordsmen in the front. This is where we make our last stand."

I don't watch as the soldiers take formation. Instead, I look inward, urging my soul into my frontal cortex, combing through my memories.

I start with the memory on the wave-skimmer—the moment when Matt first explained his theory. The memory isn't contained in a single neuron, but composed of countless interconnections. Tiny biological bridges connect each of the concepts: boat, Matt, Adamic, Library, riddle. Together, they create the memory.

Forget!

I begin severing the ties, killing off their dendritic connections. I move quickly and with little discretion.

What was I just thinking about?

"Kendra!" Diego shakes me. "You need to go!"

"Just trust me," I mutter. "I have a plan."

I reach within myself, scouring my brain. This time, I don't search for an event, but an idea.

The Lost Library.

Immediately, I can feel the strands of cognition, connecting it to every relevant concept. I sever each one as I find it.

Trench... forget!

Lake... forget!

Beneath Guard Tower... forget!

"Hello there, valiant soldiers," the Holy One's voice reverberates down the stairwell. "Firstly, I'd like to congratulate you on a gallant defense of the palace. To be honest, I'm quite impressed."

His voice draws nearer as he speaks. "Secondly, I'd like to make you a proposition...Kendra? I know you can hear me. Come forward, and I will spare your little band of survivors. Every one of them. Do we have a deal?"

Water... forget!

Dive… forget!

"Kendra! I'm waiting!" he says. "Do we have a deal?"

When I open my eyes, everyone is staring at me.

"You have to say it out loud," he calls.

"You have a deal!" I shout.

"Good!" The Holy One emerges from the mouth of the stairwell. His black hood is pulled back, revealing his joyous face as he strides down the corridor.

The feeders follow him, filling the Pit. There must be a hundred of them, maybe more.

He stops a few feet from the swordsmen, letting the feeders fill the space behind him.

He extends his index finger and curls it in a 'come hither' motion. "Don't be shy. Come on out."

Taking a deep breath, I push forward through the crowd. Bob gives me an encouraging nod as I step past him.

I stop in front of the Holy One, sandwiched between our two armies.

"Good girl," he says softly. "Now kneel."

"Nooo!" My mom pushed past the swordsmen.

I don't let her get any closer. Gripping the demon-amulet, I stretch my soul.

Sleep!

Her knees buckle and she hits the stone floor, already unconscious.

The Holy One motions at his feet. "Shall we?"

It better be enough.

I step forward and kneel at his feet. A moment later, he rests his palms on the crown of my head.

Don't worry, he whispers in my head. *This won't take long.*

Lost Library! He speaks the word into my soul, commanding it to the forefront of my attention. Immediately, the subtle associations begin to surface.

Power.

Godliness.

Holy One.

Language.

Prophets.

He fishes through the thoughts, following their connections, and the connections after that.

You clever girl. You've done some pruning, haven't you?

"Aaaaah!" I hear pattering footsteps, followed by a thump and the clatter of a sword. Whoever they were, their attempt was unsuccessful.

Where were we? Oh, yes. The location. Tell me where it is.

It's on the tip of my tongue, but I can't remember it for the life of me.

The Holy One continues deeper into my mind, crawling over the neurons like a spider in its web.

The location! he urges. I try to resist, but my brain obeys. The words surface one at a time.

Dark...

Deep...

Wet...

The Holy One hovers on the last word. *Wet.. how interesting. What is deep and wet. The well? The canal? The... Trench?*

My heart races at the last word. I can't remember why, but I remember it was a secret.

The Trench it is. Thank you, Kendra. You've kept your end of the bargain.

The Holy One lifts his hands, stepping back. "I have discovered the site of my ascension," he announces. "Unfortunately, there seems to be a dilemma." He feigns a frown, gesturing at the feeders behind him. "You see, I promised Kendra I would spare you, but I promised my servants that they would feast on the spoils of war. I made two contradicting promises, knowing I couldn't keep them both."

He turns and faces the feeders. "I'm departing. You feeders will do as you please with the survivors. Now, make way! Backs against the wall!"

Grinning from ear to ear, the feeders form two lines on opposite sides of the corridor. They stand shoulder to shoulder, each line facing toward the other.

"Now!" The Holy One orders as he passes by. "Bow to your god!"

In unison, the feeders bend at the waist, extending their necks into the walkway.

The air ripples down the entire length of the corridor. In the blink of an eye, one hundred feeder heads tumble onto the floor, severed by a thin blade of force dominion.

"There," the Holy One says, dusting his hands together as several heads still teeter. "Those beasts no longer serve a purpose. I have what I came for. Remember this mercy. You'll see me again at The Great Reviving, and I expect to hear some gratitude."

He walks slowly past the severed heads, stopping at the mouth of the stairwell. "You may not believe it, but you will worship me someday. I will save you all, and you will love me for it. I promise you that."

His footsteps echo as he ascends the staircase alone.

He's gone.

I drop to my knees, assessing my mom for any injuries. I'm still attending to her when a new set of footsteps clatter down the stairwell.

Matt stumbles into the corridor, eyes wildly flickering about. When he sees the dead feeders, he furrows his brow.

"Matt!"

I was told that he's alive, but seeing him brings a heightened level of elation.

I race to him, leaping into his arms, and wrapping my legs around his waist. He's sweaty and dusty, but a hug has never felt so good.

"Kendra!" he breathes, eyes blinking in disbelief. He squeezes me with surprising strength considering the battle he just endured. "I thought he had you."

"He did," I confess. "He knows where it is."

Matt stiffens. He opens his mouth but hesitates, knowing I won't like the words. "I have to go help them."

Already, my heart spasms. Thrice now, I thought I lost him. First, when he fed, then in Atlantia, and just now on the battlefield.

I can't endure another.

If I act fast, I could possess Matt like I did with my mother—put him to sleep before he gets himself killed—but I know it's no use.

If he wins, it's all over.

"Okay," I breathe, as my lungs begin to spasm. "But I'm coming with you."

"No!" Matt growls. "Absolutely not. It's too dangerous."

"I'm not leaving you," I cry. "You can't make me."

"I'm coming too," Diego says, stepping beside us. "We're in this together."

Matt clenches his teeth, and for a second, I think he's going to argue. Then, I feel him in my head, sampling my state of mind. I don't know what he sees in there, but he finally nods. "Okay. We do it together.

With that, he takes my hand, and we race up the stairwell, sprinting towards certain death.

37

IRIS

I stand on the measly little shore, staring into the murky water.

"Are you sure you don't want to come with me?" Sheyba asks. She's wearing her skimpy little loincloth, and a homemade bandeau. I bought her some clothes for the plane ride, but she ditched them the moment we left the airport.

"Looks like a one person job to me," I say.

She looks me over and grins. "Yeah, it's probably for the best. A shore-shrew like yourself, you'll sink straight to the bottom."

I shrug. "You just want me to take my shirt off," I accuse.

She smiles wider, completely unashamed. "So what if I do? Does that change your answer?"

I think about the moment. "Maybe if you say please."

Sheyba rolls her eyes. "Will you come with me… a debt to be owed."

I smile at the translation. "No, but thanks for asking nicely."

Sheyba furrows her brow, making sure I see her annoyance. "You know," she says, "we have a term for people like you. You're such a crab-skin."

"Meaning?"

"From the outside, you promise a tasty meal, but in the end, you only disappoint. You get my hopes up for nothing."

Before I can respond, she turns and dives headfirst into the water. Air bubbles foam on the surface, gradually diminishing until the water is glassy once again.

I wait, pacing back and forth on the shore. One minute goes by, then another… And another and another and another.

I stop pacing, staring into the depths. *You've got to be kidding me.*

I kick off my shoes first, then I yank off the shirt. When she still doesn't surface, I take a deep breath and dive in.

The water is colder and dirtier than I first gave it credit.

Light!

Even with dominion, I can barely see a few feet in front of me. The sediment illuminates bright black, and the water saps the heat from my arms, compromising my coordination within the first few strokes. Regardless, I kick downward into oblivion.

Suddenly, a hand grabs hold of my ankle, tugging me back the way I came.

"Ptuh!" I suck in the gasp the moment my head breaks the surface.

Sheyba's playful giggle tickles my ear as I splash to the side, desperate to escape the frigid water.

She treads water, a dumb little grin on her face. "So you do care about me, Iris, protector of the world."

She casually kicks to the shore. Pulling herself onto a large lava rock, she gives her body a shake to knock loose the water droplets.

She was never in any danger, I realize. She was hiding just beneath the surface, watching my reactions, testing me.

"What is wrong with you?" I demand climbing out of the water and drying myself with dominion. "Do you think this is some sort of game?"

Sheyba mirrors my emotions, glaring right back at me. "Do you?" she demands. "Some moments, I'm sure you like me, and others, I'm sure you don't. Which is it? Tell me now so I don't waste my time."

I clench my hands at my sides. This is the exact situation I've been trying to avoid. Of course, I like her; what's not to like? She's cute and fun and a little bit ferocious… but I love Jazon, and there's still a tiny chance—maybe bigger than tiny—that he'll be resurrected someday.

"It's complicated," I groan.

Sheyba shakes her head. "No, it's not. You do or you don't. Which is it?"

I look at her, but I can't bring myself to say it. "I'm not sure," I mutter.

"Great Flame! I shouldn't need the Collar of Candor to get a straight answer out of you."

"It doesn't matter right now," I insist. "We have a job to do. What did you find down there?"

"No," she says. "I'm not telling you anything until you give me an answer. Do you like me or not?"

"I liked you a whole lot more a few seconds ago," I mutter under my breath.

Sheyba ignores the quip. "Well?"

I look back at the murky water. "Fine, I'll do it myself."

I bend my knees—about to dive in—when a loud crackle echoes across the cavern. A thick layer of ice expands across the shallows, stretching several yards into the open water.

"You can't ignore me, Iris, protector of the world. Now, answer my inquiry? Why can't your feelings be revealed? I'm not moving until you tell me."

"Ugh!" I throw my hands down at my side. "I like you, okay? But it doesn't matter because I already love someone else. Got it? Happy now?"

Sheyba doesn't move, meeting my gaze with unbroken determination. "Where is this mate? If you love her so much, why aren't you with her?"

"It's complicated."

"Does she not love you back?"

"No, it's not that."

"Then what?"

I bite my cheek.

"Iris?"

"He's dead, okay? He's been dead for a long time, and even if the Holy One wins—which is feeling more and more likely—there's no way he's going to bring Jazon back. He already gave me a second chance. So it's basically official now: he's gone forever."

"Oh… I see." Sheyba exhales loudly, pursing her lips. After a moment of silence, she sits down on a rock, dipping her toes in the water. "It's complicated," she agrees.

Eventually, she gives me a quick glance, sensing the sadness I try to conceal. "I'm sorry for your loss, Iris. I can't imagine…"

I look away. "Yeah… it sucks."

Sheyba chews on her lip. "How long ago?"

"Three years next month."

An awkward silence ensues. I pace along the beach until the quiet is unbearable.

"For a long time, I thought Adamic could bring him back. I was convinced that his life depended on my standing with the Holy One. He was always hanging over me, on the verge of disappearing forever. For three years, I failed to see he was already gone."

"That's a long time to bear such a burden," Sheyba offers. "I wish I could've been there to support you."

She reaches for my hand, but I pull away, pacing back and forth next to her rock. "Yeah, well… it doesn't change anything. Even though he's gone, I can't change how I feel… I don't think I can love you the same way I loved him."

Sheyba raises an eyebrow. "I would hope not." She looks over at me, a subtle smile forming on her lips.

I shake my head. "You know what I mean."

Sheyba grows serious. "You don't have to love me in any specific way. You don't have to love me at all. The future is a clam, Iris. If you don't like what you find inside, you can always dive for another. Most of us don't find a pearl the first time."

"Are you the pearl?" I ask.

Sheyba shrugs. "I hope so, but that's for you to decide… My mom always said the heart is like a riptide. Fighting it is pointless. You're better off swimming with the current." She looks up at me with soft eyes. "If your heart pulls you in another direction, I'll understand."

"Thanks…" I mutter. My heart pounds as I hang on my next words. "I… it means a lot."

"Wonderful," Sheyba exclaims. "You officially might like me. No more ambiguity."

"Sarcasm, huh? I'm rubbing off on you."

Sheyba snickers. "I'm not even going to ask what that's supposed to mean."

I pace a second longer before taking a seat on her rock. I scoot closer until our hips are touching.

"I have a question for you now."

"About time," Sheyba teases. "Ask away."

"I, uhhh… I heard what you said in the boat. Is it true? You left Atlantia just for me?"

"Not for you." She gestures around the cavern. "To save the world, of course."

"I'm serious!" I say, openly incredulous. "You left your family, your culture… everything. And for what? The slim possibility of a relationship with someone you've only known a day? I just don't get it. I'm not worth it."

"I didn't leave for you," Sheyba corrects. "I left for myself." She twirls her finger idly, and a small whirlpool forms by her feet. "I always knew I'd leave someday. Atlantians don't believe in this kind of lifestyle. They'd kill me if they knew… or maybe they wouldn't. Who really knows. But they'd never accept me. That much is certain."

"So you were going to leave anyway?"

"Eventually, yeah. I wanted to leave for years. I'd sit in the sand and daydream about what I'd find across the Great Waters, but what I had to lose was always greater than what I had to gain…. Until I met you."

I look away so she doesn't see my disappointment. "So you did leave because of me?"

"Fine, I left because of you, but can you blame me? I mean, just look at your name: Iris, protector of the world. Sounds a bit swoon-worthy you have to admit."

Part of me wants to scoff at her decision—abandoning her family on account of a simple crush. Not even a crush, a first impression. The other part feels guilty. She gave it up for me, completely unaware of my issues.

I look away. "I know you think that you know me, but you don't. I'm not some perfect protector of the world. I'm not a hero at all; I'm a killer."

Sheyba shrugs. "So?"

"So? You don't know me, Sheyba. You don't have the slightest clue who I am. You deserve better than this." I gesture down at myself. "Trust me; I'm broken. I can't give you what you want."

"You don't know what I want," she snaps back. "You don't have the slightest clue." She holds my gaze, waiting for me to contradict myself. When I say nothing, she rolls her eyes. "The Elders have been telling me what's best for me my whole life. I'm sick of it. I don't care if you think you're a cracked hull; you don't get to tell me what will make me happy."

Something stirs in my chest.

Her outright stubbornness—her self-sabotaging determination—reminds me of Jazon. I can't help but smile as my heart flutters. It might sound stupid, but that quality, that refusal of defeat, was the reason I fell for him.

"Okay," I concede.

Sheyba looks at me and blinks. She narrows her eyes, expecting a trap. "Okay?"

"Okay," I repeat. "You're right. You're a big girl. You can make your own decisions. If you think I'm good for you, maybe you're right. Who am I to say otherwise?"

"What are you saying?" Sheyba questions. "You admit we might be good for each other?"

I nod. "I do." I bite my tongue, knowing I can't take back what I'm about to say. "The truth is… I'm glad you came with us," I finally voice.

She looks at me in disbelief, her lips gradually mirroring my smile. "I know you are," she teases. "I just never thought I'd hear you say it."

I take a deep breath, trying to settle my nerves. "And I never thought I'd kiss an Atlantian."

I relish the sight of her eyes expanding, mouth ajar with disbelief.

My heart pounds as I lean in, but I can't bring myself to go all the way. I just hover there, letting Sheyba take the lead.

Her surprise is quickly replaced with elation. She grabs me by the back of the neck and slowly pulls my lips to hers.

My heart flutters, and the world melts into insignificance.

When I start to pull away, she tugs on my neck. It's subtle, just enough and let me know she wants more.

My body responds instinctively, spurred by her desire. I lean in, closing my mouth on her bottom lip. Unable to resist, I give it a gentle nibble.

Crunch, crunch. Crunch, crunch.

We both jump apart, turning to face the source of the sound. Sandy footsteps echo from the mouth of the Trench.

About time.

Two figures emerge, stepping into the pale yellow light. Each of them is wearing an identical, gray cloak. One I recognize as the princess, the other is the king's old apprentice. If I remember correctly, he's a Guardian now.

They stiffen when they see us.

"You!" the princess reaches for her amulet.

"Me?" I ask

"Don't play dumb!" she shouts across the Trench. "You know what you did!"

The Guardian raises a pistol, aiming it at my chest.

Before he can fire, Sheyba steps in front of me. "If you want her, you'll have to go through me."

The princess furrows her brow. "Who the hell are you?"

She lifts her chin. "My name is Sheyba, defender of Iris, protector of the world."

The princess looks over at the Guardian, then back at us. "What?"

"She's Atlantian," I sneer. "Did Matt tell you nothing?"

"You betrayed him to the Holy One," the princess snaps back. "What else is there to know?"

I gesture at Sheyba. "Maybe how we saved his ass in Atlantia. Without us, Matt would've never made it off the island."

"We're on your side," Sheyba insists. "I already found the entrance for you."

The Guardian lowers his gun. He looks over at the princess who reluctantly releases her amulet.

"Where is it?" she demands.

Sheyba gestures down at the water. "Matt was right. It's at the bottom of the lake. It goes down 100 feet or so. There's a freestanding archway at the bottom. I'm guessing it forms a portal or something."

The princess approaches, never taking her eyes off me. When she reaches the shore, she takes a quick glance at the water. "The lake is big," she snaps. "Where exactly was it?"

Sheyba points. "Out there in the middle, straight down. If you want, I could lead you to it."

Princess shakes her head. "I've got it."

She still doesn't trust us.

The princess tiptoes over several boulders until she's on the very edge of a rocky outcropping. As she leans out over the water, her head bumps something invisible, sending ripples in all directions.

The ripples continue to expand, stretching all the way across the shoreline and nearly to the ceiling. The entire lake is blocked off by one enormous force field.

"Looks like I'm just in time," the Holy Ones calls out as he steps into the cavern. "To think you were so close. A few seconds more, and you might've had it. It's almost as if I was destined to intervene at this precise moment."

"Is that him?" Sheyba motions at the Holy One.

I take my amulet in my hand. "That's him."

"Go ahead," the Holy One says, splaying his hands to the side. "I know you've all been fantasizing about this moment. Do it. Take your best shot."

Antai tightens his grip on the pistol. As he raises the gun, the magazine falls free from the bottom of the stock. Then, a bolt falls loose. By the time he aligns the sights, the entire gun falls apart in his hands. The slide slips off and the barrel tumbles to the floor.

The Holy One laughs. "Those pesky handguns. Always malfunctioning."

Sheyba dives toward the lake, but her body hits the force field, eliciting a cascade of ripples.

I raise my arm as I form the command.

Lightning!

A spire of earth erupts in front of me, engulfing my arm. The electricity crackles, draining into the earth before I can direct it elsewhere.

Melt!

The stone liquifies around my wrist, and I tug my hand free. Then, the air reverberates around me as I form a shield.

Antai stands with me on the shore, looking like a startled recruit. Meanwhile, Sheyba batters the energy shield, trying to break through to her beloved body of water. The princess, to my surprise, is nowhere to be seen.

We're screwed.

Antai is moving now, drawing a longsword from its scabbard. The air ripples around him, forming a shield as he charges across the Trench.

I charge as well, drawing my dagger. The Holy One watches as we race toward him, a stupid grin on his face.

I'm close enough now, I can reach him with my mind.

Combust!

The ground explodes at his feet… or at least it starts to. The blast—a blinding void of white light—instantaneously expands to the size of a beer barrel before the Holy One contains it in an energy sphere. He holds it there, as if frozen in time, until we dash closer. Then, he releases the blast in our direction.

Ka-Boom!

The explosion obliterates my shield, throwing me backward. My ears ring, and my head throbs as I roll to my stomach and push myself to my feet.

Antai swings his sword, but the Holy One sidesteps the blade with ease.

Sheyba is still fixated on the water. She tries to pull the water toward her. Blocked by the Holy One's barrier, the water expands upward along the force field's surface.

Antai continues to swing at the Holy One, who twists away with impossible speed.

Clutching my dagger, I race to help. I take two steps before I start to sink into the ground. The earth wiggles like gelatin as my foot sinks into the earthy sludge.

Harden!

I speak to the elements, but the Holy One is already there, flattering them with his endless dominion. Somehow, even at a distance, his command takes precedence.

HARDEN!

I command with all my might, straining the limits of my soul-anchor. The ground stiffens in response, but only slightly. It's the consistency of a thick mud. When I try to lift my foot, the earth suctions around my shoes, throwing me off balance. I fall forward, and my hands plunge into the sludge.

"I must admit, Antai" the Holy One says, ducking under another swipe of Antai's sword. "I didn't foresee such resiliency. I never—" He sidesteps another thrust, "—considered you worthy of my daughter—" He rears back, narrowly dodging another swing. "but perhaps I misjudged you."

Anger boils within me. He's toying with us, no more threatened than a cat by a mouse.

I change my command, joining in the chorus of commands coming from the Holy One.

Liquify.

The ground softens beneath me, but I don't let myself sink.

Float.

My body hovers in the air as the earth drips off of my legs, splashing into the earthy puddle beneath me.

Lightning!

The blinding bolt erupts from my fingertips, but it doesn't hit the Holy One. Instead, it veers to the side at the last second, arcing into Antai.

I try to stop the command, but the Holy One has taken control of the electrons, urging them into Antai.

TZZZZZ!

I watch, helpless, as the energy courses through him.

To my surprise he's still standing. Then, he swings his sword.

The Holy One moves at the last second, barely lurching out of the way. The tip of the blade cuts across his face.

The lightning stops, and the Guardian is still standing. His entire body—face, hair, everything—is a reflective gold.

The Holy One laughs. The gash on his cheek heals before my eyes, sealing back together within seconds.

His eyes narrow. "My turn."

Antai screams as his metal limbs melt away. He floats into the air, his back arching to its anatomical limit.

Suddenly, the Holy One hesitates. In the blink of an eye, he twists around and raises a hand. His fingers close, clasping onto empty air. "Nice try."

The princess materializes as the Holy One removes her ring with dominion. Then, it melts, dripping to the floor.

TZZZZZ!

Electricity courses through the princess, dropping her to the floor.

The Holy One looks down at her. I wait for him to finish the job, but he doesn't. He only shakes his head. "Why must you put me in this position, Rose? Why must you test my convictions?"

The princess cowers as he raises his hand. After a second, he lowers it again. "You'll understand soon enough. Now sleep."

The princess slumps, and her eyes close.

Out of ideas, I glance at Sheyba. To my surprise, she's waist deep in a massive pool of water. With every second, the water continues to rise around her. It bubbles up from the ground, oozing from the rocks like water from a sponge. On the other side of the force field, the lake is several feet shallower.

Suddenly, the water rushes toward the Holy One, carrying Sheyba with it. It funnels through the narrow Trench, forming a wave a dozen feet tall.

The Holy One faces the incoming wave, a smile on his face. Just before it engulfs him, he raises a hand. The tsunami hits an invisible wall, compressing the wave against the surface, and forcing it outward in an explosive burst of spray and mist. The momentum carries the water upward into a cascading column.

As the wave stalls—momentarily balanced against gravity—the water crackles, freezing the wave in a brilliant display. The wave solidifies around Sheyba, leaving only her shoulders and head exposed.

The Guardian is already in action. He doesn't try to stand. Instead, he focuses across the Trench. To my surprise, a dozen gun parts hover in the air, arranging themselves simultaneously with superhuman dexterity. The gun parts fit together, pins and springs sliding into place. Finally, the magazine clicks into stock, and the slide racks back.

The gun, controlled by dominion, points at the Holy One. Then, the trigger flicks back.

BANG! BANG! BANG!

At the last second, the water around Sheyba lifts into the air, forming a liquid wall several feet thick. The Adamic bullets can pierce impenetrable armor, yet they slow to a stop in the water, quickly sinking to the bottom of the liquid wall.

The Holy One focuses his gaze on Antai. Before he can stop it, Antai's amulet slithers out of his shirt. Immediately, the gun clatters to the ground across the cavern floor.

"No!" Antai shouts as his amulet floats into the air and liquifies. It bubbles as the silver forms a puddle on the cavern floor.

"I should kill you," the Holy One declares as he studies Antai. "But I'm afraid Rose would never forgive me." He shakes his head. "The things we do for our daughters."

The Holy One sighs as he looks around. "Let's see… where was I?" His eyes narrow at Sheyba. "Oh, yes."

I extend my soul.

Sli—

Before I can finish the command, an energy wave hits me in the chest, cracking my ribs and throwing me back. When I hit the ground, my amulet slips from my grasp.

NOOO!

Before I can reach for it, the earth erupts around me, encasing my waist in solid stone and lifting me into the air.

The Holy One returns his attention to Sheyba, who is still frozen in the wave.

"This is not your fight, Atlantian." He waves his hand, and the ice liquifies all at once. The water flattens somewhat, but it remains coalesced around Sheyba. She squirms, and the water undulates, keeping her limbs trapped beneath the surface.

She grits her teeth as she fights for control of the water, but it's no use. He's simply too powerful.

The watery blob seeps forward, carrying Sheyba toward the Holy One, but he's not looking at her. He glances around for Antai's sword, spotting it immediately. He opens his hand, and the handle lurches, landing in his palm.

Not again! I can't lose another one.

The feelings surface. The memory of Jazon bleeding out in my arms. The feeling of ineptitude as I tried in vain to heal him. The bone-chilling, soul-crushing flood of helplessness.

The Holy One studies her. "Unlike your friends here, I don't have any tenderness toward you, Atlantian." He adjusts his grip on the sword. "I'll give you one chance to leave with your life, and one chance only. When I ascend, do not expect to be brought back."

"P-tuh!"

Sheyba spits at the Holy One. A glob of her saliva stops a few inches from his face, hovering in the air.

"Very well. As you wish."

The watery bubble bursts, splashing to the cavern floor and

draining toward the lake. The air ripples around her body, forcing her to her knees, perpendicular to the Holy One. Her head is bowed as if on an invisible chopping block.

"No!" I wail. My soul-anchor is out of reach. But I still have an amplifier beneath my shirt.

Suddenly, the Holy One pauses, as if sensing my intentions.

Don't even think about it!

The Holy One's consciousness fills me, weighing down my limbs with his endless dominion.

I extend my soul.

Combus—

It's not going to work, Iris. He speaks within my mind. *You're at my mercy now.*

I feel the dominion as he settles into my body. Pure, unbridled power rages beneath my skin. The dominion is alive. It writhes within me, coiling around my soul like a boa constrictor. It could rip me apart, devour me in a millisecond, but it doesn't. The Holy One doesn't let it.

You regret it, don't you? You could have been a goddess, Iris. I would have brought him back, you know. You would have been immortal with Jazon at your side. Now, you'll have nothing. Surely, you regret it?

Across the room, he lifts the sword above Sheyba's head.

Surely, you see the error of your ways.

My subconscious answers for me.

I do.

As the despair takes hold, I regret everything. It seems every choice I've ever made is the wrong one. In the beginning, I thought I was saving Jazon, but I was only killing others. Then, I switched sides. I thought I was saving humanity, but it was a delusion. Now, Sheyba will die for my narcissism.

If only I could go back… redo everything.

That's it!

As the sword swings, I make up my mind.

I'll come back! I'll come back in time to save her! I'll come back to this very moment.

T-Ching!

The sound of steel hitting steel rings out. I find myself smiling at the sight.

A blonde woman is standing over Sheyba's body. Not just any blonde woman—a future version of myself. She's holding an identical copy of Antai's sword, holding it out to deflect the blow away from Sheyba's neck.

Then, not even a second later, a future version of Sheyba materializes behind the Holy One, swinging an Adamic dagger of her own. Somehow, the Holy One ducks out of the way.

WOOOSH!

Wind rushes outward in all directions, the Holy One at the epicenter. Future Sheyba and future Iris are ready with shields of their own, gracefully riding the wind as it forces them back. Training equipment blows into the air and clatters against the cavern wall.

Lightning, now!

My future self speaks in my head, conveying her intentions in a split second.

Sheyba must be receiving the same message, because the four of us attack in unison.

Liiiiiiiiiightning!

The cavern erupts with energy as four bolts of lightning converge on the Holy One.

Somehow, he's prepared, intercepting the attack with a dome-shaped shield. A blinding surge of energy writhes across his force field, burning into the ground. The light is blinding. I can't even make out his form beneath the tendrils of electricity. Still, I can sense his consciousness pushing back, defying the onslaught of energy.

I continue to throw my entire soul into the attack, already feeling the strain. My head pounds, and my vision blurs, but I don't relent.

TZZZZZZZ!

5 seconds.

10 seconds.

Liiiightning!

I feel my skull tearing down the middle, but I don't stop.

Then, my mind shatters, and the world goes black.

At some point, as my mind drifts through the void, I begin to dream.

I'm standing in front of a little girl, no older than three or four. She has messy blonde hair and blue terror-stricken eyes.

I crouch down, positioning my face directly in front of hers. I reach out with hairy arms, taking her by the shoulders.

When I speak, Kildron's voice comes out.

"Alright, Iris. Daddy has to go fight bad guys. You're going to go with Zane for a little bit. Okay?"

"I don't wanna go with Zane," the little girl pouts. "I wanna go with you."

"But I'm going somewhere dangerous. When you love something, you want to keep it safe, and I love you, Iris. Does that make sense? I want to make sure you don't get hurt. That's why you have to go with Zane. Just for a little while. Your mommy will come get you soon, okay?"

Iris nods.

I smile. "Good, girl. Now, no matter what happens, remember daddy loves you, okay? You're a brave, strong, smart little girl. Now, come here."

I pull Iris closer, giving her an exaggerated peck on each cheek.

"Mwuah! Mwuah!"

I place my hands on her cheeks, lifting her chin and staring into her eyes for the last time.

"Goodbye, baby girl. I love you."

38

ROSE

The last thing I remember is my father's voice, whispering in my skull.

Sleep.

Everything is calm inside my mind. My worries are distant. My fears are suppressed.

TZZZZZZZ!

The sound shakes my sleeping soul. The ground vibrates beneath my face. Light, brighter than the sun, penetrates my eyelids, filling my mind with flashes of white.

TZZZZZZZ!

I push against the ground, struggling to lift my head. Wincing, I look around. I can't see much besides the blinding light. Multiple bolts of electricity converge in the center of the Trench.

Impossible!

My father stands at the focal point, taking cover beneath an energy dome. The entire cavern buzzes, vibrating my skin through my cloak.

As I watch, Iris slumps to the ground as her bolt fizzles out. The other three attackers continue, concentrating the electric energy on my father.

I push myself to my feet and press my hand to my chest, feeling for my soul-anchor.

Thank god!

It's still there, tucked safely beneath my shirt. Taking a deep breath, I command the elements.

Lightning!

TZZZZZZ!

Electricity flashes from my hand, joining the others.

I extend my soul into my surroundings, stretching myself to the limit. I gather the electrons, concentrating them and channeling them through my fingertips. The energy threatens to tear my flesh apart, but I don't care. I don't care if it kills me.

TZZZZZZ!

Five seconds go by… and five more.

"Ahhhhh!" I scream as I abandon all sense of restraint. Even with my soul-anchor, my mind threatens to snap.

Then, the impossible happens. I feel Zezric's shield begin to wane, weakening with every second. Finally—after a godly display of power—he's burned through his reservoir of one thousand souls.

He's running out of power!

In the blink of an eye, his shield collapses, and our bolts converge in a concussive blast!

KA-KRACK!

I squeeze my eyes shut to save myself from being blinded as the shock wave washes over me. When I open them, my stomach sinks.

My father is gone.

The ground is scorched where he once stood, but there isn't a body. There's only an Adamic sword—the steel glowing orange.

I look at my allies, blinking in disbelief.

Matt's sister is unconscious on the floor, but at the same time, she's standing next to the Atlantian. There's two of her—two exact copies of Iris.

I blink. *Impossible!*

Then, I spot a second Atlantian, standing a short way from the first.

Before I can question it, the two duplicates disappear, simply blinking out of existence.

What the...

"Bravo!" Zezric calls as he emerges from the rocky shore—an arms length from the water's edge. He rises slowly from the ground as if it were a warm bath. The stone bubbles around him, parting to let him surface.

Once his feet are at ground level, he steps backwards. His initial force field—the one stretching across the shoreline—ripples harmlessly as he passes through it. He continues to backpedal, stepping onto the surface of the lake.

I don't extend my soul to my father. Instead, I reach for my allies. I envelop Antai with my mind—Iris and the Atlantian too.

Don't let them burn!

Then, I open my mouth.

"Havak—"

An invisible force strangles my tongue before I can finish the spell.

"I must admit, you put up quite a fight," Zezric says, looking right at me. "Part of me is almost proud."

The Atlantian takes a running step and hurls her dagger. It cuts through the force field, whizzing past my father's head.

He ignores the pitiful attempt. "It's time I ascend. Goodbye, Rose. Next time you see me, I'll be your god... but I'll always be your father first. Don't forget that."

The lake surface sinks beneath his feet, leaving him suspended in the air. The water forms a bowl-shaped depression. The watery crater grows larger as my father descends, his body following the water as it sinks below him. Within a few seconds, his head dips below the waterline, and the surface of the lake flows back together.

As soon as the water converges, my father disappears from sight, concealed by the murk.

I don't waste any time.

Burn!

A concentrated flame of pure heat hisses from my palm. I try to melt my way through the barrier, but the thermal energy is reflected back at me, singing my skin.

It's no use!

I look around for a solution.

The sword!

I race for Antai's longsword, commanding it to cool as I grab the handle. Then, I bolt for the beach, swinging at the energy shield. It slices straight through, but I'm too late.

Already, the water begins to glow, dispersing the green light that emanates from the depths. Fluorescent squiggles dance along the walls, magnifying the pattern of the disturbed lake surface.

"He opened it," I gasp.

Faza Le Bakanzah

Supposedly, that's all it took. Speaking a single spell. Through the depths of the lake, I didn't hear a sound.

Then, as quickly as it appeared, the light vanishes. Instantly, the force field dissolves.

Without hesitation, I follow suit.

Repel!

I step into the water, parting the lake in front of me as if it were the Red Sea. As the water is forced aside, it reveals the lakebottom—a steep collection of boulders. I stumble over the rocks, racing toward the deepest point of the lake.

"Rose, wai—"

Antai's voice is silenced as the water crashes in behind me, but I don't have any time to spare. I race into the depths, pulling my bubble of air along with me.

Suddenly, the water parts in front of me, revealing a small archway of stacked stones, just tall enough to walk through without slouching. Dozens and dozens of Adamic symbols are carved into the stones.

I maintain my bubble, holding the water at bay. Then, I speak.

"Faza Le Bakanzah!"

Unseal Bakanzah.

I blink at the archway, but nothing happens.

"Faza Le Bakanzah!"

Nothing. No growing green light or magical portal.

"Faza Le Bakanzah! Faza Le Bakanzah!"

Then, I remember what my father once mentioned. *There's a built-in safeguard. It can only be opened once per solar revolution.*

My stomach sinks.

No! This can't be happening!

"Faza Le Bakanzah!" I shout. "FAZA LE BAKANZAH!"

Still, nothing happens.

I fall to the ground as hopelessness overtakes me. For a moment, I consider releasing my command. I could let the water crush me. End it all… snuff out my miserable future. At this point, what does it even matter?

We lost… we actually lost.

I can't go back and face my people. I can't live in a world where my father is god. *I can't… I can't do it.*

Closing my eyes, I let my bubble collapse, hearing the roar as the water rushes in.

39

MATT

Our footsteps echo off the stairwell as we dash into the darkness.

Light.

I illuminate the way, racing a few steps ahead of Kendra and Diego.

Before long, I reach the bottom, turning down a short tunnel. I quicken my pace, sprinting as I burst into the Trench.

Immediately, my stomach twists into a knot. Iris is on the floor, and Sheyba is kneeling beside her, her ear pressed to Iris's chest. Antai doesn't look much better. He's army-crawling toward the lakeshore. Rose is nowhere to be seen.

"I need help!" Sheyba shouts as she sees us. "I'm losing her!"

"What happened?" I study Iris as I skid to a stop beside them, but I don't see any injuries.

"I don't know," Sheyba gasps. "She just fell over."

"She strained her soul," Antai calls. "She lost her soul-anchor."

"Strained her soul?" Sheyba shakes her head. "What does that even mean?"

Of course, the Atlanteans don't use amplifiers. The concept is alien to them, but I don't have time to explain.

Kendra catches up, putting her hands on Iris's chest. "She's in cardiac arrest. She's fading fast. She needs—"

"Let me!" I kneel beside Iris and place my hands on her forehead. Then, I open my soul, letting Kildron's dominion drain out of me. I feel his power—his very emotions—slowly fade. Anger, guilt… contentment. It all flows into Iris.

Still, she doesn't move.

I squeeze my soul like a lemon, struggling to excrete every last drop of spare dominion. I don't stop until the world spins and my head aches.

"Ptuh!" Iris gasps, rocketing upright. "What… what did you do to me?" Suddenly, her eyes widen. "Kildron's dead?"

I nod.

She grits her teeth, looking around. "And the Holy One?"

Sheyba opens her mouth, but before she can speak, a torrent of bubbles erupts from the center of the lake. A figure surfaces, gasping for air. After a second, she slowly begins swimming toward the shore.

"Rose!"

She climbs out of the water, her clothes plastered to her body. Her head is hung, and her countenance bears the weight of surrender.

"What happened?" I ask, though I fear the answer.

"He won," Rose breathes. "He's sealed in the Library. We can't get to him now—it won't open for another year. By the time he emerges, he'll be invincible." She slumps to the ground, curling her legs up to her chest. "It's over…"

Everyone is silent.

I take hold of the chain around my neck, pulling until the hourglass falls free from my collar. "What if it's not?" I ask. "What if there's another way?"

Rose shakes her head.

Antai approaches, wearing his metal limbs once more. The chain of Diego's amplifier is visible around his neck. Diego follows behind him, his skin it's normal brown hue.

Antai narrows his eyes. "What are you talking about, MacArther?"

"This!" I hold out the hourglass. "It's a time relic. It lets us go back in time."

Kendra frowns. "But Kildron said we can't change the past. He was pretty adamant about that."

"So what? We don't have to change it," I propose. "We can learn from it. We can study the language in the past. We already know where the Library is and how to open it. Then, when we come back to the present, we'll be ready to kill the Holy One."

Antai's eyes widen. "That… that's not a bad idea."

I nod, my excitement growing. "It'll return us to the moment we left. If we go now, the Holy One won't have time to learn Adamic. We'll be a step ahead."

"He has Foresight?" Rose says. "Whatever we try, he'll see it coming."

Everyone falls silent.

"What about King Dralton?" I ask. "He had Foresight, right? He's alive in the past. He can teach us. There has to be a way to beat it."

Finally, Rose nods, her brow relaxing. "I suppose it's possible…"

"The sooner we go," I add, "the less time he has to learn spells."

Her eyes continue to brighten as she plays with the notion. Slowly, Rose nods her head up and down. "Demons, you're right… This could maybe work."

"Okay," Antai nods. "We go back in time, study the language, learn Foresight, and then return to the present to kill the Holy One. Does that sum it up?"

"That's it," I say. "My dad said we'll only have a week, but that should be enough. We just have to pick a date. Supposedly, it has to be during our lifetime. I guess any day before Dralton's death should work, right? We need him alive."

"We could go back a year," Kendra suggests. "Things were pretty calm then."

Rose is staring at the hourglass, lost in thought. "We need Titan," she mutters to herself.

Diego frowns. "Titan? As in Lunatic Titan, the old king?"

Antai nods. “He was a little off his rocker, Rose. I don’t know how helpful he’ll be.”

She looks up, face resolute. “It doesn’t matter. The Book of Life is written in Hebrew. Dralton doesn’t speak Hebrew, but I’m pretty sure Titan was fluent. We need him if we want any hope of learning Adamic.”

“He erased his own memories,” I remind her. “I’m not sure how fluent he was in the end.”

“Exactly,” Rose says. “We just have to go back far enough. I found a medical record from July 25th, 2002, describing when the amnesia started. It was the day after Hogrum Fell. That’s when he erased his memories. All we have to do is go back before that date. Even a week early would be enough.”

“That would be… what? July 18th” Antai narrows his eyes. “You weren’t even born until the 21st. Didn’t MacArthur say you have to be alive?”

“I was alive,” Rose says. “A fetus should still count, right?” She looks to me for answers.

I shrug. “We won’t know until we try.”

“Are we really doing this?” Kendra asks. “Shouldn’t we sleep on it? Think things through a little longer?”

Rose shakes her head. “Every second, he grows stronger in there. The sooner, the better.”

“Alright,” Antai exhales. “I’m in.”

“This is freaking insane,” Diego says with a grin. “I’m in.”

Kendra nods. “And me.”

Antai points at the hourglass. “Go ahead. Show us how it works, MacArthur.”

I hold out the relic. “Alright, everyone put a finger on the hourglass.”

Everyone takes hold of the relic, everyone except Iris and Sheyba. They look at each other uncomfortably.

“You’re not coming?”

“Can’t” Iris says. “We already used it to fight the Holy One. Well, not yet exactly, but we saw ourselves come back. It's already set in stone."

"But… you could try." I plead. "What if Kildron was wrong."

Iris looks at Sheyba who shrugs. Together, they place a finger on the glass.

"And we're sure about the date?" I ask.

"Positive," Rose confirms. "July 18th, 2002. One week before Hogrum fell… one week before Titan lost his mind."

Kildron… Judy… Zane!

They're alive where we're going. I'd have to get to Hogrum, of course, but hypothetically, I can see them again.

I feel my thoughts racing, exploring improbable hypotheticals. Kildron insisted that I can't change the past, but then again, I've yet to see any evidence to support him.

Maybe… just maybe… I can save Hogrum. I can rewrite everything that ever happened.

I have to try.

"Everybody ready?" I ask.

Heads bob up and down.

"Alright here goes nothing… Valiptah."

I tilt the relic, watching as the black granules accumulate on the inside of the glass.

At first, nothing happens. Then, Iris and Sheyba are whisked away, disappearing in an elongated blur of color. The cavern walls remain constant, but I catch glimpses of movement—quick flashes of bodies rushing past, like a timelapse video. Dozens of bodies zip around the room before flickering away, replaced by a new year's worth of trainees. The images flash quicker and quicker, too fast to make sense of anything. The world begins to spin.

When everything settles, I'm standing in the exact same spot, surrounded by Kendra, Rose, Antai, and Diego.

When I look up, I see a fifth individual sitting cross legged on the ground. He has long black braids secured by copper bands. He's wearing an intricate gold robe which matches the crown on his head.

King Dralton smiles, looking down at his watch. "Excellent. You're right on time."

End of Book 3: Part One

DEAR READER,

Thanks again for being recipients of an imagination transplant. I know some of you have been waiting years for this book. I hope these little black squiggles were worth the wait. As always, I would love to hear your thoughts. Please leave a review and let me know what you liked/disliked. I read every one.

As for Book 3: Part Two, it's coming along. I'm not quite sure when it'll be finished, but if you'd like to be notified when Part Two is released, you can join my email list at **devindowning.com**

While you're waiting for the next installment, feel free follow my instagram (@writing.prompt.daily) where I post short stories and original writing prompts.

Hopelessly seeking your approval,
Devin

ABOUT THE AUTHOR

Devin Downing grew up in Temecula, California, spending his childhood reading books on the beach and bashing bones at the skatepark. Today, Devin lives in Portland with his wife and newborn son. Apart from crafting complex stories, he enjoys hiking, rollerskating, and writing about himself in the third person (yep, it's me! Hi, guys!). Devin is currently enrolled in medical school, which painfully consumes all of his would-be writing time. That said, he already has several book ideas that he plans to write in the coming years.

Learn more about Devin at **devindowning.com**

Printed in Great Britain
by Amazon